The
Many Lives
of
John Stone

ALSO BY LINDA BUCKLEY-ARCHER

THE GIDEON TRILOGY

The Time Travelers (previously titled *Gideon the Cutpurse*)

The Time Thief

The Time Quake

The

Many Lives

of

John Stone

LINDA BUCKLEY-ARCHER

SIMON & SCHUSTER BFYR

New York   London   Toronto   Sydney   New Delhi

SIMON & SCHUSTER BFYR

An imprint of Simon & Schuster Children's Publishing Division

1230 Avenue of the Americas, New York, New York 10020

Text copyright © 2015 by Linda Buckley-Archer

Jacket photo-illustration by We Monsters, photograph of girl with camera copyright © 2015 by Carlos Cossio/Getty Images; other photographs copyright © 2015 by iStockphoto/Thinkstock

Use of Versailles imagery by kind permission of l'Etablissement public du chateau, du musée et et du domaine national de Versailles.

Interior photographs by Isabella Archer

For information about special discounts for bulk purchases, please contact Simon & Schuster Special Sales at 1-866-506-1949 or business@simonandschuster.com.

The Simon & Schuster Speakers Bureau can bring authors to your live event. For more information or to book an event, contact the Simon & Schuster Speakers Bureau at 1-866-248-3049 or visit our website at www.simonspeakers.com.

Book design by Laurent Linn

The text for this book is set in Electra LT Std.

Manufactured in the United States of America

10 9 8 7 6 5 4 3 2 1

Library of Congress Cataloging-in-Publication Data

Buckley-Archer, Linda.

The many lives of John Stone / Linda Buckley-Archer. — 1st edition.

pages cm

Summary: When seventeen-year-old Spark takes a summer job working at a secluded house in England, organizing journals that span centuries and all written in the same hand, she discovers her true connection to the people who live there and the trait that makes them unique.

ISBN 978-1-4814-2637-4 (hardcover)

ISBN 978-1-4814-2639-8 (eBook)

[1. Longevity—Fiction. 2. Summer employment—Fiction. 3. Supernatural—Fiction. 4. Identity—Fiction. 5. England—Fiction.] I. Title.

PZ7.B882338Man 2015

[Fic]—dc23

2014035641

FIRST EDITION

For Isabella

There is no desert like that
of living without friends.

—BALTASAR GRACIÁN

Photographs

Spark finds Mum hunched over the kitchen table, feet shoved into sheepskin slippers, hands around a mug of tea, the fridge door open for light.

"What are you doing up already?"

"Couldn't get a wink," says Mum, "knowing how early you've got to be off."

Later, as the London train pulls into the station in the frosty darkness, Spark asks: "You're gonna be okay, aren't you?"

As if she were going to say: *Don't go. Not you, too.* Nevertheless, Spark feels her heart harden, just in case, only to have it soften again.

"Will you stop your wittering and get in?" Mum says. "You'll be back before you know it."

As the train pulls out—there are only a couple of other people in the carriage, both city types—Spark puts the palms of both hands on the window and mouths, *Love you!* Although she is not sure if Mum has seen. The harsh station lights bleach all the color out of her mother's face as she stands motionless on the platform, arms hanging at her sides, watching the gap between them grow larger.

Later, New York.

Caught up in the logjam of traffic crawling toward the Brooklyn Bridge, Spark sits alone in the back of a yellow cab. Lulled by the motion of the taxi and the overheated, pine-scented air, the point of her chin slowly drops until it rests on an overstuffed backpack, which she cradles on her lap. When the line of traffic begins to move freely again, a worn-out Volvo cuts in front of them. It's a close thing. Spark's heavy eyelids snap open as the cabdriver brakes hard. The seat belt tightens across her chest and her bags slide away from her across the seat. And so it is to the accompaniment of a fanfare of car horns that Spark gets her first sight of Manhattan.

She leans forward in her seat and stares out at the dense mass of buildings that never stop coming at her, reaching up like mountain ranges. The gathering banks of violet cloud that cover Manhattan Island are so low, and so dense, that the skyscrapers seem to hold up the sky like columns shouldering the roof of some vast cathedral. "Wow!" She breathes.

The driver wants to know where she's from.

"Mansfield. Nottinghamshire . . . England."

The driver shakes his head, says he's spent a week in England. Never went there, though. Spark says she's not surprised. Mansfield isn't what you'd call a top tourist destination.

At ten to five, the cab pulls up outside the espresso bar in East Forty-ninth Street where Dan's text said to meet him. Spark monitors the meter and tries to remember how big a tip she is supposed to give. The cab pulls away, leaving her on the icy sidewalk on which snow is beginning to settle. Spark tilts back her head and opens her mouth until an American snowflake lands on her tongue.

Dan—of course—hasn't arrived yet. She scans the backs of a handful of heads sitting on high stools but none of them belong to her big brother. The penetrating squeal of the coffee machine makes her wince: Her ears are still popping after the long descent to JFK.

"What can I get for you today?" The thrill of hearing the barista's New York accent throws her and she orders a Danish pastry because her tired brain can't deliver the word "bagel" in time. She is conscious of how different she must sound. There's a mirror behind the bar. *Oh, heck,* she thinks. *I look like I've slept in my clothes.* But then, she has.

Spark settles at a narrow bench overlooking the street and wishes that Dan would hurry up. No one's taking a scrap of notice of her, yet Spark feels like she has "English" tattooed on her forehead. She licks the milk froth that has accumulated on her upper lip and her face lights up when it occurs to her that she is drinking hot chocolate on a different continent.

A movement on the sidewalk outside draws her attention. Caught in the pool of yellow light spilling out from the café, she notices a curious figure in a long dress. Spark cuts her Danish in half and licks buttery crumbs from her fingers. It is one of those moments when there is a delay while the brain processes the data. Her first impression is of a woman in an evening dress who is catching her breath between dances. By the time Spark's mind has caught up with itself, it rejects this unlikely scenario. Her gaze sidles back to the street. Sheltering under a tree is a tall, stooped woman with pale hair piled on top of her head. Although her layered approach to dressing is less a fashion statement than a means of preventing hypothermia, the result is eye-catching. Once upon a time the middle layer, a floor-length satin gown, must have been stunning. It has long, tapered sleeves, visible beneath a bulky vest, and the full skirt hangs in heavy folds. Even in this dim light, Spark can see that the hem is stained and frayed from being trailed across the streets of New York. She cannot begin to guess how old the woman is.

Abruptly the woman reaches down to the floor. Now Spark can see that she has attached a whole series of bulging plastic bags onto a cord around her waist so that they trail behind her like some bizarre accessory. The last three bags sit on the sidewalk like obedient dogs. It is in one of these that the woman is rummaging. She pulls out an aerosol can and, with a hand that is purple with cold, starts to spray the tree angrily, as if in an attempt to be rid of a bad smell.

How tragic, Spark thinks, *to end up with nothing and no one in a city that has everything.* Spark looks at her plate and wonders if she should offer the woman her half-eaten Danish. When she looks back up she notices a man in a billowing overcoat watching the woman from the opposite side of the tree. His gaze bores into her with such intensity it is as though the café, East Forty-ninth Street, and Manhattan itself have ceased to exist. Something about the little scenario sucks her in. Does he know the woman? What's the story? Spark reaches for her camera, turning off the flash and zooming in on the man. Snowflakes settle on his shoulders and on wavy black hair that is brushed back from a broad forehead. *Click.* Spark takes another shot, this time on a slower shutter speed, and frames the picture to include both people. *Click.* And another. *Click.*

Now the man approaches the woman, takes her hand, and *kisses* it. He presses some money into her palm but she throws it back at him, thrusting him away with the flats of her hands. She turns on her heels, revealing to Spark a hawk-like nose and fierce, dark eyes, and strides away in the direction of the river. The banknotes swirl across the sidewalk into the street, where passing traffic gobbles them up.

The man in the overcoat continues to observe her until she has vanished from sight, then he, too, enters the café. He buys an espresso and sits at a corner table, apparently deep in thought. Spark steals curious glances at him every now and then and notices that he is writing in a small notebook. Spark texts Dan again. Where r u? She flicks through her photos. There it is, the man's mesmerizing stare, digitized and recorded, an emotion in two dimensions. Spark is especially happy with the second shot: A car's headlights streak across the image, sulphur yellow against the gray of the street, its rapid trajectory emphasizing both figures' stillness. Yes, she is pleased with her photographs; she likes how they ask questions but provide no answers.

Paper Cut

Spark doesn't notice Dan arrive, so when he puts his hands over her eyes she leaps up like a startled cat.

"Sparky!" says Dan. He slips his bag off his shoulder and pats down her hair, like he always does.

Spark knocks away her brother's hand, like she always does. "Gerroff, Dan!"

September was the last time they saw each other. Dan hugs her awkwardly—it is not something he would normally do. Perhaps it's something he's picked up from his New York mates. Dan says hi to the barista and carries back a cup of tea, which he sloshes over the saucer. He pulls up a high stool and sits next to her in front of the window. It's dark now and Spark studies his grinning reflection in the glass.

"You're wearing a *suit*. It's *weird*," says Spark.

"Not as weird as seeing you here."

Spark pings his cup with a fingernail. "What's the point of coming to an espresso bar when you only drink tea?"

"It's my place. I like it here." He nods toward the bar. "He gives me free bagels when he's in a good mood."

Spark tells him he always was cheap and pulls out the receipt for the cab fare. "As you offered," she grins, waving it in front of his nose. "Not that I'm holding you to it." He cocks his head to one side to read it, and feigns falling off his stool.

"Dan!"

People are looking and Spark pushes him back on.

"Sorry I couldn't meet you at the airport—"

"It's okay—I got here, didn't I? Though Mum will go mental when she finds out you didn't meet me at JFK—"

"You're not going to tell her?"

Spark's eyes twinkle.

"We should text her," Dan says, suddenly solemn.

"I texted her as soon as I landed." She kisses the tips of her fingers and plants them on Dan's cheek. "From Mum."

Spark shows Dan her pictures of Manhattan taken through a grimy taxi window. Something makes her hold back from letting him see the photos of the bag lady and the man whose presence, a few tables away, she senses in the small of her back. She watches Dan stir his tea and they both look out at the street without speaking. The absence of the third point in their triangle is unsettling. She lets him do all the talking at first. How he loves New York. What they're going to do. How Ludo is letting her have his room for the week. Soon tiredness makes her wilt like a flower. She leans her shoulder against him like she used to, years ago now, when they watched telly together on the sofa after school. Spark looks at Dan's nails, which he hasn't stopped biting despite his smart suit and an internship in Manhattan. He fidgets all the while with a piece of cellophane that he scrunches up and then drops, watching it unfurl and picking it up again. Spark grabs hold of it.

"Mum's right, you're not coming back, are you?" The words slip out before Spark can stop herself.

Dan scrapes back his chair and downs the last dregs of his tea. "I don't know for sure what I'm doing yet." He gets to his feet. "Come on, let's get going."

She reaches for her backpack under the bench and berates herself. *Good move, Spark. Pick a fight, why don't you? Tell him to come home for Mum's sake while you're at it—*

"Mr. Park? I hope I'm not intruding."

Dan spins around and when Spark gets up she is confronted by the man whose image her camera has stolen. He extends his hand to Dan, who shakes it warmly.

"Mr. Stone!"

Spark watches Dan's posture alter. He straightens up, as if he is speaking to a headmaster. The man smiles and places a reassuring hand on Dan's shoulder. He's not tall—the same height as Dan, who is half a head shorter than his sister. "I was told I was likely to find you here."

Spark is again conscious of her creased clothes, her unruly hair, and the fact that she hasn't brushed her teeth in twenty-four hours.

"This is my little sister," says Dan.

Spark raises an eyebrow in her brother's direction. He acknowledges her irritation with a flicker of a smile: on, off.

The man turns to greet her and his hands go up in surprise. His eyes widen noticeably. "This is your *sister?*" Perhaps this is how people are with each other in New York. Dramatic. Over-the-top.

"Yes, Stella's over here for half term."

The man offers her his hand; he has a firm grip. "My name is John Stone. I'm delighted to meet you, *Stella.*"

There's a look in his eyes that is unexpected, like a paper cut. He doesn't seem to want to let go of her hand even when she starts to pull away. Spark wonders if he noticed her photographing him.

"Actually, no one calls me Stella. I'm Spark—S. Park. Spark."

This seems to amuse him. "Well, *Spark,* is this your first visit to New York?"

"It's my first time abroad—unless you count a day trip to Calais."

"Then you will remember it forever."

With a final squeeze John Stone releases her hand. He's not, Spark realizes, an American. He's English, or at least she thinks he is, with the kind of voice that would sound right on the stage or reading the news.

"It's a surprise to see you here, Mr. Stone," says Dan.

"Do not be concerned, Mr. Park, I am not here to check up on you!"

"The internship is great—it couldn't have worked out better—"

"Of course! I place people where I know they'll thrive. Your supervisor told me that you're an excellent linguist."

Spark watches Dan purse his lips as he tries not to seem too pleased. "Did he?"

"And that you sometimes arrive in the morning looking the worse for wear."

Dan opens his mouth and closes it again. John Stone smiles. "It's good that you're finding your feet."

"I'm grateful to you—I love it here."

The overhead lighting accentuates John Stone's deep-set eyes, which are dark—almost black—and his square, prominent cheekbones. Although his skin is rugged, and his brow furrowed, his hair is still dark—with the exception of a curious white stripe above his forehead. It's almost as if someone has taken a paintbrush and, with a deft flick of the wrist, has marked his scalp. Spark guesses he must have broken his nose at some point. It gives him the air of a rugby player, someone who is comfortable in his own skin, and who can take care of himself.

"Mr. Park, there's something I wanted to ask you before I go back to London—"

"Yes?"

"I presume you'll be returning home at the end of your internship?"

Dan shoots an uneasy glance at Spark. "I might look around for a permanent role in New York. I'd like to stay on if I could."

Spark's stomach lurches. Then he can break the news to Mum himself! *She's* not going to be his messenger. Not for this.

"Why do you ask, Sir?"

"I was about to offer you a summer job."

"Another internship, you mean?"

"Not exactly. It would not be a formal arrangement. I need someone to impose a sense of order on a collection of historical documents in my possession. Someone who can string sentences together."

"I see—"

"However, as you shall be in the city that never sleeps, and I shall be in Suffolk, where even the birdsong can seem unsociably loud—"

"It's good of you to think of me, but—"

John Stone holds up his hand to gesture that Dan need not explain.

"I need a summer job," Spark finds herself saying. "I *like* organizing, and writing's my thing."

John Stone turns his gaze on her. Dan looks appalled. Spark regrets opening her mouth even though it's all true: She does need a holiday job and she had to become good at organizing things when Mum couldn't cope. As for writing, it has helped her through everything. Until you've written it down, how can you tell what you really think?

"How old are you, Spark?" asks John Stone.

"Seventeen. If I get the grades, I'll be going to university this autumn."

"Seventeen. *Seventeen*." A slow, spreading smile lights up his face, revealing large, ivory teeth that are a little uneven.

"Yes."

"And you want me to consider you for this job?"

"Yes," she replies. "I do."

Even as she speaks Spark wonders why she is doing this. Now the full weight of John Stone's attention is on her. She waits for him to respond. Instead, he pulls out a notebook, tears out a blank page, and starts to write with a miniature silver pen. Spark scrutinizes the broad forehead etched with horizontal lines, the strong, square hands, the gold signet ring he wears on the small finger of his left hand. As he passes her the piece of paper she is seized by the feeling that she is responding to a prompt she knew would be forthcoming.

"Take some time to think about it," says John Stone. "Then, if you're still interested, I invite you to write to me. By hand. Early in the summer—in late May or early June. Tell me about yourself and how you view the world so that I can see how well you handle the English language."

"Writing's *my thing*!" repeats Dan incredulously once John Stone has departed.

"It just came out—"

"I noticed."

"Do I know him?" asks Spark. "I mean, I've not met him before, have I?"

"I can't see how. He visited me at school a couple of times. He works for the charity that gave me the scholarship."

"And he arranged your internship, as well?"

"Yes. After I graduated I went for an interview with him in London."

Dan plucks the scrap of paper from his sister's hands and peers at the precise, looped handwriting. "Stowney House, Suffolk . . . Spark, you do know he was only being polite—"

Spark snatches the piece of paper back from her brother's grasp. She folds it into a neat square and slips it into the side pocket of her new purse.

Ludo

"It's okay, Dan—let's take the underground," says Spark as he hails a cab.

"The view from the subway isn't so great."

"Well, a bus, then?"

"A sock in it, Spark. We're going by cab."

She can't remember the last time anyone spoiled her. It's strange that it should be Dan. "Thanks," she says as they clamber in.

Outside, the wind howls down the man-made canyons of Manhattan while over the icy East River screeching seagulls bicker over scraps. Inside the overheated cab, Spark's nose stays glued to the window. The Chrysler Building rises into a leaden sky and vanishes almost immediately as her sight line shifts, playing hide-and-seek with her as the cab makes its way downtown. As they head over the bridge toward Brooklyn, Spark looks back over her shoulder. It is a sight that will stay with her: the island of Manhattan at nightfall, a giant ship ablaze with lights, floating on a black sea. She thinks of Hawthorn Avenue in Mansfield, and Mum, alone, mashing tea under the fluorescent kitchen lighting while both her children are here, on the other side of the planet.

On the sidewalk of Cranberry Street, Brooklyn Heights, the wind is so cold it hurts. At first, the sight of Dan searching for his key—turning out every pocket in furious exasperation—made Spark laugh out loud. Now all she can think about is how very much she wants to get into the warmth. Dan cups his hands to his mouth.

"Ludo!" he bellows at the gyrating shadow at the top of the house that moves back and forth behind thin red curtains. "*Lu-do!*" Strains of some rock anthem, with a thumping, heavy bass, drift into the street. With each breath Dan emits great clouds of steam into the frosty Brooklyn air.

It is a tall, end-of-terrace, redbrick house, grand yet shabby. The bare branches of a huge tree scratch against the panes of the upper windows as if they are trying to get in. Dan resumes hammering on the front door. A glass panel above the lintel rattles. Spark has an idea. She begins to scrape up the scant layer of icy snow from the sidewalk.

"Stop dancing with yourself and let us in!" shouts Dan.

Spark throws her snowball at the window. Her aim falls short, but now Dan joins her. He crosses to the other side of the street to get a good run-up, then, cricketer that he is, releases the snowball in a curved shot that hits its target with a pleasing *thud*. Spark passes him snowballs. Once he gets his eye in, by standing in the middle of the street, Dan manages an accurate bombardment of the window. The red curtains twitch and finally a figure in shorts emerges onto a narrow, wrought iron balcony.

"Ludo, mate! I've forgotten my key! Come down and let us in!"

No sooner has the door opened than Dan slips through the gap, fast as a cat. Spark follows closely on his heels.

"Man, you scared me! I thought I was being dive-bombed by killer pigeons!"

Spark can't yet see the owner of the voice.

"Shouldn't you be at the airport?" asks Dan, taking off his gloves and blowing on his scarlet fingers. "What time's your flight?"

"Eight thirty."

Dan frowns at his watch as he tries to do the math. Spark closes the front door with a *click* and relaxes into the warmth. There's a smell of burned coffee, like it's dried out on the stove. She unwinds her scarf and looks about her at the hallway, which is narrow and dark and painted the color of boiled beetroot. Her fingers throb and prickle as they start to thaw. The high walls are studded with gold-framed prints of ancient maps and exotic beasts. Spark stands on tiptoes and looks over the bobble of her brother's hat at Ludo. At first she does not take in much more than a fringe of glossy hair that flops over black-framed rectangular glasses.

"Hello," she says.

"Hey. How are you doing?"

"Good. Thanks."

Spark lowers her heels and wipes her watering eyes, but Ludo's wide smile floats on in her jet-lagged brain like the fading filament of a lamp bulb in the dark, refusing to disappear.

"Eight thirty?" says Dan. "You'll never make it, mate."

"It's cool. I've got time." Spark rests her chin on Dan's shoulder. Ludo is wearing baggy shorts and a sweatshirt. He presses his hands together and bows his head, teetering about, Geisha-style, on invisible block shoes. "I make room ready for most honored guest."

"I'm calling you a cab," says Dan. "Your dad will kill you if you don't show. Tell me you're packed, at least."

Ludo's wide-set eyes flash behind his glasses. "Yes, Mom," he says to Dan. "I'm all set." Spark doesn't feel tired anymore.

Ludo's room is cavernous. More than half the size, Spark reckons, of their whole house in Mansfield. She pauses on the threshold until Ludo shepherds her in. Spotlights have been tacked onto dusty roof rafters. They are not powerful enough for the size of the room and cast long shadows. This half of the room looks like a recording studio. There's a row of empty soda bottles on a battered keyboard and a couple more on a dusty Marshall amp. Against the wall, nestled in a mess of colorful cords, are three electric guitars. One of them, she notices, is a Gibson Explorer, like the one the Edge uses in "Beautiful Day."

"Dan said you play," says Ludo.

"I'm learning."

"Feel free while you're here."

"What, even the Explorer?"

"Sure. Why not? What are you going to do to it?"

Spark thanks him, tells him she'll treat his guitars with respect. She follows him farther into the room, watching his shoulder blades move under his sweatshirt. Ludo is lithe and sinewy, half a head taller than Spark, and she's not small. He walks like a runner, arms loose, bouncing on the balls of his feet. This side of the room begins to resemble a bedroom, although it is not a bedroom like Spark's. Ludo's room has a double bed in it, and a large desk and, interestingly, a tall fridge, which hums loudly. There's a dirty saucer on the floor next to it. Spark stands in the middle of the room and slowly rotates. He has so much *stuff*: laptops and speakers, books and magazines, cardboard box files, upturned sneakers lurking in corners. When she turns back around, Ludo is watching her.

"You sure that you and Dan are related?" he asks. "He's so *dark*. And he's kinda squat, too, like he'd be difficult to push over—"

"He is!"

"Yeah? I must try it one of these days. But you. Your center of gravity is much higher. You're more like a sad Viking."

"I'm not sad! I've just got one of those faces."

"Nothing wrong with looking sad—"

"Yeah, there is."

"Not if you've had it tough."

"Who says I've had it tough? Everyone's had it tough."

"I haven't. I've had it *ea-sy*."

Looking at him, Spark can believe it. No one would say, *Don't worry, it might never happen!* to this boy. Are all Americans this easy to talk to?

"Mum's fair too, so I guess I take after her side. But Dad came over to England from Corsica. Dan takes after him. The whole of his family look like Napoleon. Even the women—"

Ludo laughs.

"It *really* irritates him that I grew taller than he did—"

"I'll file that one away!" Behind the angular frames of his spectacles, Ludo's eyes—which in this light are golden brown flecked with green—are attentive and quizzical, as if Spark is not quite what he expected and he's trying to figure her out. For the second time that day Spark feels abruptly detached from her life, like she's looking down at herself from above, a small figure in a rapidly turning world.

Dan calls up the stairs. "Lud-o! Cab's here."

Ludo goes to the door, shouts down: "On my way!" but proceeds to throw himself on the king-size bed in the corner. He appears to Spark like a young lion with his floppy hair and his large hands and feet that now drape over the sides of the mattress. The springs squeak as he bounces a couple of times.

"This bed has awesome springs."

"That's good to know!"

Ludo bounds up and points around the room as he walks to the door. "DVDs. Oreos. Cat food—don't get those confused—"

"You've got a cat?"

"Allegedly. I hardly see her. I think she's two-timing me."

There is the sound of heavy footsteps up the stairs.

"Ludo!"

When Dan's head appears in the doorway Ludo makes toward him, swooping down to grab a bulging duffel. He turns.

"Nice meeting you, Dan's sister. Shame we couldn't jam together. Some other time."

"You're going out like that?" asks Dan.

Ludo looks down at his shorts and shrugs. "It's seventy-five in the shade where I'm headed."

Spark leans out of the door and watches Ludo descend the staircase. "Thanks for lending me your room!"

"No problem."

"Have a great holiday—I mean, vacation—"

"Keep in touch," Ludo calls back. "Tell me how you like New York."

Ring Pull

February, New York.

A text wakes Spark in the middle of the night. Dad's silver St. Christopher charm—thrust into her hand at the last minute by Mum—is digging into her collarbone. She pushes herself up on her elbows. Ludo's alarm casts a lurid turquoise glow on the bedside table: 3:16. She struggles with the geography of a strange room, and when she switches on her phone she does not like how inky shadows roam around the corners of the high, angled ceiling. The text is from Mum. It says: Miss you. Is this supposed to make her feel happy because her Mum misses her, or sad for the same reason? As she can't decide what to say, apart from *Mum, don't you know it's the middle of the night here?* she puts the cell back on the table without replying. Now she's wide awake. Branches still scrape against the window and the fridge still hums.

Wishful thinking did not make Ludo late for his flight nor did it ground his plane. It's easy for her to conjure up Ludo's face in every detail. It hangs in her mind like a por-trait. Yet when she tries to do the same with Mum's, it's much harder. Her first glimpse of John Stone's face comes easily to mind too: his expression when he appeared mesmerized by the street woman. How is that? Is remembering faces more important when you don't know people? Or when you wish you knew them?

Thirsty, Spark slips out of bed and, arms held out in

front of her in the darkness, makes her way toward the door. She halts next to Ludo's fridge. Oh, to have a fridge in your bedroom! Oh, to have a bedroom big enough for a fridge! She stands in front of it, shivering in her pajamas, hesitates, then opens it. A fan of dazzling light bursts from the crack in the door, and she blinks while her eyes adjust. A six-pack of Coca-Cola sits on the middle shelf. A card has been propped up against it: FOR DAN'S SISTER.

Spark imagines the moment Ludo wrote those words for a girl he'd never met and whose name he couldn't remember. And here she is. That lucky stranger. The sound of the can opening punctuates the silence of the night: *Ps-s-s-sht!* She swallows the sweet, icy liquid down in eager gulps. Spark stands at the drafty windows, slipping behind the curtain. The street and rooftops are coated with a thin layer of glistening snow. She takes in the scene like a camera: unblinking, unthinking, merely registering at some level the foreignness of the cars and the houses and the streetlights. What she has been anticipating for so long now feels unreal. Wind agitates the bare-branched trees that line Cranberry Street; police sirens grow nearer, then fade; a woman in high heels totters down the street by herself, holding on to the cars for balance. Her stilettos make a kind of muffled echo. *I'm in New York.*

Spark finds herself tugging at the St. Christopher charm. Abruptly she reaches up to unfasten the fine silver chain. Why should she rely on a charm or anything else to ward off ill luck? It didn't do her dad any good, that's for sure. How can you enjoy *anything* if you're *afraid*? The warm metal medallion slips off the chain into her fingers. In its place she manages, twisting and pulling, to yank off the ring pull from Ludo's can of soda and thread it through.

That Spark was going to fall in love with Manhattan was inevitable. Dan is happy to show off his new city while Spark, for once, is happy to follow his lead. They walk such great distances the soles of her green ankle boots split. The days race by; when Spark slides into Ludo's bed each night she falls instantly and deeply asleep. When, finally, she plucks up the courage to pick up the Gibson Explorer, she plays it to an imaginary audience of one. Sometimes she trails the tips of her fingers across his posters, his speakers, his fridge. She cannot count on ever meeting Ludo again yet somehow does not doubt that she will.

Dan won't be returning to Mansfield—that much is obvious. Spark tries not to resent this because she can see how happy and excited he is. He has the right to live his life how and where he likes. Of course he's going to stay in New York. But there are moments when she wishes she'd never come because Dan will stay here and she's the one who's got to go back to Hawthorn Avenue.

One day, as they stand watching a yellow helicopter hovering, hawk-like, over the Thirty-fourth Street Heliport, Spark asks Dan to tell her about Ludo. It's not the first time. Dan says he's an immature smart-ass who has no notion of how spoiled he is.

Spark can't tell if he's joking. "I thought you were his friend!"

"I am! Which doesn't mean that I'm blind to his faults."

Spark interprets this as Ludo enjoys annoying Dan (a reaction she can understand), that he's intelligent (surely not a bad thing), and that his parents happen to be wealthy (should this worry her?). Dan grows weary of her defense of him. "Stop bugging me about Ludo! He's got no idea about people like us."

Spark asks him what the heck that's supposed to mean, but Dan goes silent on her.

"You mean people like *me*, who haven't had the advantage of a private education?"

Dan flashes her a warning look. As he's been so good to her all week—considerate and generous—she decides not to torment him. Besides, she can hardly complain if he feels protective toward his little sister.

Over their last meal together—noodles and pork dumplings in Chinatown—Dan asks Spark about her plans for university. "Where have you applied to, then?"

"Nottingham. They want two As and a B."

"That's harsh!"

"I know."

"You should have gone in for something obscure like me."

"But I *like* art history."

"So where else have you applied to?"

"It doesn't matter. I can't go anywhere else and still live at home. It's Nottingham or nothing. Someone's got to stay with Mum."

"Have you got to bring Mum into the equation *all* the

time? That was the idea of inviting you over. A bit of com-
passionate leave."

Spark glares at Dan. He calmly resumes eating his pork
dumplings, though she can tell he is waiting for her outburst. And she can't resist for long.

"When *you* left you knew that I'd be there to keep her
company. If *I* leave she's got no one."

"You underestimate her."

"Believe that if it makes you feel better."

Spark watches as her big brother masters his frustration.
He drinks a full glass of water without a pause and bangs it
down on the table. Spark turns her attention to identical
twin girls, opposite, short legs dangling, shoving noodles
into their mouths with red-and-gold chopsticks.

"Spark?"

"What?"

"Don't mess up your life because Mum thinks she's
messed up hers."

Spark texts Mum every day and feels bad that the thought
of returning to Mansfield fills her with gloom. She leaves
packing until the very last minute.

"Promise me you'll come back home when you can,"
she says to Dan.

"I've told you I will. Don't you believe me?"

With her brother nagging her to get a move on, Spark
makes a selection of her best photographs for Ludo. Dan
is probably right about never seeing him again, yet feeding
his cat, playing his guitars, sleeping in his bed, these acts

have cemented a bond—on her part, at least. Ludo was right about the cat—the food disappeared off the saucer every night but she's not once caught sight of the animal. Spark selects a couple of aerial shots taken from the Empire State Building, a picture of a yellow school bus with a row of kids all poking out their tongues at her, and, finally, she chooses the image of John Stone mesmerized by the street woman. On his desk, she places a tin of Cornish fudge that she brought with her from England, and a pencil sketch of Cranberry Street as viewed from his window. The sound of Ludo's bedroom door clicking shut behind her for the final time gives her an empty feeling inside. They catch a bus to the airport. A taxi is out of the question: They've both spent all their money. When she and Dan hug each other at the barrier at JFK they cannot look each other in the eye without welling up.

"See you," she says.

"See you, then. Take it easy, Spark."

The Boathouse

April 20—, Suffolk, England.

There is something wrong with the fingers of John Stone's left hand. They are twitching in a way that alarms him. He tries—and fails—to control the movement by force of will; then, when he tries to make a fist, a cold, electric pain shoots down his arm.

His hammock is tied to the posts of the old blue boathouse, where water laps beneath the rotting deck of the veranda. John Stone lies still, shrouded by rough canvas, trying to remember if this is the fourth or the fifth attack. Months have elapsed between episodes, each one a little worse than the last. Now, for the first time, it strikes him what these symptoms could mean, and his mouth goes dry with fear. He raises his left hand to the sky and stretches out his quivering fingers, opening and closing them like a fan, squinting at their silhouette, black against the setting sun.

He lowers his arm and presses his fingers hard into his thigh in an attempt to still them. To calm himself, he rests his gaze on the snaking river that flows through reed beds teeming with birds and insects. It is here that the river turns back on itself, forming a loop so tight around the ground on which Stowney House stands, that it is an island in all but name. John Stone has seen more of the world than most, but it is in this land of mists and water and silences that he feels most at ease. He strains to remember what the Spaniard said so long ago about the illness that would have killed his father had a blow to the head not finished him first. At the time the description scarcely made an impression on him. Why should it? He was a boy and had no memory of his father. Yet John Stone finds that his first teacher's words have lain dormant all this time only to emerge now, flapping at him like a bird of ill omen: *It began with his hands.*

Suspended in his hammock, he senses the pull of the earth. The ropes creak and groan as he sways back and forth, back and forth. He swings faster. It *began* with his hands. After everything he has seen and done, after everything he has *survived*. A disease inherited from a parent he never knew.

John Stone seldom used to consult Thérèse about his personal concerns—her visits to Stowney House were rarer than those of the dark-bellied geese who arrive here from Siberia every few years—but now that she is dead, who else can he turn to for advice? If his health were to fail, how could Martha and Jacob cope without him? Not from day to day, but over the months and the years. When he first brought them here they clung to Stowney House as if to a raft—and he did not bring them back from the brink for them to be cast adrift now. Absurd that he has never before doubted that he would always be there to help them.

John Stone rolls out of his hammock and walks through the wood and then across the orchard. In the distance he spots Jacob, veiled by his beekeeper's hat, walking purposefully toward the hives. Jacob will have seen him, but he is not a man to stop work for superfluous greeting. Now he enters the garden with its gravel paths and clipped box hedges. Closer to the house, through the open kitchen door, he hears the sound of Martha singing, her voice still as bright and clear as a girl's.

When he reaches the fountain, on the south side of Stowney House, he sits on the basin's edge. It depicts a river god, and reminds him of a place he used to love. Foaming jets of water used to cascade over the figure's garlanded head and flowing beard, although in recent years Jacob has diverted the water supply to irrigate the kitchen garden. An image bursts into his mind of a crowd of people, brightly dressed and laughing, and it seems to John Stone that he has entered a different landscape. He even fancies that he can hear the sound of splashing water and the excited yapping of small dogs. His eyelids close and a smile forms on his lips.

When this memory fades, it strikes him that Stowney House is not the sanctuary that it once was. He flexes his left wrist cautiously and finds that he has mastery of himself once more. Like winter shoots pushing unseen through cold earth, he senses that change is coming, and John Stone, who has cared for Martha and Jacob for so long, determines to find a Friend for them while he still can.

Your Little Life

June, Mansfield, Nottinghamshire.

Spark holds the small, fat envelope between ink-stained thumb and forefinger. She has sealed and taped it—just to be on the safe side. *Stowney House. Suffolk.* She looks around her. It's high here. The postbox commands a panoramic view of row after row of redbrick terraces, which slope steeply down toward the town, and are so familiar she rarely notices them. But she noticed them when she came back from New York, and she notices them again now.

Weeds struggle through cracks in the sun-baked pavement; she can feel the heat through her flip-flops. Turquoise ink was probably a mistake, although it seemed a good idea at the time. A handwritten letter seems so *intimate* compared with texting. And what conclusions will Mr. John Stone draw from the color of her ink, the length of her loops, the slant of her letters, the spaces between her words? Has she passed whatever test he might have set her? She contemplates the envelope and for a moment those instructions, transmitted from brain to arms to fingers, seem charged with mystery.

"I've lost my guitar pick," Spark lied when Mum caught her rummaging in the sideboard for envelopes. "The one I brought back from New York."

What was the point of upsetting her? She might not get the job. Mum looked unconvinced and lit a cigarette, blowing smoke into a slant of sunshine.

"No ciggies before lunch, you said—"

Mum stubbed it out angrily in the potted palm and left.

"I didn't say it to make you feel bad!" Spark called after her.

She covered five small pages in her wrist-achingly neat handwriting. The words spilled out and she had to rein herself in. Strange how you never know what to say until you've said it.

But now, as the envelope slips from her fingers, Spark's stomach lurches, as if it were she, and not her letter, who were falling into the black void of the postbox. Too late, it strikes her that there is no way that this rambling, personal account of herself is what John Stone had in mind. *Idiot girl!* She jams her hand into the narrow slot, trying to retrieve it. Her fingers flap about in the darkness. *Tell me about yourself and how you view life.* He didn't mean it! What he actually meant was: *Convince me that you're reliable and that you've got a couple of brain cells to rub together. Why* had she opened up like that to a prospective employer? Because he had kind eyes? Because the way he looked at the street woman in New York intrigued her? Or was it because there was no one else who said they wanted to know? But the trouble with writing about yourself and your little life is that once you start you can't stop.

A small boy walks past, shooting a glance at her assault on the postbox. Spark pulls out her hand with difficulty. The flesh above her wrist hurts like someone has given her a Chinese burn. The boy throws a pretend ball for his yappy little terrier, who chases after if anyway. There was no way, Spark tells herself, that John Stone was going to give her a job in any case. She dawdles home in the strong sunshine, convinced that she's wasted a morning and that a door to one of life's possibilities has just slammed shut.

The Good Stuff

37 Hawthorn Avenue
Mansfield
Nottinghamshire

Dear Mr. Stone,

You told me that if I was still interested in a summer job I should write to tell you something about myself and how I view the world.

   I live and go to school in Mansfield, which is a mining town in the East Midlands, though most of the coal pits have now closed. We moved here when I was still very young, after my father was killed in an accident. My parents met when my mum got a job as a waitress in the restaurant he ran in Suffolk. She says he always worked too hard and would never allow himself a day off. Coming home one night, he had a heart attack. He lost control of his van and drove it into a tree. My father originally came from Corsica. He even changed his name from Pecora to Park, which didn't go down well with his family, apparently. We don't see them—Corsica is too far away and they don't speak English. "<u>Pecora</u>" means "sheep" in Italian, so I'm relieved he didn't go in for a literal translation.

Mansfield is Mum's hometown, and after my father died she brought Dan and me back to live there. There is a photograph of Dad on our mantelpiece. When I think I am remembering him, it could be his photo that I am remembering and not my dad, which is upsetting. But I do remember the funeral: Dad's coffin behind the shiny windows of the hearse, and strangers dabbing their eyes and telling me I was a brave girl.

Mum coped until my nan—my Mum's mother—passed away four years ago. It coincided with Dan going away to university, and she became depressed. She is much better now—otherwise I would not be applying for a job that takes me away from home. For a long time the running of the house fell to me, which means that I'm used to organizing things and planning ahead. I'm good at handling numbers, filling out forms, using computers, and dealing with people. I don't have a lot of time for hobbies, but I love photography and am learning to play guitar.

I am about to sit my A-levels (art history, English lit, and French) and am hoping to read art history at university. Dan attended private school (I know how grateful Mum is to your charity for arranging his scholarship), but I went to a state school and am happy that I did. I've done well at my school and I don't feel different to the people I grew up with—which Dan definitely does.

You also asked me to tell you how I view the world. That is a difficult question to answer because how I see things is always changing. I used to think Nottingham was a big city until I saw New York. Now I feel that I've got to see as much of the world as I can. Often things aren't what they seem at first sight, so I try not to come to conclusions too soon—about people, places, music, or whatever—to avoid missing out on what could be there. Even difficult situations can have their compensations. Coping with Mum was sometimes hard, but we're definitely closer because of it.

One of my favorite photographs is a black-and-white picture of a tsunami. At first all you notice is destruction: a beach covered in debris and, behind it, most of a flattened village. But then a shape at the center of it all draws your eye in. You see that, surrounded by all this tragedy, a baby is lying on the sand, kicking her legs in the air. Stranded on the beach all by herself, you can tell that something is making her happy—maybe it's the sound of the sea or the feel of the sand. I've stuck it to my wall to remind me that no matter how bad things get you've got to be open to the good stuff.

I have a rule: I don't allow myself to be scared of anything or anyone. My dad showed a lot of courage coming to another country and making a success of his own business. I'm still thinking about what I want to do for a living—something creative, I hope—but I'd like to think that I could be as brave and determined as him. One thing I know is that I don't want to be stuck at home with a couple of kids and no future.

I'm sorry if this letter isn't what you had in mind, but if you feel that I might be a suitable candidate, would it be possible to tell me a little more about the position? If there is anything else you need to know about me, please ask.

Yours sincerely,

Spark (Stella Park)

Nothing Is More Important Than This Day

June, Suffolk.

John Stone stands at his open window, happy to let bird-song and chill, damp air drift over him. Already the horizon is streaked with pink and gold. Like Martha, he rises early, though not as early as Jacob, for whom sleep is no longer a refuge. He watches the mist rising where the river bounds his land. A new day. *Ah,* thinks John Stone. *Not so angry this morning. That is good.* He examines his hands—the dry, tanned skin, his knuckles, the half-moons of his thumbnails, the pink palms—then he makes a fist and slowly uncurls his fingers, stretching them sideways as far as they will go, and holds them for a moment. There is no trace of a tremor. Against his better judgement, hope starts to rise up in him.

In the galleried landing he examines his face in a mirror. Strands of hair hang over his broad forehead and he pushes these away, scraping a thumbnail down an unshaven cheek. *What a ruffian!* He runs his fingers down the length of his nose as if to straighten it. People tell him it gives his face character, though he does not need such reassurance: His broken nose pleases him. His complexion, however, is ash pale. He plucks out Spark's letter from his robe pocket, stares at it, and pushes it back in again, hoping that a night's sleep will have delivered a decision. Both Spark's response and his own hesitation have taken him by surprise. That he's preferred not to dwell on their encounter in New York means that time is not on his side: He cannot now keep the girl waiting. John Stone wonders how he will feel if his suspicions about Spark's identity are confirmed. He'll know more after he goes to see Edward, his lawyer. He descends the staircase, fingertips skimming the long sweep of the banister. Could he have imagined the resemblance in New York? It is clear from her letter that the girl is wholly ignorant of any connection.

The smell of Martha's home-cured bacon reaches him. Presently she will call for him, stretching his one-syllable name into two in that singsong, Irish way of hers: *Jo-ohn!* Then she will bang on a frying pan at the back door to alert Jacob, who, at the prospect of breakfast, can be depended upon to trot down the kitchen path at a sprightly pace. Martha has taken on the role of mother of the house and there are times when John Stone wishes that this were not so, because she is apt to hide behind it like a shield. A picture forms in his mind of his curious family, the two of them sitting expectantly at the table, their knives and forks held poised, waiting for the head of the house to start his meal. Guilt quickens the beat of his heart: Martha and Jacob have grown to love him. He knows that. Was he wrong to have let them depend upon him in this way? How will they cope without him when the world has roared ahead, leaving them isolated in this remote backwater? He must not delay: The task of securing a Friend for them is becoming more urgent by the day.

* * *

"How are you today, Martha?"

"I'm right as the mail, John. And yourself?"

John Stone considers how to reply, so Martha answers for him.

"You look liverish. Did you not sleep well?"

"I'm fine, Martha."

"If you say so."

John Stone holds her skeptical gaze. Martha's eyes are black and shining, and put him in mind of a clever bird. Her neat hair is pushed back behind her ears. She wears an apron over her gray dress, which reflects the current image that she has of herself. It is made from red-and-white-checked linen and is the sort that ties behind the neck and again around the waist. John Stone is still in his nightclothes, for he likes to feel at ease when he is in the country. Besides, he knows Martha likes to disapprove of his slovenly city ways.

"Martha, I'd like to have a word with you after breakfast, if I could."

John Stone catches a flicker of concern as Martha smoothes down her starched apron with the flats of her hands. "Well then, John, perhaps you could help me with the last of the apples while we talk. I will peel and you can chop. I can surprise Jacob with an Eve's pudding for his supper."

They become aware of Jacob's progress down the path; they hear the crunch of gravel and the encounter of boots with a mud scraper. The back door creaks open and Jacob enters backward, pushing up the latch with one elbow. He carries with him the odor of the outdoors, of compost heaps and cut grass, and things you wouldn't care to know about. His coarse, sun-bleached hair grows vertically, like cropped wheat. It seems to John Stone that Jacob is as unknowable as the ancient earth he tends and, like his beloved garden, never more than a season away from encroaching wildness.

"Boots!" calls Martha.

Jacob levers them off without untying the laces and pushes them into the corner of the quarry-tiled floor with his big toe. A large, dead rabbit dangles by its ears from one fist. Whatever Jacob has in his other hand, he conceals it behind his back.

"Rabbit," he says in a voice that is deep and rasping.

"In the sink, if you please," Martha says.

Jacob draws out several stems of blush-pink roses, the first of the season, which he thrusts at Martha. She buries her face in them.

"Now, isn't that better than any perfume money can buy? Isn't it the very smell of summer? Thank you, Jacob."

Satisfied, he nods. Now Jacob's ice-blue eyes swivel in John Stone's direction. His wrinkled skin is the color of walnuts. "John," he says, as if it were a statement.

"Jacob. How are you this morning, my dear fellow?" John Stone knows better than to expect a reply. He points, instead, to the rabbit, now draped over the draining board, its head lolling to one side. Dark, sticky blood oozes from the back of its skull. "Did you catch it in one of your new snares?" Jacob shakes his head and takes a stained flint ball out of his pocket. He mimes throwing it. Jacob has far and away the best aim John Stone has ever come across.

Martha picks up the animal and weighs it in her hands

appreciatively. She strokes the gorgeous fur. "Will you skin it for me later, Jacob?"

"Aye."

"And what have you got for me to put in a rabbit stew?"

"Onions," he offers. "Thyme."

"That'll be grand."

It is understood that the first meal of the day will be peaceful. In companionable silence the three inhabitants of Stowney House drink sweet tea, eat bacon and eggs, and spread butter on Martha's brown bread. Through the half-open door bees buzz around bronze wallflowers that are past their best. Jacob eagerly chews and slurps his way through breakfast. Martha and John Stone watch him wipe the egg yolk from his plate with a morsel of bread and stuff the last piece into his mouth with relish. There's a pleasure to be had in observing the satisfaction of another's appetite.

John Stone's appetite, on the other hand, is failing him. He tosses a piece of bacon to a small tabby who sits in front of the stove vigorously washing the pale fur on her chest. John Stone acknowledges Martha's thrifty disapproval with a wink and a smile. It doesn't matter that she could dine off caviar three times a day if she was so inclined. That is beside the point, for if there's one thing Martha cannot abide, it is waste. The same cannot be said about John Stone, whom life has taught different lessons, the pleasures of occasional excess being among them. The cat leaves off washing to lick the salty meat, somewhat disdainfully, with her clean, pink tongue.

"She's a mouser," scalds Martha. "If she's not hungry she'll not hunt."

"Fresh, warm blood is what she craves," adds Jacob in what strikes John Stone as a refreshingly long sentence for him at breakfast time. "It is her nature."

"I'm sure you're right," says John Stone as the cat loses interest and slopes off into the sunshine, stretching out her back legs languorously as she does so. "I merely wanted to please her."

"And that," comments Martha, "is *your* nature."

Since the weather is fine, they say their daily vows outside. They stand as one, arms around one another's shoulders and heads touching. John Stone feels the sun on his back, the warm flesh of his companions beneath his fingers, the coolness of the blades of grass between his toes. There is a robin close by, and its song, bright as glass, echoes across the orchard. Encircled by the peace of Stowney House and the love of his friends, John Stone forms the words in his mind and holds them there: *There is nothing more important than this day.* The simplicity of the ritual, which he instigated so long ago, fills him with a sense of belonging, and shields him from the biting loneliness that used to beset him. When he is away from Stowney House these words link him so strongly to his friends that he often fancies he can hear them breathing. They break apart. Jacob returns to his chores, pulling his cap from his pocket and jamming it on his head. His arthritic dog, who is no longer allowed in the house, gets up from the shady spot where she has been dozing and limps after him. By the time John Stone has walked back to the kitchen to speak with Martha the knot in his stomach has returned. *I am myself*, he says under his breath. *In me the past lives.*

Martha cores each apple and removes the peel in a continuous spiral. She is fast and accurate; John Stone takes longer to chop each one into quarters. But then, he is studying Martha's reaction. She is struggling to cope with the enormity of his announcement. Her eyes are glassy as she focuses her attention on the rotating fruit.

"We have entertained Friends in the past, Martha."

"Mais presque jamais ils ne sont restés la nuit—"

Fragments of another persona reveal themselves when Martha speaks in French—the angle of her jaw and the way she arches her eyebrows. He gets a sudden picture of a very different Martha from the current, homely incarnation that she has cultivated at Stowney House.

"Can we not accommodate one young guest in this large house? It will only be for a few weeks. Just until she gets to know us a little."

Each time John Stone has answered her in English and taken care to imbue his expression and tone of voice with warmth and reassurance.

"Is she a Friend?"

"I hope she will be. It is why I have invited her."

John Stone sees the disbelief in Martha's eyes. "But she understands about us?"

"She is young. I want her to get to know us first. If she helps us I'd prefer the first move came from her—"

"Bent u gek?"

"I'm not out of my mind, my dear Martha! Please don't make more of this than it deserves. When have I ever let you down?"

It has been an age since Martha has confused her languages in this way—which can only be a bad sign, as if the domesticated creature she has become at Stowney House does not have the words to cope with such distress. First French and now Dutch. Although he knows little of her experiences in Holland, he gathers that her time there was a particularly wretched chapter of her life. Not for the last time is he grateful that he has always been careful to remain himself. A life of multiple exiles is hard enough without changing your identity at the same time.

"Once you've met the girl, you will understand why I've invited her to Stowney House. There is something about her—"

"Oh, *John* . . ." Now Martha is wringing her hands and shaking her head from side to side. He grabs hold of her hand.

"Can't you trust me? It's for you and Jacob that I am doing this. The world is changing so quickly—"

"But why now, John? Why must you be so hasty? And why a girl? Did you not tell us you were hoping a bright young man might be a Friend to us? You said you thought he'd do well in the world."

"Daniel? He is in America."

Martha withdraws her hand from his and tucks her hair behind her ears.

"How old is she?"

"Seventeen."

"You're putting your trust in a girl of *seventeen!*" The last word becomes a wail but she clamps both hands over her mouth. "I'm sorry, John. It's the shock of it."

"Martha—I need you to remain calm. All will be well. Have I ever lied to you?"

Martha shakes her head. Now is not the time to reveal that she has met Spark before and that he is almost certain of another connection. Does that count as a lie?

"Can I count on you to welcome Spark into our house?"

Martha nods. John watches Martha sitting rigid, bracing herself, and wants to wail himself. "Please don't look so anxious. You haven't always been a recluse. You will enjoy the company—and you can try out all your best puddings on her."

Martha tries to smile. "I owe you everything, John. If this is what you want—"

"You owe me nothing, as I grow exceedingly tired of telling you. What family do we have if not each other? And now, my dear Martha, I am off to break the news to Jacob."

"John—let me tell him."

John Stone squeezes Martha's hand. "It is *my* decision and *my* responsibility. Don't worry, I'll be gentle with him."

The corners of Martha's mouth start to curl upward. "John, it is not Jacob I am concerned about." Suddenly she starts to laugh, and the relief of it sets John Stone off too. Martha dabs at her eyes with a handkerchief: "But for the love of God, John, don't tell him she's *seventeen!*"

Tree Walking

June, Suffolk.

They always bury their dogs here. John Stone is careful not to trip over the hardwood markers that Jacob lovingly carves for them and that soon become hidden under piles of dry leaves. He comes to a halt and bends over, hands resting on knees, heart thumping against rib cage. Martha is right: The city *has* made him soft. John Stone fancies he smells decay, and death—and renewal. Images form in his mind of maggots burrowing through corpses and roots curling, tendril-like, around bone. He listens to the sound of his life-blood pulsing in his temples and cannot believe that there will come a time when this old heart will actually cease pumping.

"Come back, Jacob! Things cannot stay the same forever! You don't need me to remind you of that."

Presently he rises, reaching out to steady himself against the beech tree's rough bark, and peers upward. Pinpricks of shimmering sunlight pierce its dense canopy. *Is he up there?* John Stone searches for a flash of wheaten hair, for a glimpse of a dun-colored trouser leg, or for the white of Spark's letter snatched from his grasp.

"Jacob!" he shouts, regretting the tone of anger and frustration, which he has failed to disguise. "I won't deny that there is a risk, but I have the measure of her. She is of good character."

But John Stone's words leave in their wake a silence broken only by the drone of the green metallic flies that hover above the woodland floor. He is a fool: He should have let Martha accompany him. This has been a timely reminder that a man apt to go berserk can always command a certain level of respect. His ears are still ringing.

"Jacob," he calls up, this time in a softer tone. "*Jacob. My friend.*"

He tiptoes to the other side of the tree trunk and a fleeting shape catches his eye. One of the branches springs back as an unseen foot is removed from it. Tree walking. It is an activity that Jacob has made his own—and one that promises a broken back if concentration is broken for an instant. When John Stone first suggested it to Jacob, he was drawing on his experience as a soldier during what it pleased him to call his wilderness years. The principle was simple. During times of great danger life becomes a question of staying alert, focusing on every sound and every movement. Nothing matters but the present moment—and the bullet that could be speeding toward you. Not a cure for sorrow, or regret—or, indeed, anger—but a temporary distraction, a way of letting go of the past by centering oneself in the present. Over time, Jacob has pruned these trees in such a way as to encourage lateral, weight-bearing branches. Now, if he is so inclined, Jacob can cross the whole wood undetected.

So John Stone has no time to defend himself when Jacob drops, silently, onto his back, and floors him. When he cries out, Jacob—who loves him—presses his face into the dirt without mercy.

"You are a *fool!*" says Jacob into his ear. "Little Stella will stir up memories and all Martha's children will come back to haunt her."

John Stone groans and Jacob lets him lift his head a little. He spits out earth and fragments of dry leaves. "I didn't tell you her name. . . ." As Jacob has steadfastly refused to learn how to read, John Stone is impressed by his powers of deduction. "How did you know?"

Jacob slides her letter over his mouth and nose, and inhales. "I can *smell* her."

"She is almost a woman," says John Stone as calmly as he can manage. "Martha isn't going to want to mother a seventeen-year-old."

"Is that how you think of me?" It is Martha who speaks. She stands only a few paces away, in dappled shade, a dark silhouette. "Jacob," she hisses. "You should be *ashamed.*" She spits out the last word so that it is barely audible. A wood pigeon flaps noisily skyward.

John Stone feels the crushing weight lift abruptly from his spine and he hears Jacob climbing back up into the tree canopy, scraping the soles of his boots against rough bark.

"Change destroys as much as it saves, as you of all people should know," calls down Jacob. "The girl will be careless with the life we have built here."

"And how long can we survive without change?" asks John Stone. But Jacob is already gone with a shiver of leaves.

John Stone pushes himself up onto all fours. Martha offers him her hands. He takes them and she pulls him to his feet.

"Best leave Jacob to me," she says.

"How much did you hear?"

"That I am a woman not in full possession of her emotions—"

"That is not so! If it were, I should not have suggested inviting Spark to stay with us. Martha?"

"Yes, John?"

He wonders if he should wait for a better moment to talk about Spark. No. Best to get it over with. "Do you recall the little girl who lived in the gatekeeper's cottage before I had it demolished? The one who kept coming back—"

"Little Stella, you mean?"

"Spark and little Stella are one and the same—"

"No!"

"It's true. Jacob has already worked it out." John Stone observes Martha put her hand over her mouth. "And Daniel, the bright young man I've talked to you about, is Stella's elder brother."

"Why didn't you tell me that before?"

John Stone sighs and watches a pale yellow butterfly pass through a shaft of sunshine behind Martha's head.

"Because it didn't seem important. She was a little girl who'd wandered onto our grounds. Who was she to you? Her family moved away soon after the incident with the water mill. And, I admit, it was at Thérèse's request that I have been helping the family."

Martha's eyes widen. "Thérèse?"

"Thérèse knew Spark's late father. Quite well, by the sound of it. She owned the building where he ran a restaurant. She also allowed them to live in the gatekeeper's cottage. I'd better warn you that I think it's likely Spark is Thérèse's child—"

"Oh, John!"

"When I saw the girl in New York I could have been looking at a young Thérèse. It's too much of a coincidence."

"It must have been a terrible shock to see her like that!" says Martha.

John Stone agrees that it was, indeed, very shocking. A fly buzzes in his ear. He brushes it away with the back of his hand.

"How sure are you?"

"I'll tell you after I've seen Edward. Fifteen years ago, when he told me that Thérèse had died, he gave me a letter that she'd written to me. I need to look at it again. At the time I wasn't in a fit state to give it the attention it deserved."

"Did that woman ever bring you anything but grief?"

John Stone puts a finger to his lips.

"*Little Stella!*" says Martha, shaking her head. "Life can play some strange tricks. Do you think she'll remember her visits to Stowney House?"

"She was very young," replies John Stone. "I doubt it."

Dandelion Clock

June, London.

John Stone stares down at Lincoln's Inn Fields from the high-ceilinged offices of Edward de Souza, his lawyer. Through the open window the smell of freshly cut grass reaches him. One should not be inside on a day like this. One by one John Stone's instructions regarding his will are addressed and clarified. Edward, with his neatly manicured fingers, makes indecipherable notes in pencil in a notepad. John Stone distracts himself rearranging Edward's paperweights, which pin down the fluttering paperwork. Sometimes the lawyer looks up at the sunlight dancing on the ceiling, then goes back to his notes and erases words with a pale green eraser.

Finally the lawyer takes two envelopes from a wire tray and slides them toward him. "The deeds to the gatekeeper's cottage, as requested," he says, tapping one, "and this is your late wife's letter. I thought it best to reseal it."

"Thank you," says John Stone, slipping them into his briefcase.

"It's rather a coincidence that after fifteen years you should choose to ask to look at them now. Only yesterday I was contacted by one of Thérèse's lawyers, who required me to confirm that I am still acting for you—"

"Why, for heaven's sake?"

"Apparently you can soon expect delivery of a *second* letter from Thérèse."

"Are you serious?"

The lawyer shrugs his shoulders. "From what you've told me about your late wife, posthumous control over her estate might have appealed to her. There's a legal term for it—'in mortmain'—literally, 'dead hand.' I admit to being intrigued—"

"And did her lawyers give any indication as to what this communication from beyond the grave is about? To inherit any more property would be irritating."

"Quite," says Edward de Souza, smiling. "I did press her solicitor for further information. She refused to be drawn— either that or she didn't know."

John Stone nods. "Thérèse was a woman incapable of doing anything that was not entirely on her own terms. As in life, so in death."

Once their morning's business is concluded the two men stand, face-to-face, at the door. "You were right to see me sooner rather than later," says the lawyer. "Your affairs are becoming positively labyrinthine." Edward gestures toward the far wall, lined with shelves bowing under the weight of box files.

"What will be will be, my dear fellow," says John Stone. "As we both know, life is full of surprises, some of them, alas, being more pleasant than others."

John Stone is touched to see a wave of distress pass

over the lawyer's normally composed features.

"I cannot believe that the prognosis is as bleak as you suspect," says Edward. "I wish you would consult a specialist." John Stone shakes his head firmly. "I am certain we could find a doctor we could trust—"

"No," insists John Stone. "To take such a risk is unthinkable."

"You may find that you change your mind, and if you do—"

"I won't."

John Stone reaches into his bulging jacket pocket and presses an apple-size object wrapped in tissue paper into the lawyer's hands.

"There," he says. "You thought I'd forgotten, didn't you?"

The lawyer's face lights up. He weighs the gift appreciatively in his hands. "My word, this one's heavy!"

"You've never let me down," says John Stone.

"Of course not!"

"Aren't you going to open it?"

"I hope this isn't meant to be some kind of good-bye present." The lawyer starts to tear off the paper but then stops. "I've always felt honored to be your Friend." He pulls off the last layer of tissue and smiles. Cupped in his hands, safe from the winds of time, is a dandelion clock preserved forever in crystal.

John Stone buys himself a double espresso in High Holborn and escapes back into the green oasis that is Lincoln's Inn Fields. A small reward after a morning of talk and high seriousness. Now he sits cross-legged, face tilted to the sky, sunning himself like a cat on the grass. Here, in this handsome square, society puts on its best face—grand, reassuring, civilized, benign. Of course, it is a beautiful lie. One only has to walk the streets nearby to see that.

John Stone opens his eyelids a slit and frowns in the sunlight. Office workers in a state of semi-undress are scattered randomly on the lawns: texting, eating, making calls, working on their tans. There was a time when it was the homeless of London who used to congregate here. He always did what he could for them. But they were removed, as they always are, along with the rats that feasted on their leftovers, and then new railings were erected to keep them out. The noon sun beats down. John Stone slips off his jacket and lays it on the daisies. He gulps down his tepid espresso in one gulp; the hit of caffeine feels good.

Now he flips open his briefcase and searches for Thérèse's letter, which was delivered to him along with the news of her passing. John Stone does not even know where she was laid to rest. His estranged wife's final wishes have denied him—to use a modern expression—a sense of *closure*.

Edward has resealed the narrow vellum envelope with red wax. Fifteen years ago John Stone had come close to throwing it into the fire. *Fifteen years.* The notion that he holds an object touched by Thérèse's hands unsettles him. He chases away a recollection of limpid blue eyes and the particular tilt of a chin, but her image continues to flicker in a dark recess of his mind. John Stone stands up abruptly. It is a sunny day; he will read it later. Walking away, he slips the letter into the inside pocket of his jacket—though not with any intention of keeping a vestige of her next to his heart.

Leaving Holborn, John Stone lowers the tinted windows so that the smell and sound of the city streets can penetrate the bland luxury of his hired car. At length he removes Thérèse's letter from its envelope, holding it as if it might spontaneously combust. He studies it without reading, observing the pressure and curve of her lines, the reality of her embedded in the unique flow of black ink. He feels the hairs rise at the back of his neck.

My dear Jean-Pierre, I know that you will have mixed feelings when you see my hand—I can even picture a certain apprehension in your dark eyes.

John Stone leans sideways to look at his reflection in the rearview mirror. It's true that he looks apprehensive. Once Thérèse told him (it was long ago and she was holding a knife to his throat at the time) that for all his charm he had the eyes of someone who was lost. It occurs to him that there is no one left alive who would call him Jean-Pierre.

Do not be anxious. I have no intention of visiting Stowney House. Indeed, I have no intention of doing anything or of going anywhere, suffering, as I am, from a disease of the nerves that renders me unfit to be seen in public.

A disease of the nerves—that detail had passed him by

fifteen years ago. John Stone's sharp intake of breath elicits a backward glance from the driver. But when he first read this letter he was not preoccupied with his own mortality. So, it seems that both his own father, at least according to the Spaniard, and also Thérèse, have succumbed to a weakness of the nervous system. He glances down at his hands, which currently show no sign of misbehaving.

> My purpose in writing to you is this:
> I wish to gift you a house. With this
> letter you will find enclosed the deeds to
> the former gatekeeper's cottage whose land
> adjoins your estate. I had my own reasons
> for acquiring the property but those are
> unimportant now.

What on earth had she intended to do? *I had my own reasons!* Spy on him? Drive Martha and Jacob away?

> You will be astonished to hear that I have
> caught a little of your philanthropic zeal
> and have offered the gatekeeper's cottage to
> a deserving family. The father is a cook of
> some sort on the coast. Of late he has been
> of great service to me; he has two children,
> and I would ask you to let them live in
> the house for as long as they have need of
> it. I am certain they will not bother you
> at Stowney House in any way. The youngest
> child, a baby girl, is a favorite of mine and

I would ask you to have some thought for the family's welfare.

I make this request while I can, for my health is failing. It seems unlikely that I shall survive you. Although there was a time when I found your attachment to the maxim "In me the past lives" a little irritating, perhaps now I can take some comfort from it. When the time comes, I hope that you can find it in your heart to keep alive something of me.

John Stone lets the letter drop onto his lap. Thérèse's manipulative streak gradually led him to distrust everything she said. How was he supposed to have known that on this occasion she was telling the truth? Fifteen years ago he had thought it was a ruse, a trap, details in some ingenious drama yet to be played out. It is painful to revisit her parting words. What he wanted to find is not there: She is not contrite; she does not beg for his forgiveness; there is no confession; there is no final blessing; she does not—

"Are you all right, Sir?"

John Stone realizes that he has been rubbing his forehead violently as if he has been trying to wipe something away. "Just a headache . . ."

They each address each other's reflections in the rearview mirror.

"Would you like me to stop at a pharmacy?"

"Thank you, no."

The driver turns his attention back to the road. John Stone folds up the letter and holds it in his fist by the open window. He is tempted to open his fingers and let the wind carry it away.

Why, even at the end, was Thérèse incapable of being simple and direct? *I hope that you can find it in your heart to keep alive something of me.* He is certain now that her letter concerned one thing and one thing alone: this baby girl of whom she had become so fond. Why could she not have said: *I am dying. I have a baby daughter. Will you help her if she needs it?* If she had, he would have done far more. What he *did* do for the family—a scholarship for the son and, later, an internship—stemmed chiefly from the pity he felt when he discovered that the father died not long after Thérèse's death. As far as he can tell, this Mrs. Park seems to have brought up the child as her own. That can't have been easy. In the circumstances, it's hardly surprising that she became depressed. He'll see for himself how good a job she has done when he has got to know Spark a little. If any doubt remained after he first set eyes on Spark in New York, this letter is proof enough that the resemblance was *not* a coincidence. Spark is the daughter of his estranged wife.

John Stone stares out across the sparkling, wind-rippled Thames and has an urge to get out of the car and walk awhile. He instructs the driver to pull over into a side street. They are in Chelsea, among tall, redbrick villas, and he strides out, swinging his arms, shaking his head slowly from side to side as if trying to sweep away difficult memories. Outside a small supermarket displaying boxes of fruit and vegetables on the pavement, he stops to fill a brown paper bag with some yellow plums, warmed by the sun. As he smells the fragrant flesh, a smile of recognition flashes across his face. They are mirabelles, a variety he rarely tastes nowadays, and whose sunny sweetness always conjures up bright images of his youth.

Messrs de Souza & Company, Byng House,
Lincoln's Inn Fields, London WC2.

CONFIDENTIALITY AGREEMENT

In consideration of being allowed to read the set of **eight notebooks constituting the initial part of a memoir written by Mr. John Stone, of Stowney House, in the County of Suffolk** ("the Notebooks"), I undertake and agree as follows:

i) I acknowledge that the existence and contents of the Notebooks is confidential to Mr. Stone (the "Confidential Information").

ii) I undertake not to remove the Notebooks or any part of them from the offices of Messrs de Souza & Company, Byng House, Lincoln's Inn Fields, London WC2, nor reproduce the Confidential Information in any form, whether by making notes, copies, or otherwise, and further, not to disclose or disseminate the Confidential Information in whole or in part to any third party, nor use the same for any purpose.

iii) I acknowledge that damages would be an inadequate remedy for breach of this undertaking and agree that Mr. Stone shall be entitled to obtain an injunction to prevent such breach.

iv) This Agreement shall be governed by the laws of England and Wales.

Signed: . . . .

Name:

Dated: . . . .

Prepared 28th July, 20—

Notebook 1

I

1685, Versailles, France.

They say that the grandeur of Versailles in the age of the Sun King has never been surpassed, although, human nature being what it is, one soon gets used to anything. In the middle of Louis XIV's long reign, the youngest son of a minor nobleman was brought by his father to live at court. Surrounded by art, music, and conversation of the very highest order, to receive an education at the court of Versailles, it was—as his father repeatedly told him—merely necessary for the boy to remain awake.

In the Palace of Versailles, where Louis shone at the center of a universe of his own making, the boy often felt like a spectator at a never-ending circus, relieved that the all-powerful ringmaster had not noticed him, and did not require him to perform. It was only much later that he understood what a privilege fate had bestowed on him allowing him to have observed, firsthand—and at such a tender age—the rules of the game at the court of the Sun King. The boy's name was Jean-Pierre, and that boy was me.

What I am about to describe happened so very long ago it begins to sound, even to my ears, like a fairy tale. And yet, here I am, pen in hand, holding up a lens to my own distant past. I recognize that boy but I cannot always *feel* him. Jean-Pierre is myself and he is also another. When I recall my arrival at court, for example, which was a momentous day in my young life, even though the images are bright and crisp, I see them as if I were a spirit sitting on my own shoulder. My father had often spoken of the magnificence of Versailles but his words did not prepare me for my first sight of it. I was sick after three days in a stuffy, rolling carriage, but they still had to drag me away from the blue-and-gold railings, where I clung on, spellbound, my fingers growing numb in the biting cold.

You must understand that it was an age when one's knowledge of the world was limited to a radius of a few miles from one's birthplace. It is difficult to comprehend, today, such ignorance. If anyone in our village traveled to the nearest big town, we would cluster around them for news on their return. The largest house I had ever seen was our own, which was smaller than the King's stables. And so it was that I gawped in awe at this vast palace, built of brick and honey-colored stone that glowed rose pink in the light of a dying winter sun. *Surely*, I thought, *I will not be permitted to spend my days here.*

While there was still light enough to see, my father took me by the hand and we walked to the back of the palace to view the gardens. We stood together, on the brink of a new life, our breath coming out in great clouds of steam. The sense of immense, luminous distances all leading to and from that spot was overwhelming. It was as if the cold air itself had been sculpted by a master hand. Radiating outward from the palace were wide lawns and generous terraces, all perfectly symmetrical. Topiary, statues, and magnificent fountains drew the eye to the misty distance, where a rectangular lake reflected the red evening sky like a gigantic mirror. When I beheld that astonishing vista I laughed out loud, both in delight and disbelief. This was the desired effect: the King was, after all, God's representative on earth; his power was absolute, and his home should bear witness to the fact.

"You see," said my father, "did I not tell you that Versailles is the greatest palace on earth?"

It was the only palace that I had seen—although I have seen a great many since. The scale and ambition of its creator's vision astounds me still. I had no understanding, then, of what this splendor had cost the people. A century later I saw the revolutionaries desecrate the Sun King's grave. They tossed Louis's bones into a pit along with the assorted remains of those who had reigned over France for a thousand years. I do not judge. I witness. The wheel of life revolves. To be alive is to change. Nothing lasts forever, and anyone who believes that it does is a fool.

II

I was fifteen years old. No longer a child, but skinny, long-limbed, wild-eyed. Picture me running from our lodgings in the town toward the palace, long hair flying and white stockings wrinkling around my ankles. It was my first summer at Versailles, and I was fleeing from my three elder brothers. I did not fancy my chances if they caught up with me. My father was away attending to affairs on our estate and my brothers had taken advantage of his absence by vowing to beat me to a pulp. It was not an idle threat. I was the youngest by six years and my entry into the world had coincided with our mother's exit. If I was the apple of my father's eye, I was also, according to my brothers, the cuckoo in his nest. Later I came to understand their hatred; at the time it was a situation I accepted in the same way that hens accept the existence of foxes.

I made for the Great Courtyard, where there were always lines of sedan chairs, horse-drawn fiacres, endless lines of lumbering wagons bringing in goods to supply the royal household, and, of course, the resplendent carriages of the aristocracy. Here was the din and clatter that one finds at the threshold of two dependent worlds—on the one side the town, on the other, the royal palace of the Sun King. There were many places in Versailles where a quiet decorum was required, where one spoke in a low voice, and where one did not knock on a door but, rather, scratched on it with a fingernail. But here, in the ripe stink of the crowd, you shouted to make yourself heard.

I skidded on some disgusting, putrefying thing, cracking the heel of my shoe as I did so. To stop myself from falling, I caught hold of a soft, plump arm. The arm belonged to a street hawker, a young woman who balanced a basket of fruit on her head. I grabbed hold of her waist and dragged her in front of me like a shield, peeping out to see if there was any sign of my brothers. The woman cried out as small, yellow plums tumbled from her basket. I shot out my cupped hands and caught them in quick succession, clasping them to my chest.

"I beg your pardon, Madame," I said. The woman gestured at my dripping face, pulled out a cloth, and wiped my forehead, my cheeks, my nose. She was none too gentle, and when I grimaced and spluttered she laughed. I tried to return the mirabelle plums to her, but she thrust them back at me. Women were often kind to me in my youth. She reached up into her basket and gave me another handful. "For you," she said.

So I started that fateful day hot, disheveled, my pockets crammed with mirabelles—and more than a little afraid. Hoping that my brothers had given up the chase, I slipped into the royal courtyard through one of the side gates (the main gate being reserved for the King and princes of the blood), and I hid for a long while behind a line of sedan chairs.

It was my new coat that had provoked my brothers' jealousy on this occasion. We were all in need of finery, for the King expected his courtiers to be decorative. However, we were not wealthy and it was a terrible expense to bear. My father had ordered his tailor to make me a new coat and waistcoat in blue silk while announcing to my brothers that they must make do with the outfits they already possessed. They were not pleased.

By now the Château of Versailles had become my playground, and I cannot imagine anywhere better suited to hide-and-seek. I kept out of sight for much of that day, first in the King's kitchens—where I was known, and where I played the joker, and where, in return, I was given slices of venison fresh from the spit, and handfuls of candied fruit. Afterward, I headed for the walled kitchen garden, a short walk from the palace. The garden was divided into many "rooms" and I was able to conceal myself behind rows of espaliered fruit trees. I strolled around the neat beds bursting with feathery asparagus and lines of salad, herbs, and vegetables, and helped myself to strawberries, and then to peas (a novelty much favored then by the King), which I popped into my mouth, sweet and crunchy, out of the pod.

Later I hid in the cavernous icehouse, where the cold, echoing darkness and the sound of constant dripping put me in mind of dungeons. I took to wondering when my brothers had started to hate me so. If my mother had died bringing me into the world, I reasoned, at least she had loved them for a while. Whereas I had never known her. Surely I deserved pity, not hate.

Midafternoon, I risked returning to the palace. Two young ladies, identical twins, invited me to sit with them. We played Reversi, a favorite card game of mine, although, fearful that my brothers might appear at any moment, my concentration was poor. The King, who liked to hear music wherever he went, must have been taking a stroll, for the sound of a band playing reached us through an open window. I was much taken by the melody, and the driving beat set my foot tapping. I said as much to the young ladies.

"It is by Lully," said one.

"Is it ever by anyone else?" said the other.

"Poor Monsieur Lully," said the first.

"Why poor?" I asked.

"Did you not hear? He kept such violent time with his stick during a concert last year that he struck his foot—"

"And developed a terrible ulcer—"

"Which Father couldn't cure—"

"And it turned gangrenous and then he died—"

The two *mesdemoiselles* were the daughters, as it happened, of one of the King's physicians (whose tender care everyone feared more than becoming ill in the first place).

"How very unfortunate," I said.

Presently, bored with cards, the young ladies demanded other entertainment. Unimpressed by my efforts to juggle the mirabelles, they proposed a dare, which I felt obliged to accept. An ancient duchess, fond of terrorizing her servants, was asleep in an armchair next to the doorway of the anteroom where we sat. Her jaw hung slackly open, and she was snoring, but intermittently, so that it came as a shock each time she started up again. One of the young ladies presented me with an ostrich feather from her headdress and, as instructed, I held it beneath the duchess's nose. With every breath the jewels on her wrinkled chest rose and fell.

Her lapdog, who was also half-asleep, regarded me with one bulbous, black eye, revealing a slither of white like a crescent moon. The effort of not laughing out loud made us all long to laugh even more. Suddenly the old lady snorted violently and the fluffy strands of the ostrich feather entered the dark cavities of her flared nostrils. With a start she awoke. Mirroring her animal, one eyelid snapped open and focused first on the feather and second on me. The young ladies clung to each other, helpless with silent mirth, their colorful skirts merging together like flowers in a vase. The duchess screeched for her servant and I made a swift departure.

When I reached the cool quiet of the Queen's staircase I paused to lean over the balustrade. Too late, I saw my three brothers looking up at me from below and I froze, my feet becoming rooted to the marble floor. Fear, true gut-wrenching fear, is the most terrible thing to provoke in a child—as all the bullies through time have always known and always will know. Only when I heard them clattering up the stairs, did I manage to turn on my heels and run into the Hall of Mirrors. As I darted between one group of gossiping courtiers and the next, Monsieur Grignotte, an actor with whom I was on friendly terms, called out to me in his fine tenor voice. "Jean-Pierre! Such a handsome coat, dear boy! But, you know, one does not *run* at Versailles." A long succession of golden mirrors, each the height of three men, reflected my progress across the room, revealing my whereabouts to my brothers.

I would have been wiser to stay inside the palace. Instead, I ran out into the gardens, where, as I crossed the vast terrace, I felt as a mouse must feel with a hawk hovering above it. Hunting was the thing my brothers loved most in the world and I was their favorite prey. And so I raced across the gravel paths, a film of cold sweat sticking my shirt to my back. At last I descended the long flight of stone steps to the orangery, where I was able to lose myself in the forest of fruit trees.

My plan, such as it was, was to get to the gardens—not the formal lawns and alleyways next to the palace but the *bosquets*, the groves, on either side of the royal walk. My brothers were stronger than me but I was faster than them. If I could manage to outrun them, I would hide there until they grew tired of the hunt.

We played cat and mouse for so long that I saw the first stars appear, and it was becoming cool. My brothers knew how to be patient, which was something I had yet to learn. When I thought they must have given up, I would creep out of my hiding place. Instantly one of them would appear and the chase would resume. I ran and wept, and hid, and wept some more. In the garden of the Sun King I felt alone in all the world. The suspense became so unbearable I wonder if, at heart, I had already given up the fight. They cornered me close to the fountain of Bacchus, each coming at me from a different direction. I might, even then, have got away had my damaged heel not given way. I knew it would not serve my cause to protest, or beg for mercy, or threaten to tell our father. Any retribution always came back at me a hundredfold. I do not need to bother you with their names: I would certainly rather forget them. They dragged me from view into the bushes and applied themselves to their self-appointed task. They were not stupid. They were careful not to mark my face. They threw me to the floor, one standing on my hands, which was, I recall, something he enjoyed, while the others kicked me. They stopped when I began to vomit. They hated me with such a passion: I had killed our mother in the act of coming into the world, and then I had stolen our father's love from them. It was true that when my father greeted me his face lit up in a way it never did when he saw the approach of my brothers. He made no attempt to hide which son he favored. I believe something primeval stirred in their guts that told them we were not the same. I was an alien thing: a parasite sucking the blood from their family. But for all that, they were cruel men and monsters in my eyes. I have forgiven them now, but if I'd had a sword that night I would have gladly run them through. When I crawled into the alleyway, weak as a newborn colt, it was almost dark, and Venus was shining bright in the sky.

This part of the garden was a maze of paths, and I staggered between dense hedges, clutching my ribs. One foot dragged in the dirt. The warm evening air carried the strains of violins toward me. I could make out the distant, low hum of a crowd and, rising above it, an occasional peal of laughter that echoed across the gardens. When I emerged out of dark shadows onto a broad terrace halfway between the palace and the lake, I felt as if I had returned from the dead. The world was on the very edge of night, and for the first time since the sun had started its journey across that day's sky, I was not afraid: My brothers had already done their worst. A long, double line of torches led toward the water. The King was sailing in a gilded galley with the violinists' raft following in its wake. Floating all around him, moths to his flame, a fleet of Venetian gondolas transported his courtiers. Their stomachs full, their limbs tired after an afternoon's hunting, they listened to sweet melodies while trailing their fingers in the cool water; they feasted their eyes on heavens dense with stars. My balance threatened to give way and the soles of my shoes scraped across the gravel as I dragged myself down the path. As darkness fell the boats became invisible, but I could see their torches from afar, creeping across the lake like glow worms in a meadow.

Soon my head was spinning so much I could scarcely put one foot in front of the other. The effort of keeping upright was becoming too much. Spotting a giant stone urn a short distance away, I shuffled toward it, arms outstretched: a toddler lurching toward its mother's knees. My teeth chattering inside my skull, I clung to the cold, smooth stone. My fingers started to slide down the marble.

I heard a voice. "Please! Mademoiselle! By the ur-rn!" The voice was deeply accented, the *rs* rolled richly on the tongue, and it seemed to come from very far away. "Be so good as to catch him before he falls!"

At that same instant I felt small, soft hands support me and a slim shoulder maneuver itself under my arm. As this person gently levered me into an upright position, I caught the scent, I thought, of rosewater. I wanted to open my eyes but I could not.

"Monsieur," a girl's voice called out, next to my ear. "He trembles as if he were very cold!"

The girl, who merely happened to be passing, was Isabelle d'Alembert, though I did not know it then. The first voice belonged to the Spaniard, and he, it transpired, had been searching for me the whole day long. I was destined from birth to encounter the Spaniard, but Isabelle fell into my life like a blessing.

III

There was nothing halfhearted about the Spaniard: His opinions were definite, his reactions extravagant. My first teacher seemed old to me then. Now I would not think him so. He was full of vigor and appetite. I can hear him still, calling to me across a crowded room: *Jean-Pier-r-re! Why do you not answer! Is it cabbages you have for ears?*

He was a well-built man, yet there was an elegance about him, and his expressive hands were as articulate as his tongue. He loved the company of women and was always the most courteous of men. When he spoke, he would spit out his words like heavy hail, and the way he r-r-rolled his rs behind his teeth for emphasis was catching. Too much time in his company and I would start to do it myself. In private he revealed himself to be a quieter, more considered, subtler character, who in reality had a perfect command of French. He taught me to embrace the world at the same time as protecting myself from it. Over time I formed a deep affection for him although at first I was suspicious of him, despite his apparent kindness.

The day after my brothers beat me, I did not awake until midafternoon, and found myself in a room I did not recognize, and in such pain that I could not bear to move. I lay quietly and watched fingers of light creeping through the cracks of tall shutters. All was peaceful. Motes of dust danced in slanting rays of sunshine that sliced through the shadows; a clock ticked in an adjacent room; doves cooed outside the window. My precious blue jacket hung limply over a chair. I took stock of the stains with calm resignation: dirt, blood, vomit. One of the finely embroidered cuffs was ruined, while sticky juice from the crushed mirabelles had seeped through the pocket linings. It was clearly beyond repair. What my punishment would be for such carelessness I did not like to imagine. Then I discerned a sound that until that moment had escaped me: the slow in-and-out of someone else's breath. I tried to push myself up, and let out an involuntary cry on account of the agony this movement provoked. The Spaniard's strong nose and dark, soulful eyes loomed at me from the shadows.

"My boy," he said, pressing a damp cloth to my forehead. "You are awake."

"Who are you, Sir?" I asked by way of a reply.

He rested a reassuring hand on my shoulder. "I am your friend, Jean-Pierre. Your very good friend." I was not reassured. Indeed, this struck me as an odd remark for a stranger to make. "My name is Don Vincencio Miguel de Lastimosa, and you are in my apartment, in my own bed, and you are safe."

"I do not understand," I said.

"Alas, your brothers did not spare you. I do not think it is wise that you continue to live under the same roof with them. When your father arrives, I will suggest that—as it does not appear he can control his sons—you should come to live here, in the palace, where it would be my pleasure to watch over you."

Reassured to hear that my father had been sent for, I

thought it best, in the circumstances, to make no comment. While there was no denying that I was unlucky to have such brothers, I told myself that my father loved me and would never agree to such an arrangement! Besides, what made this stranger presume he could interfere with my family in this way?

My father did love me: When word reached him that I was hurt, he returned at once to Versailles. In the meantime the Spaniard and his valet nursed me. They spooned broth into my mouth and applied hot poultices scented with herbs to my chest and back. Given the number of beatings I had suffered at the hands of my brothers—though admittedly this was the worst—I was bemused to receive such tender attention. Indeed, I almost regretted it, knowing that the next time my brothers turned on me I would be obliged to suffer once more in secret, and would have to cure myself like a wild beast, alone.

The Spaniard even went against his better judgement, as he later admitted to me, and summoned a doctor, who called on his great medical experience to pronounce that I had suffered a beating. He advised bleeding me. After all, where was the harm in shedding a little more? It was a procedure he performed with great skill, insofar as he relieved me of a quantity of blood without letting a single drop stain the linen. He cut into me with a stained blade and pressed my flesh to encourage a rich, red stream to flow into a porcelain bowl. It was decorated with a colorful floral motif on which I tried to focus my attention. I fainted and came to with a pounding head. Curiously, the treatment made me feel worse, not better. I should probably thank that doctor for making me unwilling to submit myself to his colleagues over the years. He has undoubtedly saved my life many times over.

At some point during my convalescence I awoke from a nap convinced that I could smell roses. The Spaniard's valet told me that I had missed a visitor, a certain Isabelle d'Alembert, who had enquired after my health and left me a bowl of peaches. I resolved to seek her out when I was recovered.

On the fourth day my father arrived. He did not appear to be the least surprised to find me in the care of the Spaniard, who greeted him with warmth and affection.

"Do you know Signor Lastimosa, Father?" I whispered to him when the Spaniard left the sickroom for a moment.

"Oh, yes," he replied. "Since you were a newborn."

The Spaniard instructed his valet to remove my shirt in order that my father could see the full extent of my injuries. The flesh that covered my rib cage was hot and visibly swollen, while a flowering of great purple bruises, tinged with yellow, spread, impressively, over my abdomen toward my back. My father stood at the foot of the bed, tight-lipped.

"Did your brothers do this?"

I did not want to lie, nor did I wish to condemn my brothers—partly because I was no telltale but also because I could easily picture the consequences. I therefore remained silent. When my father was angry, a vein would appear that ran down the center of his forehead; I saw it now. The Spaniard drew him to one side and they both retired to the adjoining room, where they spoke loudly enough for me to hear snatches of their conversation. Had I been able to, I would have rolled out of bed and listened at the door.

The Spaniard, I gathered, was keen to be of service. Why he should have formed such a strong and swift attachment to me I could not comprehend, but I overheard him offer to become my tutor and to introduce me to the ways of the court. He also repeated his suggestion that I come to live with him. When my father—naturally—refused, I sensed the angry disappointment in the Spaniard's voice. He warned my father that it was his responsibility to keep me safe, a remark that struck me as impertinent. Yet my father did not protest and presently he returned to my sickbed to take his leave of me, promising to fetch me home the following day.

By the time I returned to the house, which my father had rented for us in the town, my brothers had already been dispatched back to our estate in disgrace. I had thanked Signor Lastimosa for his kindness, and had bid him farewell, believing that our paths were unlikely to cross again. Now, to my astonishment, my father informed me that he was, after all, to become my tutor. "But why?" I demanded. His reply was vague and, being a dutiful son, I did not question his decision further. It puzzled me, nevertheless, that my father seemed to be in such thrall to the Spaniard.

Little by little, my father and I learned to do without each other for longer periods of time, weaning ourselves, with a kind of sweet melancholy, from a stage of life we both sensed was drawing to a close. A small attic room was found for me above Signor Lastimosa's apartment, where, increasingly, I would sleep instead of returning to my father's house. My father was not a remarkable man, but he gave me my most valuable gift: I knew, even before I was old enough to speak, that I was loved by another human being who enjoyed spending time in my company. He taught me how to laugh. Everything good starts from there.

And so began my education with the Spaniard. He taught me languages—ancient and modern—history, philosophy, mathematics, and the art of rhetoric. His strategy was always to finish while I still wanted more. A favorite game was to riddle his lessons with mistakes so that I, the pupil, could have the satisfaction of correcting my teacher. Then he would praise me excessively, so that, even though I understood it was a game, I always looked forward to my lessons. If my eyes glazed over he would pluck the quill from my hand. "Come, Jean-Pierre," he would say. "Let us find something to divert us." His approach produced an eager and diligent student, although I had my own reasons for being attentive. In the court of the Sun King, the art of conversation was highly prized. Indeed, wit was mostly the weapon of choice, and we courtiers feared public ridicule more than a beating: Its wounds were messier and took longer to heal. Besides, there was a particular young lady whom I hoped to impress.

IV

The spell that Isabelle d'Alembert cast on me was initially due to simple curiosity. Twice we had met, yet I had not seen her face, and the only words I had heard her utter were: "He trembles as if he were cold. . . ." If the sweet voice that continued to resonate in my head had a dreamlike quality, it was doubtless because I had been barely conscious when I heard it. Equally, though there were any number of ladies at court who doused their gowns with rosewater, it was a scent that, as far as I was concerned, now belonged irrevocably to her. I was feeding a daydream. I knew it but I did not care to stop. Her very name, Isabelle d'Alembert, acquired a patina of mystery, and I assigned qualities to her that her actions did not necessarily deserve. I *had* to meet her.

And so I resolved to write a letter of thanks to my unseen visitor. The Spaniard, who, as I was discovering, was most particular in questions of etiquette, asked if I would allow him to look over it. I saw the page tremble as he tried to conceal his laughter.

"I cannot allow you to send this, Jean-Pierre."

Having spent an afternoon composing it, I was not pleased. "Why should I not send it, Monsieur?"

"The young lady brought peaches—"

"For which I thanked her—"

"So profusely that your letter reads like a declaration of undying love!"

"I assure you that it does not!"

"And I assure you that this young lady's family will think

that it does. If her father sees your letter you may have cause to regret your words."

Insulted, I stood with my back to the Spaniard, and read it again. My cheeks burned: How easily our words betray us. I crumpled the letter in my hand.

"That young lady is beyond your reach," said the Spaniard sternly. "The Comte D'Alembert plans a glittering match for his only child. At court your reputation is your most valuable currency. Lose it, and you may never get it back. Jean-Pierre, I cannot allow you to make your entrance onto its stage in the role of a fool. Do you understand?"

"Yes, Signor," I replied flatly. "My reputation is my currency." The Spaniard flashed his big white teeth at me, and slapped me on the back, as was his way, knowing full well that I had only the barest notion of what he spoke.

I allowed the Spaniard to dictate a short and appropriately worded note of thanks to Isabelle d'Alembert. I duly signed it with my most flourishing signature.

Later, in need of some air, we took a turn around the orangery. The sun blazed down; heat bounced off the pale walls of the palace and rose up from the gravel paths. The Spaniard fell into a pensive mood and we walked, mostly in silence, down an alley of citrus trees in their high, square containers. All at once he stopped to dig his thumbnail into the pith of a ripening lemon in order to release the zest. He inhaled deeply and beckoned for me to do the same.

"It reminds me of my childhood in Madrid," he said. The sharp tang of citrus always made him homesick.

"Will you ever return to Spain, Signor?"

"Not until I have passed on to you what knowledge I can."

"It must be hard to live in a country that is not your own," I said. "If you miss your home you must not stay in France on my account."

He turned to look at me square in the face, and his incredulous gaze discomforted me. "But Jean-Pierre, it is precisely on your account that I remain in France. Nothing is more important to me than your education and your welfare. Do not doubt it for an instant."

Despite the Spaniard's warning, I did not, of course, stop thinking about Isabelle d'Alembert. Often some beauty would catch my eye—fluttering her fan, or strolling through the *bosquets*, the shaded groves, arm in arm with her chaperone—and I would wonder if this was my Isabelle. As I had no clue as to what she looked like, it was frustrating to think that I might already have encountered her. I cannot tell you how distracting I found the scent of rosewater in a crowd. But in the end it was not perfume that led me to her.

One evening, at the end of my first summer at Versailles, I overheard a conversation. There had been a performance of a comedy by the late Monsieur Molière, and a colorful crowd of us swept like a roaring tide into the Hall of Mirrors. Our voices rose up to fill the echoing space; crystal chandeliers sparkled in great slabs of slanting golden light.

"Who is that plain creature?" said a woman's voice close to me.

"Which one?" asked another.

"In the gray silk—so unbecoming."

"You mean, Isabelle d'Alembert? My dear, there is a girl who does not have to worry about her looks. She was the only one of the brood to survive, and her father owns vast estates in the South."

"I grant you that she has fine eyes. But as for the rest . . ."

If it were possible, my heart leapt and sank at the same instant. I whirled around to find the speakers of these unkind words and to see where they were looking. They were women of a certain age, wearing tall headdresses that obscured my view. Their attention was fixed on a group of young persons who commanded a prominent place in the center of the room. I moved through the crowd to gain a better vantage point. Some of them were known to me, by sight, at least. They belonged to the most powerful families in France, and they were all in high spirits, their voices carrying across the glittering room, loud and shrill. It seemed to me that this privileged band strutted, peacock-like, among us lesser mortals, and that if anyone was ignorant of their pedigree, the quantity and quality of their lace and jewels announced their status to the world. A blond-haired young man in dark blue silk was striking an attitude. He was telling an anecdote that provoked gales of laughter. I glanced down at my own old-fashioned surtout, a tight-fitting jacket made of some drab, inferior stuff, and wished that my father were richer.

Then I caught sight of the person I presumed to be Isabelle d'Alembert. She stood a little apart from the rest of the group. She was of medium height, slight, and was dressed in shimmering, pearl-gray silk. Unlike most of the ladies in the room, her dark hair was arranged in a simple style and she wore no headdress. I think she must have been the youngest in the group by several years: I guessed she was about my own age. The young lady was not conversing with any of her companions but nor did she look ill at ease. In fact, she was staring out of a window, apparently deep in thought. She did have fine eyes. They were large and gray, the color of storm clouds.

I stared at her for far longer than was polite, coming to my own conclusions about her looks. A sixth sense must have told her that someone was observing her, because she turned to look straight at me. For a moment I sensed her puzzlement and then her eyes widened and I was certain that she recognized me. She smiled, and such was the electric effect of that first acknowledgement that I had to turn away. When I trusted myself to look again I saw that a haughty-looking man, rather stiff around the shoulders, had offered his arm to Isabelle and was leading her away. I wondered if this could be her father. As the pair proceeded down the room, I noted how the crowd parted in front of them. On the point of disappearing into the Salon de la Guerre, I saw Isabelle pause and turn under the plaster relief that portrayed a triumphant King Louis trampling his enemies into the ground. Her eyes searched the crowd where I had stood a moment before. I told myself that it must have been my face that she had hoped to see.

Giant Colorful Birds

July, Mansfield.

Spark is astonished to learn that she used to live so close to Stowney House when she was a child. Mum casts an eye over John Stone's letter and shrugs before passing it back. She resumes drying the cutlery. "He's got nice handwriting, I'll say that for him. No one ever invited me to Stowney House. I've never met John Stone."

"Do you think I'll remember it? How old was I?"

"Four? Maybe five? You know what I'm like with dates. Anyway, what does it matter? It's ancient history."

"Come on, Mum! Don't you think it's a coincidence? A random guy whose picture I took in New York turns out to be the man who arranged Dan's internship. Then he offers me a holiday job. And now I discover we were neighbors in Suffolk when I was little—"

"No. You were in New York *because* he arranged Dan's internship. And it was *you* who asked *him* for a holiday job. Though why you couldn't have got a job at the canning factory like everyone else, I don't know. You could have had a five-minute walk to work. If you wanted to go away, you could've saved up and gone off somewhere hot with your mates. Somewhere with a bit of nightlife. Not *Suffolk*."

"It's not about the nightlife—it's about getting some experience!"

"Don't talk to me like I'm stupid!"

"Oh, *Mum!*"

Spark hangs mugs on hooks under the blue Formica shelf. *Why do families have to be so difficult?* Mum sorts cutlery into the drawer, throwing in each knife, fork, and spoon with more force than is necessary. Spark walks over to her and gives a hug. She's rewarded with a smile.

Presently Mum says: "We weren't neighbors. It was a good half mile to Stowney House. And it was a registered charity that helped our Dan. John Stone just works for them."

"But it was John Stone who organized it, wasn't it? I know you're not thrilled about Dan being in New York, but it was a brilliant internship to get—"

"So you're saying I should tug my forelock to him? The gentleman from the big house taking pity on us poor folk? John Stone is nothing to me."

Spark watches Mum staring fixedly out of the kitchen window and it occurs to her that John Stone's help—for which she's supposed to be forever grateful—in fact took her son away from her. Mum pulls at the collar of her blouse, her gaze resting on the abundant hanging baskets, still dripping from watering, that adorn the concrete wall. Lilac petunias and pink geraniums scramble for supremacy in the sweltering yard. *What a shame,* thinks Spark. Mum had been in such a good mood this morning.

"Have you got something against John Stone? Because if you have, you'd better tell me now. You haven't changed your mind about letting me go, have you?"

"Don't be daft."

Spark doesn't entirely believe her. *Oh, heck.* But it's hardly as if she's going on a polar expedition. If Mum can't cope, she can be home again in a couple of hours like Dan says. In any case, if she gets lonely it might even encourage her to go out.

"Mum, did you ever meet a woman called Martha?"

"Who?"

Spark follows the lines of the letter with her finger until she finds the right place. "Listen—John Stone talks about her. He says: 'In fact, I met you on one occasion, though I was away for much of that summer. However, I heard from my housekeeper, Martha—'"

"*Housekeeper.* Nice for some—"

"'. . . that you broke into the garden of Stowney House so often that she became quite attached to you. If it had not been for an incident with our water mill you would probably have continued to visit, but we felt, at the time, that our land was not safe enough for such a young child, so Martha took you back to your mother to tell her what you had been doing. Of course, you were extremely young, so you may have no recollection of your adventures at Stowney House.' Do you know anything about a water mill, Mum?"

"I suppose you think I was being a bad mother—letting a five-year-old run wild in the middle of the countryside. Letting strangers get 'attached' to her child."

"No!"

"You were always wandering off. I couldn't stop you. You were adventurous. But you always came back—"

"Mum! This isn't about *you*. It's about John Stone." Spark flashes a broad smile at her. "Your mothering skills have always been perfectly adequate."

"You little . . ." Mum chucks a tea towel at Spark.

Spark catches it and throws it back. "So *do* you remember meeting Martha?"

"Vaguely."

"And?"

"There's not much to tell. I opened the door and found a woman on the front step doing up the buckles of your sandals. You were patting her hair—it was very curly and black, I remember. She didn't say much—she just handed you over. It was embarrassing."

"Was she nice?"

"I don't know! I suppose she must have been good with children. I could see you'd wrapped her round your little finger."

In just two days Spark will be at Stowney House. She tells Mum she's going to make a start with her packing. Instead, she lies flat on her back on her narrow bed. The room is hot and airless, and soon her book slides out of her fingers and falls to the floor. She is drifting in and out of a dream: a dream that seems so real she wonders if sleep has nudged some long-forgotten memories into the light of day. She rolls off the mattress and starts to pace up and down in the gap between her bed and the window. With each pass she tugs at the patterned curtains. How do you tell the difference between remembering something that *happened* and remembering something that you *imagined* because you want to remember?

She tries to retain the random images that keep appearing, like the fragments of colored glass that shift and fall as you rotate a kaleidoscope. It occurs to her that these images are familiar: This isn't the first time she has dreamed about these places. It's just that she's never before made the connection.

A watery landscape, with a sky that went on forever, and reeds that towered above her and whispered and swayed in the wind, and the call of birds. A land choked with brambles and birch saplings. She was sliding flat on her belly under arching, barbed canes, holding them with the tips of her fingers so they didn't spring back. Vicious, clawlike thorns tore at her bare legs and snagged her cardigan, pulling out long threads, which she had to unhook one by one.

What she recalls most vividly, though, is a thorn that caught deep in the delicate fold of her eyelid like a cat's claw. She had to hold the bramble cane still so it didn't rip her skin. Finally she pulled out the thorn with fingers made slippery by tears. What made her carry on, beating her slow, painful path through the brambles? Did she know what lay beyond?

There is a second memory, and this one conjures up a sound of splashing. A man—he has his back to her—stands in front of a fountain that sends a jet of foaming, sparkling water high into the air. Somehow she knows that a fish glides beneath the surface in the mossy green shade. It is large and white, and its scales gleam like silver.

In her cramped bedroom Spark runs her fingers through her wavy, fair hair so that it stands up on end and she looks like a dandelion clock. The fish had a name, and one that made her laugh, but it has slipped her mind. Could that man have been John Stone? Is that why, in the coffee bar in New York, he looked at her so strangely? Yet how could he have recognized her? Even if he has a good memory for faces, she was only four or five.

Spark hears Mum climbing up the stairs. She braces herself for a sarcastic comment about how much packing she hasn't done but, instead, she hears the bathroom door open and close. As she stares at the light filtering through her curtains, more fragments of the past rise up; the memories adhere to one another, like drops of mercury. She is sure she can remember a *second* man in the gardens of Stowney House. And a *woman*. They were moving from tree to tree like giant, colorful birds.

Mum pushes open the door. She heaps towels on top of the wicker chest of drawers.

"In case they expect you to provide your own," she says, eyeing the empty suitcase but holding her tongue.

"Thanks, Mum."

"Anything else you need? I don't suppose they expect you to bring your own sheets—"

"Mum?"

"Yes?"

"Tell me you're going to be all right."

Mum stoops to kiss Spark on the top of her head. "You worry too much, Stella Park."

Spark flings her arms around her. Mum pushes her away to examine her face. She wipes away a tear from Spark's warm cheek with the sleeve of her cardigan. "Crocodile tears! Don't start, love, or you'll set me off."

Spark gets on with her packing. Mum reads the paper in the sunny yard and the smoke rises up and enters Spark's bedroom through her window that will only ever open a crack. By the time Spark has finished, the unsettling images from her childhood have submerged once more, diving like ocean creatures down into the deep.

Homing Pigeon

July, Suffolk.

"Martha! *Martha!*"

When John Stone arrives back home at sunset, there is no sign of Jacob in the garden, and his calls echo through a deserted house. He places the mirabelle plums and some green exercise books he purchased in Holborn on the kitchen table. Then he goes off in search of Martha. He is accustomed to her hurrying out to welcome him. Now, as he strides from room to room, opening and closing doors, an old anxiety starts to creep over him. Martha normally avoids entering the long gallery, but he puts his head around the door to check all the same. From her carved and gilded frame, a dark-haired girl with eyes the color of smoke looks down at him; he blows her a kiss before retreating into the hall.

"Martha!"

Long ago he would return to an empty house, knowing that he and Jacob would soon be scouring the riverbanks and marshes for Martha. It was grief for her lost children that drove her there. Sometimes they would hear her calling out their names into the wind, children who had never set foot in Suffolk, and whom she would never again greet on this earth. Yet she was not mad. John Stone and Jacob came to understand that she was compelled to do this, over and over again, until her sorrow had run its course and she could permit herself to forget them. Each time John Stone would wonder if they would find her, facedown, floating in the river. But his fears proved groundless: Martha never wanted to die.

It is in the breakfast room that he finds her, singing to herself as she makes up a bed for Spark. He loves the purity of her lilting voice; he stands on the threshold and listens. When Martha turns she jumps at the sight of him.

"John! You gave me a fright! I didn't expect you back so soon!"

"It's seven o'clock."

"Upon my life I thought it was half past five at the outside."

"This is a surprise. I thought you said one of the attic rooms would do for Spark—"

"It's a woman's prerogative to change her mind. She'll be grand here."

John Stone looks around him, at the hand-blocked wallpaper, the Japanese prints, and the twin ormolu mirrors, tall as a man, that reflect the fountain. "It's the most beautiful room in the house. Do I gather that now you know who she is, you're feeling happier about entertaining our visitor?"

Martha tucks in the flap of the linen pillowcase. "Of course I am. I'm curious to see how little Stella has turned out. She was a precious child. Is she still bonny? I bet she's a beauty—but then, that would hardly be surprising."

"Well, you'll see for yourself soon enough. When I told you who I thought she was, I thought it might—"

"Turn me against her?"

"Yes."

"No one gets to choose their parents. And her mother

gave her to a stranger to raise, after all. So, did you find out for sure that Thérèse is her mother?"

"I have her letter. Thérèse didn't admit to being Spark's mother—that would have been far too simple—although, in truth, the girl's face is the only evidence you need. What she did say was that the father was a cook of some sort on the coast and that he had been of great service to her—"

"I see. And this cook's wife took little Stella in?"

"Apparently."

"That was good of her. And does the child know who she is?"

"No."

Martha, hugs the pillow to her for a moment. "Then, for the love of God, John, we should not be the ones to break it to her. It wouldn't be right."

"And if Mrs. Park decides to say nothing?"

"Would it not be kinder, in any case, to leave the girl in blessed ignorance? Let her be satisfied with the family she thinks she has. She can still be our Friend."

"If it were you," says John Stone, "wouldn't you prefer to know the truth about yourself?"

"What you don't know, you can't grieve about."

A scraping sound in the hall announces Jacob's arrival. Grunting a little, he maneuvers a heavy upholstered armchair across the threshold. Martha has asked him to fetch it from an upstairs study. John Stone steps forward to help him and they place the chair in front of the French windows.

"John." Jacob greets John Stone with a slight incline of the head. His expression is grim. "She'll be trouble."

"Good evening, Jacob," says John Stone pleasantly. "I see you've made a start on the hedges—"

Jacob interrupts him. "It's not too late to tell her to stay away."

"Actually, it is," he replies.

"She'll be comfortable here," says Martha, glaring pointedly at Jacob, who ignores her.

"If you'd have told us it was Thérèse that put up the family in the cottage, we'd have driven the child away from the start."

John Stone sighs. "I wanted to spare you from unnecessary anxiety. What was I supposed to do? Evict an innocent family from their home? And, if you remember, I was away most of that summer, and when you told me about her visits I advised you to discourage her from coming—"

"I didn't invite her, John!"

"I'm not blaming you, Martha."

"The sweet thing had the instinct of a homing pigeon. She kept coming back. Perhaps she sensed, child though she was, that there was a connection of sorts."

Jacob grips the back of the green velvet chair. "I thought you had more sense. It will turn out badly."

"It will turn out well!" John Stone almost shouts at him. "Do you truly think I would bring Spark here, to the home I have shared with you all these years, if she didn't have my trust?"

Jacob aims a large gob of spittle into his handkerchief and heads back toward the hall. "She doesn't have mine."

John Stone shouts after him. "I would ask you to make her welcome! Don't drive away a potential Friend!"

When John Stone turns around he sees that Martha is star-ing at his left hand. He draws it quickly behind his back and squeezes the twitching fingers tightly in his good fist.

"What's the matter with your hand?"

"It's nothing. I'm tired."

"Will you not let me have a look at it?"

"It's nothing that a bite of supper won't cure."

"Oh, I'm sorry, John. You must be half-starved after your journey. I'll set to right away."

"Martha—"

"What is it, John?"

"When Spark arrives, remember to protect yourself a little. You have such a warm heart. Will you do that for me?"

All the happiness drains from Martha's face. She nods briskly, walks out of the door, and doesn't look back. John Stone listens to Martha's offended retreat back to the kitchen. He has picked at the scab of her pain. Worse, he has implied— again—that he does not have confidence in her. She deserves better from him. And what if Jacob is proved right? What if, in trying to help the two of them, he is about to make a cata-strophic error of judgement? *You are tired*, John Stone coun-sels himself. *Eat. Rest. Sufficient unto the day is the evil thereof.*

He sits on the edge of Spark's bed, looking out at his silent fountain, and presses his juddering left hand between thigh and mattress. In the absence of the soothing play of water, John Stone allows his mind to wander back to a time when the world seemed new and he was yet to discover that he was different.

Good Timing

July, Compartment D, 14:30 to Ipswich, Suffolk.

Spark has spread herself out at an unoccupied table in the quiet compartment of the train. She has neglected to turn her phone off. When it starts to ring people crane around to glare at her. She drops *Jane Eyre*, leaps out of her seat, and darts into the drafty corridor. The automatic doors whoosh closed behind her.

"*Mum!* I've been gone a whole hour!" Spark puts a hand over her other ear to block out the noise.

"I couldn't wait to tell you—I've just come off the phone with Dan. He's taking a couple of weeks off. He's coming home!"

"When?"

"At the end of the week."

"I thought he couldn't afford it—"

"That's why he rang. Dan's landlord says if we can put up his son while he's here, he'll buy them both their airfares."

"The son? Ludo?"

"Yes, Ludo. I've told Dan to say to him that he can have your room."

"Ludo's coming to Mansfield?"

"Can you believe it? Dan's coming home after all!"

"But I'll be at Stowney House—"

"I know, love. But at least *you* saw Dan in February. I haven't seen him in getting on for a year."

Spark switches off her cell and watches the countryside sweep past with glazed eyes. A flock of crows lifts above a field of ripening corn. Black-and-white cows graze in green meadows. Hedgerows and ancient trees hurtle by. She unzips the deep side pocket of her handbag and slips her hand inside, probing with her fingertips until she can feel a sharp edge of cold metal. Spark stares down at the ring pull from Ludo's can of Coca-Cola and lets her forehead knock against the glass of the window. *Great timing, Dan.*

Notebook 2

V

It was during that time—at the Spaniard's suggestion—that I began to keep a journal in a shorthand of my own devising. Over the years I refined my technique until I could write as quickly as I could speak; it had the advantage of being impossible to read by anyone who did not possess the cipher. I have those first, clumsy attempts before me now, and I see that it is of the agonies of adolescent love that I wrote. The browning, mottled paper might smell of decay, but the fading ink still conjures up all the freshness of youth.

What had started as a daydream had, by now, transformed into something that threatened to overwhelm me. The longing made me ill. I could recognize the tilt of Isabelle's head when she was little more than a speck in the distance; it felt as if I were constantly pushing through crowds trying to reach her, and she would always be carried one way and I in another. I could conjure up her face at will; she appeared constantly in my dreams; often I looked in a mirror and it was Isabelle's features that I saw. She mixed in such elevated circles that it was impossible for me to approach her without provoking ridicule. Now I understood why the Spaniard had advised me to banish her from my thoughts. Naturally, I became excessively sensitive about my status: It was a sickness to which all we courtiers were prone. The Spaniard used to compare the courtiers of Versailles to hens in a coop:

while humbly deferring to their superiors, nothing made them happier than pecking at those of a lower status than their own. Pity, he said, the hen at the bottom of the pecking order. That wretched creature, I vowed, would not be me. Somehow I would prove myself worthy of Isabelle's regard.

I was beginning to despair of ever speaking with Isabelle face-to-face when fate intervened to bring us together. It was on the evening of a ball that the Grand Dauphin—Louis's son and heir—had arranged in honor of the newly constructed grove of the ballroom, and it was to be a splendid affair.

Beforehand, my father and I dined with the Spaniard. My father chose the occasion to make an announcement: "Your brothers are anxious to return to court. I have agreed to their request on condition that they formally beg your forgiveness."

I recall choking badly on a pike bone. The Spaniard, who was sitting next to me, came to my aid; it took several hard slaps between the shoulder blades before I could dislodge it. I could scarcely blame my father. However my brothers had treated me, we were all his sons and it was his duty to help us all make our respective ways in the world. As I dried my watering eyes, the Spaniard and I exchanged glances.

"Naturally Jean-Pierre is welcome to live under my roof," said the Spaniard. "Should your own accommodation prove crowded—"

"We have more than enough room for all," said my

father quickly. "But thank you, my dear friend, for your most generous offer."

"Do you not think it might benefit Jean-Pierre to live with his tutor in the palace itself?"

I saw a vein appear in my father's forehead. "One day, perhaps. Not yet."

I recall looking from one to the other as each tried to disguise his anger and avoided my questioning gaze.

Night had fallen and the ball was well under way by the time we reached the grove of the ballroom. Like all the *bosquets*, it was concealed from view, and was entered via an alleyway of tall, clipped hedges that led from the royal walk. It resembled an ancient amphitheatre and my father and the Spaniard were excited to see it. As for me, Versailles was so full of splendors that I could raise little enthusiasm for yet another one. There were tiers of circular seating, arranged around an open space. The focal point was a cascade that was encrusted with thousands of giant shells. The water burbled over it like a mountain stream, cooling the air that circulated around it. An orchestra had been installed above it: I could see the tightly curled wigs of the musicians poking up over the trellis, and their horsehair bows, which caught the moonlight as they moved in unison. The Spaniard adored dancing, especially the gavotte, which he executed with grace and delicacy despite his size. His heavy black wig flapped about his shoulders as he jumped and turned. My father, however, turned increasingly melancholy, and I found him a seat next to the cascade, where we listened to the sound of falling water and watched the Spaniard dance.

"Your mother," he commented, "would have loved to have come to this ball. I don't believe I gave her the opportunity to dance as much as she would have liked. And now it is too late."

I caught the Spaniard's eye between dances, and signaled to him. When I whispered into his ear that I did not think my father had the heart to stay for very long, he left the dance floor without a trace of ill humor, and proposed a visit to the recently completed Colonnade.

He led us down the royal walk toward the Apollo Fountain, and then left through a leafy alleyway where the moonlight did not penetrate. Torchlight marked the entrance and we groped our way toward it. Presently the sound of water reached us through the foliage; it grew louder as we approached the Colonnade. On entering the circular clearing a member of the Swiss Guard, the King's household regiment, saluted us. We found ourselves in a kind of open-air temple. I stood at its center and slowly rotated: I counted thirty-six pale marble columns; in between each column was a fountain; from each fountain pulsed a jet of water, the height, perhaps, of two men. The whole space reverberated with the sound of splashing. Torches had been placed behind each of the fountains so that the water sparkled yellow and red, like liquid fire. I had never seen anything more magical. I expected, at any moment, nymphs and satyrs to appear and move among us mortals.

I had presumed that, aside from the guard, we were alone, but I was mistaken. For a moment I wondered if a herd of pigs had found their way into Versailles, for above the sound of water I heard snorting and grunting. Then came the sound of bodies crashing through the under-growth, as if men were hunting wild boar. I half expected to hear hounds baying as they do when they have cornered a wounded animal. Instead we saw a crowd of panting young men and women, perhaps fifteen or twenty, darting through the pillars into the moonlit Colonnade, where they stood clutching their sides and bending over as they caught their breath. The grove exaggerated every sound: I could even hear the rustling of silk. Someone grunted like a pig, caus-ing a wave of laughter that subsided only to start up again when someone else took up the call. The young ladies in their tight corsets pleaded with the gentleman to stop mak-ing them laugh before they fainted clean away.

The Spaniard shook his head and smiled indulgently.

"Ah, to be young," commented my father.

I recognized some of them; the young man to whom I had taken such an instant dislike in the Hall of Mirrors was among them. Out of the corner of my eye I saw a movement in the shadows and two more figures fell into the circular space. There was the sound of sobbing and, with a thrill of recognition, I realized that it was Isabelle d'Alembert; she was supporting the arm of a young woman whose face was entirely obscured by a fan.

"Shame on you!" cried out Isabelle.

The laughter stopped.

"Don't be such a *bore*, Isabelle. I'm sure Mademoiselle de Cluny does not begrudge us our little joke." It was a young woman who spoke; her black curls tumbled over her pale shoulders.

"It's not a very amusing joke," said Isabelle. I sensed the distress in her voice. They were an intimidating group and she suddenly appeared very young.

"Actually, my dear Isabelle"—it was the self-styled wit speaking now—"I think that anyone with a sense of humor would find that it is—*grunt*—quite—*grunt*, *grunt*—amusing."

The Colonnade echoed once more to raucous laughter; bejeweled bodies shook with mirth, and fluttering fans, like oversize moths, cooled flushed faces. Isabelle and her sobbing companion left the arena, vanishing into the black shadows beyond the curved sweep of the pillars.

"Please excuse me," I called to my father and the Spaniard, and ran after Isabelle and her weeping friend. They had not gone far, and I could make out Isabelle's voice.

"How can he be so *hateful*! My father says he would make a good suitor—I don't mind telling you that I would rather *die*!"

"Can I be of service, Mesdemoiselles?" I cried.

I thought it best to show myself, so I ran in front of them toward a patch of torchlight that spilled out onto the path. Isabelle's face loomed out of the darkness. I only had eyes for her.

"You!" she exclaimed.

"Mademoiselle," I replied. "I would like to repay your kindness, if I can. May I be of service to you?"

"You could teach that vile wretch, the Prince de Montclair, a lesson!"

So, he was a prince. His high rank only made him more hateful in my eyes. "Very well," I said. "I will." And I turned on my heels and sprinted back to the Colonnade.

"Monsieur!" Isabelle called after me. "No! I did not mean for you to—"

But it was too late: My blood was up. I had had my fill of bullies. I tore past my father and the Spaniard, then halted a few paces from the glittering group, the blood pounding in my ears. I marched straight up to Montclair—he was half a head taller than me—and words came out of my mouth that I had not had time to plan. Silence fell on the party. All we could hear was the splashing of the fountains.

"You have insulted Mademoiselle d'Alembert and her companion, Monsieur," I declared roundly.

If he was rattled he did not show it but affected to brush some dirt off his shoulder. He replied coolly: "Have we been introduced, Monsieur?"

"I demand that you offer your apologies to Mademoiselle d'Alembert."

"Monsieur, you are impertinent!"

His tone was purposefully disdainful. I never took my eyes from him. "It is *you* who are impertinent," I cried.

He rounded on me, grabbing hold of the collar of my jacket, his face so close to mine I could smell the wine on his sour breath. Behind me I could hear my father and the Spaniard calling my name.

"What have the affairs of Mademoiselle d'Alembert to

do with you? I am certain that the concern of a young person such as yourself is nothing more than an embarrassment to her." Montclair spoke slowly, injecting threat into every word. "I advise you to take your leave before I am forced to teach you a lesson you won't forget."

He let go of my collar and then stood, chin thrust out and shoulders thrown back, trying to stare me out. At that moment I don't believe I knew if it was the Prince de Montclair or my brothers whom I attacked. The protests of my father, the Spaniard, and Isabelle, behind me, did nothing to dampen my desire for vengeance. I flung myself at my adversary's chest and pushed, teeth clenched, with every last ounce of my strength. Although the Prince was taller and stronger, he struggled to find purchase on the wet gravel in his high-heeled shoes. He lost his footing and staggered backward toward one of the fountains. Where the jet of water had splashed over the rim of the basin, a puddle had formed on the ground. I could not resist it. Spinning him around so that the Prince had his back to me, I grabbed hold of him by both elbows, then whispered into his ear, rather more loudly than I had intended: "You should know that Mademoiselle d'Alembert has said she would rather *die* than have a suitor such as you."

Without waiting for him to respond, I kicked him in the rear so that he fell forward, face-first, into the dirt. Many of the courtiers let out small *ohs*, which spread, in an audible, breathy whisper, all around the Colonnade. I watched the Prince push himself up on all fours, his white breeches and pale surtout soiled and wet. He remained there, immobile, for an instant like a cowed beast, and all at once, before I could stop myself, I grunted like a pig. Someone gave a single, nervous laugh. This, in itself, provoked a short-lived wave of snickering. When I grunted again, the whole drunken party erupted with repressed laughter. Montclair stood up and made as if to advance toward me, but saw that my father and the Spaniard had now positioned themselves squarely between us. Nostrils flaring and eyes glassy with rage, he strode off to the opposite side of the Colonnade, stopping when he reached the pillars. There he turned on his heels and hissed like a snake at me. My father and the Spaniard took hold of my arms and marched me out of the grove. I craned around at Isabelle as I was pulled past her. Isabelle returned my gaze, her glittering eyes reflecting the torchlight, though her expression was difficult to read. Her companion, on the other hand, curtseyed deeply, and when she arose she was beaming. Someone, at least, was happy.

VI

I awoke late, feeling like a hero, the morning after my encounter with the Prince de Montclair in the Colonnade. Still, I
made a small effort to look contrite when I arrived at the
Spaniard's apartment for my daily tuition. His valet told me,
however, that his master had left early on urgent business.
It was our custom to start the day with some broth, and as
the valet ladled me some into a bowl, in a pointedly offhand
manner, there was a look in his eye that said he did not think
I deserved it. I did not care. I may only have kicked over an
arrogant youth, but I felt as if I had crossed some invisible
barrier into manhood. A message had arrived for me, which
the valet passed to me with his white-gloved hand. When I
discovered it was from Isabelle, I was scarcely surprised: I had
defended her honor, after all. *Meet me as soon as you can
at the Fountain of Apollo. I shall wait for you.* My broth was
pushed aside and I flew out of the apartment, down the flight
of stone stairs, and into the soft morning light.

The gardens of Versailles had been transformed by the
prospect of my meeting: I seemed to tread outside the geo-
graphic universe. Fine rain cooled my face; blood coursed
through my veins; life was about to begin! I wanted that
short walk to last forever. The Fountain of Apollo soon
came into view, although I was barely conscious of having
moved my legs to get there. No jets of white water curved
over the circular pond—only the approach of the King
miraculously caused every fountain to spout forth. Even
so, Apollo, god of the sun, surged up from still, green

waters, ready to drive his chariot across the sky.

As I drew closer, I saw that Isabelle was waiting for me on the opposite side of the fountain. Her eyes acknowledged me but she immediately started to walk away, motioning, with a discreet wave of her hand, for me to follow her. Three spaniels, a breed popular with the ladies at court, ran alongside, barking their excitement and pausing to leave their scent on every marble statue we passed. Not once did she turn around, and she walked so briskly a rising anxiety warned me against catching her up. Her full skirts swished and billowed in front of me. When she reached a lightly wooded spot south of the orangery, she stopped to survey the gardens. I halted a few yards behind her and glanced around me. Aside from a Swiss Guard at his post some distance away, there was no one nearby. I understood that she should have been attended by a chaperone and did not wish to be observed talking to me alone. She had taken a risk: I was flattered. I walked up to her and gave a deep bow. It occurred to me that we had never been formally introduced.

"What were you thinking of yesterday evening, Monsieur?" she said tersely. "Your behavior was *outrageous*."

Did she toss her curls? I believe she may have done. She was not tender with me. She certainly was not grateful. More to the point, she seemed *angry*—and I, of course, could not take my eyes from her. It seemed to me that the finest veil of freckles had been smoothed over the ivory skin of her forehead, and the rosy skin of her plump cheeks. Her teeth were white and small.

"*Outrageous?* But—"

"Is it because you love Mademoiselle de Cluny?"

"*No!*"

"You do not! Then I am relieved to hear it—as she is betrothed to the English Milord and his two thousand spotted pigs."

"*Pigs!* Ah! Now I understand."

"You mean you didn't *know*?"

"No!"

"Then what reason had you to attack the Prince de Montclair?"

"Because you asked me to, and because she is your friend."

"I did not ask you to!"

"Forgive me, Mademoiselle, but you said that I should teach that vile wretch a lesson—"

"I didn't mean it! Do you always believe what people say?"

"Yes. No . . ."

Her dogs had begun to take an interest in me. They clustered around, pink tongues lolling, standing on their hind legs and leaving dirty prints on my stockings. I thought it best not to throw them off. I even patted their tiny heads.

"You had been fighting the first time I saw you—"

"You helped me when I was in need—I shall never forget it—"

Isabelle laughed. "I stopped you from falling—anyone would have done the same. I suppose that you enjoy provoking arguments—"

"I assure you that I do not."

"I cannot quite believe you. . . . You realize that Mademoiselle de Cluny is now convinced she has an admirer?"

My jaw dropped, provoking a broad smile that lit up Isabelle's face. "I see," she said.

"But it was not for her!" I exclaimed.

"Then you made the Prince de Montclair look ridiculous on *my* account?"

I nodded. We stared into each other's eyes trying to fathom what lay beneath. I couldn't breathe.

"Come!" she called to the dogs, and turned—I think to conceal her blushes. Isabelle could never hide what she was feeling. I wanted to shout!

I followed her. She moved so quickly, her skirts trailing over dry leaves, that I had to scurry behind her, jostling for position with her brown-and-white spaniels. When she stopped, I stopped too. We looked about us at the peaceful glade. We listened to a blackbird singing overhead, to the buzzing of invisible insects, to the strong pulse of blood in our temples. When she walked, I walked too, and then I would catch the scent of rosewater in her wake. Weak sunshine broke through the clouds, filtered through birch trees, and traced a constantly moving pattern on Isabelle's back. I caught up with her, and we continued side by side. We did not speak. Presently I reached out to stroke the back of her hand with mine. It took courage to bridge the distance between us. The slightest, most thrilling, of touches. When she did not pull away my heart soared.

"You must understand," she said, "that the King himself

has suggested to my father that the Prince de Montclair would make an appropriate suitor for me. The d'Alemberts are wealthier by far, but the Montclairs come from a most noble and ancient line—and the Prince's father holds great sway at court."

I took her hand and held it in mine. She turned to me and smiled. "But you would rather die," I said.

"I would rather die," she repeated. "Though it is unfortunate that the entire court is now privy to my feelings. Come!" she called to her dogs and, squeezing my fingers, slipped her hand from mine.

"Please may I see you again?" I asked her.

"Perhaps—"

"I promise not to believe everything you say."

"Well," she said, "in that case, I can assure you that I never, ever want to see you again." And with that she hurried away from me, past the lonely Swiss Guard, and back toward the palace and the company of those of whom her father approved.

VII

Returning through the gardens of the Sun King after my tryst with Isabelle, the world seemed to throb with the dazzle and promise of life. My elation was not shared by the Spaniard: When I entered my teacher's apartment, his disappointment in my behavior was tangible.

The previous evening, after leaving the Colonnade, the Spaniard had not trusted himself to talk about the incident. My father, too, had accompanied me back to our town house in near silence, and I had left the house before he had risen. It was the first time, I think, that his youngest child had truly displeased him. I would have preferred an angry reprimand to his silence. As for me, my feelings for Isabelle, as well as my satisfaction at seeing that bully Montclair with his face in the dirt, had made it easy for me to push to one side those difficult emotions. Now they came flooding back. When the Spaniard demanded that I explain myself, I displayed little remorse. It was hardly, I said, as if I had injured the Prince.

"Do not play the fool! That is not the point—"

"I pushed him into a puddle," I protested. "He deserved it—he had insulted Mademoiselle de Cluny—"

"However *he* behaved, Jean-Pierre, *you* showed disrespect to someone belonging to a higher rank than yourself. Considerably higher."

"The young lady was in tears, Signor."

"And do you intend to defend the honor of every victim of an unkind word at Versailles?"

"I hope that I would try—"

The Spaniard raised an eyebrow. "Would you have lifted a finger to help her had a certain young lady not been her friend?"

The Spaniard expected no answer and I looked at the floor.

"Jean-Pierre, listen to me. Sooner or later the Prince de Montclair—or more likely his father—will make you pay for your behavior."

"Let him try," I said.

The Spaniard threw down his napkin and scraped back his chair. He started to pace up and down in front of a tapestry depicting Saint Sebastian pierced with arrows.

"Did I not expressly warn you against cultivating false hopes with regard to Isabelle d'Alembert?"

"I believe she likes me, Signor," I said quietly. "Whereas she does not care for the Prince de Montclair at all—"

"No!" exclaimed the Spaniard. "Apparently *she would rather die* than have him as her suitor! Those were her words, were they not?"

"Yes—"

"Let me share with you a conversation I overheard this morning as I waited in the antechamber of Monsieur. The Princess Palatine asked one of her ladies-in-waiting if she intended to go hunting this afternoon. "Oh," came the reply, amid much laughter—not to mention *grunting*—"I should rather *die*, like the fragrant Mademoiselle d'Alembert. . . ."

I put my face in my hands.

"You have made a grave error of judgement, Jean-Pierre,"

said the Spaniard, rolling all his *rs* for emphasis. "I shall do my best to placate the young man's father but I doubt that I shall succeed."

For the first time I realized what consequences my behavior might have for Isabelle and I felt sick with guilt. "How can I make amends, Signor?"

"Your brothers are shortly to arrive in Versailles. I suggest that you take their place and return home to your estate until the incident is forgotten."

"Leave Versailles? Now?"

The Spaniard coolly returned my stare and nodded.

"I can't!"

How could I leave? I had to meet with Isabelle and lend her my support after the trouble I had caused her.

"You *must*. I shall accompany you."

"No!" I shouted, running to the door. "It is not possible—"

"It *is* possible, and I must insist that you do it for the sake of your reputation."

"No!" I cried. "I shall not. By what authority do you order me to leave?"

I did not wait for the Spaniard's reply but ran through the door. All of that morning's happiness had already leached away. My memory, then, is of running: running away from the palace with its courtiers, its rules and restrictions, and notions of rank, and out into the streets of the town, past wagons, and street hawkers, and men on horseback; never stopping until I reached a part of the town where the streets were emptier, and where I came across a gaggle of child beggars who sat listlessly in the gutter sheltering from the sun, which was already high in the sky. They sprang up when they saw me, and I threw a handful of coins high in the air for them to catch. I ran on, pursued for a while by a line of ragged children with nothing better to do. They fell away when I reached the Church of Saint Symphorien, and there I caught my breath, head hanging over my knees, listening to the wagons rumbling past and the sorrowful beating of my heart. I had defied the Spaniard. Now what was I going to do? What *could* I do?

Clumps of dry grasses and poppies grew through cracks in the paving so that my vision was filled with glossy, scarlet petals poised on wiry stems, a whorl of golden anthers at the center of each flower. No sixth sense told me I was in danger. Nothing had alerted me to the presence of another. But all at once a movement caught my eye. A shadow—it was the shadow of a figure with a raised arm—fell across the dusty flagstones above my own crouching silhouette. For the merest instant I observed the arm hang, poised to strike, then it came slicing down, the pitiless blow of an executioner. It felled me. The pain was beyond imagining. I heard my skull crack; I heard, as if it were not my own, an unearthly scream. All the light was swallowed up by an oily darkness. The last image that I saw was the glowing scarlet of the poppies splattered with the darker, viscous red of my own blood.

Anything Red
June, Suffolk.

The car John Stone sent to collect Spark from the nearest station speeds across a flat, watery landscape. The roads are poor and Spark, tired after the long journey, starts to feel nauseated. She scans the horizon for signs of habitation but sees none. It's gone seven by the time they swing into a single-track road that is rutted and edged with deep, reed-filled ditches. Some way ahead, Spark sees what appears to be a small wood or, at any rate, a mass of trees; as they draw closer a ribbon of water comes into view, and then, marking the end of the track, a small bridge spanning a stream. A heron, frozen in its one-legged pose, eyes them as they pass over the bridge and into a tunnel of trees. Now the tires crunch down a gravel drive. At first, branches smack against the windows of the car, but gradually the tunnel grows wider and lighter. Spark leans forward in her seat. This must be it. The prospect of meeting John Stone again, only this time without Dan, unsettles her. Presently, green shade gives way to sunlit lawns, brightly colored flower beds, and high, dark hedges. The gardens, which are sheltered from the marsh and invisible from the road, shield, in their turn, a stone-and-brick-built house—actually more of a mansion than a house—which Spark can only assume is John Stone's home. He works for a charity—surely he can't live *here*.

They come to a halt in the broad courtyard and the

driver opens Spark's door for her. As she clambers out she catches a fleeting glimpse of a man with a wheelbarrow: He is retreating rapidly to the far side of the lawn. At the same time, a slim, dark figure is hurrying out of a side door to greet her.

"Little Stella!" the woman exclaims. The biggest smile lights up her face. "By all the saints, just look at you!" Spark holds out her hand but the woman is transfixed by her.

"I'm pleased to meet you," says Spark, her hand hovering uncertainly now in midair.

Martha reaches for it and clasps it in both of hers. "You don't remember me, do you? I can see that you don't. I'm Martha."

"Sorry, I don't—I was quite young when we left Suffolk—"

"Well, of course you wouldn't! You were a baby!" Martha continues to search Spark's face. Her dark eyes are bright and her tanned cheeks smooth and a little flushed. Spark had expected her to look older. In fact, she seems younger than Mum. "But just *look* at you!" Martha repeats, shaking her head.

"Do you recognize me?"

"Oh, yes. Indeed I do."

"Really?" says Spark, not sure how to react. "I thought I might have changed quite a lot!"

"Let's say there's no mistaking who you are. But where are my manners? You'll be awful tired after your journey. Give me your case and I'll show you to your room."

* * *

Martha leads the way over the lawn; she carries Spark's suitcase and walks with a smart, brisk step. They pass a fountain of classical design, which features a stern and powerful figure with a flowing beard. Spark stares over her shoulder as she keeps pace with Martha, and is struck by the statue's haunting gaze. His tragic, staring eyes speak of having witnessed extraordinary things, no doubt terrible things.

"What an amazing fountain. Is it Neptune?"

"It's not Neptune, no. It's a river god or some such thing. Does it appeal to you? I can't say I've ever taken to it, myself, although John is *very* attached to his fountain."

They enter the breakfast room through a pair of French doors. It is flooded with light: the paneled walls are parchment white and three immense golden mirrors reflect the garden, making what is a large room seem even larger. There is a marble fireplace and a bed made from polished wood; there is a mass of velvety roses in shades of shell pink and crimson, which arch from the neck of an oriental vase; there are paintings of landscapes glazed with yellowing, cracked varnish. Above Spark's head, suspended by a long brass chain, hangs a crystal chandelier.

"I hope this'll do for you. You've got a fine view of the garden and the fountain, at least—"

Spark turns full circle in the center of the room. "It's *beautiful!*"

Martha's face flushes with pleasure and Spark observes her lowering her eyes, a little coyly, as if she is unsure, momentarily, what to say to her guest. When Martha proposes unpacking the suitcase, Spark—picturing with embarrassment its crumpled contents—hurriedly refuses the offer. "I've brought so little," she says. "But thanks anyway."

"Well then, I'll let you settle in. I'll return with some supper for you in a little while."

"Should I say hello to Mr. Stone?"

"John will see you tomorrow. He's given me instructions to let you into the archive room myself in the morning."

Once Martha has gone, Spark unpacks her things then prowls around her new territory like a cat. At home she doesn't have the floor space to do push-ups; here, she could do a cartwheel if she felt so inclined. When she tries out the mattress, the scent of lavender water rises up from thick linen sheets. Yet she can't settle: The room is so much bigger than she's used to. Finally, she takes a pillow and one of the cushions from a green brocade armchair and places them in the corner of the room. Here she makes herself comfortable, resting her head on the side of a chest of drawers, and surveying her new domain in wonder. She wishes she could share this with someone.

Late the next morning, emerging from the house, Spark spots the gardener. He stands at the other side of the lawn in front of the dark yew hedge, which, as Martha has explained to her, separates the formal garden from the kitchen garden. Spark feels she should make an effort to be friendly so waves energetically. He doesn't turn. "Hello!" The gaunt figure, whose straight back is angled over a wooden barrow, ignores her and keeps on pushing. This is the second time the gardener has done this to her. Spark stops waving and lets her arm drop to her side. She supposes that he could be deaf.

Crouching down next to the fountain's wide basin, she plunges her arms into the cooling water up to her elbows. She rinses away the dust from her hands then wipes them on the grass. The old book smell—mold, must, whatever you call it—that permeates the archive room has made her headachy. There are no windows in there, and no electricity. She's been dusting and reshelving the books, as instructed in John Stone's note, working by the glaring light of an old-fashioned bulb clipped onto a stepladder. Each time she accidentally looked at the glowing filaments, which was impossible *not* to do, fluorescent shapes, migraine green, spread over her vision like an oil slick, making it difficult to decipher the dates on the manuscripts. The touch of the ancient paper reminded her of the powdery underside of moths' wings. Happy to be outside, Spark stretches her aching arms above her head, interlocking her fingers and rolling her shoulder blades. When she tips back her face, the sunlight is dazzling.

Martha, like Mum (who can't even be trusted with a remote control), must be a technophobe. Only Martha is probably even worse. This morning, while she was trying to set up the lightbulb in the archive room, Spark stood in the doorway holding the long, orange extension lead, hoping that Martha would plug it in for her.

"Would you not be better off with candles?" Martha asked in her lilting accent.

"Better not—I don't want to set fire to Mr. Stone's man-uscripts on my first day! Could you maybe show me a socket it would be okay to use?"

Martha looked troubled, and instead of taking the plug that Spark offered to her, she gestured vaguely at a spot on the wall beneath a narrow console table. "There," she said. "You can do the business there, if you want to—"

"The business? Plug it in, you mean?" Spark couldn't help smiling.

"What else?" Martha replied stiffly before walking off.

Spark isn't yet sure what to make of Martha, but one thing is clear: She has gone to a lot of trouble to make her feel wel-come. Spark wants Martha to know that she's noticed, and that she is properly grateful for the effort she's made. When Mum was at her worst, she rarely noticed what Spark did for her. Spark understood that taking her daughter for granted was a symptom of Mum's depression, but feeling unappre-ciated was still hard. So, after breakfast (which she'd found laid out for her on the kitchen table—the others, apparently, rose with the sun), Spark had set off in search of Martha. She found her walking back from the orchard, barefoot in the grass, an empty wicker basket swinging from one hand. Her calves, beneath her plain black skirt, were tanned and strong.

"Martha! Hi!" Spark called out, running toward her.

"Spark! Did you sleep well? Was your room comfortable?"

"It's the most comfortable bed I've ever slept in! I *love* my room. Thank you so much!"

Spark watched an array of emotions fan over Martha's expressive face.

"Well, that's grand . . . grand—"

Abruptly Martha announced that she had better get back to the kitchen before her pastry burned. "It was feeding Bontemps that put it out of my mind—it's not like me to be absentminded—"

"*Bong Tom?*"

"Oh, the tortoise. I'll show you later. He's a big fellow— but you don't have to be scared of him. John brought him back from his travels."

What opinion had Martha formed of her? Did she seem the sort of person who'd be scared of a *tortoise*? "Oh, I don't let myself be scared of anything."

"No, you don't," said Martha over her shoulder. "You were always bold." And before Spark could ask her what she meant, Martha started back for the house.

When Spark pulls the sleeve of her T-shirt to her nose there's a whiff of mold. She is beginning to regret not bringing more changes of clothes, for she's uncomfortable asking Martha about the laundry arrangements. As far as she can see, there is no washing machine, which is worrying. Surely the wringer in the scullery is for decorative purposes only? It had better be—she's never washed anything by hand in her life.

"Come here, you varmint!"

Spark springs up. Jacob is running across the lawn toward a flower bed on the opposite side of the fountain. Her eyes open wide in surprise. The tortoise Martha mentioned is of the giant variety and has waded into a herbaceous border in full bloom. It's huge—the length and height of a Labrador but twice as wide. It is demolishing the flowers. Jacob clambers on top of it, though it's a struggle to stretch his legs that wide.

"Martha! *Martha!*" Jacob shouts.

Spark thinks this probably isn't the moment to introduce herself. She looks on in awe at the tortoise's prehistoric face, his wrinkled stalk of a neck, the four stiff legs protruding out of the shell at improbable angles. It is as though once, long ago, he had tried on this carapace by accident and could never slip out of it again. Martha appears from the back of the house, wiping her hands on her apron. When she spots Jacob astride the animal, trying to wrench him away from his prized plants, she watches, hands on hips. "For the love of Michael! Why do you always have to do that? He's not a horse!"

Jacob dismounts, and the tortoise, losing interest in the plant of his own accord, lumbers away, like some arthritic old general, following the path that leads to the front of the house. He vanishes around the corner, a bright green leaf stuck to his back foot.

Martha tells Jacob she'll tempt him back to his pen with some baby carrots and beetroot, not that she hasn't got enough to do this morning. Spark volunteers to lay the trail for her. "Why, thank you," Martha says. "If you're sure you can spare the time—"

"It's not every day you get to meet a giant tortoise!"

"Then come with me to the kitchen and we can find some scraps for him. Something red. The old fellow can never resist anything red."

"Someone left the pen open," complains Jacob. Now that he is no longer scowling at the tortoise, he is scowling at Spark.

"Well, I'm sorry, I'm sure," says Martha. "I've been at sixes and sevens all day—I don't know what's got into me."

"I do," says Jacob.

Spark looks from one to the other and decides that if no one else is going to do it, she had better introduce herself. "Pleased to meet you, Jacob. I'm Spark."

"I know who you are."

Martha gives him a sharp look. "Jacob, will you help Spark get Bontemps in his pen when she's tempted him back to the orchard? Well, will you?"

Jacob gives a curt nod and retreats to his green domain. He whistles for his dog, who presently limps into view under the yew arch that leads to the kitchen garden and, beyond it, the orchard.

Spark walks backward, talking to the giant tortoise, coaxing him, throwing slices of red apple, beetroot, and carrot onto the grass. She crouches down next to him and observes his strong, beak-like jaws open wide and snap shut. "You are one messy eater," she says. His shell gleams like polished hide; his sturdy legs seem to be covered in dragon skin. Occasionally he swivels his pewter eyes and looks right at her, and they seem to convey such a wry view of the world it delights her. By the time she has got to the pen she has dared stroke his leathery neck, which he tolerates, at least, though she cannot tell if he likes it. Jacob has appeared out of nowhere and is already holding open the door of the pen. For a moment Spark fears he's going to lock her inside the chicken-wire cage too. She steps out quickly and Jacob clangs the gate shut.

A tinkling bell sounds from the direction of the house. "Luncheon," he says and aims a large gob of spittle an inch from her foot. Spark takes a step backward, offended. He continues to stare at the grassy spot on the ground.

"Last time you were here you caused Martha grief."

The anger in his voice goes deep. Spark is unnerved. "Did I? I can't remember."

"You know what people say about leopards."

She finishes off the saying in her head. What spots does she have that she can't change? Who does he think she is? Jacob walks back to the house without waiting for her. Spark stares after him, recovers herself, and follows in his footsteps.

In the kitchen, a fat, golden-crusted pie sits steaming in the center of the table. Spark cannot face being alone with Martha and Jacob and excuses herself, saying that she is not hungry. Martha looks crestfallen; Jacob bristles. Spark says she's sorry and flees the kitchen. Now she sits in the malodorous archive room in the dark. For a while she feels like the little girl Jacob has implied that she still is. She wants to go home. What can she have done that was so bad? She was five! One tear rolls down her cheek, which is all she allows herself. She refuses to give Jacob the satisfaction. You stand up to bullies. It's only fear you should be frightened of. Then she switches on the light and resumes the work she is being paid to do. Half an hour later, Martha arrives with a covered tray—in case Spark regains her appetite, she says—and places it carefully on the floor between piles of manuscripts. When Martha gets up Spark has the impression she is about to hug her, but she changes her mind at the last moment. Instead Martha touches her cheek with the crook of her finger. "Don't you fret about Jacob. His bark's worse than his bite." After Martha has gone, Spark wolfs down her chicken pie and feels more cheerful. She has a friend.

Water Mill

Taking a break, midafternoon, Spark sits on the edge of the still fountain and decides that this is not the sort of house you buy, this is the kind of house you inherit. She cools one hand in the light-spangled water and watches a solitary fish glide in and out of the feathery weeds. It's a ghostly white. It must be the same one—she knows koi carp live for years. She still can't remember its name, though.

It's good to be out of the archive room. Its location, right at the center of the house, is strange: It is accessible only from the tomb-like corridor next to John Stone's study. You'd think the whole building had been built around this one airless, circular room. And, try as she might, Spark cannot decipher a single word of the manuscripts. It would be great if they contained something exciting, some dark secret, but she supposes they'll turn out to be something dull.

She looks up at the house, shading her eyes from the sun. The colors are honeyed: all golden stone and soft red brick. Some kind of tree has been trained up between the diamond-paned windows. It has dark, glossy leaves and waxy, saucer-shaped flowers whose marzipan fragrance drifts on the warm air. A sudden, gusting wind sweeps into a crescendo, blasting through the circular rampart of tall trees that shields Stowney House from the marsh. All around, a million fluttering leaves glint silver against cloudless blue. Strangely, here, close to the house, the air is almost still. She feels the tension release from her shoulders, her back, her stomach; she feels warm and safe, as if nothing bad could happen to her here. It is as if this house has a tender spirit.

Slipping her phone from her pocket, she switches to video mode and points the lens at the fountain—at the garlanded river god and those invisible mysteries at which he stares—and then, in a long sweep, captures the gardens, the back of the house, and the tall stained glass window, whose soft colors—violet, red, and gold—stream across the floor of the entrance hall. In a minute she might walk up to the orchard to get a few shots of the tortoise: close-ups of its shell—which she is sure that Martha must polish—and its extraterrestrial face.

Something prompts her to flick through her photographs until she finds the image of John Stone and the street woman in New York. She frowns at it, still intrigued, and wonders if she had sensed, all those months ago, a connection of some kind. Had she not witnessed that scene, would she have put herself forward like she did? Would she be here now?

Her eye is caught by a wonderful sight: A vast number of honking geese pass over the sunlit, swaying treetops in a perfect V formation. Spark switches back to video mode and starts to raise her hands, preparing to press the record button. At that instant, John Stone himself appears at the front door. He walks toward her, captured on her tiny screen. Spark obeys an impulse to continue recording—to own the moment, to show Mum, actually she's not quite sure why. He is just as she remembered; his face has got this comfortable, lived-in quality to it; he has such an easy way with him. John Stone coughs gently, clearly amused that she doesn't appear to have noticed him.

"Spark! Hello at last. Welcome to Stowney House."

Spark stands up hurriedly. "Hello, Mr. Stone—"

"Call me John." He shakes her hand briefly and motions for her to sit back down. "We're living in the twenty-first century, after all."

Spark nods, although if she were honest, she'd rather not. "All right—*John*."

"I'm sorry I was not able to greet you on your arrival—I hope Martha and Jacob have been looking after you—"

"Oh, yes. Yes, they have."

"So, tell me how you're getting on."

"Good—I think."

"Could you understand my notes about the dates?"

"Yes—I think I've got the hang of it now. I still can't make out any of the writing—"

"You wouldn't: there's a trick, which I'll show you next week. The manuscripts were written using a cipher." John Stone sits down next to her on the edge of the fountain. "You picked my favorite spot."

"Do you ever switch the fountain on?"

"Ah, now that's a sore point, I'm afraid. Jacob has diverted the water supply for his vegetables."

"Couldn't you divert it back sometimes?"

John Stone laughs. "I thought you'd met Jacob—one must choose one's battles!"

The wind roars through the tall trees that seem to Spark to guard Stowney House; it is a sound that puts her in mind of the sea. "It's so beautiful here," she says.

"I'm happy it pleases you. This house is unique. And her charms become increasingly difficult to resist. Martha tells me you helped recapture our tortoise."

"He's massive! How old is he?"

"We think he could be a hundred and seventy years old."

"A *hundred and seventy*! That's incredible!"

"He was sired by a tortoise who was kept on the island of Saint Helena while Napoleon Bonaparte was held prisoner there."

"How long has Tom been at Stowney House?"

"I don't recollect—a long time. Actually his name isn't Tom: It's Bontemps. A French name. *Bon*—good. *Temps*—time or weather—"

"I should have known that," says Spark. "I sat my French A-Level exam only a couple of weeks ago."

John Stone smiles at her. "You've nothing to prove here. As it happens, Bontemps is named after several generations of *valets de chambre* who served the kings of France. They prided themselves on being men you could rely on."

"And *is* the tortoise reliable?"

"I suppose he is!"

John Stone leans over to pluck a daisy from the lawn and drops it in the water; the flower floats on the sparkling surface and Spark sees the carp swim up to inspect it. Disappointed, it disappears with an impatient swish of its tail.

"Does the fish have a name?"

"If it does, I don't recall it."

John Stone's hand rests on the sun-warmed rim of the carved stone basin. When he shifts position, a ray of sunshine bounces off the golden signet ring he wears on his little finger. Spark tries to work out what is engraved on it and decides that it is a tree. It appears to be studded with minute diamonds that lie, like fruit, in its branches. When she looks up again, John Stone meets her gaze. Spark feels as if she is made of glass and he can see straight through her. He doesn't offer to tell her about his ring.

"Dan and I had hamsters when we were little. They were always dying on us—we must have had seven or eight. We still had to have funerals for each one of them, though. Our backyard is concreted over, but we have an old water trough that Mum filled with flowers. It got to the point when she couldn't plant her geraniums without digging up a hamster skeleton. We should have kept a tortoise instead."

Her story provokes a rich laugh. "How right you are—creatures who insist on dying on you are certainly best avoided!"

Spark grins, pleased to have amused John Stone. "There was that giant tortoise—Lonesome George—did you hear about him? I think he was a type of Galapagos tortoise. The very last of his kind." She reaches for her phone to look for a picture before she remembers there's no Internet. Her nail catches in the back pocket of her jeans where the phone is slowly wearing a hole. "They tried mating him with other types of giant tortoises but he refused to have anything to do with them. And then, not so long ago, he died. So, no more Lonesome Georges. Isn't that incredibly sad? The very, very last one."

When she looks up John Stone does, indeed, look incredibly sad. He changes the subject, telling her that after she has finished cleaning and shelving the manuscripts he'll teach her the cipher. She might even like to have a go at transcribing some of them. But all in good time.

"The important thing," says John Stone, "is that you start to feel at home here, find your feet. It's such a pleasure to see someone young at Stowney House. If anything bothers you, anything at all, I want you to say. Will you do that for me?"

"Yes."

"Good. And is there anything that you need?"

"No—Martha's gone to so much trouble—"

John Stone gives her a searching look. "Sometimes you may have to be patient with my friends. We haven't entertained a lot of guests here of late."

My friends, she notes. *Not housekeeper, not gardener. Friends.* Life at Stowney House is not how she'd imagined it to be.

"Incidentally," John Stone continues, "I think you were trying to use your phone just now. I'm afraid there's no reception here." Spark doesn't say that she'd worked that out within minutes of arriving. "And I'm afraid we have no landline, either. Stowney House remains disconnected from the world. Though if you walk a couple of hundred yards up the road you can usually get a weak signal."

Spark has already discovered that, too. "Do you like being cut off from everything?" she asks.

"I suppose I do. At Stowney House the world may enter only at my say-so. I suspect you feel differently."

Spark nods. "I can't stop checking for texts. It feels wrong! Like I'm no longer a part of the world."

This appeals to John Stone. *"Like I'm no longer a part of the world!"* he repeats. "Does a thing have less value if we experience it alone?"

"Isn't it good to feel a part of something bigger? Mostly I hate to feel cut off from people—but not always. Like when I'm taking photographs and then it's as if I'm on the outside looking in."

John Stone nods. "Interesting . . . though even if the photographer might *feel* alone, what a photograph does, above all, is freeze a moment in time—a first encounter between two people, for example—and make something that is unique and personal available for all the world to see. One incident could be reproduced an infinite number of times through a lens that inevitably distorts. I can scarcely imagine, now, a world before photography existed, but there is a part of me that feels that such intimate moments preserve their value and meaning precisely by *not* being shared with those who did not experience them."

A feeling of mild guilt washes over Spark and she lowers her gaze. Her employer is not talking about her videoing him, is he? Surely not—she would have been able to tell if he'd noticed. And it's not as if she's about to share it with the world.

From the house comes the sound of Martha singing. She must be doing something that demands attention because she starts, trails off, starts, and stops again.

"Your arrival has put Martha in a good mood!"

Spark hesitates, then says: "Can I ask you something?"

"Ask me whatever you like!"

"When I first came here—when I was little—did I do anything to upset Martha? Jacob seems angry with me."

"Ah. What you must understand about Jacob is that he is utterly devoted to Martha. With Jacob, everything follows from this simple fact. A long time ago, when I first met them both, Martha helped Jacob through a particularly difficult period of his life."

Spark pictures Jacob as an alcoholic or drug addict, plucked off the streets by John Stone. Maybe *that's* what was he was doing in New York; he does work for a charity, after all. Yes, there is something about Jacob that reminds her of a feral dog—cowed yet ferocious at the same time.

"Your visits made Martha happy," continues John Stone, "and I believe she became very sad when they stopped. It's not for me to tell you her story, but Martha used to be a mother, and your arrival . . . created conflicting emotions in her."

"I see. . . . I'm sorry."

"Being likeable isn't a fault. Nor is liking children when you've lost your own."

"So I didn't actually do anything bad?"

"No!" he laughs. "How could you? You were so young. Of course, there was the incident at the water mill. Martha hurt her shoulder—not badly—when she rescued you—"

"A water mill? Here? I don't remember."

"We rarely use it now. I can show it you if you like. It might jog your memory."

Spark and John Stone stroll through gardens and dappled woodland. Presently they can see the river glinting through the reeds. John Stone points out the old blue boathouse with its hammock; he tells her that if she ever goes there she must watch out for the decking because some of it is rotten. They take the river path and soon arrive at the water mill. John Stone opens the door for her and she steps into the dark interior, where splinters of light pierce the gloom through cracks in the wood. The giant water wheel looms up in front of her, but it is the smell that hits her, a particular combination of dust and damp hessian sacking, and it works like a key to unlock a long-forgotten memory. A mouse the color of soot scuttles across the dirt floor into deep shadow.

"Are you all right?"

"I think I *do* remember. . . ."

Inside her head there is the residual echo of thundering water and the creaking of a great, rotating wheel, that same movement of moist air that you get at the foot of a waterfall. She watches John Stone peering upward. It would be a long way to fall from the top of the wheel. Today all she can hear is a songbird on the roof.

"Martha said she found you clinging on by your fingertips, little feet kicking," he says. "She prized you off but you both fell backward and she caught her shoulder on something on the way down. Jacob has always acted like a guard dog around her. I was away when it happened, but I suspect it gave Jacob more of a fright than Martha."

"Is it that . . ."

"Go on," John Stone encourages.

"Is it that Jacob is anxious that Martha will get too attached to me again?"

Spark sees something in John Stone's eyes that makes her want to cry. "Yes."

"You can't run away from life because you've been hurt by it," she says.

"And where did you glean that piece of wisdom, young Spark?"

But Spark doesn't want to talk with him about her mother. Not yet, at any rate. John Stone doesn't know her. He wouldn't understand. So Spark shrugs her shoulders, not trusting herself to speak. Returning through the wood John Stone, echoing Martha, tells her that she mustn't worry: Jacob's bark is far worse than his bite.

Spark is tempted to say: *So he does bite, then?* but restrains herself.

All at once Spark stops in her tracks. A short way ahead, she sees first Jacob and then Martha climb up the trunk of a large tree as fast as if they were climbing up the rungs of a ladder. They are soon clothed in foliage, but Jacob's legs and stout boots are visible as he walks across a sturdy horizontal branch. Then she sees Martha's bare feet tripping along behind him. Wide-eyed, Spark directs a questioning look at John Stone.

"Martha and Jacob are both excellent tree walkers. I don't recommend that you try: It's harder than it looks."

Spark notes how careful he is to react as if there were nothing unusual about this activity. "I've seen them do that before!" she exclaims. "When I was little. I thought they were giant birds—"

"Well, we won't disturb them. It's a kind of meditation. There is no place for anxiety or sadness when one false move will send you crashing to the ground."

Spark's mind reels. What kind of anxiety and sadness are these people trying to escape? "Do you think it would be all right for me to eat in my room tonight? I'd like to walk up the road to call Mum, and there's a letter I have to write."

She catches the merest suggestion of disappointment on John Stone's face. "Of course. Would you like me to let Martha know?"

A pang of guilt pricks at her. On top of having a flaky housekeeper and a grouchy gardener to deal with, now he's got an antisocial intern. "I don't mean to be unfriendly."

John Stone takes her hand for a moment. "It can't have been easy to leave home and come here by yourself. Well done for today."

"Thanks," she says, and out of nowhere comes the thought that if she can't hack her holiday job, and runs back home, Mum will be cross because there'll be nowhere for Ludo to sleep.

"Tell me, do you like the sea, Spark?"

"The *sea*? Yes, I love the seaside. I don't go often."

"Good. Then tomorrow morning—early—I'll drive us to the coast. It's not far. We can all start the day with a swim."

As they draw closer to the house, Spark has the feeling that there is something not quite right with John Stone's left arm. He clutches it to his side as he marches away. Spark returns, a little reluctantly, to the archive room and wonders how long it would take to transcribe all these dusty manuscripts.

Notebook 3

VIII

The Spaniard feared for my safety, otherwise I should not have traveled. He had obtained—from a Turkish scholar of his acquaintance—a small quantity of dried, cinnamon-colored root. As he had been instructed, the Spaniard ground the root into a smooth paste, then, pulling away my lips to expose my teeth, rather in the manner of a farmer looking to buy a horse, he rubbed the paste into my gums with the back of a small metal spoon. It had a bitter, faintly perfumed aroma that was not unpleasant, and on account of its powerful and long-lasting sedative effect, what would have been an unbearable journey given my injuries, I experienced as if it were happening to someone else. I was unconscious of any pain; I was unconscious of the passage of time. If I dreamed, it was of Isabelle, of following her through the interminable corridors of Versailles, of longing to see her tender face, but never being able to catch up with her. At some point my father laid a moist cloth on my forehead, and when my eyes flickered open he forced a smile, which failed to conceal his anxiety. We traveled continuously, I later learned, for three days and three nights, stopping only to change the horses which pulled our carriage-and-six, the two postboys taking it in turns to walk ahead with a lantern during the hours of darkness. My strongest recollection of the journey was the smell of the paste, and the cold caress of the spoon on my gums.

I awoke in an airy chamber I did not recognize. A high window gave me a view of azure sky; a current of air—it was hot and dry—swelled the bed curtains so that they breathed in and out like lungs. I felt safe, yet on the verge of alarm at the same time. Comforting sounds drifted into the room: someone was sweeping the path below; a cockerel crowed; there was bleating, and a bright metallic clinking of distant bells, the type worn around the necks of goats. This was the South. I could smell it. I could sense the difference in the air. Half-concealed by the billowing curtains, was that the Spaniard who sat in old green armchair at the bottom of my bed? The book, balanced precariously on one knee, I recognized as his treasured copy of the works of Baltasar Gracián. Was it my fate to be knocked down by life and his to pick me up again? I lifted my head to speak. The intense pain that seared my skull rendered me unconscious once more, though not before I heard the Spaniard cry to my father: "Jean-Pierre is awake!"

The following dawn, though my head was still pounding, I was recovered enough to prove to my father that I had not lost my wits: He had me say my name, and his name, and the Spaniard's name, which was difficult enough to remember at the best of times, Don Vincencio Miguel de Lastimosa, then he asked me to count to twenty and name the months of the year. As for how I came to be in this pitiful condition, I admitted that I had no recollection. My last memory was of nodding, scarlet poppies.

My father fed me some broth, scraping my chin with the spoon to collect any escaping drips. When I explored my face with my fingertips, I discovered that my nose was numb and alarmingly swollen, and that a strip of my scalp had been shaved. My head was wrapped in a turban of bandages. I asked for a mirror, a request that my father refused, while assuring me that I would regain my looks soon enough. When I demanded to know what had happened, he put me off and called, instead, for the Spaniard.

Through the half-open door, I watched the two men embrace in the corridor. "The Lord be praised," I heard my father say. "He is able to form his words at last."

"Does he recognize you?"

"Yes! It is as if he's just woken from a long sleep."

"What did he say?"

"That he wants a mirror—and that he wishes to know what has happened to him."

"He can have a mirror if he likes but explanations can wait—"

"No!" I called through the door. "Tell me!"

The Spaniard laughed out loud as he drew near. "Jean-Pierre! What trouble you have caused us!" I watched him examine my face, paying close attention to my eyes. I gathered he found me much improved, for he stood back up and flung his heavy black wig across the room, as was his custom when he was particularly pleased.

"You have been injured—badly," he said, rubbing his hands joyously back and forth over his shaved head. "But now I can see that you *will* recover. That is all you need to know for the present."

"Please, what happened to me, Signor?"

"There is little to say and little to know. Alas, you were

found in a pool of blood in front of the Church of Saint Symphorien. You had been robbed. The thief's identity remains a mystery."

"Robbed? I had nothing worth stealing!"

"To those with nothing, anything is worth stealing."

The effort of listening and speaking was making my head spin. I lay back on the pillow, bands of pain squeezing my brain. My father saw and laid his cool hand on my forehead, as he used to when I was feverish as a child. His touch comforted me.

"Where am I, Father?"

It was the Spaniard who answered. "I have brought you to my own house, close to the gorges of the River Tarn, thirty leagues south of your father's estate. It is an ancient country. When you are recovered I will show it to you."

I had imagined that his home was in Spain. When I said as much, he commented that he had several homes and that I would be safe here. The Spaniard fetched an ebony hand mirror, inlaid with mother of pearl, which he said I could keep by my bedside to watch how quickly I healed. My father held it for me as the Spaniard gently lifted an edge of the dressing. I could not recognize myself! Two rat's eyes peered out of whorls of swollen purplish-red flesh; my nose was bent and twice its normal width; where my hair had been, bristles poked out of a pale scalp. The beginnings of a tightly sewn seam, a lurid scarlet line, peeped out from under the bandages. The skin was puckered and weeping.

My father tried to be lighthearted. "There, you see? Not so very bad!"

"You were fortunate that you lost no teeth—"

"I am a *monster*," I cried, wondering if Isabelle would ever again be able to stomach the sight of me.

"No, Jean-Pierre," said my father. "Trust your body to heal itself."

I was lucky to have survived the attack, but it was a long time before I could walk unaided, or speak without feeling that my next sentence was slipping away from me. At the end of two weeks my father announced that he needed to return to our estate, and would then travel on to Versailles to meet my brothers. In my weakened state I became tearful, and even jealous of my brothers. I begged my father to stay longer. Why, I asked him, could he not have taken *me* back to our estate so that I could have recuperated in the house where I grew up?

"You are almost a man, and no longer my own. Though I hope you will continue to think of me with affection."

"What are you saying to me, Father?" I cried, wringing the bedsheet between my hands. "Have I done something to displease you?" I watched a vein appear in the middle of his forehead. "*Please* take me with you!"

"You are not well enough to travel."

"You brought me here when I was worse!"

"Honor the Spaniard, my boy. You have more to thank him for than you know."

Then my father kissed me on the forehead and, in so doing, accidentally caught the edge of the long dry scab that traversed my scalp with his stubbly chin. I flinched, and before we both pulled away, our eyes met and each perceived the pain the other felt. "I'm sorry!" I exclaimed, at the same instant that he said: "Pardon me, Jean-Pierre." For a moment he looked down at me, slumped on my sickbed, dabbing tearfully at my oozing wound with a handkerchief. Then my father turned abruptly and left. I could only think that he was punishing me for my behavior in the Colonnades. Had my treatment of Montclair brought such shame on our family? I wept, and tasted the salt of my tears, though I hid them from the Spaniard.

IX

Summer was sliding into autumn and my precious rectangle of sky was often filled with banks of purple, rain-laden clouds. I suffered the fitful sleep of the invalid: Dreams and feverish imaginings filled my nights, and leached into my waking hours. I experienced again the cruelty of my brothers, heard Montclair's hissed threats in the Colonnade, witnessed my father's melancholy in the bosquet of the ballroom. Sometimes, in the silence of my bedchamber, I imagined I could hear the music of fountains. How tired I grew of my own company, tired of beef and chicken broth, tired of staring out of my small window at the stars, tired of waiting for the Spaniard to announce that we were returning to Versailles.

Reading caused my head to ache. Words refused to reveal their meaning, stubbornly remaining shapes on the page. At first, even holding a book was more than I could manage. To keep up my spirits, the Spaniard read to me every day. He was fond of *Don Quixote*, particularly the earthy humor of Sancho Panza. He read the role with such comic flair that I would cry with laughter, causing the Spaniard to stop midsentence in order to observe me with his sensitive, dark eyes, fearful for the state of my damaged skull. For his wisdom and humanity, we read the essays of Montaigne. In my darkest hours he has saved me: I read him still. Another favorite author, though for very different reasons, was François de la Rochefoucauld. The Spaniard knew all his maxims by heart, admiring the precision of his language and his cruelly insightful wit. I recall that if ever I tripped, or hurt myself, he would unfailingly quote him:

We all have the strength to endure the misfortunes of others.

I tell you this because I do not wish to imply that I was always unhappy during my enforced stay at the Spaniard's house. Nevertheless, as my body regained its strength, my spirits flagged. The delight I took in taking my first wobbly steps and exploring a new place, soon evaporated like summer rain. *When can we return to Versailles?* was my constant refrain. *Be patient* was always the reply. I was blind to the beauty of the landscape and deaf to the Spaniard's kind words. Even after a night's good sleep I awoke tired and was rarely good company. If the Spaniard asked me to accompany him on one of his long walks I would invariably refuse.

It saddened me that Isabelle had not written to me, although I comforted myself with the thought that she had been forbidden to do so. When I was well enough to form words with a quill, I wrote to her. I dared not express my deepest feelings but said that I was recovering and thought only of returning to Versailles.

Early one morning, I encountered the Spaniard in the hall. I caught him covering the contents of a large straw pannier with a piece of cloth. At the sound of my voice he stood up and positioned himself in front of it. The basket had a curved bottom, and he was obliged to press it against the stone staircase with his white-stockinged calves to prevent it from toppling over. From the pressure he needed to exert I guessed that the basket was heavy. "Good morning, Jean-Pierre," he said. "I am happy to see you up so early." I did not want to ask him what he was doing.

The following dawn, a gust of wind slammed shut the heavy front door. The deep boom resonated like canon fire through the house, waking me up and prompting me to rise from my bed to look out of the window. Down below, the Spaniard was walking up the path that led toward the river. On his back, fastened tightly around his shoulders with leather straps, was the same pannier. The weight of it made him stoop forward.

Curiosity lifted me from my melancholic frame of mind, and when the Spaniard returned at dusk, I walked out into the gardens to greet him. His face was pale with fatigue, and he hardly lifted his feet from the ground as he walked. The basket, I noted, was now empty, and swung on his back from side to side. Pieces of twigs and dry leaves clung to his clothes.

"Have you had an agreeable walk?" I asked.

"Yes, thank you, Jean-Pierre. This country air is—"

"Exhausting?" I suggested.

He gave a wan smile but did not volunteer any further information. That evening he excused himself and supped alone in his room.

When the next day followed a similar pattern, I asked his valet where his master had gone.

"I could not say, Sir."

"He was carrying a heavy load."

"Indeed, Sir?"

There wasn't a more discreet man alive than the Spaniard's valet, and if he knew his master's secret he was clearly not going to divulge it to me.

* * *

When my teacher set off with his basket the following morning, hat jammed over his flowing black wig, I decided to follow him. It was a more difficult task than I had supposed. I needed to leave a considerable distance between us, which meant that the Spaniard was forever disappearing from view while I, anxious not to take my eyes from him, constantly stumbled over tree roots. The first leaves of autumn were falling and they fluttered through the air like a rabble of yellow butterflies, creating a scene in constant movement. I found it easiest to focus on the pale flash of the Spaniard's stockings, which, little by little, took on the appearance of two white sticks luring me giddily onward to who knew where. We walked quickly, and if it was hard for me, it must have been harder still for the Spaniard, who carried a heavy burden.

The Spaniard's house stood in woodland some ten minutes' walk from the dramatic cliffs that rose up above the River Tarn. I soon found myself standing on a precipice above a calm stretch of the river. An extraordinary shade of turquoise, and smooth as a pond, the Tarn sparkled under a bright sky. When the Spaniard stopped to rest, I pressed myself to the side of the path, hoping that if he were to turn around I would be hard to spot. Below me, stunted trees sprang from crevices in limestone cliffs the height of a cathedral. The deep canyon shifted constantly from sun to shade and back again as fast-moving islands of cloud scudded across the sky. The effect, as I looked down at the river, was dizzying.

Before long the Spaniard was on the move again. I was lucky, for not once did he feel the need to check behind him. We walked on steadily, the Spaniard rarely stopping to regain his breath. By midday we came upon a squat stone bridge that spanned the river with its broad arches. A man was struggling to maneuver his boat in the green shade at the foot of the bridge. Since the canyon magnified the smallest sound, I could hear his every grunt. He was unaware of our presence, and I was sorely tempted to greet him so that I could hear my own voice bounce off the cliffs and echo down the gorges of the Tarn.

When I looked up the Spaniard had vanished. Alarmed, I ran along the path to catch up, but even after I had left the village far behind, there was no sign of him. Loath to turn back, I pushed on. The path led me to a bare plateau, where I clambered to the top of a giant block of limestone. Arms outstretched for balance, I slowly turned in a full circle, searching the rugged landscape for any sign of my teacher. I saw nothing but rocky outcrops, trees, and sky. I had lost him.

The wind raked through what sparse vegetation clung to this exposed spot. It was desolate here. Leaning against a tree, long years dead—time and the elements had stripped it of every scrap of bark—I wiped the sweat from my brow and wondered what to do for the best. A shape passed in front of the sun, causing a shadow to flicker over me, and when I tilted my face skyward I saw a large black bird, gliding in a column of air, descending slowly from the heavens in vast circles, powerful and free. I slid my back down the bleached trunk and sat on the hard ground. I watched that bird for a long time, and forgot for a while that I was thirsty and tired.

I asked myself why I had bothered following the Spaniard in the first place, and soon my mind returned to the hurt, still raw, that my father's departure had caused me. I recalled a happier time, remembering how, when I was an infant, my father would set me in front of him on his high horse, and we would ride together to the bustling village square. I would look down from that great height and smiling faces would greet me, and hands reach up, holding out apples or sweet-meats. I would say my childish thank-yous, twisting around on the horse's neck to wave and smile as we trotted away, and then I would feel my father's hand ruffling my hair and would hear him calling me his treasure, his sunshine. But now, even though I had come close to death, my father had abandoned me to a tutor's care. *You are no longer my own.* Might my father ever change his mind? Could I persuade him to take me in again were I to return somehow to our estate? Or should I go back to Versailles, where I at least stood a chance of seeing Isabelle, and where I could prove to my father that I had learned my lesson?

It was getting late and I was a long way from the Spaniard's house. I resolved to retrace my steps. Away from the river, and with the sun blanketed by thick cloud, I lost my bearings. The path had petered out and a growing anxiety gnawed at me. Even after two months of recuperation my health was not recovered. My scalp was painfully sensitive to any cold and I could sense a damp chill rising from the ground. I needed to drink and to rest but, having no choice in the matter, I pressed on. Presently, however, an uncanny sensation crept over me: The hairs rose on the back of my neck, and my heart began to race. I found myself constantly looking over my shoulder and straining to listen for signs that I was not alone. The wind continued to roar through the trees, and the unrelenting sound of it exhausted me. Was it only the wind that I could hear? Increasingly I could not ignore the sixth sense that told me that I was in danger. In mortal fear I spun around.

Running directly at me in a straight line through the trees was a lone wolf. Head held steady even in motion, its keen eyes were locked onto its target. In that heightened moment of terror, I seemed to escape the confines of my body and looked down at myself. I saw, with the dispassionate gaze of an observer, the wolf speeding soundlessly toward me, its long-legged gait smooth and efficient. This image of impending death mesmerized me: I saw its pricked black ears, its teeth that protruded from snarling jaws, its powerful claws, its coarse black pelt and the paler undercoat. Above all, I was drawn into the beam of its amber gaze that sapped my will to escape.

"Jean-Pierre, you fool! *Run!* Climb into a tree!"

The Spaniard's words catapulted me into flight. I lurched toward the nearest tree, fear spurring me to leap higher than I had in my life. I caught hold of a stout lateral branch, clinging on at first by the tips of my fingers, and then, once my hands had found purchase, I swung my legs back and forth until I had worked up enough momentum to hoist myself up. Now I found myself bent double, the air knocked out of me, the branch digging into my belly. The whole tree bowed and shivered with my weight, causing a flurry of leaves to rain down. Out of the corner of my eye I detected a dark shape approaching fast. Grunting with the effort of holding on to the rough bark of the trunk, I heaved over a leg and straddled the branch, gripping it hard between my thighs. As the wolf leapt,

I thought to retract my feet. Its jaws snapped shut on thin air. A ribbon of drool dripped from black gums. It started to pace impatiently beneath me, sometimes jumping up to snatch a bite at my dangling legs. Oh, how my skull ached! I gritted my teeth, and prayed that I would not faint, never taking my eyes off the wolf for an instant.

We both—predator and prey—became conscious of the Spaniard's low whistle. There was silence, then the air below me began to vibrate with a succession of menacing snarls as the wolf raised itself on its haunches, ready to spring. I saw the Spaniard approach, carrying a long stick in each hand. He seemed to glide rather than walk toward us, rotating the sticks, all the while, in the smallest of circles. The wolf turned his attention away from me and toward this other disconcerting two-legged creature. I wondered if I would have the courage to jump on the wolf's back if it sprang at my teacher. But the wolf remained crouching on the floor, transfixed and growling. Presently its head started to move as it followed the circles the Spaniard made in the air. Now he made gentle clicking noises and took a step or two closer. For several minutes the Spaniard held the wolf's attention in this manner, his gaze holding the animal, his voice soothing and sweet. Finally he stepped so close to the wolf he could touch him. For a moment he held his hand, palm outward, in front of the animal's face, and then, very slowly, brought it to rest between the wolf's ears. When he applied a little pressure, the animal slumped down so that he lay, flat and docile, on the ground. The Spaniard crouched down and dragged two fingers down the length of its muzzle several times in succession. When he took his hand away its yellow eyes were barely half-open. Now the Spaniard drew the tip of his finger in a straight line down the beast's nose. With a slight flicker, its eyes closed. The prostrate wolf let out a long and breathy whine.

The Spaniard stood up and gestured at me to stay where I was and to make no noise. He stroked the wolf's thick pelt as if caressing a favorite dog, then bent over to whisper into its ear. The animal awoke—not with a start, but calmly—and looked about him, barely acknowledging with a movement of its ears the presence of the man standing at its shoulder. The Spaniard patted the wolf firmly on its rump. "Go, now," he commanded, pushing it forward, and the animal trotted away into the wood. When the animal had vanished from sight the Spaniard instructed me to climb down, holding out his arms to support me. I slid down the tree trunk.

"How did you do that?" I exclaimed.

"It is not so very difficult. A wise man taught me. If you can manage to keep alive for long enough I will show you the secret."

"What a happy coincidence that our paths crossed at that moment!"

The Spaniard laughed and thumped me on the back. "Come, the light is fading and I still have not completed my errand. Will you accompany me?"

X

"Commit the path to memory," the Spaniard said. "In case you ever need to return."

When I asked why I should wish to do such a thing he told me to be patient: All my questions would be answered presently. As we walked from the river into higher ground, the wood became sparser, and here he started to point out any distinctive features: large boulders or fern-lined gullies, or a change in vegetation that might help me to recall the route. The Spaniard even plucked leaves from aromatic plants and had me crush them between thumb and finger, the better to recognize their scent. He indicated the position of the river behind us with his long-nailed thumb. "Notice too," he said, "how sounds change close to the ravine."

I nodded but was too tired for my teacher's words to hold my full attention. I asked myself why, from the first moment he had encountered me, the Spaniard had devoted himself so wholeheartedly to my care. It was not the first time I had pondered this question and I had never found a satisfactory answer. I wondered too why this lively and companionable man saw—and, for that matter, trusted—so few people. And why had he not taken a wife when he clearly enjoyed the company of women? The Spaniard was a puzzle: an intriguing man who was full of contradictions. I also sensed that, for reasons I could not understand, the Spaniard had contrived to come between me and my own father. So, for all his kindness, I resented him.

"Jean-Pierre, are you listening to me?"

The Spaniard's voice dragged me back into the windswept wood where the trees shook their branches like angry fists and caused storms of leaves to swirl around our feet.

"I must tell you that it was no coincidence that I was on hand to rescue you from the wolf. You were never out of my sight."

"You were watching me!" I exclaimed.

"Watching *over* you."

I came to a halt, shocked and offended—though in the circumstances I had no right to be. "Then why didn't you come to my aid sooner? I was lost—"

The Spaniard shrugged his shoulders. "Error makes the best teacher."

He commented coolly that had I agreed to accompany him on one of his walks there would have been no need for such a tedious ruse.

"When did you realize that I was following you?"

"I could hear you even before we had left the grounds of my house."

"You heard me!" My pride was hurt. I had been so careful. "How could you hear me over the roaring of the wind in the trees?"

To stalk their prey in the mountains, the Spaniard told me, hunters listen *beneath* the wind. It is the same with fishermen: They look, at a slant, *through* the surface reflections in order to see what swims in the shallows. "Can you not hear your wolf?" he asked. The wind was agitating the trees, keening through the sandy undergrowth. I said I could not. With his forefinger, the Spaniard traced a rising note in the air, a distant wolf howl. At first I detected nothing and frowned, shaking my head. But then I caught it: *Aa-ooooh!* Like a hovering hawk spots the movement of a field mouse within the movement of rippling grasses, I heard it as a sound within a sound. All at once I understood. There was no trick to it. The wolf's cry had always been there. It was a question of paying *attention*—a word that was constantly on the Spaniard's lips.

"Listen, even when you think you have already heard. *Especially* when you think you have already heard. On city streets, in crowds, in conversation with someone you *believe* you know. Listen *through* what you *think* you hear. Cultivate the habit of paying attention."

Then the Spaniard instructed me to lick my finger and hold it up.

"From which direction is the wind blowing?" he asked.

I raised my hand and pointed through the greenish gloom.

"Was the wind blowing across the gorges of the Tarn toward you or away from you?"

"Away."

"So where is the river?"

Again, I pointed, and he nodded his agreement.

"You see? It is not so difficult. . . . Did you know that you were walking in a circle?"

"I was not!" I protested. "I'm not a fool—I walked in a straight line."

He ruffled the hair on the back of my head, good-humoredly. It was a gesture I associated with my father. And

I said, before I could stop myself, "You are *not* my father, Signor! And never will be!"

With these words I surprised myself and hurt the Spaniard. I witnessed the effect of my outburst in his dark, liquid eyes. It was a look that reminded me (I admit it was an unworthy thought) of a faithful dog unjustly kicked. I thought too of the day in the orangery when, nostalgic for Spain, he had implied that he remained in France only on my account. The Spaniard swung away his gaze and stood with his back to me some ten paces away; I stared at his broad shoulders and bowed head but could not bring myself to apologize.

He turned around to face me. "I have only ever desired to be of service to you." He pulled out a hip flask from his pocket, took a swig from it, and offered it to me. I declined. The wind carried the smell of brandy to me. Wiping his lips with the back of his hand, he said: "I have delayed long enough. You are strong enough now to hear what I have to tell you."

I sensed the muscles in my neck contract into two taut cords. The Spaniard's expression was solemn. If whatever he had to tell me was this upsetting, I might prefer to remain ignorant of it. He reached inside his green surtout and pulled out an object, which he put into my hands. I recognized the familiar touch of soft leather.

"My purse?"

"You were not robbed, Jean-Pierre."

"I don't understand—"

The Spaniard sighed once more. "It was not a thief

who attacked you, but an assassin. Alas, we do not know his identity—"

"An *assassin!*"

The idea was absurd. Why would anyone want to kill *me*? A long silence passed between us.

"Surely it couldn't have been my brothers?"

"All your brothers were three days' ride away on your father's estate."

"Surely not Montclair! Unless pushing over a prince demands a death sentence!"

"The Prince de Montclair and his father were playing cards with Monsieur at the time."

"Then if you don't know who it was, how can you be sure that it was an assassin?"

"Because a Swiss Guard happened to witness the attack. It is how we know that a hooded and masked figure brought a rock down upon your head. From his description, it is a miracle the blow did not kill you. He believed that something had caught your eye, something on the ground, because the angle at which you held your head meant that the rock glanced off your skull, slicing through your scalp instead of crushing it."

The Spaniard thrust his arms into the air and drew them violently down, reproducing the action of a man intent on removing the life from my body. There was something affecting about the way in which he did this. It was clear to me that he had tried to picture the details of my attack many times over. All the same, his mime was difficult for me to stomach, and summoned up waves of nausea that conjured up the weakness and pain I felt in the first days of my recovery.

"You were doubly lucky because then a remarkable thing occurred. As the assassin lifted the rock a second time—to finish what he had started—a gang of beggar children rushed at him. By the time he had recovered his balance the Swiss Guard had arrived and he fled—"

"But I still don't understand why you think his purpose was to kill me. He could have been a thief who was interrupted as he tried to steal my purse."

The Spaniard held up a forefinger and shook it from side to side in the manner of a dowager declining the soup course. "The Swiss Guard insisted that his cape was made of excellent cloth, and that he wore the boots of a gentleman, the boots, perhaps, of a courtier. No, this was not a man who would risk his skin for a few paltry coins."

Now it was my turn to relive the details of the scene: the quiet, cobbled square, a distant rumbling of wagons, the soaring voices of the choir through the open church door. I pictured myself felled by that excruciating blow. Suddenly I tasted the blood in my mouth, could *smell* blood, saw fat, glistening drops of it splattered over stone and over scarlet petals. And, there, looming over me, was my hooded assailant, hands raised high, clutching his murderous rock. Merciless . . . What *was* I to him? What expression did his mask conceal? Hate? Exhilaration? Indifference? And then to be saved by a pack of child beggars! The same, I supposed, who had scampered after the coins I had thrown into the gutter.

"Signor," I asked, "did he hurt any of the children? I should like to repay them for their courage—"

"I have already rewarded them." The Spaniard permitted himself a smile. "Though I hear they were on the point of rewarding themselves before the Swiss Guard intervened. If they managed to hold on to their bounty, which I doubt, none of them will have gone hungry since that day—"

"They saved my life—"

"True. Salvation often comes from unexpected quarters. One of them also gave chase. He witnessed the assassin mounting a white horse. He had paid a boy to hold it for him, in readiness for a swift departure."

A gust of wind shook a fresh crop of leaves from the tree canopy, and they skittered over the sandy ground at my feet. "Who do you think attacked me, Signor?"

"It is a riddle whose answer I have been unable to discover. Until I can, I cannot permit you to return to Versailles."

We fell silent and presently I began to tremble—with physical exhaustion, with the chill wind, with the shock of it. The Spaniard removed his surtout and wrapped it around my shoulders. This time, when he pushed his brandy flask toward me, I accepted. I was little used to strong liquor and my eyes watered as the fiery liquid burned its way into the pit of my stomach. I pulled the jacket tight around me. Who would want me dead, and why? I was no one.

"Could you manage to walk a little farther?" the Spaniard asked. "We are close to a place where I shall build a fire and where you can rest."

XI

I had little strength left. Thankfully our destination was, indeed, but a short walk away. No one could have guessed that here lay the entrance to the Spaniard's cave. Using branches as makeshift shields, we forced our way through a dense thicket of thornbushes, which the Spaniard himself had planted several years previously. Once through this first barrier, I watched him lever to one side the boulder, which concealed a narrow slit in the rock face. Taking out a tinderbox from his basket, he proceeded to disappear, arms first, into the cave, contorting his body to squeeze through the opening. *It would be much easier for me,* he'd said. The entrance was fringed with hart's tongue ferns that shone, emerald green, in the twilight. Striped snails, ivory and golden brown, clung to the rock in a line that marked the position where the boulder had been. The Spaniard's distorted call echoed through the cave: "Jean-Pierre! Follow my voice!"

I took a deep breath and crawled in after the Spaniard, brushing away quantities of trailing cobwebs that stuck to my face and hair. There was an immediate drop in temperature, but the cave was well ventilated and its walls were dry to the touch. I could smell fresh wood ash. Tunnel-like at first, it opened out into a yawning space of perfect darkness so that it was my ears, rather than my eyes, that grasped its scale. Soon a yellow glow appeared in front of me. The Spaniard had plunged several tallow candles into the ground while others were spiked on makeshift holders wedged into crevices in the rock. Once he had lit them all, I saw that the cave was comparable in size to a small ship, and once that comparison had struck me, I took a fancy to the idea that we were sailing into the night, gliding on calm, black waters. There was a natural vent in the cave's ceiling and the Spaniard had constructed a rudimentary stone grate directly beneath it. He made a fire in it, and placed a blanket on the ground next to it; I lay there, slowly roasting, mesmerized by the tongues of pale flame that licked the crackling logs, and by the fire's glowing heart that seemed to pulse in a current of air. I slept. At some point he took hold of the edges of the blanket and slid me over the rough ground, farther back into the cooler shadows. I drifted in and out of sleep. I watched trails of blue smoke rise in a neat column toward the vent, some ten or twelve feet above, where it was sucked away, through deep layers of rock, into the outside world. Every now and then I was aware of the Spaniard tossing handfuls of aromatic herbs onto the flames. As their juices boiled, they hissed and whined, and the cave was filled with their scent.

I lay there, heavy-limbed and staring into the middle distance, present and absent at the same time. It was as if the Spaniard had cast a spell on me, preparing me in some way for the story that, after long years, he was finally on the brink of telling me: a story that would cause the earth in which my life was rooted to shift, and fall away, like a landslip down a gently crumbling slope.

"Are you awake, Jean-Pierre?"

I became conscious of the smell of roasting meat, and

my mouth started to water. I nodded, blinking, and pushed myself up on my elbows. "Yes, Signor. I am awake."

"See what I have caught for our supper. If you want to hunt rabbit, sunset is the best time."

"It's a fat one," I agreed. "As big as a hare."

"I can see a little more blood in your cheeks. Are you hungry?"

"Very hungry. Is it day or night, Signor? I cannot tell in this cave."

"Night. Your wolf is howling at the moon."

The rabbit was not quite cooked, but I stole a large morsel anyway, and ate it greedily, blowing on my burning fingers. The Spaniard started to talk to me about his childhood, a subject that he had never broached before. I found it impossible to picture him as anything but a strong, barrel-chested man in his middle years. He told me that, in fact, he had been a delicate child.

"I was often ill. When I should have been playing with my brothers, I spent my days studying instead. Languages came easily to me—I was better able to defend myself with my tongue than with my fists. Then, when I was eleven, my father took me to see a man of letters who had agreed to instruct me in the classics. His name was Juan Pedro de Atenas, and he was attached to the court of Philip IV in Madrid. It was a very great honor, although I did not appreciate this at the time.

"My father was devoted to Juan Pedro. He spoke of his self-mastery, his *grace*, his insights into the human heart. Unlike many clever men, he never used his wits to belittle others. What is more, he always spoke the truth—whereas most men say what they want to hear, or what they think others want them to say. Juan Pedro was an extraordinary man, and for twenty-two years—until his death—I was a Friend to him, just as my father had been, and his father before him."

"Twenty-two years! Why haven't you talked to me about him before?" I asked.

"Let us say that the time was not right to speak of him."

Warm, and with my hunger sated, I pressed the Spaniard to tell me more.

"What distinguished Juan Pedro de Atenas from other men only became apparent over the course of time. He passed from childhood to adolescence to manhood in a wholly unremarkable manner. However, once he was an adult, the years did not mark him as they did his peers. Indeed, when Juan Pedro was fifty he still looked twenty; at one hundred he had barely reached middle age; at two hundred he was past his prime but still full of vigor. Alas, he died before his time, otherwise who knows how long he might have lived. Yet he was neither immortal nor a magician. Nor was he the devil himself—a repeated accusation that drove him into hiding. No, Juan Pedro was a man like any other except in this one single respect: Once he had attained maturity, he aged exceptionally slowly.

"His father, whose name was Alfonso, had always predicted this fate for him, insisting that he and Juan Pedro were the last survivors of a remarkable, long-lived line. For a great many years, however, Juan Pedro remained unconvinced, dismissing his father's claims as flights of fancy—"

I had been lying on my side, basking in front of the flames. Now I sat up, all attention, and demanded: "So how old *were* Juan Pedro and Alfonso?"

The Spaniard answered that Alfonso had lived to an enormous age but had refused to keep count of his years, being persuaded that it did him no good to dwell on such matters. Juan Pedro too felt that the delicate matter of his age was not a subject for discussion. Nevertheless, the Spaniard was certain that Juan Pedro was more than two hundred and twenty-five years old at the time of his death.

"How wonderful to live to such a great age!" I said. "To be able to plant an acorn and outlive the tree!"

The Spaniard was not so sure. Alfonso, he said, viewed his longevity with a kind of humble acceptance, but his son suffered greatly before coming to terms with what most would regard as a blessing.

"A long life exacts its own payment. A sempervivens will inevitably endure loneliness and loss."

"*Sempervivens?*"

"'Sempervivens' is the name Juan Pedro used for his own kind. It means 'always living,' and although not strictly accurate, it is a word to which I am accustomed and shall continue to use."

I remember repeating the word to myself so that I would not forget it. And now, in these pages, I teach it to you. I doubt that you will have difficulty remembering it. The Spaniard also spoke to me about Alfonso's theories about the sempervivens: that only a union between two long-lived parents could produce a long-lived child, whereas a mixed union *never* produced long-lived offspring. Alfonso himself had survived three brothers (they had all perished in combat), and all of them were sempervivens. Curiously, however, his only sister did not inherit the trait of longevity, but grew old like the rest of humanity.

It was only after the still youthful Juan Pedro had witnessed the death of two wives, eight children, and countless friends that he was finally forced to accept that his father had told him the truth. The Spaniard never forgot Juan Pedro confiding in him that he seemed to have spent his entire life dreaming about the dead.

After Alfonso's death—Juan Pedro was then more than a century old—he abandoned his home in the mountains, as well as the many graves he tended, and took to wandering from place to place, never settling, nursing the lonely ache in his soul. Having rejected his father's advice as a young man, Juan Pedro now found himself shaping his life in ways that Alfonso had suggested. He moved on frequently to avoid arousing suspicion and, at the same time, began to study in earnest, recording what he had witnessed on his travels and writing about the lives of remarkable individuals and significant events. Most importantly, he wrote down everything his father had told him about the sempervivens, and began a lifelong search for other members of his dying race.

To be entrusted with such a secret! That night in the Spaniard's cave, by the orange glow of the fire, my teacher held me in his thrall. I did not care to dwell on this darker side of the fate of a sempervivens but pictured, instead, the riches and knowledge such a person could acquire in a single lifetime. Gradually, however, like the flicker of a stranger's shadow passing in front of a doorway, a sense of dread stole over me. *Why* was the Spaniard telling me this now? Perhaps my anxiety merely mirrored that of the Spaniard himself, whose jaw was set tight, and who was plainly ill at ease, even though he was trying hard to disguise it. I watched him turn the rabbit on his makeshift spit, for one side was beginning to char. The juices were running freely now, and dripping fat spat and sizzled, filling the cave with blue smoke. He wiped his greasy hands on a handkerchief.

"What happened to Juan Pedro, Signor?" I asked. "Had he found happiness when you knew him in Madrid?"

"Juan Pedro spent many years traveling across Europe in search of other sempervivens. He all but despaired of ever finding a companion. You can imagine what an impossible task it was—any sempervivens would soon learn the need for secrecy—"

"So he never found anyone?"

"Finally, he *did*. I had the honor of being present when Juan Pedro returned from a pilgrimage to Santiago de Compostela with a wife. His prayers had been answered. He saw her, quite by chance, standing in front of the cathedral, a lone figure, and he sensed an immediate connection. Even though Juan Pedro's health was failing by then, he returned ablaze with joy. Never had I seen him so happy. Her name was Berthe and she originated from France. She was spirited and full of life; Juan Pedro called her his gift from God."

"So you knew her?"

"I knew her well."

"Did they have children?"

"Berthe died giving birth to her first child. A boy."

"No—"

"Alas, five days later I discovered Juan Pedro dead outside his own house. It is possible that he stumbled on account of his illness, but it is also possible that someone wanted him dead. It was a blow to the head that killed him."

"And the baby, Signor? Did the baby survive?"

"Yes, by the grace of God, the boy survived. And I have to tell you—"

"What is it, Signor?"

The Spaniard's chest heaved with emotion and he could not look at me but stared, instead, into the glowing heart of the fire. Then I knew why he had brought me to his cave and I guessed what he was about to say.

"Jean-Pierre, you are not who you think yourself to be. You know that your mother departed this world the same moment that you entered it. But it was Berthe who died giving birth to you. Juan Pedro was your father."

In the silence that followed the Spaniard's revelation, I felt nothing. "That is not possible, Signor, for you *know* who my father is. He is your friend!"

"He *is* my friend, and he brought you up as his own because you were born on the same night in the same city that he lost his own wife and child. Fate brought us together in Madrid."

The Spaniard read the disbelief in my face. "He loves you as his own, but you are not related in any way to the man you know as your father."

"*If* this is true, why didn't *he* tell me?" I cried. And at that moment, I realized that he already had. *You are no longer my own.*

I stared at the fire, at the glistening flesh of the rabbit, at its once-twitching muscles now contracting in the flames. The fire crackled, the fat spat, the world continued to turn, and nothing was the same.

The Spaniard took hold of my hand. "You understand that it is more likely than not that you are a sempervivens?"

I withdrew my hand and stood up. "You are mistaken!" I shouted. I was scarcely aware of crashing the flat of my foot onto the spit, causing a shower of golden sparks to rise into the air, and of kicking the burning logs, scattering them, along with our supper, over the floor of the cave. The Spaniard made no reaction apart from calmly beating out the glowing cinders that burned into his britches. I fled, crawling on my hands and knees through the darkness and slipping out of the narrow entrance into the night air. The Spaniard called out after me:

"I swore on your father's grave that I would keep you safe! It is possible that you hold within you an eternal legacy!"

XII

I ran into the night under a sky rinsed clean of clouds and awash with stars. I ran blindly through the woods, tripping over roots and kicking up drifts of leaves. I ran until I could run no more. When I reached a clearing, I surprised a fox. Here moonlight poured down in a wash of blue, so that the animal was silhouetted, pin-sharp, in front of clumps of swaying ferns. I stood still, catching my breath. All the while we studied each other, fellow travelers, equals, and presently he sloped off to resume his business, ears pricked, tail held rigid behind him, a perfect horizontal.

The wind had not let up; if anything, it blew stronger than before. The tree canopy creaked and groaned like a ship's rigging. I was glad to be out of the Spaniard's cave, and here, in this wild wood, where I could be alone with my thoughts.

It is not an easy thing to discover that you are not who you thought you were. The Spaniard's story had crashed into the life I thought I owned, shattering it into countless shards, too sharp to pick up, impossible to repair. Now my brothers' words drummed an accusing rhythm in my head: *Cuckoo! Cuckoo!* They had been right all along. I *was* the cuckoo in their nest. Had they sensed my difference, or had one of the servants let slip the secret? They were not my brothers. Their father was not my father. Their mother was not my mother. Now I grasped the meaning of my father's words: He was handing me back. So many lies, over so many years, to conceal my true parentage! I added my cries to the howling wind. *Lies!*

While the Spaniard spoke of the sempervivens, I had hung on to his every word, convinced and entranced. Now I questioned the truth of it. Men don't live for centuries. The Spaniard's devotion to Juan Pedro had made him gullible. It was a tall tale and I would not demean myself by believing it. Even so, as I reeled from the shock of the Spaniard's revelations on that fateful night above the Tarn, a small part of me recognized that he had told me the truth. Already I grasped that the certainties that, my whole life long, had told me who I was, and what I was, and where I belonged, had gone: They had been cut away at a stroke, with all the benign violence of a surgeon's knife.

"Jean-Pierre!"

The yellow glow of a lantern blinked as the Spaniard moved through the trees. I was tempted to remain silent but after he had called out three more times, I answered. After causing me such pain it would have pleased him to comfort me with word or gesture but I held myself back and would not give him the satisfaction. And so, guiding me with one hand on my shoulder, he led me back through the wood. We did not speak. Once more in the cave, I saw that he had mended the fire, jointed the rabbit, and placed it on a pewter dish. I would not eat. Presently the Spaniard picked up a candle and gestured for me to follow him to the side of the cave farthest from the entrance. When he lowered the flickering flame, the entrance to a smaller inner chamber was revealed. The Spaniard stepped back to allow me to enter first. Its roof was too low to make standing upright possible. I was struck by the way he gestured, rather grandly, with his hand—as if I should be awed in some way by the contents of this cave. But all that I saw, barely visible in the semidarkness, were some scrolls—perhaps two dozen— and a great many piles of books stacked on bare wooden shelves. I looked on, unimpressed. The Spaniard fetched his pannier and started to unload its contents, passing them to me through the small entrance hole. He asked me to place them on the empty shelf nearest to me.

"Aren't these your journals, Signor?" I had often seen him write in them, though the quantity of them surprised me. "Is *this* the secret you wanted to show me?"

"Did you hope for something else? Caskets of gold, perhaps?"

"No," I lied. "I did not know what to expect."

The Spaniard knew me too well and a half smile formed on his lips despite the uneasiness that had grown between us.

"All the books bound in red leather are the journals of Juan Pedro. The few bound in green are my own. Though not sempervivens, I wished to record something in the intervening years—"

"The intervening years? What do you mean?"

"Until you were old enough to—"

"What? Contribute to them myself?"

"It is too soon to speak of such a thing, though it is something your father would have wished. The scrolls you see in the far corner were written by Alfonso—your grandfather—"

"The man you *say* was my grandfather—"

"There is no doubt, Jean-Pierre. I stood in the adjoining

room the night you were born. I heard your first cry. When you were barely one week old—and already an orphan—it was I who placed you in the arms of the man who was to bring you up, a man distraught after the death of his own wife and newborn child. It was I who gave you your name."

"*You* did!"

"Juan Pedro was inconsolable after your mother's death. And he was not a well man. He had succumbed to a disease of the nerves. It started with his hands. . . ."

The Spaniard looked at me sorrowfully, with all the respect due to grieving relatives—except that these deaths had taken place fifteen years ago, and I had only that night learned of the existence of Juan Pedro, his allegedly long-lived race, and our alleged relationship. Nevertheless, the idea that, in the act of coming into the world, this baby (I could not accept that it was me) had caused the death of Berthe, provoked in me an acute distress. My throat constricted and I crawled farther into the inner cave, focusing my attention on the long line of journals bound in Juan Pedro's red leather. I ran my finger along their spines. That there were so many was a measure, I supposed, of his longevity. The Spaniard crawled in after me, and pulled a journal at random from the shelf.

"Queen Mariana of Spain often confided in your father and had she learned of their existence would have doubtless taken his journals. I smuggled them out of your father's house the day he died and hid them here. You will never own anything more precious."

I made no comment. He opened the volume and placed

it on the floor between us. "Look," he urged, and held up a candle, taking care to avoid dripping tallow on the precious pages. Reluctantly I lowered my eyes and saw for the first time Juan Pedro's beautiful hand though I understood not a single word of his elegant and finely drawn script. Wonderfully executed drawings peppered the densely written pages: There was a woman's face in three-quarters view, her eyes shrewd and lively, looking out at me from the journal, and a sketch of a ship, a glorious Spanish galleon in full sail. A growing emotion, a fragile thing—which I took pains to conceal—took me by surprise. I reached out my fingers and stroked the marks Juan Pedro had formed long ago on the coarse paper.

"And what color leather will you use to bind *my* journals?" I asked. "As that, I suppose, is your purpose. Blue perhaps? Or yellow?"

My tone was harsh and mocking—the false face of pent-up distress. I saw the Spaniard wince. "It is not a question of *my* purpose, Jean-Pierre. Your father, and your grandfather before him, saw the acquisition of knowledge and experience over long years as *their* purpose and, I believe, their personal salvation. You are young and it is enough that you know of the existence of their journals. I will contribute no longer to this enterprise. I hope that you will consider following the example set by your forebears, but you will, as we all do, forge your own path in life."

"Then I wish to return to Versailles as soon as possible," I said, "for I would prefer the company of Isabelle d'Alembert and the man I believe to be my father, to that of journals written by dead men who are nothing to me."

The Spaniard's patience was at an end. His face turned thunderous. "You will show some respect, Jean-Pierre, if not to me—a true Friend who has devoted his entire life to your family—then to Juan Pedro and Alfonso, whose blood, whether you care to acknowledge it or not, you carry in your veins! And as for returning to Versailles, I cannot permit it."

"And by what right do you confine me to your house?"

The Spaniard took a deep breath to calm himself. "Listen to me, Jean-Pierre, I have no proof, because there is a possibility that he stumbled and hit his head against the corner of a wall, yet I am convinced that Juan Pedro was murdered. Someone knew who he was. Someone brought down a rock upon his head. *That* is the reason I made arrangements for you to be brought up in France by a man who does not know your true identity. It is the reason I left my home, and everything I knew, in order to come to the court of the Sun King, to prepare the way for you. And now someone has attempted to murder you in precisely the same way. Surely you can understand why I am reluctant to allow you to return to Versailles?"

"You think someone tried to kill me because I am Juan Pedro's son?"

"I do."

I shook my head. "No. I can't believe it—"

"I hope I am wrong. . . . There is one last thing I must admit to you."

I stared at him, doubting I had the strength to bear any more revelations. And so, calmly, and without a trace of remorse, the Spaniard said that, given the high probability that I was sempervivens, he judged it unfair, both to Isabelle d'Alembert and to myself, to allow any intimacy between us to develop. He had intercepted and destroyed my letter to her. He had also burned the two letters that Isabelle had sent to me. The impact on me of this last admission was instant and violent. As I lunged forward the Spaniard grabbed hold of my wrists and forced me back down. He was the stronger by far and he looked pityingly into my eyes—which I found unbearable—and he said: "You must feel that I have stripped everything away from you. Your home, your family, your first love—"

I did not have the strength to reply.

"And I am sorry for it. Many men would kill for what, at this instant, you would throw back in my face. Yet I *do* understand. I have imagined this moment for many years. Please believe, at least, that I understand your pain."

I turned my back on him and the Spaniard fell silent for several minutes. At last he said: "I shall be your Friend and teacher for as long you desire it, but you are the master of your own fate. In the morning I shall return with a horse. For now I will take my leave of you. I can see that you wish to be alone. Good night, Jean-Pierre."

He left the cave. I heard his footfalls as he returned to the world. When I was alone again, I rolled into a ball at the foot of my father's and my grandfather's journals, pinched out all the candles, and stared into the impenetrable darkness.

Daddy Longlegs

As Martha scrapes out the last spoonfuls of Sussex pond pudding from the basin, they hear Spark's footsteps crunch past the back door in the direction of the footbridge. John Stone notes the hopeful gleam that comes to Jacob's eye and holds his gaze. He explains—just in case anyone happened to be wondering—that Spark intended to call her mother. She will doubtless be walking up the lane to get a signal for her cell phone (a strange activity, also beloved of John Stone in recent years and to which Martha and Jacob have become accustomed). Spark isn't jumping ship. Not yet, at any rate.

Jacob rises from the table, sucking sticky lemon syrup noisily from one finger, and nods his thanks to Martha. The remaining pair sit together at the long kitchen table, Martha folding and refolding her checked napkin while John Stone stabs at a curl of lemon rind with his fork and moves it around his plate. Both are lost in their own thoughts. Presently Martha scrapes back her chair and announces that she is going to put the peelings on the compost heap. John Stone offers to do it for her, but Martha shushes him. He watches her go and thinks it will be good for her to have a young woman in the house for a while.

He stands at the open kitchen window, sipping mint tea. The evening sky is milky, almost pearlescent, and the sun burns red through gaps in the trees. Resting his cup on the draining board for a moment, he holds out both hands, fingers straight and slightly spread apart, checking for tremors—a habit he must learn to control before Martha starts noticing. Spark was good company this afternoon. He enjoyed her conversation and the glimpses of her character it afforded. She strikes him as wise beyond her years. But then, she's had to cope with more than she should: the death of one parent and the demands of another. And if Spark is the image of her mother at the same age, at least she shows no sign of having inherited Thérèse's personality—that particular combination of dazzle and manipulation that made her so difficult a companion. Indeed, Spark seems to possess a well-balanced disposition, and—unlike her mother—is an amateur when it comes to the art of concealing her emotions. True, she did not admit to having taken his picture earlier, but the contrite expression on her face when he brought up the subject of photography all but made him laugh out loud. The "cook of sorts, on the coast" (as Thérèse described Spark's father) was probably an agreeable sort of character. Difficult and complex feelings rise up inside John Stone, feelings that he immediately suppresses. Fate may have seen fit to deny him the companionship of a wife and the consolation of a line that will continue after him, but he learned long ago the lesson of not dwelling on a thing that cannot be changed. Jacob makes no secret of resenting Spark on account of her parentage but John Stone, who has better reason, will rise above such base and shortsighted emotions.

What must Spark be saying about his bizarre household to the woman she believes to be her mother? The girl is clearly devoted to this Mrs. Park—he only hopes the woman appreciates how lucky she is. John Stone feels a sudden stab of guilt and questions, for the first time, the rightness—for *Spark*—of bringing her here to Stowney House. But the imperative of finding a new Friend means that it's a little late in the day to be entertaining doubts. He runs his fingers distractedly through his hair. How is he going to manage this?

Outside, the swifts swoop and dive. It is the sound of summer. And, thanks to the treacherous hook of memory, it is also a sound that transports him to the day Isabelle died. Afterward he rode into the fields and stood with bowed head, statue-still and thigh-deep in a fast-flowing stream, paralyzed with grief and incomprehension. Out of nowhere, scores of these beautiful creatures suddenly arrived, surrounding him with their flitting forms, engulfing him with their sibilant cries. He had believed himself to be familiar with death until the day he confronted Isabelle's lifeless body, then he understood that death remains a stranger until it takes away someone we love. Yet, just as Isabelle had told him it would, his heart had continued to beat. And here he is, centuries later, facing his own end—and all the responsibilities that brings. Please let him not have made a terrible error by inviting the girl here.

John Stone reaches up for the bottle of Armagnac on the cracked oak lintel. Someone has carved a date into the blackened wood: 1695 (he likes to think it was the Spaniard, but he does not know for sure). As he pulls out the cork with a satisfying *pop*, Martha flounces back into the kitchen, eyebrows knitted together in fury. She disappears into the pantry and emerges with a broom and a small butterfly net.

"What is it?"

"Spark's room is full of daddy longlegs. Jacob's been in there. I saw a cunning look on his face while she was batting one away earlier. He's a bad man, so he is. And you can be sure I've told him what I think of his antics."

John Stone hurries out after her. Jacob has switched on every light and has left the French doors wide-open. Martha caught him standing in the middle of the room swinging around the stinking carcass of some roadkill that he had found. Martha chased him out, but now there are horse flies, moths, and a quantity of daddy longlegs circling the room, colliding with the sparkling chandelier. There are also dozens of white maggots wriggling and squirming about on the floor. John Stone sweeps up the maggots while Martha leaps up high into the air, expertly catching the winged creatures in her net. Afterward she squirts lavender water about the room, hoping to camouflage any lingering odor of rotting flesh. By the time they're done they can hear Spark's footsteps crunching down the drive. John Stone switches off all the lights and they slip out into the dusk, closing the doors silently behind them.

The scent of burning tobacco leads John Stone to Jacob. He is smoking a clay pipe in the kitchen garden, the stem clenched between his teeth as he crouches in the earth, training pea shoots up a cane wigwam. He lifts his head and regards John Stone defiantly.

"She'll blab," says Jacob. "Send her home before we all have cause to regret it."

John Stone shakes his head. "No."

"I'll drive her off if I can—"

"Surely you can see that we need a new Friend?"

"I can see. It's you who's blind. We've got your lawyer."

"And he's over sixty. Can't you give her a chance?"

Jacob stands up and walks toward him, resting the pipe between horny thumb and forefinger, and fixing him with his pale eyes. "What's changed that makes you so reckless now?" For all that Jacob is mostly hot air, John Stone feels the hairs rise at the back of his neck. He smells the tobacco on his breath. "There's something you're not telling us."

"I've told you all you need to know," says John Stone. He won't reveal his illness. Not here, not now.

"And why does she have to *live* here?" Jacob is too close, and speaking too loudly. "She's *Thérèse's* daughter! If I'd known who she was, I'd have—"

"You'd have done *what*, Jacob?"

"I'd have wrung her neck, years back, when first I clapped eyes on her."

John Stone exclaims angrily. "It's my late *wife* you're talking about Jacob, for all her faults—"

"*Wife!*" Jacob snorts. "How long did she ever spend under your roof? She'd blow in on a storm and be gone as soon as the sun shone—"

"That's enough, Jacob!"

"And every last time she came it'd set Martha back. You don't know the half of it."

John Stone pushes at Jacob's chest with the flats of his palms; Jacob's eyes narrow, and he starts to push back. Suddenly the two men are locked into each other like rutting stags. John Stone becomes conscious that a part of him has been spoiling for a fight since he first talked to Jacob about Spark. However, as Martha has reminded him often enough, there's a reason Jacob has survived as long as he has. John Stone is no match for him and his feet start to slide backward in the dirt path. It occurs to him too that Thérèse would laugh out loud at the thought of him defending her in this way. He breaks eye contact and steps backward.

"You know, my friend, if Spark comes to any harm, Martha will never forgive you." It is the truth. Jacob does not reply. "Can't you see that I'm doing this for your own good?" He nearly adds, *you fool*, but stops himself in time. Jacob's sense of humor (and he has a good one in the right mood) does not extend to his mental states. "I *swear* I will keep you and Martha safe."

When Jacob pointedly takes out his penknife and starts to whittle a piece of wood, John Stone decides to leave him to his sculpting and retreats down the path. He reminds himself that there is a reason why Jacob behaves as he does—not that this makes him any easier to deal with. Out of the three of them, Jacob is the oldest; he is also the only one of them to have been brought up in a community of his own kind. Alas, the defining experience of Jacob's life was to have witnessed, as an adolescent, the bloody slaughter of his family and everyone he knew. As sole survivor, the massacre taught him to conceal his difference, trust no one, and keep moving. Even now Jacob insists that he would have moved on long ago, if it weren't for Martha asking him to stay. Stowney House has helped to heal him, but even so, as his nightmares testify, Jacob still battles with the fear that, sooner or later, "they" will find them out—and come for them again.

Somewhere in the orchard a blackbird is singing, celebrating the close of another day. Its liquid notes rise up into the dusk. John Stone can't resist one last attempt to make his case and turns back. He finds Jacob taking a long, slow draw of his pipe. The tobacco in the bowl crackles and glows red in the gloom, illuminating for an instant his rawboned face.

"Do you remember how it was when they invented the telegraph? How it changed *everything*? Suddenly we knew what was happening on the other side of the world, and people on the other side of the world knew what was happening to us. It gave us a sense of *who* we were, and *where* we were, and *what* we were."

Jacob puts down his penknife. "What are you trying to say, John?"

"That Stowney House is almost an island, but not quite. Without a bridge, we're lost. I tell you, Jacob, not since the telegraph came have I sensed such a *shift* in how people think about themselves. Spark's generation is the first who are strangers to solitude and silence. They know only noise and a constant need to be connected. Despite my efforts to adapt I find myself floundering. Spark could be your— our—link to a new world."

Predictably, Jacob grunts. "People are people. Spark will blab. Perhaps she won't mean to, but she will."

"I think you're wrong—"

Jacob isn't listening to him. "They'll pin us up like

butterflies, and poke at us. And they won't stop till they've worked us out. I'd throw myself in the river before I let that happen, and Martha with me."

"*I* won't let that happen to you. Haven't I kept you safe all this time? *Trust* me." But he can see that Jacob can't. And if John Stone were in his shoes, would he?

Headlights

John Stone, it appears, likes to drive. Spark grips the edge of the tan leather seat as they hurtle down narrow, sandy-edged lanes toward the coast. It is her first time in a convertible: The wind slams into her face and plows shifting white furrows through Martha's short, black hair in front of her. Spark, to her surprise, is the only one to wear her safety belt. John Stone's reactions are sharp. Twice now he's swerved to avoid rabbits, and both times Spark screwed her eyes shut tight. When he brakes, going round a blind corner, he shouts: *Brace yourselves!* And the others laugh!

Martha and John Stone start to sing folk songs. Even Jacob consents to join in after a while. Spark, who knows none of the words, feels as embarrassed as the time a Spanish guitarist serenaded Mum when they took her to a tapas bar for her birthday. At the same time she is impressed: Her companions can actually sing. Even Jacob's rasping voice is somehow transformed into something melodic. Their voices soar. They know how to harmonize. They clap their hands, beat out a rhythm on the steering wheel, the dashboard, stamp their feet. When, finally, she dares clap in time with them, John Stone smiles at her in the rearview mirror. As the car cuts a track across the flat landscape, it is as though their music is being shed into the winds like thistledown.

They park in a field and then walk in single file for a few minutes, John Stone leading the way, through dunes where tufts of marram grass spike through powdery sand. There is a steep path cut into a crumbling, brick-colored cliff that is home to a colony of sand martins. It is high tide, though the sea is retreating, and they decide to sunbathe for a while. John, Martha, and Jacob lay out their mats in a line on the remaining ribbon of shell-strewn beach. They strip under Martha's modesty towels, which are gathered at the neck, standing on one leg, holding on to one another for balance, pulling off pants and socks and handing each other their bathing costumes. Then, once they are changed, and like a routine they have followed a hundred times before, they all lie flat on their backs, tail to toe, toe to tail, their arms at their sides, their eyes closed tight, an expression on all their tanned faces as calm as deep water.

Unsettled and lonely, Spark feels that she may as well not be with them; she nearly goes for a walk by herself, but talks herself out of it. Reluctantly she peels off her jeans and yellow T-shirt, revealing her bikini. The fresh breeze buffets her pale flesh and brings her out in goose pimples. She wraps her arms around her midriff and half crouches, locking her knees together. Spark surveys the beach. They are alone. She stares out at the sea, a pale opal green under a sky of deepening blue. Small, crested waves race to the shore like enthusiastic dogs. A foaming line of surf constantly teases, threatening to engulf her friends but always receding at the last moment. John, Martha, and Jacob lie like ripening chrysalises, soaking up the sun's rays.

Spark decides she may as well join them and stretches herself out on her striped blue towel. Already her skin feels dry and salty. At ground level she is sheltered from the wind and wraps some of the towel over her. The tufts of cotton feel warm and comforting. The continuous roar of the sea makes her chest vibrate. She closes her eyes. Cool ozone fills her lungs; the cry of a gull speaks of vast distances. In her dream, Ludo is asking her something, though she can't concentrate on what he is saying. Instead she is noticing the gold hairs on the back of his hand and the way his eyelashes curl.

When she awakes, the tide has gone out and a broad tan beach has appeared. The smell of the sea is in her nostrils and she is very warm. Someone has draped an extra towel over her, which she throws off. The sand is wet and glistening; it reflects and elongates the forms of the people who have now started to congregate here. Raising herself up on one elbow, she observes the transformed scene. A toddler trots unsteadily across the sand, all energies focused on not tipping her slopping bucket; a man flies a giant red kite, pulling alternately on two wires that climb high into the sky; a golden Labrador splashes through the surf, barking at a herring gull. And Martha, Jacob, and John Stone are playing volleyball like champions. They are so good a small crowd of children have gathered to watch.

Spark stretches out on her towel and waves at them. Soon she'll have a swim, but first she must read through what she wrote yesterday evening. She unzips her bag and takes out a pencil and the picture postcard of Suffolk she bought for Ludo at the station. If she mails it today, it should be waiting for him when he arrives. She tells him her room isn't much bigger than his fridge; she explains that the mattress will prove tricky for anyone who doesn't have the physique of a twelve-year-old girl; she promises to try and get back for a weekend.

Spark sighs. Too jokey. Too much emphasis on smallness of room. And set against the tone of the rest of the postcard, the initial *Welcome to Mansfield!* now sounds sarcastic. But in the sunlight it's really obvious how many times she's rubbed out sentences and rewritten them. It's just going to have to do.

That evening, at John Stone's request, the four of them eat alfresco in the orchard, under a starry sky. It has been a good day: She has swum in the sea and made good headway with the archives. Things are more relaxed with John Stone around. Martha, who is clearly a stranger to the *ping* of a microwave, has roasted a chicken in butter and herbs. It smells delicious, but Spark's stomach is beginning to tie itself in knots on account of Jacob. He sits opposite her and has reverted to a sullen, glowering presence. He also keeps sliding the oil lamp toward her, which she hates because of all the buzzing, fluttering creatures with a death wish that are attracted to the light; they hurl themselves at the scorching glass, and she's got a horror of them catching in her hair. Each time Jacob moves the lamp toward her, John Stone moves it away again, without comment, to his side of the table. There is no way Jacob isn't doing it on purpose.

John Stone and Martha do their best to draw Spark into the conversation. Martha points out the cluster of glow worms under an apple tree, and at one point John Stone recites a funny limerick about James Joyce and a tortoise. Spark doesn't mean to be so quiet, but it's difficult to ignore Jacob's spiteful behavior.

Suddenly, and with no warning, John Stone collapses forward onto the table, his face landing in his plate. Spark springs up, terrified, a hand over her mouth. Martha, although concerned, does not seem overly alarmed.

"Fetch a blanket, can you?" she says to Jacob, who immediately runs toward the house.

"I'll call an ambulance," Spark cries.

"No!" exclaims Martha. "No! John has no truck with doctors."

Spark can only think about her father. "But he might be having a heart attack!"

"Lord bless you, his heart's fine. John is apt to fall into a deep sleep, as suddenly as turning out a light." Martha clicks her fingers for emphasis. "And you can't shake him out of it, no matter how hard you try. The first time I saw it, I thought he must be peloothered—but it's not the drink that does it to him. He's done it since he was a boy."

Martha gently lifts John Stone's head and starts to clean the grease from his chin with a napkin.

"Here, let me hold him," says Spark, gripping his skull between the palms of her hands, trying not to dig her fingernails into the flesh of his face.

Martha shifts the plate and finishes wiping John Stone's nose. Spark is amazed how heavy heads are. "Sometimes it's for a few minutes," says Martha, "and sometimes it's for hours. It's his nerves—though John insists that it's not. He won't remember a thing when he wakes up."

"Don't you think we should call a doctor—just to be sure?" says Spark.

"Certainly not. He'd have our guts for garters if we did."

Returning to the house through the orchard, Spark holds the oil lamp high while Jacob takes John Stone's shoulders and Martha takes his feet. She opens the doors for them as they carry him into the drawing room and deposit him on a couch. Jacob unties John Stone's laces and levers off his shoes.

"We can manage now," says Martha, turning to Spark. "But, Lord, look at you, you're as white as a sheet!"

Spark becomes aware of the tears rolling down her cheeks and wipes them quickly away with the back of her hand. But the tears keep coming. Nodding to Jacob to stay with John Stone, Martha guides Spark to the kitchen, an arm around her waist. To have another grown-up take responsibility. To not be alone when difficult stuff happens. The tears come faster. She just can't stop herself.

"I thought he might be dead."

"Hush, now. Drink this."

Spark sips warm milk laced with a tot of whisky, which Martha has prepared for her. When she looks up, Martha is smiling at her, maternal and reassuring.

"Don't you be worrying yourself about John. I'm not worried about him, I promise you. Let's get you to bed and you'll be right as the mail in the morning—as will he."

* * *

In her room, Spark undresses in the dark, can't be bothered to draw the curtains, lets her clothes lie where they fall on the floor, sinks instantly into a deep sleep. But in the middle of the night she is wakened by the sound of tires crunching on gravel. An engine is running. Spark opens her eyes and screws them shut again, dazzled by a strange light. *Oh no,* she thinks, *it's an ambulance!* She rolls out of bed, lands on all fours in front of the French doors, and for a moment, stares out at the floodlit garden. The fountain casts an immense shadow over the lawn, and every blade of grass is sharply defined in the powerful yellow beam. Spark slips out into the night, making her way toward the courtyard. But it's not an ambulance. She stands shivering on the path, unsure whether to show herself. A long, black car is parked in the courtyard. John Stone, in suit and tie, climbs into the backseat while a uniformed chauffeur places a suitcase in the boot. Martha, in her dressing gown, looks on. The rear window glides down and muffled words pass between John Stone and Martha. Spark fancies she hears her name, but she's not sure over the purr of the engine.

Spark tiptoes back to her room and eventually goes back to sleep. She awakes late and wonders if she dreamed it.

Notebook 4

XIII

It was early spring before we left the Spaniard's house on the banks of the River Tarn. He had urged me to start a new life outside France, but I steadfastly refused. Finally we struck a bargain. If, despite my doubts, I agreed to continue my education and training in a manner of which Juan Pedro—my supposed father—would have approved, then the Spaniard would do all that was necessary for me to resume my life as a courtier. He would also, in addition, arrange a meeting with Isabelle d'Alembert. The Spaniard was unhappy with our bargain—he was still concerned for my safety and regarded my feelings for Isabelle as a youthful infatuation—nevertheless, he kept his word.

Returning to Versailles, we stopped in a small town north of the Cévennes where we saw a troop of soldiers—*dragonnades*—march through the streets. Their task was to "persuade" the protestant Huguenots, by any means necessary, to convert to Catholicism, a religion that was hateful to them. They were there by order of an increasingly devout monarch. For me, it was a timely reminder of the long reach of the Sun King's hand, a reminder that words uttered in some antechamber in far-off Versailles transformed, inexorably, into actions that could shatter lives.

What I witnessed that day became the first entry in the first of my journals—written to fulfill my part of the bargain.

Reading it today, I see that what preoccupied me was a question: Where did the truth lie in that scene? Was it in the arrogant swagger of the officer leading his men? Or was it, rather, in the ashen face of the Huguenot mother, gathering her children to her skirts as she backed into an alley? Should I write about the soldiers blowing kisses at girls in the crowd, or the cat, terrified by the commotion, and crushed under the wheels of a military wagon? And how was I to interpret the stern expression on the catholic priest's face as he looked on, hands locked so tightly in front of him that his fingers grew white? I did not understand, then, that we see things not for what they are, but for how *we* are. Even so, that first attempt was enough to show me that to be a witness is not a simple thing.

My meeting with Isabelle d'Alembert was to take place in Rambouillet. It would then be a mere half day's ride from her aunt's square manor house to the court of the Sun King at Versailles.

I was shown to a whitewashed sitting room, sparsely furnished with three armchairs and a card table. Tall windows looked out on one side over the lush forest of Rambouillet—where I had left the Spaniard hunting wild boar—and, on the other, over a gently rolling landscape dotted with sheep and newborn lambs. *Meh-meh! Meh-meh!* Their shrill cries penetrated the drafty windows. The calmness of my surroundings made the waiting worse. My ears strained to hear the footsteps of the girl who had inhabited my thoughts for so long. How would she be with me? And, for that matter, how should I be with her?

There was a mottled mirror hanging at the far end of the room that reflected the chalky morning light. I placed myself in front it and took stock. My new mint-green waistcoat (I was excessively proud of it) had ridden up my waist, and my hair was in disarray. As for my neck, it poked out of my cravat at an angle resembling a heron waiting for a fish. I did what I could to improve matters. I retied my hair, straightened my waistcoat, and—a futile gesture—pinched my broken nose between thumb and forefinger. It was at the instant I forced the broadest of smiles, baring all my teeth, that the door swung open. It was Isabelle d'Alembert. Before I could adjust my expression, our reflections met in the mirror. Just as I remembered, her eyes were the smoldering gray of storm clouds. As the idiotic grin vanished from my mouth a smile appeared on hers. How foolish I felt, but how *alive*. I tried not to stare but could not tear my eyes away from her.

"Welcome to Rambouillet, Monsieur. I hope that your journey was agreeable and that your health is much improved."

"Thank you," I replied. "It was. . . . It is."

Isabelle held out a creamy hand. I kissed it, and held on for a fraction too long, for she had to pull her fingers from my grasp. *Rosewater!* I breathed her in.

Isabelle was speaking, but the sound of that longed-for voice had mesmerized me, so that her meaning seemed to slip through the net of her words.

"My aunt is kind," she said, "and promised us a few minutes alone."

"A few minutes," I repeated, like a fool. There was

laughter in her eyes. The speech I had rehearsed that morning in the fields fled from me, refusing to return. I flapped about hopelessly in the shallows of our conversation until Isabelle came to my rescue.

"I feared for your life when my letters remained unanswered—"

"Forgive me, I—"

"There is no need to apologize, I assure you. Signor de Lastimosa explained that you could not read on account of your injuries, and that he could not risk writing to me directly in case he provoked my father's anger." She paused, and added: "He was right, of course. My father reads all my correspondence and he would not have approved. . . ."

A small frown appeared on Isabelle's brow—concerned, I suppose, in case I should be offended at the idea that her father considered me unsuitable company. In truth, I cared little what her father thought of me. On the other hand, how I longed to share with her how utterly my life had changed since our last meeting. I longed to tell her that there was a possibility that I would outlive everyone I had ever met, and their children, and who knew how many generations of their children, and that I was supposed to use my time wisely, putting service to others above my own personal happiness. I wanted to tell her that although I could not quite believe it, I could not quite disbelieve it either, and that I no longer felt carefree but was forever wondering if I was a sempervivens or an ordinary boy wasting his precious life wondering if he was different. And, even more than that, I wanted to tell her that despite everything that had happened to me, the only thing that made me truly happy and gave my life meaning was the thought of *her*. I wanted to tell her that the bloom on her freckled skin reminded me of the texture of a butterfly's wings, and that when she looked at me with those eyes—which spoke of such tenderness and intelligence—I felt as if she could see my soul. I wanted to tell her that it was my determination to be with her once more that gave me the strength to recover from my injuries. I wanted to say that just to stand next to her was to live life more intensely. Of course, I said none of this, but asked if her father would be angry if he knew that I had come to Rambouillet.

Isabelle nodded solemnly. "After that night in the Colonnade, my father felt obliged to send a written apology to the Prince de Montclair and his family on my behalf. But, you see, what happened made people laugh, and so they like to repeat it. They are still taunting the Prince—mostly behind his back. It infuriates him."

"What do they say?" I asked, unwilling to summon up a scrap of sympathy for the fellow. "That, like Mademoiselle d'Alembert, they would—"

"Rather die? Yes." Isabelle bit her lip but her eyes, at least, were laughing. "He hates me now—whenever I enter a room, he leaves immediately."

"I admit that I should not have repeated what you said about him—and for that I am sorry—but, all the same, it was *nothing*! I'm certain the Prince de Montclair says worse things about people several times a day."

"It was nothing yet something. . . . It is not *nothing* to ridicule a prince. Papa says we have made enemies of the Montclair family—and he has made it clear that he blames me."

"And me, I suppose?"

"That goes without saying."

"Ah . . ."

She reached out to point to my nose. "Was it broken?"

"Yes."

She stretched out her arm a little farther and, very gently, ran the tip of her finger over the scar that protruded from my scalp and down over my crooked nose. Her touch sent shivers of pleasure skittering down my spine.

"Did it hurt very much?" she asked.

"When you are no longer in pain it is difficult to remember what it felt like."

Isabelle pointed to a spot on my scalp. "May I?" she asked, and then, resting both hands on my head, she teased out a few strands of hair from my ponytail. I felt the warmth of her breath on my cheek. I could see every golden freckle. It was overwhelming.

"Do you know that you have a small stripe of white hair over the scar?"

I did know. I have it still. "Yes," I said and, hearing footsteps in the corridor, and unable to resist any longer, I stole a kiss. Isabelle stepped backward and shot a look behind her as a soft *rat-ta-ta-tat* sounded at the door.

"I came back to Versailles for *you*," I whispered urgently.

Isabelle's eyes were shining. "Come in, Aunt," she called and retreated to the window. It was only for a second or two at most, but it was enough: She stood calmly, a figure against a landscape, her hands folded neatly in front of her. But her eyes disclosed to me what she felt. The rush of joy was hard to contain.

Her aunt swept into the room along with Isabelle's three silly spaniels. Their bright, black eyes sparkled, their claws *click-clack*ed on the parquet floor, and they put their eager little paws on our knees. She was a refined woman with an elegant bearing, just as I expected. We exchanged pleasantries; she gave me a tour of her house, pointing out some of her treasures, including several portraits of prominent figures at court. One was of Monsieur's second wife, the Princess Palatine. She was a good sort, she said, but so *ungainly*. Did I not think so? And such ruddy cheeks from all those afternoons of hunting without protecting her skin behind a veil! A shocking lack of vanity, would I not agree, for a princess of the blood?

"Shocking," mimed Isabelle from behind her aunt's back.

"Oh, shocking," I repeated, keeping my face very straight.

As we walked through the house, Isabelle and I contrived to lag behind so that we could exchange glances and hold hands for a few precious seconds. We were not careful enough, for I saw the color heighten in her aunt's face. She then began to interrogate me about my family and my father's estate, and it suddenly struck me that not only was my true identity a mystery even to me, I would be obliged, from now on, to lie about it to the rest of the world. This distressing thought made me even more tongue-tied in the face of the aunt's searching questions. Soon my nerves were in shreds, and I started to stutter and pull at my tight cravat.

I overheard her whisper into Isabelle's ear: "Whatever were you were *thinking* of, my dear, asking me to receive this young man?"

Ignoring Isabelle's silent protests, her aunt brought up the incident at the Colonnade. The whole affair, she said, had distressed Isabelle's father exceedingly. Why had I attacked the Prince de Montclair so recklessly? She opened her painted fan and beat the air beneath her chin while she waited for my response.

"He insulted Mademoiselle d'Alembert's friend, Madame. I had no option but to defend her honor."

"Monsieur, I was hoping, in the circumstances, that you might express some remorse. The fact that you show none indicates, at best, a lack of good judgement and, at worst, inexcusably poor manners. I gave you the opportunity to redeem yourself. Alas, you have not availed yourself of it."

Closing her fan with a *click*, Isabelle's aunt indicated that my visit had come to an end. She shepherded me out of the room, making it clear to Isabelle that she was not to follow. Isabelle's expression was difficult to read as she curtseyed her farewell. Her aunt accompanied me to the entrance hall, where she stopped and turned to face me.

"A word before you leave, Monsieur."

Her expression was perfectly pleasant. "Yes, Madame."

"My niece is a d'Alembert, with a glittering future ahead of her. It is only because I dote on her that I permitted you to call on her today. You must understand that you will not, of course, be welcomed at Rambouillet on another occasion. Adieu, Monsieur."

As my carriage moved away, I wondered if Isabelle's aunt had planned to warn me off from the start, or if I had failed whatever test she had set for me. Never had I felt the sting of humiliation so acutely. I was not worthy of Isabelle and her aunt had made this plain to her. What ridiculous conceit had made me think that I could win her? Yet a sixth sense made me look back at the house. I saw the pale oval of Isabelle's face appear at an upstairs window. She blew me a kiss. And then I flung my head and shoulders out of the carriage window and waved joyfully until she had disappeared from view.

XIV

As I stepped into the inn, with its pervading odor of wood smoke and roasting mutton, I heard a clatter of boots descending the wooden staircase. It was the Spaniard. New guests had arrived and I watched him pick his way through teetering piles of luggage, their dogs, and their fretful children, until, finally, he stood before me. "At last!" he said, and grabbed me by the shoulder.

He led me outside, into a meadow, where only black-faced sheep could overhear our conversation. My meeting with Isabelle and her aunt, still at the forefront of my own mind, was clearly the last thing on his. He did not even ask how the visit had gone. Instead, he announced that during my absence a messenger had arrived from Versailles with instructions for me. The King's *valet de chambre*, Monsieur Bontemps, wished to speak with me, and I was to wait for him, at midnight, at the crossroads outside Rambouillet. He would be traveling in a carriage that bore no armorial markings. I was not surprised that the Spaniard was agitated. Monsieur Bontemps—a man whom the King trusted above all others—desired to talk with *me*! This was astonishing news.

"But *why*, Signor? What could be the purpose of his visit?"

"Have you truly listened to nothing I have told you?" said the Spaniard in exasperation. "It has always been a possibility that the King knows about you."

The Spaniard was right to be angry with me. At that

age I was still apt to listen only to what I wanted to hear, and my preoccupation with Isabelle had made me deaf to his concerns. He had often told me how fond Queen Mariana of Spain had been of Juan Pedro. I was also aware that, owing to the suspicious circumstances surrounding Juan Pedro's death, the Spaniard had enlisted her aid, and she, in turn, had approached the King of France. Louis consented to Queen Mariana's request and offered his protection to the infant and his guardian who had fled Madrid and now sought refuge in France. Queen Mariana and the Spaniard had never spoken directly to each other about Juan Pedro's longevity, so neither could be certain how much the other knew. But the Spaniard—who had now benefited from the Sun King's hospitality for over fifteen years—lived in fear that Juan Pedro's secret might have been passed from one monarch to another.

"Do you think that the King believes me to be a sempervivens?"

The Spaniard shrugged his shoulders. "I cannot say. But we are about to find out. Perhaps the King believes the time has come for him to inspect his goods. . . ."

I looked at him, taken aback by the unpleasant turn of phrase. "How could Monsieur Bontemps know where to find us?" I asked.

"As I have told you before and repeat now, nothing happens at Versailles without the King being told of it sooner or later. Besides, where there's a will, these things are simple to find out."

The Spaniard reached into his pocket and pulled out

a small leather pouch. "Here. You are required to present *this* to Monsieur Bontemps to prove your identity."

The pouch was decorated with three fleurs-de-lys. When I tugged opened the fine drawstrings I found a signet ring wrapped inside a piece of scarlet silk. I held it up at eye level. The Spaniard joined me, and standing at my shoulder, gripped my wrist in his large fist, turning it this way and that in order to observe every detail. It was made of gold, and its octagonal head was embossed with an apple tree whose roots had been depicted in as much detail as the branches, so that the two halves of the tree mirrored each other. Minute rubies represented the fruit with which its boughs were laden. Spiraling around the inner surface of the ring was an inscription, which I read out loud:

"'*Sapiens vivit quantum debet, non quantum potest.*'"

"Seneca!" the Spaniard exclaimed. *"The wise man lives as long as he ought, not as long as he can."*

We exchanged a glance and saw the look of alarm in his eyes. "So the King *does* know!"

"He may," agreed the Spaniard, letting go of my wrist.

As the Spaniard walked away from me I noted the despondent tilt of his head. But it was not dismay that I felt. Rather, a throb of excitement started to pulse through my veins. What plans might the King have for me? The Spaniard was deep in thought. Presently I asked: "Will you accompany me tonight?"

"My presence has not been requested, Jean-Pierre." He held my gaze for a moment. "This is not the first time Monsieur Bontemps has attempted to see you. He sent a messenger to the Cévennes soon after we arrived. I sent word to him that you were unable to speak and that you could receive no visitors—"

I was indignant. "Why didn't you tell me this before?"

"I had hoped to dissuade you from returning to Versailles."

"I do not understand you, Signor. What if King Louis does know my secret? Is it not a good thing to have his protection?"

"It is what comes with that protection that concerns me. The blood of the sempervivens might run in your veins, but you are still a boy. When Juan Pedro came to the Spanish court he had already acquired wisdom in the world and knew his own mind. Louis has all the instincts of a powerful king. How are you to hold your own in his presence? He will bend you to his will; he will *train* you into a form that pleases him like the topiary that adorns his gardens. He will be the master and you the servant and you will soon forget that it could ever have been otherwise—"

"I am not feeble-minded, Signor!"

"That is not what I said—"

"Forgive me, Signor, but are you implying that I could learn more from you than from the Sun King?—"

"No, Jean-Pierre! My only thought is to place you where you can grow freely. In Versailles, I fear you could be pruned and shaped to the King's design—a king whom *you* will out-live. Do you understand me?" My look of incomprehension provoked an impatient sigh. "You will need all your wits about you this evening," he said abruptly. "I suggest you return to the inn and rest."

My teacher's words had unsettled me. Nevertheless, still smarting from the disdain Isabelle's aunt had showed me only that morning, I could not help but regard the Spaniard's predictions as excessively gloomy. Indeed, as I stared up at the luminous clouds scudding across the moon, and warmed my hands under my armpits, it seemed to me that, given my lowly place in the pecking order, I was fortunate to have been noticed by the master of Versailles. All the same, when I heard a rumble of wheels announce the arrival of Monsieur Bontemps, something held me back from stepping forward and showing myself immediately. A spot of light—the glow of a lantern—swam toward me through the darkness. What did the Sun King want with me? *Could* I withstand the will of a king? I heard the single peal of a bell ring out over miles of dew-sodden pasture and sleeping lambs.

"Who goes there?" called the driver as I stepped out in front of the royal carriage. I felt the heat coming from the horses' steaming flanks and heard the jangling of reins. No sooner had I announced myself than a rectangle of light spilled onto the dirt road and a large, broad-shouldered man stepped out of the carriage. I had seen Monsieur Bontemps from a distance at Versailles. He seemed larger in person, and stooped a little, in the manner of those who are taller than the rest of us.

"I am Alexandre Bontemps, *premier valet du chambre du Roi.*"

For a thickset man his movements were graceful. I rose up from my own bow, and the open and charming smile I observed on his face endeared him to me at once. When I presented the pouch to him, he extracted the ring, took hold of my wrist, and, to my surprise, placed the ring on the little finger of my left hand.

"As I suspected. Too large. I shall have it altered. Come," he said, pocketing the ring and guiding me into the carriage by my elbow. "Let us get out of this damp night air."

We scrutinized each other in the yellow light cast by two lanterns. Monsieur Bontemps had an easy manner. He demanded to know if I had dined, and when I said I had not, he picked up a basket from the floor that contained a plump roast chicken. Pulling off a leg with a moist squelch, he offered it to me in a napkin. Availing himself of the other leg, he sank his teeth into the meat and I listened to the sound of his chewing. Soon Monsieur Bontemps smacked his lips, threw the leg bone out of the window, and wiped his glistening chin.

"You will be wondering why you have been summoned in the middle of the night to meet with the King's servant."

"Yes, Monsieur."

"Then let me tell you at once that the King requires me to make certain arrangements for your welfare. Like my father before me, my life is dedicated to the service of the King, and has been for a quarter of a century and more. I tell you this because you need to know that you can rely—with absolute certainty—on my discretion. Does the chicken please you?"

"Thank you, yes. It is excellent."

"Good. We have a new head cook at Marly—the last one came to a bad end. I am persuaded that his kitchens can roast poultry, at least." He placed the basket on the seat next to me. "Please, serve yourself. . . . The King has informed me that your identity is known only to his Majesty and Queen Mariana of Spain—and, of course, your tutor—"

"Then the King knows that I am—"

"*Stop!*" cried Monsieur Bontemps, clamping his hands over his ears and causing the driver to appear at the window to enquire if his master needed assistance. He waved him away. "Forgive me, but you must not—you must *never*—divulge anything about yourself. The King has commanded it. This is of the utmost importance. Do you understand? *No one else must know who you are.*"

"I understand, Monsieur. I am sorry."

"Secrets are a burden and I am *very* happy to be spared yours. As far as the world is concerned, the man who adopted you is your father. Now, tell me, to the best of your knowledge, has the redoubtable Signor de Lastimosa, who protects you with such zeal, ever spoken of your secret to anyone else?"

"I do not believe so, Monsieur."

"Have *you* spoken of it to anyone else?"

"No, Monsieur."

"Good . . . good. The King will be pleased."

"May I ask what you *do* know about me, Monsieur Bontemps?"

"Very little. I know that I failed to keep you safe, despite having the Swiss Guards watch over you."

"The Swiss Guards?"

"It was for your own protection."

"Did I *need* protecting?"

Monsieur Bontemps gave me a curious look. "Clearly you did!"

I touched my skull instinctively. "Then you did not fail me, Monsieur. If it hadn't been for the guard outside the Church of Saint Symphorien, I should not be here now, eating chicken in your carriage."

"If you will permit me?" Monsieur Bontemps removed the chicken bone from my greasy fingers and tossed it through the window. He drew one of the lanterns close to my face. "May I?" he asked. He pushed the hair away from my forehead to examine my scar. Then he tapped my crooked nose and gave a broad smile. "It gives you the air of a fighter. You were lucky: I can see that. Are you quite recovered?"

I told him that I was.

"The King desires to establish you at court, but at first you are to live quietly, for we do not wish to provoke curiosity."

I listened, round-eyed, as Monsieur Bontemps described how my new life would be. I was to be offered a secretary's position in the household of the King's younger brother, whom everyone knew as "Monsieur." He would pay me a generous allowance. My father would also be granted a pension but only on condition that he remove my three brothers from court. The King, it appeared, was well informed, indeed.

Then Monsieur Bontemps told me something that sent

shivers down my spine. "From time to time," he said, "the King intends to talk with you alone. His Majesty prefers to keep this arrangement secret. Bearing this in mind, you will be permitted to use a private staircase that connects the King's apartment and that of Monsieur, where you will be lodged. Each Sunday morning, while the King attends mass, you will climb the stairs and let yourself into the first room you come to. In the far corner you will see a small, gilded desk inlaid with tortoiseshell. Pull down the lid and you will see a sun motif, which, when rotated, reveals the escutcheon of a concealed drawer. There are only two copies of the key that will open it: One is in the King's possession and *this* is the other." I took the key, which he held out to me. It had been threaded onto a fine golden chain. "If your presence is required, you will find a note informing you of the time and place in the drawer."

"May I ask a question, Monsieur?"

"Pray do." Monsieur Bontemps looped the chain around my neck and gestured for me to tuck it into my shirt.

"What will be the purpose of these meetings?"

"That is something you will need to find out for yourself."

Presently Monsieur Bontemps rapped on the roof with his cane and called to the driver to take us to the inn at Rambouillet where I was lodged. When the carriage lurched forward, the basket fell to the floor and the legless roast chicken rolled back and forth between us. It bothered me, but my cheerful host did not seem to notice it.

"By the way," he said, a twinkle coming to his eye. "I understand that you are fond of a certain Mademoiselle Isabelle d'Alembert." Even the dim light could not have concealed my embarrassment. The Swiss Guards must have been spying on us! "Such a pity that you insulted the Prince de Montclair. However, I have a talent for smoothing ruffled feathers. . . . I'll have to see what I can do."

Bidding me farewell as I climbed out of his carriage, Monsieur Bontemps tapped my chest where the gold key now lay next to my skin. "Not a word about this to Signor de Lastimosa," he said.

The good opinion I formed of Alexandre Bontemps that night did not change over the years. Versailles had a way of corrupting kind hearts, but somehow the King's *valet de chambre* managed to keep his. He continued, throughout his life, to bestow his favors generously, and I remember how much he hated to be thanked. His discretion was legendary—indeed, anyone at court refusing to reveal a confidence would be accused of "doing a Bontemps." Five generations of his family served the Sun King and his descendants. After the last one died, some eighty years after the conversation I have just described, a court without a Bontemps in it no longer felt the same. But by that time, the royal dynasty, to which they had devoted their lives, was about to be swept away. Alexandre Bontemps never once asked me who I really was. My guess is that he believed me to be an illegitimate child of the King, and if he did, he wasn't alone in suspecting such a thing.

One thing I did regret on that first evening was not asking him why I had to keep my meetings with the King secret from the Spaniard. Perhaps I sensed, without being told, that I would not have liked the answer.

The Way She Looks at You

The morning after John Stone's curious departure, Spark sits cross-legged on the sunny lawn, finishing her breakfast. She becomes aware of Jacob creeping stealthily toward her, like a tomcat stalking a sparrow. Spark looks at him out of the corner of one eye as she bites a corner of toast. He plunges his trowel like a dagger into the flower bed behind her. When she says hello, he grunts an inaudible reply. She attempts to read her book, but Jacob flings uprooted weeds onto the grass next to her, sucks loudly on one of his boiled sweets, clacking it against his teeth, and presently begins muttering to himself. The muttering gets louder. Spark can't decide if he's talking nonsense, or speaking in a language she can't understand. Either way, it unnerves her. Although, in principle, Spark refuses to be driven away like this by Jacob, when he begins to hiss, too, she decides that enough is enough. She closes her book. Actually she would have liked to slam it shut, but it's a paperback. Martha appears behind Jacob just as Spark is preparing to stand up. She is barefoot and carries a bowl of cubed beetroot for Bontemps. Frowning, Martha looks first at Jacob, and then at Spark, putting a finger to her lips. Jacob, squatting among yellow and white lupins, is unaware of her arrival. Spark and Martha listen to the gibberish that pours out of Jacob's mouth. After a moment Martha taps him smartly on the shoulder. He starts visibly. She leans down and speaks into his ear: "Now, just you stop this nonsense. Don't think you're fooling anyone."

Jacob plays the offended innocent and retreats to his domain on the other side of the yew hedge. Martha watches him depart and tells Spark—again—that she mustn't worry about Jacob. He'll soon get used to having her here at Stowney House. Spark smiles and nods, but doubts that *she* will ever get used to Jacob.

Spark accompanies Martha to the orchard to feed Bontemps. Inside his wire enclosure, Spark watches the tortoise lower his ancient head into the bowl. He opens wide his jaw and clamps it shut again on the beetroot. It's a hit-and-miss affair. The purplish-red juice stains his wrinkled face. Martha pats his head. "You're fond of beetroot, aren't you, old fellow?"

Spark scratches his wizened neck, something he seems to like. "Martha," she asks, "do you know when John is coming back?"

"Oh, John will be back before you know it."

"What does he do exactly? He works for an educational charity, doesn't he?"

Martha reflects for a moment before answering. "John talks to important people. When they have a problem, he listens. And he always knows what to say. You can rely on him to give the long and the short of it, the he and the she of it. Oh, John's held in high regard, I assure you, and in the very best circles."

Yes, but what does he actually do? Spark wants to say, but decides against it. She has a feeling Martha doesn't really know. "Aren't you tempted to get a cell phone—so you can keep in touch with him? You can get an okay signal a couple of hundred yards up the lane. It must get tricky never knowing where he is."

"You're a funny girl," says Martha, black eyes twinkling. "I don't need to know what John is doing every minute of every day! Where would we be if we all knew each other's business from dawn to dusk? A person would go mad!"

Returning through the orchard, something brushes against Spark's legs. "Hello," she says, and bends over to stroke a small tabby cat. The cat pointedly ignores her and brushes itself, instead, against Martha's legs.

"Shoo!" says Martha, clapping her hands. "Shoo!" Spark—like the cat—can see that Martha means it. The cat dives under the yew hedge.

"Don't you like cats?"

"It's a stray. John likes it, so I tolerate it for his sake. She's a mouser. Or supposed to be."

"The cat seems to like *you*."

Martha shrugs. "Cats have bad associations."

Spark looks at her askance. "I don't understand—"

Her remark seems to have irritated Martha. "Ah, you do. People don't trust them. They say they're witches' accomplices, and hang them by their tails from maypoles."

Spark is horrified: "You've seen people do that?"

"Haven't you?"

"Not in Mansfield, I haven't!"

"When I was younger I lived in Paris. Once I saw . . ."

"What?"

"I shouldn't say. It'll only upset you—"

"I'll imagine something worse, if you don't tell me!"

Martha shrugs. "Well, our quarter of the city was home to a lot of printers. And they all had apprentices. They were forever disgruntled. Though when they complained that their bosses treated their pet cats better than them, it wasn't so far from the truth. Anyway, one night the apprentices decided to make their point. They staged a mock trial with a judge and a jury. Only they didn't try their bosses, they tried their *cats*—for all the world as if the wretched creatures were responsible for their woes—"

"But why?"

"People do wicked things—and senseless things. No doubt because they felt sinned against. And, of course, the cats couldn't fight back—"

"I thought most people loved cats—"

"Well, I'm only telling you what happened. It was a long time ago. Times change. Naturally they found them guilty."

Martha puts on a spurt as they walk back to the house. Spark has to jog to catch her up. "What happened to them?"

"Ah, you can guess. I saw them the next morning strung out in a long row. It's not something you forget in a hurry."

Spark feels sick and has no idea what to say.

"You see. I shouldn't have told you," says Martha. "Though there's no point pretending there isn't any ugliness in the world."

It's Saturday. The archive room, cool even during the heat of the day, already feels like Spark's territory. She has imposed her own sense of order on it, and she has taken it upon herself to reshelve the journals closest to a wall that (just like their partition wall at home) shows signs of rising damp. She should probably mention this to John Stone, as he doesn't strike her as being the kind of person to be interested in house maintenance.

She picks up another journal from the pile and carefully brushes the dust from its leather binding, taking special care with musty paper edges and the embossed numerals on the spine. Spark mostly avoids opening them, but with the red journals she sometimes risks it. Unlike the blue ones, they're illustrated. This one contains a drawing of a magnificent horse's head, with flaring nostrils and wild eyes rimmed with white. She carefully closes the browning pages and stacks the journal on the growing finished pile.

Spark's mind begins to wander. It occurs to her that she has managed to survive at Stowney House for nearly a week. And Ludo will have spent his first night in Mansfield. She hopes her postcard arrived in time. The thought of Ludo emerging from sleep between her floral sheets brings a slow smile to her face. She pictures his long legs sprawled across her mattress, his feet hanging over the edge of the bed. When John Stone gets back she'll tell him she'd like to go home next weekend.

Martha calls to her from the hall: "Have you got a moment to give me a hand?"

Spark, who had promised to help take the washing in earlier, says she'll come right away. Confirming all Spark's fears, Martha washes by hand, bent over a huge copper tub of steaming soap suds. The wringer is *not* decorative. Spark turned the handle this morning (as her shoulder muscles now testify) and afterward helped hang up the smalls. They draped the sheets over a long, low hedge, which Jacob keeps pruned for the purpose.

The sun has shone down all morning so the laundry is already bone-dry. They talk as they take it down, sorting it into piles on the sun-warmed lawn. Martha enquires how Spark is getting on in the archive room.

"Oh, fine. I've got into a rhythm now. It'll help once John has taught me the cipher. I thought the dates referred to *when* the journals were written. But they can't do—not unless something very weird is going on! I've probably misunderstood his system."

"Ah well, I couldn't tell you anything about that. You'll have to ask John."

Martha suddenly grows tired of talking and makes a game of folding the sheets, throwing them up in the air and shaking them out. She asks if Spark can do cartwheels. When Spark nods, Martha whispers, as though it's the biggest secret, that she *loves* doing them.

"It's been ages since I tried," says Spark, putting down her basket of sheets. "But I'll have a go."

Martha shouts out encouragement. Spark turns an adequate, if lopsided, cartwheel. Her next one is a little better. "Your turn," she says.

Martha composes herself for a moment then propels herself sideways. Spark observes her execute an immaculate cartwheel, revealing, to her amusement, a bizarre undergarment that reaches to Martha's *knees*.

"Was that a fluke or are you really good?" laughs Spark.

Martha's face lights up. *"Fluke?* Ha!" She turns out one perfect cartwheel after another, cartwheeling all around the perimeter of the lawn. Spark's whoops draw Jacob out of the kitchen garden. He stands next to the yew hedge admiring the poise and grace of his friend's acrobatics. The ghost of a smile appears on his face.

"Wow. Did you train as a gymnast or something?"

"Oh, get along with you!" Martha laughs. "I've just had a lot of time to practice."

Spark helps Martha take the bed linen upstairs. It's the first time Spark has seen Martha's bedroom. It's necessary to climb a second flight of narrow stairs to get to it. The room is long and low, and furnished simply. The walls are whitewashed, and the wardrobe, chest of drawers, and small cabinets are all made of a dark, polished wood. There is a patchwork quilt in shades of red and blue, and a bed that is not much bigger than hers in Mansfield. All is spotless, tidy, and wholesome. In fact, there's something of a young girl's room about it. There's even a china doll propped up in a cane chair by the window.

Spark holds the pile of folded sheets while Martha takes them, one at a time, and stows them in meticulous order in a large linen cupboard. A black-and-white photograph on the wall catches Spark's attention. She cranes her neck to get a better view. Martha has her arm around the shoulders of a stooped and deeply wrinkled old woman, who looks up at her. There is a strong family resemblance: The proportions of their heart-shaped faces are *identical*. Both wear simple blouses with high, round collars edged in lace, and both have their hair tied back, although Martha's hair is black while the old woman's hair is pure white. Martha is smiling straight at the camera, her dark eyes shining. She looks younger, although it's difficult to say how old the photograph is. What strikes Spark is the expression on the old woman's face: Her milky gaze focuses on Martha, revealing a tenderness and a pride in the younger woman that is so affecting Spark's eyes grow misty. As the weight of the last remaining sheet disappears from her outstretched arms Spark asks: "Is this your grandmother, Martha? It's such a beautiful photograph. The way she's looking at you . . ."

Martha does not reply, and when Spark looks down at her, still kneeling next to the linen cupboard, she is shocked by the change in her. Her mouth has opened and its corners are pointing down like a tragedy mask; her empty hands lie open and helpless in her lap, as if she has lost whatever she had been holding. There is something about the cast of Martha's crumpling face that speaks of a very young child who has tripped and grazed her knee; there's that same ominous silence which heralds the inevitable scream. A single, heart-wrenching sob erupts from Martha's trembling lips. Whatever nerve Spark has touched, it's red raw. "I'm sorry," gulps Martha. "I'll be myself again presently."

Spark is dismayed. She crouches down and puts her arm around Martha. Beneath her hand the slim, warm back heaves. "Oh, Martha. What is it?"

Martha is trying to hold back the tears and Spark can

sense that she's losing the battle. "*Please* go!" Martha whispers in a cracked voice. "You weren't to know." Spark hesitates. "Please!"

Now Spark runs downstairs and into the garden, past the fountain, and onward to the orchard. She finds Jacob taking an axe to a tree stump. His old dog is lying nearby, its head resting on its paws; with every blow its tufted ears turn.

"Jacob!" she pants. "Something's wrong with Martha—"

Jacob drops his axe and sprints toward the house, Spark following on his heels. Back in Martha's room, Jacob crouches next to her. She has not moved, and she is weeping silently, taking deep breaths to calm herself. He cups Martha's hands in his. "What has the girl done?" Jacob asks. Somehow it worries Spark that his rough hands are encrusted with dirt. He might soil Martha's apron. Martha releases one hand and waves vaguely in the direction of the photograph.

"I don't know why I haven't taken it down," she says.

Spark stands in the doorway pulling at the hem of her T-shirt. "I'm so sorry if I upset you," she says.

"*You* should never have come here!" barks Jacob, and his pale blue eyes connect with her, like an ancient force, and she feels the full heft of his fury.

Spark descends the narrow staircase two steps at a time. She hears Martha calling out for her to come back, that she wasn't to know. But Jacob is unrepentant:

"You don't belong here! You should never have come!"

Monsal Dale

Spark walks for an hour under a high sun then breaks a rule and hitches a lift. She's lucky: A farmer's wife takes pity on her and drops her off at the nearest railway station. She's not so lucky with the trains. The connections are bad, and it takes forever to leave this flat landscape, which she tells herself she wishes never to see again.

It's seven by the time Dan returns her text, instructing her to change trains at Nottingham and travel on to Derby. He, Ludo, and Andy Theology are on a pub crawl through the Derbyshire Dales. By the time the train comes to a squealing halt in Derby, the sun is a pink smudge above the platform shelters and there's damp in the air. Spark sees Dan at the same moment that he spots her. Brother and sister thread their way through the crowd of people milling about on the station concourse.

"Spark!"

Spark throws her arms around him. Family. A member of her own tribe. Dan pushes her away so that he can see her face.

"What's up?"

"I couldn't hack it," she says. "I wanted to come home."

"You okay?"

"Yeah. Just glad to be back."

"Where are your bags?"

"I left in a hurry."

Spark hears Dan's intake of breath. "Nothing . . . bad happened, did it?"

"Not like that. It was just an awkward situation. John Stone was nice to me, but then he had to go away, and he's got this gardener and housekeeper, and they're—*odd*. I couldn't seem to do anything right. . . . Dan?"

"Yes?"

"Thanks for coming to get me."

They walk through the ticket hall. "A bit different to Grand Central Station," says Spark. "Is it good to be back?"

"It is, as it happens. Mum's pleased I'm home—"

Spark laughs. "Like she's not been waiting for you to come back since the minute you left!"

"Does she know *you've* come home?"

"Not unless you've told her." Spark wrinkles up her nose. "You smell of beer."

"What do you expect?"

"I hope you're not driving—"

Dan taps the side of his head with his finger. "Why do you think I brought Andy Theology along?"

Andy Theology, so called because of an early crush on a Sunday school teacher, has been Dan's best friend since they were both in short trousers, and long before he abandoned him to go to his "posh" school. Because Andy has spent half his life coming over to the Park household, he is accustomed, like her brother, to ruffle Spark's hair in greeting, and she is accustomed to pushing him off. He's big-boned, and dressed in baggy combat gear and a fly fisherman's hat, into which he has tucked all manner of feather lures, like exotic insects.

"Ay up, our Spark," he says. "Are yer all rait? Eeh, we've supped some stuff tonight."

Spark frowns at this strange accent. Andy Theology gives a slight backward nod of his head by way of explanation. Spark gets it. "Greetings, Andrew," she says, enunciating properly, in the Queen's English. "How are you doing?"

And there he is. Ludo. Standing in the litter-strewn station car park in his rectangular shades. Floppy, sun-bleached hair lifting in the breeze. There's an easy smile on his face. In contrast to Andy, he wears tight-fitting black everything, with the exception of his Converses, which are lime green. As he leans against Andy's dusty station wagon, he puts two fingers to his forehead in a salute. Spark's mouth is dry. She manages: "Hey. How are you doing?"

At Monsal Head, deep in the Dales, which they reach as the light is beginning to fade, Andy insists they walk over the old viaduct before he allows Dan and Ludo to sample any more local ale. The four of them stand in a line, high up over the valley, a warm, gusting breeze at their backs. Spark is at one end, Ludo at the other. Dan points at a hawk hovering level with them. They watch as it plunges downward, swooping over the herd of black-and-white cows that are grazing in a verdant meadow, and diving straight into the rushy margins of the River Wye. The image of Martha's distress flashes into Spark's mind. She switches it off like a lightbulb. The hawk flaps its wings and soars up again, clutching its prey in its strong talons.

"Water vole," comments Dan.

"Rat," says Andy.

It's as if they are contractually obliged to disagree. The sound of rippling water rises up from the bottom of the valley. "This is awesome," Ludo concedes. As he and Dan break away and continue across the viaduct, Andy tries to imitate Ludo's limber gait. "Awe-some," he drawls.

"You're only jealous," comments Spark.

"True. I can see myself in New York."

"How long are you going to keep up this daft accent?"

"Wash yer mouth out. It's not daft—it's Mansfield—"

"*Phony* Mansfield," corrects Spark.

Andy reaches out to ruffle her hair again. She steps to one side.

"Ludo thinks I married at sixteen and I've got three kids," says Andy. "I've got a whole scenario worked out."

"And you think that's *funny*?"

"I owe it to myself to keep myself amused."

"He's our guest, Andy—"

"Oh! I thought I detected a gleam in young Spark's eye. . . ."

Spark walks off to the sound of Andy chuckling. "Idiot," she says, under her breath.

In the pub at the top of Monsal Head, Spark watches Ludo negotiate the uneven stone floor as he carries four full glasses to the table. She shuffles over to make room for him. Their arms touch briefly and her nerve endings register the contact minutes later. There is a lot of masculine banter about real ale and American football to which Spark does not contribute. Andy stays in character throughout. Ludo asks him about his children, and Andy makes up names and far-fetched family anecdotes; Spark has to look away and bite her lip, while Dan, a master of the straight face, kicks her foot under the table.

When Andy asks about Suffolk, Spark tries to describe life at Stowney House. Her audience is particularly impressed when she gives the age of the resident giant tortoise. It's good to have something interesting to talk about. But she doesn't mention John Stone collapsing over dinner, nor Jacob being so protective of Martha that he drove her away. Nor does she mention the growing sadness she feels for upsetting Martha and for letting down John Stone, both of whom tried to make her feel welcome. Ludo asks how old the manuscripts are that she's been cleaning.

"Some of them are ancient. *Centuries* old. Though I haven't got the hang of John Stone's dating system yet—"

"*Yet?*" says Dan. "You're going back, then?"

Spark realizes that she hasn't totally made up her mind. "I *do* like the work . . . but . . . Oh, I don't know—"

"Do you want me to get in touch with John Stone?" asks Dan.

"No! . . . Thanks for offering, but I can handle it."

Dan holds up the palms of his hands. Spark looks away. An awkward silence is broken by Andy insisting that Ludo try a specialty Blue Stilton crisp. He corrects his American English: *chip*. Ludo takes one, sniffs it suspiciously, and crushes it between his back teeth. He nods his approval.

"Yeah, I could eat a ton of these." He offers one to Spark, who shakes her head.

"Working in a private archive is pretty cool," Ludo says.

"If only the gardener and the housekeeper weren't so difficult to get on with . . ."

Spark becomes conscious of how pathetic this must sound and, embarrassed, can't bring herself to say anything more about Stowney House. But when Andy and Dan go to the bar to get another round of drinks, Ludo returns to the subject.

"Why don't you try hanging on in there for a while longer? Even if it doesn't work out, at least you'll know you gave it your best shot—"

Spark turns to face him, and Ludo surprises her with a look that is so open, and so warm, that she loses herself in his hazel-flecked eyes. Such a small thing to hold another person's gaze, and yet so intimate. When Andy returns, and sets down her bottle of Coke and a brimming glass of ale, Spark has to wrench her eyes away. Did something just happen between them? As she surveys her surroundings to calm herself, it is as if someone has turned up the volume, and the laughter, and the conversations, and the clinking of glasses, are all far too loud. The smell of ale nauseates her and it's too hot.

"You okay?" asks Andy.

"Why wouldn't I be?"

A conversation starts up about life in New York and when Spark remains silent Andy tells her to cheer up—it's only a holiday job, after all.

"Honestly, I'm okay," she replies. "Just a bit tired after the train journey." She picks up the bottle of Coke, wet with condensation, and presses it to her hot cheek.

Dan starts to yawn loudly. "You're not the only one. My body is telling me that my brain is lying about what time it is."

"Where's yer stamina, lad? We've barely got started," says Andy.

Spark, too, doesn't want the evening to end. "It's only jet lag, Dan. You've got to tough it out."

Ludo, however, says, "You should listen to your body, man. If you're tired we should go."

"I'm okay," says Dan.

"No, we should go," says Ludo firmly.

Spark looks from one to another, trying to decode the subtext of this exchange, perplexed that Ludo seems to want to cut their evening short. When he slides out from the table, her side feels cool where the warmth of his body had been. Her heart sinks. Why does she have to be so foolish? They troop out of the pub in a line, stooping a little to avoid the low beams, catching the loose threads of strangers' conversations, passing through the threshold into the hushed splendor of a starry night.

They crunch over rough ground on the way back to Andy's car. It's chilly now, and there's a smell of damp grass. Spark walks between Dan and Ludo. At one point she trips over a stone. Ludo catches hold of her arm and pulls her up, and when he doesn't let go of her arm immediately, she feels a stab of hope. She was so distressed only a few hours ago, but already this morning's events at Stowney House seem to have lost their sting.

There is no moon, so although they are parked at the top of Monsal Head, the valley below is invisible. A deep darkness presses in on them. Suddenly Ludo starts to holler: "Wo-wo-wo-wo-woh!" Spark listens to the sound travel across the dale and ricochet back again. Andy joins in, then Dan. "Come on, Spark," says Ludo. "Make some *noise!*" She whoops in unison, and for a minute the four of them fill Monsal Dale with their cries. Spark's spine tingles as the void throws back their voices. When they stop the silence is monumental.

Back in the car, Andy turns the engine on and comments cheerfully: "Eeh, it's like life, in't it? A bit of a racket followed by a long silence." Spark, sitting in the passenger seat, flicks his ear with her finger and thumb. "Oi!" he says. "And pain hurts." She glances back at Dan and Ludo. Neither notices her. Her brother has closed his eyes and Ludo is straining sideways, peering at Dan's face.

Mortmain

At half past nine London is still heaving with commuters, but John Stone's work is already done. In the coolness of his hotel bedroom, he tosses his jacket over a chair, kicks off his shoes without untying the laces, and falls backward onto the sprung mattress, flexing his back and flinging his arms over his head. He listens to the muffled sound of London traffic that penetrates the room and contemplates sending a text to Spark, telling her that he has been called away on business. He retrieves his phone from his jacket, pausing to look out over Hyde Park through billowing gauze curtains, and remembers that he never thought to ask her for her cell number. In any case, he can trust Martha to explain—she's coped better than he had hoped so far, and Spark seems to have taken to her. Perhaps he has been wrong to worry. He switches his phone off—he must sleep—and lets it drop through his fingers onto the bed.

John Stone doesn't feel as tired as, by rights, he should. The driver reached London at dawn, and delivered him to an eerily deserted Whitehall Street. After the requisite security clearance and a certain amount of hanging around in ministerial corridors—only to be expected—the meeting took place on a hastily chartered boat between Westminster and Putney Bridge. He had found his client frozen with indecision, mistrustful of those around him, and unable to embrace the changes he knew were coming—a predicament with which John Stone felt some sympathy. The two of them leaned over the side of the boat, side by side, and watched the sun burn off the mist that clung, in mysterious patches, to the banks of the Thames. John Stone has played the role that, he supposes, defines him: a constant in a changing world, a living reminder of the long arc of history. *In me the past lives.* By the time he left him, his client was calm and resolved as to what had to be done.

It is only after taking a shower that tiredness hits him. He watches the television news distractedly, just in time to catch sight of his client climbing into a car in Westminster. It is hard to believe that this man is the anguished soul who, only hours before, was pouring out his doubts to John Stone. He watches him call out comments to the assembled press pack in the same way that he, long ago, used to throw coins to beggars.

As soon as he lies down, a profound sleep overcomes him. Midafternoon he is woken by the discreet buzzing of the hotel telephone. He is vaguely aware that this is not the first time it has rung. Disorientated, he swings his legs over the side of the bed and realizes that he is not in his bedroom at Stowney House. The ringing stops. He has been dreaming of his own death; his skin feels clammy and cold. Given his state of health, John Stone reassures himself that it is not a premonition, but merely evidence that his unconscious mind is attempting to come to terms with its own end. Indeed, now he comes to think of it, the Sun King often dreamed of dying—and Louis died bravely and well. A few images of his dream linger, guttering like a candle. Sunset in Paris. His three surviving clients walking across the Pont Neuf, bearing an urn. He seems to see his ashes raining down softly onto the Seine as it journeys toward a cold sea. There are swifts—of course. They swoop low, skimming the water, filling the air with their cries. He notes that there is no one present in his dream who truly loves him. There are no grieving relatives. No wife. No children. A sempervivens: as anonymous in death as in life. No doubt his clients will dine well afterward and exchange reminiscences about the "fabulous cuckoo of Versailles." *Enough*, he counsels himself. *It is a dream.*

When the telephone rings again, he pulls his bathrobe about him and, frowning, picks up the receiver. "Yes?"

"John, my apologies for disturbing you, but I've been calling since midday and I was becoming concerned—"

"Edward! Our appointment! It should be me apologizing. What time is it?"

"Two forty-five."

"I'm afraid I was catching up on my sleep—it's been a rather eventful twenty-four hours. Is Thérèse's lawyer with you?"

"Yes, she's been here for some time. Look, why don't we come over to you?"

When John Stone opens the door, half an hour later, he is tempted to put up his hands in mock surrender. Four people stare back at him. As well as Edward, he sees a well-dressed woman in her forties, with a shining bob of chestnut hair; a stocky man in blue overalls, who carries what looks like a toolbox; and, finally, a gray-ponytailed biker in leathers, who clutches a small wooden crate to his chest. John Stone thanks them all, very much, for accommodating him by coming here, to his hotel.

"Is that for me?" he asks the biker.

"If you're John Stone, Esquire, it is. Where do you want it, Sir?"

John Stone stands to one side and gestures to his room. The biker places it inside the door and fishes out an electronic pad from his fluorescent waistcoat. John Stone scribbles his signature on it, and the messenger departs down the long, plush-carpeted corridor that seems to absorb all sound. John Stone ushers his remaining three guests into his room while thanking them again for being so accommodating.

"Allow me introduce your late wife's solicitor, Ms. Foster," says Edward.

The woman offers her hand and explains that Thérèse had left detailed instructions in her will regarding a letter and certain personal items. "The will specifies that on this precise date these items are to be delivered to you in the presence of her legal representative. It also requires you to examine them without witnesses."

"Ms. Foster, I should warn you that I feel under no obligation to do anything my late wife's will *requires* me to do. Especially since Thérèse died fifteen years ago."

"I do realize that this is an unusual situation, Mr. Stone, although not without legal precedent—"

"Mortmain," adds Edward quietly. "Posthumous control over one's estate."

John Stone nods, recalling their conversation in Lincoln's Inn Fields.

"Should you prefer *not* to take delivery of the letter and the gift, that is, of course, your prerogative. In such a case, I am under instructions to destroy them both by fire at the earliest opportunity, and preferably in your presence."

John Stone raises an eyebrow and exchanges glances with Edward. "I can see why you thought it wise to wake me," he says.

"I am, of course, legally bound to follow my instructions to the letter," says Ms. Foster.

"Then," says John Stone, "let's get on with it."

"The crate was nailed down and sealed in your late wife's presence," says the solicitor. "I thought it might be useful to bring along Jim, our firm's handyman, so that he can open it for you."

John Stone acknowledges him with a nod of the head. The handyman, who has composed his face into as disinterested an expression as he can manage, roots about in his toolbox. He makes short work of levering open the crate and, kneeling down next to it, removes quantities of crumpled paper onto the carpet. John Stone and Edward exchange bemused glances; when they look back, the handyman has plunged his arms deep into the crate and is lifting out a small wooden chest. Jim places the chest on a glass coffee table as carefully as if it were a bomb. He then stirs around the paper in the crate with his screwdriver. "Looks like that's it," he says. An aromatic smell pervades the air.

"Cedarwood," remarks John Stone. "Insects don't like it. It keeps away moths." As Jim busies himself breaking up the packaging and putting it into the heavy plastic sack he has brought here for the purpose, John Stone steps toward the glass table and makes as if to lift the lid of the box.

"Please, don't," says Ms. Foster. "The will specifies no witnesses. I should also say that you are requested to read a letter from you wife *prior* to examining the contents of the box."

John Stone shakes his head and laughs. "Oh, Thérèse!"

Ms. Foster opens the clasp of her handbag and draws out a long vellum envelope that has been secured with Thérèse's own seal. She holds it out to him. The glossy wax is black. John Stone hesitates before taking it. For an instant, his imagination plays tricks with him, and the lawyer's hand is transformed into the hand of his late wife. Her almond-shaped nails, her creamy, freckled skin and prominent knuckles. Mortmain. He pulls Thérèse's letter from her lawyer's grasp and feels his stomach lurch.

"My thanks for your forbearance," says Ms. Foster. "We wanted to be scrupulous in carrying out the wishes of our late client. She was a remarkable woman."

The solicitor's comment unsettles John Stone. At Stowney House, where Thérèse did so much to antagonize Martha and Jacob, he never hears a good word said about his estranged wife. He feels a pinprick of guilt.

"You met her, then?"

"Oh, yes. On several occasions. We were grateful to

her—we had only recently set up our firm. All the lawyers in our firm are women—and she was very supportive of our venture. In fact, she put a lot of business our way. If I might say so, she was quite a character."

John Stone has a sudden vision of a whole life about which he knew little and rarely enquired. He feels his face drop. "Yes, Thérèse was . . . quite a character."

Edward de Souza, ever attentive, steers everyone out of the room as soon as he can then returns to ask his client how he is bearing up—physically and emotionally. "I'm sorry I couldn't spare you this pantomime, John—I hope it hasn't been too upsetting for you."

"Thérèse always had a flair for drama."

Edward looks at the letter pincered between his client's thumb and index finger. "Well, I suggest that you burn it or read it as quickly as possible and then get on with your life. You know where I am if you need me."

"Thank you," says John Stone and, as lies are sometimes more expedient than the truth, he adds: "Don't worry, my friend, Thérèse can't hurt me now."

Thérèse's Gift

My dear Jean-Pierre,

Of necessity this must be an exercise in prediction, for I have the arrogance (as you will doubtless judge it to be) to attempt to direct my affairs when I am no longer a part of this world. Of course, no one knows where lightning will next strike, and I can only pray that you, and another person of whom I must speak, are safe and well on the date that my lawyers will attempt to deliver this, my final letter, to you.

You see, I have a gift for you—a late gift—and one that I hope, from the bottom of my heart, that you will cherish. But first you must allow me to unburden myself of certain matters. We have each long been a constant in the other's life and for that I am grateful. Nevertheless, I am not prone to sentimentality and do not fool myself that ours was a love match. It was in the spirit of revenge for my mother's incarceration that I first sought you out, and in the hope of children who would survive you that you married me. Fate arranged our union—after all, what other choice was open to us? No one, Jean-Pierre, has a higher opinion of you than I, but even you have the propensity to be blind when it concerns your

own situation. You have said at one time
and another that you have found me to be
difficult, cruel, unpredictable, and proud. I
willingly admit to the sin of pride—how else,
as a woman born at the time that I was,
could I have held my own in a world run by
men? But as for the rest, I say to you that
the heart, like everything else, is subject to
the laws of cause and effect.

Did you truly not notice your young wife
falling in love with her own husband? It is
better that I believe that you did not. Your
recent discovery of Martha in the workhouse,
and your efforts to bring her back from the
edge of insanity, preoccupied you. I understood
this and tried to be patient, which is not
(as I do not need to tell you) in my nature.
Unrequited love weakens and diminishes, turns
sweet to sour. It was around that time that
I discovered the cipher for your journals. As
you kept them hidden from me, naturally I
read them all. I learned about the woman
with whom I could never compete, and of
whom you never spoke—except in a thousand
oblique ways to which I now held the
key. It was a veiled allusion to Isabelle
d'Alembert, following a lapse in temper on
my part, that caused me to leave you in the
first year of our marriage. And it was while
I was nursing my wounds that I discovered
I was carrying your child. How overjoyed I
was! I told myself that even if you might

255

find me wanting in comparison to your first love-who lived but a few paltry decades-at least I could bear you a sempervivens child. Soon afterward I miscarried. I stayed away until I was myself again. My pride would not permit me to admit to you my failure. Over the course of our union there were other reconciliations and other miscarriages. Suffice it to say that I was driven to a secret despair. It was easier for me to deceive you. The last thing I wanted was your pity, nor did I wish to see your heart break. I saw how you yearned for a child you would not have to bury. Doubtless it is your longing for family that leads you to tolerate the company that you keep at Stowney House. Let us both acknowledge that it was better for me to live apart. In truth, dependence made me weak. Alone, I refused to be afraid.

Then, three autumns ago (as I write this letter) we met in Saint James. You offered to take me back with you to Suffolk, and I, against my better judgement, found myself agreeing. Call it a premonition, a woman's instinct, a flower's last chance to bloom. And so we were reconciled for a few short weeks. For the very last time, although we did not know it-and I regret that I did not know it. Then a remarkable thing happened: I started to exhibit all the symptoms of being with child once more, even though

256

I believed myself to be past childbearing age. More convinced than ever that I could not carry a child of yours to full term, I made the decision to leave. I picked some trifling argument with Martha as an excuse and when I announced my departure I recall that you made little effort to persuade me to stay. My intention was to give myself up to calm and solitude in the hope that I could persuade the baby inside me to cling on to life.

I was not hopeful, yet, to my astonishment, the baby continued to grow and thrive, while my own health faltered. These ill-formed words are testament to the now-constant tremors caused by a disease of the nerves whose first symptoms revealed themselves during my confinement. I envisaged a birth at Stowney House. This baby would be a late triumph, an atonement, a beacon of hope. But as the weeks passed a growing conviction held me back from writing to you. One day I awoke and I knew that if my own life was slipping away, I could not allow my unborn daughter (I never doubted that I was carrying a girl) to be brought up at Stowney House.

You will feel that I stole our daughter's early years from you—but do I not return her to you now? Your instinct would have been to protect her from the world. Mine was to let her be a part of it. And so it was that with my cuckoo's instinct I thought to spare her from a childhood too laden with the cautious weight of years. After all, did not your beloved Spaniard put into place precisely such a stratagem?

After my previous request, I wonder if you have paid much attention to the family of the hardworking man whom I installed in the gatekeeper's cottage. My guess is that, unsure of my purpose, you will have kept your distance. You will have had more sense than to give them money, though perhaps you will have done something with regard to the children's education—most likely you will have done something for the son. It may be that you will have done nothing, and left well alone: We have both learned long ago the folly of trying to direct the lives of others. God willing, Stella Theresa Park's upbringing within that family will have been less careful than the one you would have given her—though I hope it will have allowed her more freedom to grow. Heaven forbid, in any case, that I should have let Martha and Jacob influence the character of our precious daughter. By the time you read my letter, Stella will be approaching eighteen years of age and more than capable of judging them for herself.

I accept that you remain determined to hide from the world for Martha and Jacob's sake. However, I beg you, Jean-Pierre, to allow our daughter to decide for herself whether she wishes to follow in your footsteps. With a new generation, consider the possibility of change. And in your final judgement of me, grant me this, at least, that despite my opposing views, I never did anything to endanger the anonymity of our race—even in these final stages of my illness, when I have been sorely tempted to submit myself to a surgeon's care.

Soon I shall retreat to some peaceful spot until the end comes, for I no longer judge myself fit to be seen. You would come to me, I know, but I prefer you to remember me in my prime. Besides, my pride will not suffer any deathbed comparisons. . . . I forbid you to pity me—I have led an extraordinary life, and it gives me joy to picture our daughter on the cusp of womanhood.

I have been the grit in your oyster shell, Jean-Pierre. Without me, you might not have become the man that you are, a man with whom I could not share my life, but whom I have been proud to call my husband. It pleases me that, finally, I was able to bear you a sempervivens child. How I envy you, Jean-Pierre, for you will know a daughter's love.

Thérèse

Mine!

There are no words!

No words!

John Stone feels that he is viewing the world through something solid and transparent, a block of glass. This astonishing news! All he can do is obey a powerful urge to move, to *run*. A strong, hot wind blows as he speeds past strolling tourists in the sun-dappled park. He loosens his billowing white shirt and tugs it out of his belt; he pulls at the neck until the top button flies off.

When he can run no more, he jogs, and when he can no longer jog, he sinks to his knees and bends double, panting, leaning forward until his forehead presses into prickly, dry grasses. His cheeks are slick with sweat and tears—of joy, he supposes. For most of his life he has despaired of ever having a sempervivens child to make sense of his absurdly long existence. "She's mine!" he whispers to the earth. *"Mine!"*

Later, when he has mustered the courage, he slowly lifts the lid of the cedar chest as if it were a trapdoor to another time, another place. He is greeted by a sea of tissue paper, which the ceiling fan overhead causes to ripple with miniature waves. A pulse thumps in his neck as he carefully removes the tissue. Growing impatient, he plunges in his hands and his fingertips touch something soft: It is a baby's shawl. He holds it to his cheek: cashmere, he thinks, or

finest lamb's wool. With it he finds a smocked and embroidered newborn's dress and a pair of socks whose cuffs are
threaded through with satin ribbon. John Stone lays them
out on the low glass table and kneels in front of them.
The dress is so small. The silk embroidery, he knows, is
Thérèse's work. He presses his fingers down on the spot
where Spark's baby heart would have beaten eighteen years
ago. Now he picks up a sock and imagines the size of her
newborn feet, the immaculate toenails, the delicacy of her
skin. How long did Thérèse risk keeping her? And when
the time came to part from her beautiful child, where did
she find the strength? She must have told herself that it was
an act of love.

He reaches into the chest again: Now his fingers close
on a small silver casket. It contains Thérèse's wedding ring
and the golden locket, engraved with an apple tree and studded with rubies, that he had made for her in the first year of
their marriage. These items too he adds to the collection on
the glass table.

The last object to be relinquished by the cedar chest is
a black-and-white photograph in a silver frame. The resemblance shocks him anew. Thérèse wears a velvet maternity
dress; her long, elegant fingers support her rounded belly.
She must have been close to full term. The image of this
once-vibrant and infuriating woman regards John Stone.
He understands that, as she looks into the camera, she is
picturing *him*, the father of her precious unborn child; she
is sending to him a message that must travel through time
and an uncertain future to reach its mark. Thérèse used to

insist that she did not want to bear him children and he had believed she said it to hurt him. Now, finally, he understands why. A throb of sorrow, tinged with guilt and regret, rises in his gullet, as he remembers an errant wife whom he has not, until this moment, been able to mourn.

That evening he walks for several hours before retiring to bed. London's streets are crowded with people he seems to have met before: shuffling old men, their spines drooping like wilting flowers; lovers, latched on to each other, tenderly oblivious of the rest of the world; city men, self-assured and seemingly invincible, ignoring the cracks growing beneath their feet. He wants to put his hands on their shoulders and say: *I understand. Live well. Be happy while you can.*

When John Stone awakes with a start in the middle of the night, he is still unable to articulate his thoughts. An emotion pulses in a place he cannot reach. He retrieves the shawl from the cedar chest and stands on his balcony, holding it to his cheek. He gazes at the swaying treetops, opposite, in the orange glow of the streetlamps and listens to the distant whine of police sirens.

Notebook 5

XV

Like migrating birds follow the course of a river home, when I survey the vast expanses of my own past, I am forever searching for a line of meaning. If I had listened to the Spaniard—ignored Monsieur Bontemps's promises and turned my back on France—would I have been a different man, a better man? Who can tell? But when I was young, *my* line of meaning, *my* river's course always led me back to Isabelle. For better or for worse, the man that I am now was forged by my first experience of love in the court of the Sun King. Of course, we all present our stories in a particular light, hoping to shape how we are perceived, and desiring, above all, to be *understood*.

And so I returned to the palace of the Sun King and learned the trick of remaining invisible. Like a young deer left to graze in safety within tall bracken, I moved among the giant characters of Versailles and, as long as I didn't reveal myself in the open, drew little attention to myself at court. I was now living in the household of the King's brother, the Duc d'Orléans—known as "Monsieur"—and his second wife, the Princess Palatine, Elisabeth-Charlotte—known as "Madame."

Sometimes I looked at Monsieur and thought I was gazing at a smaller version of the King, for the resemblance was remarkable: He had the same physical poise, dark features, and strong nose. Slighter than his brother, and with a small potbelly, Monsieur was always exquisitely dressed. In principle, I was to play the role of secretary; in practice, Monsieur rarely required me to do anything at all. I was admitted to his household as a favor to his brother, and since he was not permitted to know the reason, I think he felt at a disadvantage. In any case, he largely avoided my company.

As for Madame, his German wife (we knew her as Liselotte), it was an entirely different matter. My arrival in her household raised her spirits, or at any rate provided some distraction. Theirs was not an ideal marriage given that Monsieur preferred the company of men. Moreover, in a court that valued beauty, style, and grace above all things, Liselotte was plump, inelegant, and loathed dancing. She lived, instead, for her hunting, for her dogs, and for the quantities of letters she would write daily. I liked her: She spoke her mind and knew how to enjoy herself. In the right mood Madame could be extremely vulgar, which always made me laugh.

The Spaniard came to tutor me daily, and would tease me on account of the grandeur of my new surroundings. It was true that there was so much gold in my room, it seemed full of sunshine even on a cloudy day. Best of all was the luminous goddess who smiled down at me from panels in the ceiling. Garlanded with flowers, she cavorted with plump cherubs against a sky of heavenly blue. I would let the Spaniard's words drift over me and gaze up at her instead.

One morning he arrived with a copy of his favorite book

in his hand. As he had been unable to dissuade me from returning to Versailles, he was determined, at least, to teach me the ways of the world, and introduce me to the earthly wisdom of Baltasar Gracián.

We were interrupted by Liselotte, who flounced into the room with her ever-present lapdogs. We caught a glimpse too of her son and daughter—the two surviving heirs she had dutifully produced before resigning from that particular royal duty. The children peeped in at us before their mother gestured for them to hurry along, and they clattered away down the corridor. Young Elisabeth-Charlotte, who was fascinated by my broken nose (I would tell her outlandish tales about how I got it), lingered long enough to give me a solemn wave. Her mother flopped, red-faced, into a gilt armchair. Five or six small dogs instantly jumped up onto her lap and snuggled into her.

"Don't give them that disapproving look of yours, Signor," Liselotte scolded in her German accent. "They are the best people I have come across in France . . . and no eiderdown is as cozy. Though, in truth, my darlings"— she was addressing her dogs in a voice she reserved only for them—"I am quite warm enough after all that exercise."

She peeled the spaniels off one by one and dropped them on the floor. I offered to call for refreshments.

"No, no, no," she said. "I have no wish to interrupt your lesson. Continue as if I were not here. I shall lie here quietly and listen. I'm steaming like a spent horse after my walk."

Liselotte folded her hands across her ample stomach and closed her eyes expectantly. I grew self-conscious: Jolly though she was, the Princess Palatine was a highly intelligent woman who prized the art of conversation. I did not wish to appear stupid in her eyes.

The Spaniard asked me to describe Gracián's book. I mumbled something about good advice. When he pressed me for more, I suggested that it was a series of lessons about surviving in a world that wants to break you.

"Ah, so it is about *surviving?*" asked the Spaniard.

"Perhaps not only surviving. Succeeding. Winning," I said.

"Good," said the Spaniard. "Go on."

Liselotte half opened her eyes and scrutinized me through her eyelashes. I continued.

"Gracián talks about cultivating prudence and good sense. Self-mastery. Coolness. He says: Don't reveal what you are thinking; don't reveal what you are feeling. You should keep your secrets tight to your chest and conceal your abilities and intentions from your adversaries in order to win—"

Liselotte snorted quietly: "I can think of several people who follow those rules—and I can't say I'm fond of any of them—"

"With respect," said the Spaniard, "at court one's reputation is everything. One must pay careful attention to how others perceive you. Jean-Pierre, who has a kind, open character, must learn how to protect himself."

Liselotte held her tongue while the Spaniard listed some of Gracián's advice: Get to know the great people of your age; make people depend on you while avoiding outshining those on whom *you* depend; don't expose your weaknesses;

only excellence counts, only achievement endures.

Liselotte heaved herself up noisily from the chair. "I have to say I find it all a little depressing."

"Not all of them are depressing," I said, feeling that I should come to the Spaniard's defense. "The one I like best of all is: *There is no desert like that of living without friends.*"

Liselotte pouted and said: "Well, it seems to me that this is the kind of advice to give to a man with enemies, a man who is struggling to make his way in the world. But Jean-Pierre has been welcomed into the court by the King himself. Why should he beat at a door he has already entered?"

The self-evident truth of Liselotte's casual remark struck us both, I think. When I looked over at the Spaniard I caught a forlorn look in his eyes, which I was unable—then—to understand. He did not want this for me. What the world saw as success, he viewed very differently.

Liselotte paused with her hand on the door handle. "Would you care to come hunting with me this afternoon, Jean-Pierre?"

I accepted her invitation with thanks, but when she did not extend it to the Spaniard, I felt as if I had betrayed him.

We left off our lessons early that day, but not before the Spaniard had given me a piece of advice. One day I might speak with the King, and on that day, he said, I must not admit the small possibility that I might not be a sempervivens. I am certain that Baltasar Gracián would have agreed with him. As for me, unconvinced as I still was by the Spaniard's story, my greatest fear was what would happen to me when, sooner or later, I was found out.

XVI

After some weeks in my new position at court, I became anxious that the King had forgotten about me. Louis attended mass at the royal chapel every day, leaving his apartment at ten in the morning, but it was only on Sunday, as Monsieur Bontemps had instructed, that I dared climb the private staircase that allowed me to pass, unseen, from Monsieur's apartment to that of his brother. The King, who loved music, insisted that the chapel choir perform a new piece every day, and I had got into the habit of opening my windows and sticking my head out, straining for the sound of singing coming from the north wing of the palace. When the music reached me I knew it was safe to climb the stairs and look inside the secret compartment of the tortoiseshell desk.

Ten o'clock had already struck that Sunday morning and I leaned out of my window at the broad courtyard. There was a smell of summer rain. A stooped, ancient gardener was scraping his rake over damp gravel, making it difficult for me to make out if the choir had started to sing. When someone tapped my shoulder I jumped, grabbing hold of the sill for balance. I turned to see Liselotte smiling at me.

"So this is what you do while the rest of us are at mass! You daydream and look out of your window."

"Madame! You startled me!"

She narrowed her eyes. "What *do* you get up to on Sunday mornings? I've noticed that you avoid the chapel—"

Protesting that I was up to nothing, really nothing at all,

I changed the subject, and asked if she intended to hunt that afternoon. She asked if I had seen a ring that she had misplaced and might have left here. I said that I had not, although I did not believe Liselotte's explanation for her presence any more than she believed I had no reason for being here. She walked over to a mirror and adjusted her headdress, which was slipping to one side. Our eyes met in the mirror and she said: "Who precisely are you, Jean-Pierre?"

My heart sank. It had never occurred to me that she might be suspicious of me.

"But you know who I am, Madame!"

"Do I?" Her eyes slid from mine and she made a face at herself in the mirror, wrinkling up her nose and blowing out her cheeks. "I don't know which I resemble most—a badger, a cat or a monkey, or all three at once. . . . You know, I was at the theatre last night. Were you there? I don't recall." I told her I was not. "It was Monsieur Racine's *Bérénice*. Oh, how I lost patience with her! All that *wailing*. Anyway, the King took me to one side during the interval. And do you know, he was actually rather *stern* with me."

"I'm sorry to hear that, Madame."

"It was on your account." I must have looked suitably anxious because she started to laugh. "Never fear—his Majesty was stern but gentle: I shan't be carted off to the Bastille quite yet."

Strains of angelic singing reached me through the window. If I was already agitated, that feeling now intensified. Monsieur Bontemps had insisted that the only safe time to use the private staircase was during Sunday mass. What if a message awaited me? It would be a *disaster* to miss an appointment with the King!

"You may have noticed," said Liselotte, "that I am fond of corresponding." It was true. When I think of her now, the image that comes to mind is of her ample frame bowed over a sheet of paper, calmly dipping her scratching quill into an ink pot, oblivious to the children crawling over her feet and to the courtiers making merry around her. Often, she would write a dozen letters in a single afternoon.

"I am interested in people," she said. "I *enjoy* writing about them. But recently I have been reminded that one has to be careful about what or rather *whom* one writes about. *Nothing* is private at Versailles. I wrote about my husband's new secretary to my aunt: I said only agreeable things about you—at any rate, I was not unkind. But do you know what the King said?"

I shook my head uncertainly. I often felt out of my depth in Liselotte's company. "No, Madame. What did the King say?"

"His Majesty forbade me ever to mention your person again in any of my correspondence. What is more, he prefers me to avoid speaking about you at court. My letter, it seemed, never reached my aunt. He has also spoken to my husband in similar terms. Monsieur's new secretary is someone the King desires to remain as inconspicuous as possible. Indeed, he is *counting* on us. What do you say to that, Jean-Pierre?"

I gulped. "I do not know how to answer, Madame."

"I find it all most puzzling and mysterious. If discretion is so vital, why does not the King remove you from the court to some country house and have done with it? What I want to know is this: What is your true purpose here? Monsieur clearly has little use for another secretary—"

"I beg of you, Madame, do not ask me to comment. The King has forbidden it."

Liselotte scrutinized my face until I felt compelled to look away. "If I am not allowed to know your true identity, I should at least like to know this: Do I have anything to fear from you, Jean-Pierre?"

"No, Madame! I swear!"

"Would it be true to say that your identity is a *delicate* matter?"

"Yes," I said, without hesitation, "it *is* a delicate matter. But please believe me when I say that I am grateful for my position within your household and undertake to serve you as best as I am able."

Liselotte's expression softened—the transformation in her demeanor was abrupt. She leaned forward, took my hand, and squeezed it. "Then, as we both love the King, even though I am sorely tempted to tease all the details out of you, we will speak no more of it. Agreed?"

"Agreed, Madame."

As she made to leave the room, I could almost see an idea beginning to form in her head. Her small blue eyes twinkled in her florid face. "I happened to hear last night that Mademoiselle d'Alembert is recently returned from her aunt's house. I have a fancy to invite her to keep my daughter company during her dancing lessons. Charlotte-Elisabeth, like her mother, does not take easily to learning new steps.

Perhaps I could persuade you to partner Mademoiselle d'Alembert. What do you think, Jean-Pierre? Is that not a good plan?" She took the broad smile that lit up my face as agreement. "Excellent, then that's settled."

In fact, it was only weeks later that I understood Liselotte's sudden change of heart with regard to the *delicate matter* of my identity. I overheard her use a somewhat vulgar phrase for the illegitimate children of the princes of the blood (she called them *mouse droppings in the pepper*) and at that precise moment I saw her flick an apologetic glance in my direction. I am certain she believed that the King was, in fact, my father. She loved Louis—chastely, I hasten to add—and he, in turn, was always a great support to her. It was for this reason, I think, that she always showed me such consideration. Liselotte admired the King's noble profile, and I often found her gazing sadly at my broken nose. What a terrible thing, she must have thought, to have damaged such a valuable legacy. On the other hand, my own "shapely calves" (her words, not mine) and other attributes it would be too immodest to bring up, were clearly down to *good breeding*. And who was I to contradict her?

No sooner had Liselotte left the room than I charged up the narrow staircase to the King's study. With the tip of my finger I pushed open the creaking door, peering through the crack, until I could be certain that the room was empty. At least the tortoiseshell desk was familiar to me by now. There was a catch that fastened the narrow lid (it doubled as a writing surface), and beneath it I knew to find the small golden escutcheon engraved with a sun motif. I pried it open with my fingernail and, pulling out the key from under my shirt, inserted it into the lock. As it engaged with the mechanism, and the small drawer come loose, I heard a sound behind me. Sweat pricking at me, I slowly turned around. It was one of the King's hunting dogs: a snowy white creature, apart from one ear, which was tan. This was no guard dog, but an animal accustomed to being fed by the King's own hand, an animal that slept in rooms fit for a duchess and that had only known kindness. It padded toward me, sniffed my hand with its apricot nose, and settled at my feet with a sleepy whine. When I slid open the concealed drawer, this time it was not empty. I locked the drawer, closed the desk, slid my shoe, very gently, from beneath the dog's jaws, and fled down the cool stone staircase.

In the safety of Monsieur's apartment I inspected the note. The seal bore the imprint of three fleurs-de-lys. It was signed *Louis*, although it could have been the work of his trusted scribe, who, over decades, had perfected the signature of the King. I was commanded to present myself by the water mill on the banks of the Yvette River at four o'clock that very afternoon.

XVII

The King! The King! His approach would set off a wave, first of whispers, and then of deep, sweeping bows. There would be a delicious sound of rustling silk, like water lapping on the shore, as ranks of ladies sank to the ground and rose up again, marking the royal progress across the room.

I had often seen him from a distance, walking in the gardens, a troop of dignitaries and musicians in his wake, or sailing in the royal barge on the Grand Canal, but only once had I gotten close to him. More precisely, I had made out the top of his black wig in the Hall of Mirrors as I peered over several rows of heads. Even so, the knowledge that mere yards separated me from the King had been enough to raise the hairs on the back of my neck. Louis was, after all, the architect of Versailles, God's representative on earth, he who could raise you up or destroy you on a whim. *I know him not*—that single phrase, uttered from the lips of the Sun King—would cast you into permanent shadow.

A face-to-face encounter was more than some humble subjects could endure. On one occasion I met a cousin of my father's, shortly after he had been introduced to the King. All the color had gone from his face, and he was so drained by the experience he could barely stand. The Spaniard and I sat him down and brought him brandy. He was usually a levelheaded fellow, but all he could say for some considerable time was: "The King! I have met the King!"

* * *

And so it took all my nerve to wait for him alone on the grassy banks of the Yvette River. I had arrived far too early, and was as jumpy as any soldier waiting for the order to charge. There was enough time for me to question my choice of outfit and doubt my ability to form words in the royal presence. I became embarrassed by the Spaniard's poorly groomed mare, and decided to tether her upstream, out of sight. In so doing I got mud on my shoes and, wishing to keep my handkerchief clean, I wiped off the dirt as best as I could with a handful of grass from the riverbank. I realized, too late, when I felt something move, and heard an angry buzzing, that I had grasped hold of more than grass. A large hornet stung the palm of my hand two or three times before I managed to fling it into the stream. Its venom inflicted a searing pain, and as I watched the current carry it away, my hand began to throb alarmingly, as if the insect had somehow injected a pulse into my palm. The skin swelled up before my eyes, becoming blotchy—a vivid scarlet on white.

The shock of those hornet stings somehow burst a bubble of distress that had been steadily growing since my meeting with Monsieur Bontemps. Why had I gone along with this absurd tale of long-lived men and women? And even if I believed the Spaniard's story, he still could not tell me if I had inherited my parents' longevity. Yet here I was, supposedly the last in a line of sempervivens, about to have an audience with the Sun King. At that moment, I would certainly have chosen another encounter with my brothers over *this*.

I wrapped a dampened handkerchief around my hand,

trying to compose myself while I watched the river glide slowly by. All at once the world seemed to hold its breath: The mill abruptly stopped turning, and the moorhen chicks, which I had been watching skate in and out of the reeds, vanished from sight. The sound of galloping! Many horses were headed this way; flocks of birds were rising into the air above the tree canopy at their approach. I saw a Swiss Guard appear from behind a tree (the distinctive blue-and-red uniform was unmistakable). I wondered how long he had been there, and if he was here to protect me or the King?

It was Louis himself who drove the hunting carriage. Four small, black horses thundered through the trees, the wheels throwing up sods of grass and mud. Two boys accompanied him. One rode postilion while another followed on with the reserve horses, for the King, who adored hunting, often wore out three teams of them in an afternoon. I stood stock-still, knowing that I was his quarry, and braced myself, sensing the rush of air and the vibration of the earth as the carriage swerved and the horses came to a halt inches away from the riverbank. At the same time, a movement caught my eye upstream. I had assumed that I was alone here in the woods, but I saw four men emerge from the water mill, carrying a chair, a table, and a rug. Now the Sun King was climbing out of the carriage. Now he was standing before me. The sun that poured down from behind his shoulders was dazzling, so that I had to squint up at a face familiar yet unfamiliar at the same time. A tang of eau de cologne cut through the smell of the river. Nothing seemed quite real. And although my head instructed my body to bow, my body failed to follow orders. Instead, I gawped, wide-eyed, taking in the luxuriant wig, the black hat with its white ostrich feather, the strong nose, the exquisite surtout—black, white, scarlet, a flash of gold—the slow, spreading, amused smile—

"You appear to have hurt your hand, Monsieur."

"Sire!" I gasped, feeling as if someone else were speaking my words. "Sire, a hornet stung me." Now I bowed long and low. His calves were as shapely as Liselotte always insisted they were, and encased in scarlet stockings.

The King tugged at the loose corner of the handkerchief and held it up between the tips of his fingers; he peered at the red lumps on my hand—the flesh was already so swollen, and the skin so tight and shiny, that I could not close my fist. He returned the handkerchief to me and motioned to the postilion rider to approach. The latter was instructed to return as soon as possible with a poultice for hornet stings. At a signal from the King, the men disappeared back into the water mill, and the second boy led away the carriage and horses. We were alone. Louis sat down, and even in that simple act impressed upon me that I was in the presence of a King—for it is difficult to convey the extraordinary grace with which Louis lowered himself into that chair. If majesty was a mantle that he wore, I never knew him to let it slip.

A small table had been placed next to his chair: On it was a silver bowl filled with peeled hard-boiled eggs of different sizes, some grayish, some tinted blue, others the brightest white. He took one, sniffed it with flaring nostrils, and bit into it, never once taking his eyes off me. There was an attentive, discriminating look on his face that put me in mind of my father when choosing horses at market. I watched him raise his arm a little and turn his head in the direction of the water mill. A moment later the creaking wheel started to rotate again, filling the riverbank with noise.

"To thwart prying ears," the King said. "And, of course, to supply water for my fountains. I shall address you as Jean-Pierre. Given your ancestry, I should prefer not to use your family name—even though it will be necessary for you to keep up the pretense at court."

My poor father. How it would have hurt him to overhear such a thing. "Yes, Sire," I said.

"Tell me, do you walk in my gardens? Do they please you?"

"They are magnificent, Sire. I walk in them every day. The fountains are a wonder." This was true, though it is in my nature to try to please.

"They are, indeed. I shall have you meet Monsieur Le Nôtre, their creator—a most agreeable person." The King spoke slowly and often paused between sentences, as he did now. "Your nose is broken, I see." He gestured vaguely with his hand. "And your hair. This *tuft* of white. The attack on you, I presume?"

"Yes, Sire, I was fortunate to survive it."

"The promise of a long life is no protection against a hard rock, it seems—or, indeed, a hornet."

"No, Sire."

"And you have no idea why anyone would wish you dead?"

"I do not. I can only hope that he will not try again."

"Then allow me to reassure you. The assassin is incarcerated in a dungeon in Marseilles. Interestingly, it was not a he, but a she—a woman dressed as a man—who wielded the rock—"

"I do not understand, Sire," I exclaimed—I could not stop myself. "Monsieur himself investigated the crime. No culprit was found—"

"A child beggar led us to her. A public trial was unthinkable: The utmost discretion was required. With the exception of Signor de Lastimosa, not a single person at the French court knows your true identity. And no one will. You are to be my secret. I have therefore issued a *lettre de cachet*. The assassin—whoever she is—will trouble you no more."

A *lettre de cachet*! We all knew what that meant. A person could be locked up at the King's pleasure, without trial, or any right of appeal. There was one notorious prisoner, known as "the man in the iron mask," whose face no one was allowed to see, not even his jailer, and who was doomed to decades of incarceration. Now, it seemed, a similar fate had been reserved for my would-be assassin.

"Do you have any idea who she might be?" asked the King.

"No, Sire! None at all."

"I am persuaded that she is insane. Under torture she would admit to nothing. She raved and continues to rave. The personal guard I had assigned to her tells me she talks of her affections having being spurned by your father in Madrid."

"Juan Pedro, Sire?"

"Evidently. However, I tell you this purely to put your mind at rest. I lived through dangerous times as a child. I know what it is like to be forever looking over your shoulder."

"Thank you, Sire."

"You will not talk of this with the Spaniard or with *any-one*. To have the ear of a king, is to hold one's own tongue. Do you understand?"

"I do, Sire."

"I shall hold you to your word. Do not disappoint me."

He turned from the waist to regard me and I felt my flesh grow cold.

"Tell me, Jean-Pierre, what sort of man is your Signor de Lastimosa? What are his motives for helping you, do you suppose?"

As I stood before him, I instinctively made a fist with my one good hand, a gesture that was not lost on the King. On the Spaniard's behalf I felt suddenly terrified. "He is a good man! He has devoted his life to my father and now to me!"

"I repeat my question to you, Jean-Pierre. What are Signor de Lastimosa's motives for helping you?"

I cast about for an answer. "I . . . It is as if we were *family*."

The King patted his lips with a napkin and helped himself to another egg. "And yet, you are *not* family. Your situation has changed. It seems to me that Signor de Lastimosa can do little for you now."

I lowered my eyes and remained silent. Presently he rose from his chair in the same kingly way that he had lowered himself into it. He re-created himself in his own image, every minute of every day. He was a living example of Gracián's advice: Always present an impenetrable surface to those who could harm you. Civil war raged during Louis's youth, and the Spaniard always maintained that the seeds of his greatness were sown at this time. Unlike his descendants—or at least until it was too late—Louis took nothing for granted.

"Come, let us walk awhile," the King said. "What Queen Mariana has told me about you intrigues me. She says that you come from a long-lived race and that you are the last of your line. Is this true?"

I smelled the grass crushed by a king's feet and hesitated for a fraction too long before answering. The King caught my eye, and held it, arching one eyebrow. A stern note came into his voice, no doubt the same tone that he had used to warn Liselotte.

"You must tell me the truth, Jean-Pierre. *Do* you come from a long-lived race? *Are* you the last of your line?"

"It is probable, Sire," I burst out. "But I cannot know for certain. It is what I have been told."

"Queen Mariana implied as much. It is also what Juan Pedro told her—and it pleases me that you are a truthful young man. But your discomfort is eloquent. Perhaps you were advised against admitting the possibility of doubt?—"

"No, it is just that—" What a poor liar I was in those days.

"I thought as much," said the King. "Nevertheless, we will proceed as if you will be as long-lived as your father and grandfather. If it transpires that you were a poor bet, well . . ." The King shrugged his shoulders and smiled serenely. "However, my gambling instincts are rarely wrong.

I shall think of you as my *unicorn*. For what other sovereign can count among his subjects that rarest of creatures, a man who can outlive an oak tree?"

His description disturbed me. We walked in silence for a while, and when he rested a royal hand on my shoulder, the sensation chilled me. The realization grew that I was locked, henceforth, inside a secret.

"I am a gardener, Jean-Pierre, but I am no longer at an age when I create a garden for myself. I plant for my heirs, and it is for them that I should like to cultivate you. I can offer you royal protection and privileges while I—and my heirs—live. In return there is something I would ask of you. I want you to become my witness. We will talk, and you will note down my thoughts and opinions on kingship, and on other matters as I see fit. Then, long after I have departed this earth, you shall continue to be my mouthpiece."

It seemed to me that I could hardly say no to the arrangement he proposed, though I had not the least notion of what would be entailed. The King said that my father's insights had been of great help to Queen Mariana, and he hoped that I, similarly, could aspire to a similar role.

"You are young, Jean-Pierre, and will therefore learn far more from me than I could ever hope to learn from you. But the day will come when you will be able to speak of my reign to those who will rule France after me, and, in so doing, you will be both a comfort to them and a great source of wisdom."

It goes without saying that the Sun King left his mark on the world without any help from me. Yet only a hundred years later I watched a revolutionary tide wash away a monarchy its people had grown to hate. An oracle, or a philosopher, would have been far more use to him than a boy destined to live a long life. But any notion of the horrors (deserved or no) that would befall his successors before the next century was out would have seemed absurd to those two figures who strolled, so very long ago, along the grassy banks of the Yvette River.

"So Jean-Pierre, will you pledge allegiance to me and to my heirs?"

He made a gesture with his hand that I was to kneel before him. The Spaniard's words came back to me, and I had to acknowledge the mesmerizing force of the King's will. Who was I to withstand him? I stared down at the muddy turf strewn with buttercups, and once more caught the scent of the eau de cologne used to rub the royal skin clean every morning.

"Give me your right hand, Jean-Pierre."

I removed the handkerchief and lifted my hand, and the Sun King pushed the signet ring onto my finger, forcing it over the knuckle and into the flesh—swollen on account of the hornet sting—until it would go no farther. The oak tree with its tiny rubies glittered. The stretched, red skin bulged over the gold band. Monsieur Bontemps had done as he had said, and had arranged for the ring to be tightened. The King bid me swear allegiance to him, and him alone.

"Repeat these words," he commanded, in a tone that caused my heart to miss a beat. "*In me the past lives*—for this shall be the rule by which you shall live your life."

"In me the past lives," I repeated.

He then placed his hands on my head in a blessing. "In you, Jean-Pierre, the past shall survive in a future that I shall not see. We were both marked at birth to live extraordinary lives: I to rule, and you, God willing, to outlive many generations of men."

The sound of hooves announced the arrival of the postilion rider, who carried a muslin cloth containing a poultice for my hand. The King summoned his carriage. As he climbed up—as energetically as a much younger man—a thought seemed to occur to him, and he told me to expect a visit from his tailor. My waistcoat, he said, was in execrable taste and it was not right that his brother should be subjected to such vulgarity.

After the King's departure, I stood for a while on the riverbank nursing my swollen hand. It seemed to me that I was not the same person who had arrived here an hour before. My life was no longer my own. When I unpeeled the cooling poultice, the beautiful signet ring that bound me to the Sun King was covered in white paste. It dug into my flesh. *In me the past lives?* But my own life was barely begun! I found myself tugging at the gold band, for it hurt me, and I told myself that the King had not said that I must wear it *all* the time.

Like Father Like Son

Spark wakes up to find Mum stroking her hair. "You were dead to the world. I thought I'd better wake you up before it's lunchtime. The chicken's been roasting half an hour."

Spark has been sleeping on the leather sofa, buried under a couple of jackets, face squashed into a cushion. She groans and raises her head. "What time is it, Mum?" Her hair is sticking to her forehead.

"Gone eleven. It amazes me what you can sleep through. Your phone's gone off a couple of times. Didn't you hear it?"

"No. Pass it to me, can you?"

Spark props herself up on her elbows and blinks at it. "Unknown number," she says, reaching out to push the phone back onto the coffee table with her fingertips.

"Shove up," says Mum, squeezing onto the edge of the sofa. "Well, this is a turn up. I'm bracing myself to be on my tod for a month and by the weekend the whole family's back for Sunday lunch!"

"I know," says Spark. "It wasn't exactly planned—"

"So, is everything going all right with your job, then?"

Spark hasn't worked out her story yet. "Oh yeah, I just—"

"I *knew* you wouldn't be able to resist coming back to see Dan—"

"How are you, anyway, Mum? Has everything been okay this week?"

"Well, I've kept myself busy—which is a good thing. I

seem to have spent half the week cleaning and shopping. You know how your brother can eat!"

"Are they up yet?"

"Dan's having a shower, and I've sent Ludo down to Morrison's for a few bits and pieces."

Spark sits up, clutching the coat to her chin. "Oh, Mum! You sent Ludo *shopping*! You should've asked me, or Dan—"

"He didn't mind! I'm sure he's not too grand to buy some spuds. Anyway, he's dressed—which is more than I can say for you. If you get a move on you can get changed in your room before Ludo gets back."

With Ludo's stuff everywhere, Spark's room looks like the inside of a cupboard. Damp from the shower, and smelling of Dan's shampoo—an unfortunate fragrance choice, in her opinion—Spark pulls on a clean pair of jeans and finds a T-shirt that doesn't look too crumpled. As she perches on the foot of her bed, patting her hair dry with a towel, she receives a text. She glances down through strands of wet hair. Same number as the two missed calls this morning. Now she drops the towel and brings the phone to her face, giving the text her full attention. The sender is John Stone. How did he get her number? She never gave it to him. He must be back at Stowney House. Spark pictures him pacing up and down the lane under a wide sky, the wind whistling through the rushes on the marsh. The last thing she wants to think about right now is Stowney House and its inhabitants: This is an intrusion into her world. She considers deleting his text. Droplets of water fall onto the tiny illuminated screen and roll over John Stone's words, which, inevitably, she reads.

My dear Spark, I hope that you will forgive me for contacting you in this manner, but I need to be certain that you are safe. The last thing I would wish to do is to worry your mother, but if I have not heard from you by one o'clock, I feel that I must contact her. Spark goes hot and cold. Suddenly she sees her actions from John Stone's point of view. He must have arrived home to find Martha upset, Jacob angry, and no sign of the useless intern whose safety he will have felt to be his responsibility. For all he knows she could be dead in a ditch—and she did not even leave a note to explain where she was going. *Oh, heck.* He goes on to mention Jacob's outburst: He hopes that Spark can try to forgive it; he also apologizes for his own, unexpected departure; above all, he asks her to consider returning to Stowney House—if only to be able to leave on better terms. If, on the other hand, you wish me to have your luggage sent on, he writes, I will, of course, make the necessary arrangements. He ends his text with: Affectionately yours, John Stone. Spark smiles despite the heavy guilt: This is not a man who is accustomed to sending texts.

Downstairs she can hear Mum opening the front door for Ludo. Spark quickly taps out her reply with two thumbs. Sorry to have worried u. Arrived safely home last night. Can I let u know what I'm doing later?

Dan has bought Mum a good bottle of wine to drink with Sunday lunch and, with help from Ludo, has been regaling her with New York stories. Mum has sat entranced, sipping her rosé, listening to Dan's jokes, nudging Spark with her elbow, and wiping the corners of her eyes with a tissue. Dan could always make Mum laugh. With lunch finished, everyone helps bring the dirty plates and the remains of the Sunday roast into the kitchen.

Spark should have known that it was a mistake to scold Mum for sending Ludo to the shops. Now, on principle, she'll allow him no special privileges. Mum throws the tea towel at him. "Here, I'll wash, you can dry."

Ludo's face is, as Mum would say, a picture. Dan rolls his eyes dramatically toward the heavens.

"Less of your cheek, Daniel Park," she says, and flicks soap suds at him. Maybe it's worth the embarrassment to see her in such high spirits. Spark plucks the tea towel from Ludo's grasp.

"Here, let me."

Ludo, for once, looks awkward, unsure how to react. You've got to be careful with other people's mothers. Mum washes, Spark dries, Dan puts away, and Ludo watches. Spark notices a meaningful look pass from Ludo to Dan. In response, Dan shakes his head. There's something about this exchange that makes Spark's heart skip a beat and presently she nudges her brother. *Is something up?* she mouths at him. He shakes his head. She doesn't believe him.

"By the way," Spark says out loud, "you didn't give John Stone my cell number, did you?"

"Me? No. Has he been in touch, then?"

"He texted me this morning—he wants to know if I'm going back."

Mum stops washing up. Soap suds drip off her yellow rubber gloves. "Are you thinking of quitting, then?"

"I'm not sure—"

"Well, if you're not happy, love, no one's forcing you to go back."

"I'll need to pick up my things in any case. You've got to promise not to say *I told you so*, if I don't stay on."

Mum resumes washing up. "As if."

Spark aims a conspiratorial look at Dan: There's no way that Mum will be able to resist. But Dan doesn't connect with her—he's miles away. Ludo, however, does, and gives her a sympathetic smile. It is a smile that sets all her alarm bells ringing. "Dan?" she says. "What's up?"

Mum turns around and Spark lowers her tea towel. Dan looks from one to the other. Spark does not like the set of his face. "Sit down, Mum," he says. "You, too, Spark."

"Do you want me to leave?" asks Ludo.

"No, you're all right," says Dan. "You've come all this way. Stay."

Ludo leans against the kitchen sink, staring fixedly at the wood-effect doors of the kitchen cabinets. Dan, Spark, and Mum sit around the blue-topped table, the same table she and Dan stood around dipping their fingers into cake mix, and where she learned to read her first words. Spark watches Mum: She looks as if all her fears are rising up from the kitchen floor like phantoms.

"Well?" Mum says. "Spit it out, Dan." The tendons in her neck are taut as wires.

"Okay. I went for an interview for a translator's job—in the financial sector—and they liked me." *Oh*, thinks Spark, with relief, *it's about a job!*

"That's wonderful, Dan! Congratulations!" says Spark.

"Well, good for you," says Mum. "If I were in New York, in your shoes, I don't suppose I'd want to come back to Mansfield either—"

Spark gives an inner cheer. *Well said, Mum.*

"Thanks—but it's not that. I had to have a physical. For insurance purposes."

Spark stops breathing. Mum puts her hand over her mouth and speaks through her fingers. *"What did they find?"*

"They found . . ." Dan must have rehearsed this scene but, now that it comes to it, he stalls. Spark wants to hug him. "They found what they think is a heart abnormality. *But,* and this is why I'm asking you—*please*, Mum—not to not overreact, the results *weren't* conclusive. They need to do more tests to be sure—either way. They wanted to know about my family history, and when I told them about Dad, they said I should really get myself checked out by a heart specialist. Because if it's what they suspect it is, I could have inherited the condition—"

"You can *inherit* a heart condition?" says Spark.

"They'll have to wire me up to a machine to monitor my heartbeat, and I'll need an MRI scan, and I don't know what else. The thing is, this firm's health insurance won't cover me if I'm high risk. They've promised to hold the job open for me, but they need a medical report that proves I'm fit before they'll sign the contract—"

"Oh, Dan," says Mum.

"Yeah, I know. So, anyway, I telephoned from New York, and the GP's surgery has fixed me up an appointment with a heart consultant in Nottingham. It's tomorrow afternoon."

"And I thought you were here for a nice holiday," says Mum.

"If you *have* inherited something, did they say what that means?" asks Spark. "I mean, what will they do? What *can* they do?"

"That's what I'm about to find out. I'm not convinced anything's wrong—I feel absolutely fine."

Mum has fixed a lopsided smile to her face, which is fooling no one. "It'll turn out to be nothing. Anything to do with insurance, they're always cautious. They're happy to take your premiums, but the last thing they want to do is dish out any cash." She scrapes back her chair. "I'll put the kettle on. Thanks for waiting to tell me until *after* the meal."

Spark grabs hold of Dan's arm from across the table and squeezes it. "You'll be fine," she says.

Dan doesn't respond. He's observing Mum's back and how it is starting to heave over the kitchen sink as she holds the spout under the tap.

How can *Dan* have anything wrong with his heart? He runs, and plays cricket, and you've only got to look at him to see how healthy he is. Mum's head is drooping now and water is cascading from the spout. Ludo steps forward and gently takes the kettle from her hands and puts it on its stand. Spark wills Mum not to make a scene. For Dan's sake. *Please, please don't lose it. He hates it so much. Distraction tactic. Say something. Anything.*

"So if it's an inherited weakness, should *I* be tested, too?" Spark asks.

Dan meets her gaze and frowns. "D'you know, I'd not thought—I suppose it does—"

Mum swings round, her cheeks glistening with tears, and glares at Spark. "It's always got to be about *you*, hasn't it?" she thunders. "This is about Dan and *his* health!"

Mum's words are like a slap. "We're all upset, Mum—but there's no need to—"

"*You* won't have inherited it—you're from different stock," snaps Mum.

"*Different stock!* What are you talking about?" cries Spark.

"I mean you've only got to look at you to see you didn't take after your dad. Not like Dan. . . ." There's a pause and suddenly Mum collapses into breathy sobs. "I'm sorry," she says. "It's brought it all back."

"Great," says Dan. "Just great." He turns to Ludo. "Now do you see why I wanted some masculine support?"

Spark excuses herself, and slips out of the kitchen door and into the back alley. She stands as far away as possible from the stinking dustbins and stares, glassy-eyed, at the dandelions growing through the gravel, distress rooting her to the spot. After a while Ludo appears at the back gate. He wraps his arms around her and gives her a hug.

"Dan is going to be all right," he says. "*You* are going to be all right."

Ludo smells of warm skin and soap. But Spark doesn't want to be held by him under these circumstances. To allow herself to be comforted is to admit that there could be something wrong with Dan, and she can't do that. So she pulls away, allowing Ludo to keep one arm draped lightly around her shoulders.

"Dan says he wants to spend time with your mom. I guess it would be a good idea to give them some space."

Spark nods. "If that's what Dan wants."

"You know," says Ludo, "if you need to go back to Suffolk to pick up your stuff, we could go this afternoon. I could drive you."

Spark disengages herself to look at him. She sniffs. "I can't ask you to do that."

"Sure you can. It would be my pleasure."

"Have you any idea how far it is?"

"It can't be that far—you can fit the whole of England into New York State."

"That can't be right! Is it?"

"Yep. Andy told me."

Spark smiles. "It must be true, then!"

"And I'd like to see Suffolk and your Stowney House. You can give me the full tour."

Spark thinks about it. Well, she can't stay at Stowney House now. She may as well pick up her bags and get it over and done with. "Really?"

"Yeah. Shall we go?"

"All right. Thanks."

Bad Dog

It cuts deep that Martha and Jacob, after he has kept them safe from the world for all this time, should have been so *careless* with his daughter.

John Stone keys in the number and listens to the ring-tone, pressing the phone hard against his ear. A southerly wind whistles through the rushes, a forlorn sound. He prays for Spark to answer. She doesn't. For ten minutes he walks up and down the lane, kicking up lumps of dried mud, trying to keep calm, reasoning with himself, trying to decide whether to call the police, or Mrs. Park, or wait. He watches the wind plow sinuous paths through the reed beds and tries to halt his rising panic.

He had returned to Stowney House as soon as he could, heart singing. The fact of Spark's existence had been seeping slowly into his mind and soul like water into layers of permeable rock. A daughter of his own, this late gift, this *miracle*. Then, as he climbed out of the car, he saw Martha's face as she stood on the threshold: anxious, defensive, eyes red-rimmed. In dismayed silence he listened to her account of what had happened, every last drop of joy pooling away. It has been eighteen hours since Spark left Stowney House. No one went looking for her. Cold sweat sticks his shirt to his back. "Spark is a young woman, after all," Martha said. "She has the right to go where she chooses. By the time we realized she wasn't in her room, she could have been anywhere."

John Stone made no reply but immediately ran to the lane, where, for a time, he screamed his frustration at the sky and the billowing white clouds that sailed serenely over the marshes. At least a contact in Whitehall has proved helpful. He tracked down Stella Park's cell number and texted it anonymously to John Stone in less than a minute. If it comes to it, John Stone will not hesitate to ask this same contact for help in searching for her. For now, however, he will be steady. He will not overreact. When he can resist no longer, he calls Spark's number a second time. As he waits to get through, Martha and Jacob appear in the distance. He waves them angrily away. Spark does not pick up. There is no invitation to leave a message. Images of what could befall a young woman, alone and unprotected, crowd in on him. John Stone sinks to the ground, tormented by his powerlessness to act. He sits among feathery grasses, face in his hands, surrounded by crickets. *Zig-zig-zig-zig.*

Presently it comes to him what he must do, and he composes a text message. If he has not heard from her by one o'clock, he will telephone Mrs. Park. He presses send, and stares at the small screen, willing a reply. When, only minutes later, Spark's text arrives, he clutches the phone to his chest and, for a brief moment, rocks backward and forward in relief.

Later, Martha, Jacob, and John Stone stand in a circle by the silent fountain, heads bent and touching. "In me the past lives," says John Stone softly. "There is nothing more important than this day." It is Jacob who breaks away first.

John Stone felt the need to make his peace with his friends. Never have their actions caused him more distress, but he cannot yet tell them why. Spark will be the first to know that he is her father, and the timing of that revelation will depend on Mrs. Park—although he will do his best to persuade her to act sooner rather than later. Until then, he must keep Martha and Jacob in the dark.

"Will Spark ever come back, do you suppose?" asks Martha.

"If she does, she'll be wary of you—of us. Let's wait and see."

The three of them take an evening stroll along the riverbank. Grise limps at Jacob's heels. A cormorant catches a large eel in front of them, and they stop to watch the bird shake its head this way and that, forcing the wriggling thing down into a stomach that can barely be big enough to contain it. This section of the riverbank is choked with brambles, and when a young rabbit vanishes into impenetrable thorns, Jacob hurls a stone after it. Unusually for him, he doesn't hit his target.

"You're losing your touch," says John Stone.

"I aimed to miss."

"Wasn't it here that Spark got into the grounds that first time?" asks Martha. "I've got a memory of picking barbs from her cardigan."

"Aye," says Jacob.

"How on earth did she get through those brambles?" asks John Stone.

"Painfully," says Martha. "She was a determined little thing."

Grise's arthritis is bad today; she's finding it difficult to keep up with her master. Jacob picks her up, holding her in his arms like a baby.

"Poor old girl," says Martha, stroking the dog's tufted ears. "Spark gave her a fright that day, do you remember?"

"She's still wary of her."

"Why?" asks John Stone. "What did she do?"

Martha describes how Grise, who was young and fierce back then, caught the scent of a stranger and ran ahead, barking. They found her snarling and baring her teeth, a mere hand's breadth away from the face of a small girl with a cloud of blond hair. But the child, far from fearful, was standing her ground. *Bad dog,* she shouted, and, taking hold of Grise's jaws in her small plump hands, bit her nose. The dog let out a howl that sent the rooks flapping from the trees, and bounded back to Jacob, where she cowered, whimpering, between his legs.

"Extraordinary!" says John Stone.

They walk on, John Stone leading the way with a smile of paternal pride on his face. It occurs to him that, while he is no coward, he suspects Spark inherited that side of her temperament from her mother. John Stone wonders how well, in the end, he knew Thérèse. Those black moods and her petulance—which, over the years, all of them had learned to dread—had they been, all along, the consequence of jealousy on a proud nature? The truth was that many of Thérèse's departures had been preceded by outbursts directed at the raving creatures her husband had plucked from the gutter and who now "stuck to him like ticks to a dog's back." She would have driven them from Stowney House if she could, but John Stone had always stood squarely between them. At the time he had thought Thérèse deeply unreasonable and cruel. Now he sees how his wife must have felt usurped. If only her ridiculous pride had not prevented her from confiding in him! If only he had *known* that she'd read his journals! Having taken the decision never to talk about Isabelle in order to spare her feelings, had he, in the end, inflicted a greater hurt? John Stone recalls some of the entries Thérèse might have seen and the blood leaves his face.

Martha peers at him with her dark currant eyes. "You seem out of sorts, John."

John Stone shakes his head vigorously and walks on. He becomes aware that the others are talking quietly together. When he turns around he sees Jacob encouraging Martha to speak. John Stone braces himself. *What now?*

"We know that you get the shakes. I've seen it, and so has Jacob. You've got no cause to hide it from us. We're not children, John."

He protests that these episodes are nothing. Predictably they don't believe him. Yet he's been so careful! Does he tremble without realizing it? Now, there's an idea that rattles him.

"We think you should go and see a medical man," says Martha. "Doctors aren't the butchers they used to be. They can even cure people sometimes."

John Stone sighs. "It's a trapped nerve." He holds up his

right hand, the good one. "It comes and goes. But why do you even waste your breath suggesting I see a doctor? Why would I take that risk?"

Martha and Jacob exchange glances. Then Jacob says: "Let's suppose you're not ailing, John. Then it seems to us that you're in too much haste to find another Friend."

"No." John Stone shakes his head firmly. "I happen to disagree with you—Edward isn't getting any younger—"

"Well, you see, John, we don't want *her*."

Her! John Stone feels a crackle of anger ignite in his gut.

"Edward is a lawyer and a man of the world. But this girl . . . With a mother like hers, what makes you think this girl will ever amount to anything?"

"Jacob!" Martha is mortified.

But Jacob has not finished. "Thérèse caused us nothing but grief and her child will be no different. Spark will bring trouble to Stowney House. Look at us now—she already has—"

John Stone lunges at Jacob. Martha darts between them. "No!" she cries. "*John!*"

Jacob drops Grise, who lies where she falls, staring fearfully up at them. The violence of John Stone's reaction is so out of character that Martha and Jacob seem unsure what to do. He is panting and glassy-eyed. The three of them remain curiously frozen in this tableau until Martha breaks the silence. She snaps at Jacob:

"For the love of Michael, haven't we had enough trouble for one day? You can see John's not himself."

"Good friends speak the truth. Maybe John needs to be

reminded that we deserve a say in how we live our lives."

Martha purses her lips. And how could John Stone possibly argue with such a sentiment? He exhales slowly and lets his fists unfurl. There are rows of scarlet marks where his nails have dug into his palms.

"I'm sorry, Martha. Jacob. Let us talk tomorrow, when I shall be in a calmer frame of mind."

He walks slowly back toward the house through the birch wood and the orchard. Martha, Jacob, and the limping dog follow on behind, walking in single file. They pass through the yew arch into the formal gardens. No one has the heart to speak.

Goldilocks's Accomplice

To drive for hour after hour through a summer landscape with Ludo at the wheel. To rest her arm on the open window and feel the wind tug at her hair. To share their favorite music so that it becomes the sound track of their journey. It is a scenario that Spark would have scripted if she could. Except that here she is, less present than absent, with an anxiety that keeps tapping her on the shoulder, reminding her that she's here because her brother might have inherited the heart condition that killed her father.

The round trip will take close to seven hours. She observes Ludo's tanned fingers draped around the steering wheel of Andy's station wagon, and how smoothly he guides them through narrow, winding roads. That Ludo would do this for her! She stopped being tearful at least fifty miles back, but Ludo continues to check on her before flicking his eyes back to the road. She smiles back at him.

"Just keep reminding me which side of the road to drive on," he says.

Spark tries not to dwell on Mum's hurtful words, but her mind is trapped in a loop. Norfolk, and then Suffolk, sail by in a blur of hedgerows dotted with scarlet poppies. They pass an ancient oak tree that stands at the center of a vast field. A flock of sheep shelter under its boughs. It puts her in mind of the tree that tore her family apart. Spark never saw the scene of the crash. She knows that Dad's car smashed into an enormous tree, and wonders if it's still standing. Dogs who maul people are put down. Trees that fail to get out of the way of oncoming vehicles, and kill with their inert massiveness, are they condemned to be felled? It would be only fitting.

Spark has never worried about Dan. Nor has Mum. Not really. From this day forward, she knows that every time he's late, every time he's forgotten to get in touch when he said he would, every time he looks pale and tired, they'll think: *His heart, is it his heart?* As if he could read her thoughts, Ludo says: "You know, this checkup, it's a precaution. Dan's been most worried about how your mom will take it."

"And you came all the way to England to give Dan moral support?"

Ludo shrugs. "It was the free trip to Europe that clinched it—"

Spark shoves him with her elbow. "But you'd be daft not to take advantage while you're here. Is there anywhere you want to see?"

"Paris. Florence. London—of course. As it happens my tutor is over here. I promised I'd hook up with him."

"When's that?"

"I'll see how things go with Dan. It doesn't take long to get to London from Nottingham, does it? Why don't we meet up one day?"

"Oh," says Spark, heart leaping. "Cool."

The shadows are long and almost violet by the time they arrive at Stowney House. Spark had intended to go in by herself, on foot, but Ludo leaps out to open the gate and immediately drives over the wooden bridge that spans the stream. The tires crunch down the gravel drive. She hopes John Stone is at home. If not, Martha will be terrified and Jacob will appear brandishing a garden fork or something. As she gets out of the car Spark feels the heat radiate up from the courtyard that has basked in sunshine all day. The scent of the saucer-shaped flowers drifts over from the front of the house. Rows of diamond-paned windows mirror the evening sky. Ludo snatches off his sunglasses and rotates three hundred and sixty degrees. "This is *incredible!*" he says, pulling out his phone and taking pictures of the house, the gardens, the fountain.

"Martha!" Spark calls. "Mr. Stone!" But the only sound is the low roar of the wind in the trees. "I'll try the kitchen."

Ludo follows on her heels, eyes everywhere, touching the beams, the heavy oak furniture, and the old plaster walls, picking up the heavy silver candelabra, running his fingers over the date, 1695, carved into the beam above the inglenook. "There's no electricity in here," he says.

"There is in most of the house," says Spark. "But Martha prefers candlelight and the stove burns wood."

"That's a little weird, don't you think?"

Spark feels a tug of defensiveness. "Is it? I suppose Martha is an old-fashioned sort of person. I wouldn't say she was weird."

Still no one arrives to greet them. Spark feels uncomfortably like Goldilocks, only Goldilocks with an accomplice. "Martha!" Ludo goes into the hall and explores the sweeping staircase with its galleried landing. Growing anxious in case Martha or Jacob should appear, Spark strains to hear sounds of their presence. She really should not have let a stranger into their home without permission. Ludo is studying all the pictures in the entrance hall. He takes out his phone and photographs them. Spark is a little taken aback.

"He's an art lover, your Mr. Stone," he says.

"Yes," Spark says, indicating with her thumb a door leading from the hall. "Martha says he's got a whole gallery of pictures in there."

"What sort of pictures?"

"I don't know—it's his private place. No one disturbs him in there. But you can see my room, if you like. Martha says it's the most beautiful room in the house."

"Sure."

"It's normally the breakfast room but she brought down a bed for me."

She leads him to the door and lets him open it. Ludo exclaims loudly. "This is some bedroom." He looks over his shoulder at her. "Have you ever seen pictures of the Hall of Mirrors at Versailles?"

"No," says Spark.

"Well, I'm telling you, whoever designed this house *definitely* has."

Spark busies herself packing up her things. She gives him sidelong glances, admiring his relaxed gait as he moves around the room, lingering over every detail. Presently he returns to the hall and she hears him climb the stairs. Ludo wasn't kidding about wanting to see Stowney House.

"I'm going to the car," she calls up to him. Then she adds: "To put all my bags in the trunk."

But Ludo doesn't take the hint. "Okay!" comes the reply.

Andy's trunk is full of fishing gear, and it takes Spark a while to jam everything in. She checks the time. Already half past seven. Returning to the breakfast room across the lawn, a movement catches her eye. John Stone, Martha, and Jacob are walking in single file through the yew arch. Jacob brings up the rear, carrying his dog. Martha has brought a hand to her mouth and points at the breakfast room. The French doors, which Spark did not shut behind her, are opening and closing in the breeze.

"Hello!" shouts Spark, jogging onto the lawn so that they can see her, and won't think that a thief has broken into the house.

Martha and John Stone both call out her name and hurry toward her, but Jacob, grim-faced, stands staring upward at the house. Spark looks quickly over her shoulder. Ludo is taking pictures from the window of the galleried landing, upstairs. *Jacob is going to* kill *me*, she thinks. With everything that has happened since she left Stowney House, Spark has had no time to agonize about facing the people she left in such awkward circumstances. Now she prickles with self-conscious unease. They meet in the middle of the lawn like enemies in no-man's-land: Martha, neat in a knee-length black skirt and lips parted in surprise; John Stone, as usual, in an immaculate white shirt, his eyes shining a welcome. The angle of the sun seems to accentuate his crooked nose and that familiar stripe of white hair above his forehead. He takes her hands without hesitation.

"Spark! I am delighted that you've come back!" Actually, he does seem genuinely delighted to see her.

"I'm sorry for leaving the way I did. I honestly didn't mean to worry you. I didn't think—"

"Martha explained what happened. I understand."

Martha plants a kiss on her cheek. "Thank the Lord you're all right."

Spark glances back at the house. "I hope you don't mind me inviting Ludo in. He drove me here from Mansfield. He's a friend of Dan's from New York."

If John Stone is unhappy that a stranger has felt free to explore his home, he doesn't show it. Instead, he suggests to Martha that she provide some refreshment for their guests. As for Jacob, Spark watches him vanish, without a word, into the kitchen garden with Grise. At least she knows where she stands with him.

The presence of this handsome young man in her kitchen unsettles Martha. His sheer physicality is hard to ignore. In this enclosed domestic setting, Ludo does seem to take up a lot of space. Spark notices Martha glancing down at Ludo's sprawling long legs, at his feet that tap and jiggle in his lime-green shoes while John Stone engages him in conversation. Martha mostly keeps her back to him: It is as though if she can't see Ludo, Ludo won't be able to see her.

"Here, let me help you," says Spark, reaching up for cups and saucers. Then, leaning in toward Martha, she whispers:

"I'm ever so sorry about yesterday. I didn't mean to upset you."

Martha's features soften. "It's me that ought to know better. The dead are dead. You've just got to be grateful for the life they've had."

"Yes," says Spark, without meaning it. It seems to her that death is much more complicated than that.

Clearly uncomfortable in this company, Martha soon excuses herself, and heads for the orchard with some scraps for Bontemps. John Stone, in the meantime, has got the measure of his guest. Ludo, or so it seems to Spark, is putty in his hands. In the space of the time it has taken for the kettle to boil, John Stone, with that easy manner of his, has found out all about his family, the fact that Ludo is an only child and wishes he weren't, that he has big ambitions in the world of software design, and that he is due to meet with his university tutor in London. As Ludo intends to stay in South Kensington, John Stone tells him about the museums; the architecture; the cinema at the French Institute, which has the best legroom in London; and suggests a brasserie where Ludo could take his tutor for lunch. He recommends the risotto.

Ludo makes a note on his mobile. "Thank you, Sir."

Spark places the teapot on the table and sits down. Ludo is so drawn in by John Stone, he does not acknowledge her. It was a good feeling being at the center of his attention this afternoon; suddenly she feels eclipsed.

"So, Ludo, did Spark tell you about Stowney House?"

"Her description didn't do it justice," says Ludo.

John Stone winks at Spark. "Didn't it? Oh, *dear—*"

"Can I ask how long you've lived here, Sir?"

"For much of my adult life—on and off," says John Stone. "I grew up in France."

"I can see that you admire Versailles."

"You are an observant fellow."

"I can see that you're an art lover too. The pictures in the hall, of London street scenes, I'm sure I recognize them. Aren't they eighteenth-century? They're not Hogarths, are they?"

"An observant and *inquisitive* fellow," remarks John Stone with an affable smile. "Yes, they are Hogarth prints—full of wit and uncomfortable truths."

He shifts in his seat to face Spark, who sits on the edge of her chair taking small sips of Earl Gray tea. "And now, if you don't mind, Ludo, I should appreciate a quiet word with . . . my employee. Would it be very rude of me to ask you to take a short stroll in the gardens? I promise you that I shan't keep Spark long."

"No problem." Ludo scrapes back his chair but instead of walking immediately toward the kitchen door, he takes out his phone and prepares to take a photograph. "Could I take a picture of you and Spark—as a memento of her stay at Stowney House? I'm sure her mom would like to—"

But before Ludo can finish, John Stone gets to his feet and holds up the flat of his palm. "No," he says, as abruptly as Spark has ever heard him speak. "I would ask that you do *not* take any photographs of my property. Indeed, if you have taken any already, I would ask you to delete them. We value our privacy here."

"Of course, Sir," Ludo replies and, turning to Spark, adds, "Take your time. I'll be in the garden. Thanks for your hospitality, Sir."

"You're very welcome."

Spark is almost certain that Ludo was taking a picture of John Stone even as he spoke. She opens her eyes wide at him but he merely says, "See you later."

Spark and John Stone sit at opposite sides of the kitchen table. When she looks expectantly at him, a powerful emotion passes over his face that Spark cannot decipher, and she presumes that Ludo's behavior has upset him. Presently he seems to recover a little. She supposes that she had better tell him that she's not coming back. Get it over and done with.

"Did you ask Ludo to bring you here?"

"No, he offered," says Spark.

"Is he . . . a *friend?*"

Spark blushes furiously. "He's a friend of Dan's. We met in New York."

"I'm sorry, that was impertinent of me." John Stone takes Spark's cup, refreshes it, and pushes it back toward her across the old grain of the table. "You know, I have the feeling that Ludo is a young man who likes to get his own way." She is not sure if John Stone is expecting a response—and would not, in any case, know what to reply. Spark hides her blushes, as much as it is possible to hide them, behind her bone china teacup, whose rim feels so thin between her lips.

John Stone tells her what great progress she has made in the archive room and asks, very gently, if she intends staying on at Stowney House. His manner is so warm and considerate that Spark wishes that she could say yes, but now . . . How can she be away from home *now*? Despite her best efforts, her eyes start to well up.

"Something's wrong," says John Stone, his face full of concern. "Would it help to talk about it? Or are we, at Stowney House, the problem?"

"It's Dan." Spark bites her trembling lip. "His doctor is worried that he might have inherited my dad's weak heart."

John Stone straightens his back and studies the backs of his hands. "Is there a definite diagnosis?"

"No, we have to wait for him to have some tests."

"Then there is no point in expecting the worst," says John Stone. "The old saying about crossing your bridges when you come to them is a wise one."

Spark dabs her eyes with the sleeve of her T-shirt and John Stone hands her his handkerchief. "Here, keep it," he says. "We won't even discuss your position at Stowney House. For now you need to be at home with your brother."

As Spark covers her face with the cool cotton square, and dries her tears, they hear footsteps hurtling down the stairs. "John! John!" Martha's cries are urgent and getting closer. John Stone pushes back his chair to get up and at the same moment the door flies open. Spark sees the fear in Martha's eyes. "Quickly! Before Jacob hurts him!"

Fight in the Marshes

John Stone told Spark to wait in the house but he can hear her footfalls behind him. Martha, who is fastest, has gone on ahead. By the time they reach the birch wood, John Stone has to stop to catch his breath. Spark does the same. He looks over at her and Spark's blue eyes find his. She's scared. This is not the reunion he had hoped for.

"I hope you meant what you said about Jacob's bark being worse than his bite."

"Let's just find out what's happening, shall we?"

They've lost sight of Martha. John Stone shouts at the top of his voice, "*Martha!* Where are you?"

Her reply is only just audible. "Here! The boathouse!"

The old blue boathouse lies a little upstream on the open riverbank. Martha stands on the decking, shading her eyes from the low sun as she scans the marsh. The light is dazzling after the wood: Spangles of sunlight bounce off the river's surface. Behind her, as if some ghost is keeping her company, the old hammock rocks in the wind.

"There!" she cries, and points. John Stone looks in the direction Martha indicates.

"I see them!" cries Spark, and now she, too, is pointing. "Where the river snakes around—inside the loop."

John Stone spots them, two figures struggling through the golden reed beds, rising and falling, up to their thighs in water. Jacob is chasing Ludo; he's wielding something above his head.

"What happened?"

"I wish I knew, John. There were shouts, and then I caught sight of the boy tearing across the lawn, running as if all the hounds of hell were after him."

"What's Jacob holding? I can't make it out."

"His axe," says Martha, and adds quickly, "but you know Jacob—he's all bluster."

Not entirely true, thinks John Stone.

"This is my fault," Spark says. She holds the sides of her head in her hands, transfixed by Ludo's plight. "I should never have come back—"

"Stay with her, Martha. *Don't* let her follow me."

He doesn't hesitate and plunges straight into the fast-flowing stream, wades across the chest-high water, and clambers up the far bank. The ground is marshy here: He squelches through mud that sucks at the soles of his sodden shoes. He can't see anything but can hear Jacob's roars. Then the wind carries Ludo's voice to him: He's screaming something at Jacob—he can't make out what, but he sounds panic-stricken, a little manic.

John Stone hesitates—these marshes can be treacherous— and resolves to avoid the open water and force his way through a dense reed bed, parting the stiff stems with his arms, sometimes sinking up to his armpits in water. For a while his vision is obscured by foliage but presently both figures come into view. Whatever Ludo has done to provoke him, Jacob is out of control: chest puffed out, shoulders hunched high, jaws clenched. He has caught hold of Ludo's T-shirt and is reeling him in. The boy, who is holding his phone high above his head, suddenly shrugs out of his garment, causing Jacob to lose his balance and stagger backward. Ludo darts at his attacker while he has the chance and kicks him in the groin. Jacob lets out a terrible yell and collapses backward into the water. At the same time, the axe flies out of his hand and vanishes with a splash into the marsh. John Stone is almost upon them now.

Ludo, a demented expression on his face, half crouches, shifting his weight from one leg to the other, his eyes fixed on the swirling patch of sludgy water that swallowed Jacob up an instant before. John Stone plows toward them as quickly as his tired legs will go, ready to yank Jacob out. All at once, Jacob explodes out of the water, covered in green weeds, spluttering and roaring and clutching his groin.

Ludo shrieks and flails his arms around.

"Enough!" cries John Stone and steps squarely between the two of them. "What is going on?"

Jacob shakes himself like a dog, golden-red sunlight catching in the needles of water that fly off him. John Stone wipes his eyes with the back of his hand.

"Keep him away from me!" Ludo's pupils are so dilated his eyes appear black.

"He's a thief and a spy!" says Jacob. "He was skulking in the long gallery."

"Is that right?" asks John Stone, turning to Ludo. "What were you doing in my gallery?"

"*Nothing!*" Ludo keeps his eyes fixed on Jacob.

John Stone considers for a moment. "I have a suspicion, Ludo, that it was not only on Spark's account that you came here today. Am I right?"

Ludo meets his gaze for the merest instant, but it is enough time for John Stone to make a judgement.

"Just call off your lunatic, can't you!"

It is an unfortunate choice of words. Jacob pushes past John Stone and launches himself once more at Ludo. He brings him to his knees and forces his head forward into the water. Ludo finds enough purchase on the floor of the reed bed to shove Jacob away from him. He spits out a mouthful of marsh water, flicks back his wet hair, and pushes his glasses back onto the bridge of his nose. By some miracle he has managed to keep his cell phone clear of the water. He still holds it away from him at shoulder level. Now John Stone stands over Ludo and Jacob, like a mother over squabbling toddlers, as they face each other on their knees and up to their chests in water. He asks himself what could be stored on Ludo's phone that makes protecting it such a priority; he wonders how many pictures Ludo has taken here today, and what he intends to do with them. John Stone makes the decision to intervene while he can. With his right hand, he restrains Jacob by squeezing a specific nerve in his neck (it makes him yelp—he will apologize to him later), and with his left hand he wrests Ludo's phone from his slippery grasp and flings it far out into the marsh. Too late, John Stone notices the sound of someone thrashing through the water behind him.

"What are you *doing?*" Spark screams. "Who *are* you people?"

There is horror in her eyes as she looks from Ludo to Jacob to John Stone and back again. Ludo stands up and starts backing toward her. Spark grabs hold of his arm and pulls him.

"*You!*" Spark shouts at John Stone and Jacob, pointing her finger first at one and then at the other. "Don't move. Stay exactly where you are."

John Stone opens his mouth to speak, but Spark silences him with a look. "I *saw* what you did."

John Stone stands watching the concluding moments of this evening's little drama. He's so still the avocets, with their curved beaks and black-and-white plumage, ignore him as they trawl through the shallows for food. He feels utterly spent. Spark and Ludo have almost reached the boathouse. He can hear the *slap* and *whoosh* as they wade through the water. Spark is supporting Ludo: She holds him around his waist and has draped his arm around her shoulders. From the way he is staggering he can tell that Ludo is in shock. He is bare-chested, and his T-shirt, which Spark retrieved and tucked into his belt, trails in the water. He'll live, though. He might have swallowed a quantity of marsh water. Perhaps there'll be some bruising around his neck. But, frankly, thinks John Stone, he's seen much worse happen to spies. Jacob is busy raking through the slimy mud with his fingers looking for his axe. It is an old one and he doesn't want to lose it.

"The girl blabbed," says Jacob.

"Spark doesn't know anything to blab about."

"How come the boy reckons he knows something, then?"

"*That* I shall need to find out—"

"But it was *her* that led him to us."

"He's not the first and he won't be the last."

Jacob finds his axe and lifts it up in triumph, dripping with water and weeds. They walk toward the house. A movement catches John Stone's eye and he watches Martha dart along the riverbank to help Spark with Ludo. He had forgotten about Martha. When she reaches the two young people, however, John Stone sees that she freezes. Spark is shouting at her. He can hear some of what she is saying and can guess the rest: that Martha is one of them, one of the crazy people, and not to be trusted, that she must stay away from them. He watches Spark hold up the palm of her hand in a warning gesture not to approach. All at once John Stone starts to shake, so violently he stands no chance of hiding it from Jacob, so violently that Jacob drops his axe and holds his friend in his arms, squeezing him in a vain attempt to quell the nervous spasms. Defeated and ashamed, John Stone doesn't even struggle. Over Jacob's shoulder he watches the receding figure of his daughter. *Spark is lost to me,* he tells himself. *Lost before I've even found her. How right Thérèse was to keep her away from Stowney House.*

Notebook 6

XVIII

Liselotte was as good as her word, and arranged for Isabelle and me to attend her daughter's dancing lessons. Isabelle was as graceful and quick to learn the steps as I was clumsy and slow—something that the dancing master never tired of telling me. Isabelle was endlessly patient. Thanks to her, I mastered the gavotte and the minuet, and even the volta, which I knew she loved. Liselotte was always present at our lessons, looking on while refusing to dance herself: hands resting on her stomach, her good-natured face glowing. The Spaniard would also attend, being a good and graceful dancer for a man of his size. The dancing master was terrifying—just as young Elisabeth-Charlotte had told me he was. He walked among us, keeping time with his long black stick, adjusting a shoulder, straightening a leg, shaking his head in disbelief (especially at me), pouring down the most imaginative insults on us—always out of earshot of Liselotte—comparing our dancing skills to those possessed by various farmyard animals. I was the perfect fellow pupil for Elisabeth-Charlotte, being the worst dancer in the room, by far. The instructions somehow entered my ears without conveying any meaning: *Three demi-coupés . . . three full coupés . . . once forward . . . once back . . . open pas de bourée . . . to the left . . . to the right . . .*

"Poor Jean-Pierre," Isabelle would tease. "How hard it

is to dance when one's head cannot talk to one's feet." You must not imagine that to dance with Isabelle was to take her into my arms and sweep her around the room. Dancing was an altogether different affair then. It was a question of display, elegance, control—and memory. Nevertheless, we always found the means to communicate. Isabelle would flutter her fan in front of her face and draw it down to reveal her smiling eyes. Whenever the gavotte demanded that we turn our backs, we held hands and mouthed sweet nothings. Over the weeks we grew more daring. Once, as we stood behind the dancing master and Liselotte—they were watching the Spaniard and Elisabeth-Charlotte perform—I cupped Isabelle's face in mine and kissed her long and hard. The little girl saw us, and her jaw dropped, but she did not give us away. Later, she came up to me and said: "You are very *bold*, Jean-Pierre. But I shall not tell Mama." I did not doubt—I have never doubted—that Isabelle's love for me was as strong as mine was for her. She filled my heart and mind and soul. It was very simple: When I was young, the existence of Isabelle d'Alembert gave my world its meaning.

In the meantime, the King started to speak with me more regularly, always in secret. I grew accustomed to our conversations, though never lost a sense of awe in his presence. Sometimes he would take a pause while hunting, and we would ride in his carriage through the woods. Sometimes I would be smuggled into the Château of Marly, where he would go to escape the court and all its formalities. We would meet in the gardens, far from the house and the rows of guest pavilions that looked out over the lake.

He liked to talk to me about his childhood. Out of five babies, Louis was the first to survive. His mother, Anne of Austria, understandably thought of him as God-given, and refused to be parted from her precious son. Because she adored the theatre, Louis grew up loving spectacle and drama and dancing. In fact, he soon gained a reputation as an excellent dancer himself. "I would appear as Apollo, god of the sun, dressed all in gold," he told me. "For I understood at an early age the importance of *dazzling* my courtiers. It is a lesson I would have you pass on to my heirs."

But I also know that he lived through moments of terror and anguish. His father died when he was only four years old (a clock in the courtyard at Versailles forever marked the hour of his death to remind Louis that life is short). Then, when he was ten, during the Frondes—it was a period of civil unrest—an angry mob broke into the palace. A circle of threatening strangers entered Louis's bedchamber and crowded around his bed. He pretended to be asleep, and eventually, they drifted away. But while he lay, terrified, beneath the sheets, Louis tried to prepare himself to behave with dignity whatever might befall him. The child being father of the man, Louis resolved to transform himself into a monarch whose hold over his subjects was absolute.

Occasionally he would move me to tears. One day, as we stalked a lame stag with broken antlers (the sight of it, he said, offended him), he described how he sat with his beloved mother during her final days. She died of a cancer and the stench of the sickroom was nauseating, which distressed him greatly. Louis was a devoted and dutiful son, and he put aside the affairs of state as she finally slipped away. The doctors could do nothing for her. He broke down as he remembered the scene, and I was struck, not for the last time, by this ruler's equal capacity for love and ruthlessness according to circumstances. Afterward he went on alone, and hunted down the stag.

The Sun King taught me how to keep secrets, and made me swear, on my honor, that I would never, during his lifetime, betray his confidence. I did not. What sort of man are you if you cannot keep your word? Nor, for his part, did he betray *my* secret.

He was less guarded, I think, with me than with anyone other than his faithful Bontemps. The difference being that he treated Bontemps as a friend. I often felt that, as he unburdened himself to me, he would forget that I was actually there.

XIX

As my second summer at Versailles wore on, life took on a pleasant rhythm. The Spaniard still tutored me daily and, if I lived and breathed for my dancing lessons with Isabelle, I also started to look forward to my conversations with the King. However, as autumn loomed and the days grew shorter, Isabelle often seemed preoccupied. I would take her hand and ask if she were sad, always fearful in case her father, or her aunt, had found her another suitor. But she always insisted that there was nothing wrong, and it was easier to believe her.

It was during this time that I received some unexpected news. Liselotte had been in a temper all morning after she discovered that Monsieur had asked me to deliver an extravagant gift to a handsome acquaintance of his. On my return to the apartment I found that she had regained her good humor. She tapped my arm playfully with her fan. "Come, Jean-Pierre. While you were away a gift arrived—only this one is for *you.*"

She led me up the private stairs to the King's study. On top of the tortoiseshell desk I knew so well was a linen bag containing something bulky and of irregular shape. There was also a letter, sealed with wax and impressed with the face of Apollo.

"Open it!" urged Liselotte.

I broke the seal and unfolded the thick paper with eager fingers. There was the King's signature—*Louis*—written in an untidy cursive hand, and underlined. I read: "We have decided to confer a barony on your father. You are invited to present yourself tomorrow morning in the Hall of Mirrors, where we shall be happy to greet the son of the soon-to-be Baron de Chamborigaud."

"There!" exclaimed Liselotte. "By ennobling your *'father'* — a word that drew a smile to her lips — "there will be fewer questions about your elevated position at court."

"But what has my father done to earn this honor?" I asked.

Liselotte shrugged her shoulders. "I don't believe that is the point, do you? He has fought in several military campaigns, has he not?"

"Yes, in the Netherlands, when I was very young."

"Well, then. Or perhaps he has rounded up some Huguenots—"

"I'm sure he has not," I said, recalling the march of the *dragonnades* through the town in the Cévennes.

"Stop looking so anxious!" Liselotte said, laughing. "The King intends to acknowledge you publicly. And look, he has sent you a gift!"

I loosened the drawstring and the scent of new leather met my nostrils. *"Oh,"* I gasped, never having seen a finer pair of shoes in my life.

"You must try them on!" urged Liselotte.

I sat on the floor and did as I was told. They were black leather, the long tongue pluming out and over an ornate, rectangular buckle, which was fashioned from silver. The heels were high and, more significantly, dyed *red*.

Only the nobility were permitted to wear heels of such

a color. Red to announce my rank, red to show that I had no need to dirty my shoes, red, no doubt, to conceal the blood of those I might crush beneath my feet . . . I leapt up and strode up and down the room, heels clicking, buckles sparkling. They pinched my toes, but what did I care. "I feel like a prince!" I said.

"Of course! And why shouldn't you?"

It was not my intention to mislead, but how could I contradict her?

We were all Louis's creatures at Versailles, jumping through hoops, and forever hoping for some tasty morsel. In my own eyes those shoes—I admit it—increased my stature by far more than the three inches the King's red heels allowed.

"I shall find Isabelle and show them to her," I said. And then the thought struck me that with my new status, even the d'Alembert family might look more favorably on me.

Liselotte's expression changed and I could see that she was on the verge of saying something but stopped herself.

"Is something wrong, Madame?"

"Ah, it is something I heard this morning. But I shall not pass on tittle-tattle."

I was scarcely in a position to insist. We returned downstairs and Liselotte took her leave of me, promising to be present the next morning in the Hall of Mirrors.

Once back in my room, I flung myself on my bed and lay stretched out, flat on my back, hands supporting my neck. I stared at the plump cherubs who cavorted across my ceiling and marveled at my change in fortune. I even wondered if I dared bring up the subject of Isabelle with the King. Although it had been Louis who had first suggested a union between the Montclairs and the d'Alemberts, the incident in the Colonnades had put an end to that. The Sun King, as I had seen with my own eyes, always took good care of his own: his mistresses, whom he showered with jewels and houses and titles; his family; and likewise all his favorites at court. Why, even his dogs led a privileged existence, sleeping in their own quarters, and being fed specially prepared food by the royal hand. So why should the King not take care of his unicorn? Perhaps if I told him what my feelings were for Isabelle, he could intercede on my behalf with Isabelle's father.

That night I slept fitfully. I longed to be able to talk about my dilemma for I did not know what to do for the best. But by then I was locked into so many secrets, there was no single person with whom I could be entirely open.

XX

You could be hundreds of miles from Versailles, but if you could see a clock, you would know what Louis was doing at that precise moment. The court revolved around the rising and setting of the Sun King. His life played out in a series of rituals for all to see. Each morning only those of the highest rank were permitted to observe him being washed and shaved. Later, the Officers of the Chamber and the Wardrobe attended as he was dressed and ate breakfast, so that this middle-aged man would sip broth from a bowl in front of an audience of a hundred men or more. At Versailles, to have the honor of passing his shirt to the King was a mark of influence and power. It was absurd—but it was an absurdity that Louis imposed and we accepted. So I knew that at the stroke of ten, prior to holding council in his cabinet at eleven, Louis would walk through the Hall of Mirrors on his way to mass. There was always a crowd since he believed that all his subjects had the right to approach their King. It was during the short walk between his apartment and the chapel that he would acknowledge me.

When I arrived in the Hall of Mirrors that morning I may as well have been invisible, but I told myself that if Louis did what he had promised, when I left, every eye would be upon me. I waited with Liselotte and her well-trained children, who stood to attention and did not fidget at all. In comparison, when I caught sight of my own reflection (it was difficult not to in that room), even my features seemed ill-disciplined. I shuffled from one leg to the other in the crush of people, unwilling to engage in conversation. There was no sign of either Isabelle or the Spaniard, although I had sent messages to both early that morning.

A Versailles crowd had a unique smell: It was somewhere between fragrant and rank. It was a cold morning but at least we rivals for the King's attention kept one another warm in that vast, echoing space. Preferring to keep my own company in my nervous state, I sidled through chattering groups until I reached a window overlooking the gardens. I tried to gather my thoughts while watching the sun evaporate the dew. In the hazy distance, the Grand Canal, a long slab of water between banks of trees, glittered like a bed of diamonds. I stared at the skin on the backs of my hands, trying to imagine it wrinkled and slack, and wondered, not for the last time, if my position at court had its foundation in a fiction.

When ten o'clock struck, quiet descended on the Hall of Mirrors. I threaded my way back, still hoping that the two people with whom I should have liked to share this moment would arrive in time. But there was sign of neither Isabelle nor the Spaniard. All at once, like a stage curtain, the crowd divided, and I saw the King emerge at the head of a small cortège, long black wig draped over his shoulders. Heads bowed and ancient knees creaked. The King's approach had the same effect on his courtiers as does a magnetic charge on iron filings. It was impossible not to gravitate toward him. Until he chose to move on we could not be free of his influence.

I heard someone beg for an invitation to the royal retreat: "Marly, Sire?"

"We will see," was the King's careful reply. He was always polite, even when provoked. My view of him was blocked by someone in an ill-fitting wig and apricot-colored surtout. After several months in Monsieur's household, and after the embarrassment my mint-green waistcoat had caused me, I had developed an eye for court fashion. The surtout, I knew, displayed lamentable taste. The King would disapprove. I could picture the flaring of his sensitive nostrils. Now a woman was making a complaint about her late husband leaving a property to his sister. She had been left without means, but her pronounced lisp made her sad story sound comic. The King leaned in toward her so that I saw him give his smiling reply: "Ah," he said. "We could sooner reconcile all Europe than two women." Everyone crowed with laughter except the widow.

As the King moved closer, Liselotte reached out for me as if to capture an errant child. She grabbed me by the elbow and pushed me forward. I resisted. All at once the anticipation, the grandeur and the spectacle of it, the sparkle of glass, the blaze of gold, the heat of bodies, the sharp tongues and cutting glances, the stink of decay and the scent of flowers—in short, this royal theatre—was too much for me. What raw ambition I sensed in that room, what yearning, what cruel disappointment.

"Calm yourself!" Liselotte hissed into my ear. "Take deep breaths. It would not do to faint."

I nodded, my mouth too dry to speak. Would the Sun King even notice me in this sea of faces? A trickle of cold sweat ran down my temple. *Versailles c'est moi*, Louis once said to me—*I am Versailles*—and I never understood more clearly what he meant.

The King's shapely calves glided ever nearer over the polished floor. I became mesmerized by them: His stockings were scarlet, and a line of golden fleurs-de-lys ran up the side of his leg. A cane, held with the lightest of touches, marked the beat of his step and added a flourish to his gait. Now he was addressing the fellow in the apricot surtout. The figure bowed deeply, sweeping off his hat with a gesture that all at once I recognized. My heart skipped a beat as I glimpsed his profile: It was my father! The last time I had seen him I believed we shared the same blood.

"Our heartiest greetings, Monsieur!" said the Sun King in a clear, ringing voice so that all could hear. "We are pleased to recognize your invaluable assistance with regard to the enforcement of the Edict of Fontainebleau in the South."

"Sire, I am *overwhelmed* that . . . my very modest actions have attracted the attention of your Majesty." My father's halting tone betrayed, for anyone who knew him, the depth of his unease.

"Come," said Louis, resting his hand on my father's broad shoulder, "let us also greet your son, who will be delighted to see you here today."

My father scanned the crowd until our eyes met, both of us astonished that we could have been in the same room without having noticed the other. The King was fond of surprises. I was rooted to the spot, but Liselotte placed her hand on my back and thrust me into the empty space that had formed in front of the King and my father.

The King beckoned me to join them. We stood in a row with Louis at the center. "Ladies and gentlemen of the court, we present to you the newly created Baron de Chamborigaud and his youngest son."

There was a smattering of applause led, I think, by Liselotte, and a flurry of whispers behind fans. New favorites always caused a stir. Would they be rivals, or a route to the King's affections? The King spoke into my ear so that I felt the heat of his breath: "See how your King looks after his unicorn."

The moment was over. The King moved on. Liselotte beamed at me, satisfied that the royal seal of approval had been given as promised.

Leaving the Hall of Mirrors with my father, we received half a dozen invitations from people who greeted us as friends but who were, to the best of our knowledge, strangers before that morning. Afterward we headed for the gardens. As we walked, he took my arm, just as if he were my father and I were his son, which made me sad. And I realized how much I had missed him, and was overcome by a longing for my life to return to what it had been before I encountered the Spaniard. It was my father who spoke first.

"I am glad that you know the truth about your birth. I was never fond of secrets."

My throat constricted and, not trusting myself to speak, I nodded my head vigorously. He saw how I struggled to hold back my tears and did not press me to talk further. Instead, he gripped my arm more tightly and we walked in peaceable silence, my father guiding me down steps and along paths, always away from the palace.

"It wasn't true," said my father presently, "about the Edict of Fontainebleau. I haven't destroyed Huguenot churches, or closed Protestant schools, or whatever it is I am supposed to have done. My *ennoblement*—it has everything to do with you and nothing to do with me."

"I know," I said. "And I am sorry for it."

"I cannot deny that it pains me: I should have preferred to have been recognized for something I *have* done. Something of which I am proud . . . Although, in a sense, I have. I count bringing you up in the way that I did—without my wife— among the achievements of my life. . . . And at least it has made your position at court secure. Have you been told that the King does not require my presence at court?"

"No!" I exclaimed. "But why?"

My father shrugged his shoulders. "I cannot say that it makes me very sad—except insofar as I shall not see you as often as I should like. I've had a bellyful of mouths that say one thing and eyes that say another. I'm getting too old for the games they play at Versailles. I'd rather sit at ease in my own house and kick off my boots when it pleases me."

We strolled on past splashing fountains, my own noble red heels crunching through the freshly raked gravel.

"But *why* has the King ordered you to stay away? I don't understand."

I watched the furrow deepen between his brows. "It is my opinion that the King wishes to avoid divided loyalties. I believe he wants you for himself. I hope that he treats you well, at least—"

"Oh, do not worry on that account, Father! The King has been most kind—and generous. See, he sent me these shoes." I balanced on one leg and waved my foot in front of him. He eyed them, unimpressed. "And I won't be alone. I have the Spaniard to keep me company—"

"For the present—"

"What do you mean?"

"I wonder how long you can rely on the presence of Signor de Lastimosa."

"He has promised to be my tutor for as long as I wish it—"

"Yes, but have you ever asked yourself why the King should play host to a man with connections to the Spanish court, someone who did his best to dissuade you from returning to Versailles?"

"But he had good reason!"

"The King might see it from a different perspective. He might wonder if Signor de Lastimosa intends, one fine day, to return to Madrid—and take you with him."

I supposed it was true that neither the King nor Monsieur Bontemps had spoken of the Spaniard with any warmth. In fact, on the banks of the River Yvette, the King had asked about him with a degree of suspicion. For the first time I contemplated the possibility that the Spaniard might not be welcome at court. I picked up a handful of gravel and flung it into the green waters of the Latona Fountain. And where *was* he? *Why* had he left no word? In addition to being disappointed that he had failed to lend his support in the Hall of Mirrors, I also now felt a twinge of concern. My father pulled me around to face him.

"Listen, my boy, I first carried you in my arms on the same day that I buried my wife and my stillborn son. I was half-mad with the grief of it, yet when the Spaniard held out to me this swaddled newborn, and I felt your life beating between my large hands, it was an act of *grace*. I took you for my own and was able to turn away from my despair. The circumstances of your birth didn't matter to me then—and they don't matter to me now. I am not your blood father, and I do not care to know why you have attracted the attention of a King, but it was *I* who raised you. I may not know your secret, but I do know your truth. So I say to you while I still can: Don't allow the politics of Versailles to tarnish the brightness you were born with. You have it within you to become a *good* man, and there are few enough of those—"

My father was not a demonstrative man, so to hear him speak these words moved me greatly. I came very close to sharing my secret and risking the King's disappointment. But I did not. "Thank you, Father," I said.

"I do not say these things to compliment you, Jean-Pierre. I mean what I say. Nevertheless, now that you are a courtier, I would urge you to be . . ." My father searched for the right word. "More *guarded*. You have always had a trusting nature, whereas in Versailles what you need most is eyes in your back."

He embraced me and I told him that I would always think of him as my father. He did not release my shoulders immediately but turned me around slowly with his thumbs.

"I've been trying to lose him since we left the palace," my father said. "He is a tenacious fellow. Though it is a comfort, I suppose, to know that you are protected."

A Swiss Guard entered my angle of vision, and when our eyes met, the young soldier immediately averted his gaze. I should have liked to inform him that taking my chances with would-be assassins was preferable to suffering the constant company of the King's guards. I reasoned, however, that neither of us had any say in the matter.

XXI

Three times a week, between the hours of seven and ten, intimates of the King met in his apartment to divert themselves with cards, billiards, and conversation. I arrived that evening at the royal apartment at the invitation of Liselotte, who was almost immediately called away to have a word with the King. Feeling ill at ease in such illustrious company, I stood in a corner listening to the musicians play. Liselotte was admitted to an adjoining room, and as the door opened, I saw the King taking aim in a game of billiards. He was putting all his weight on one red-stockinged leg, while stretching the other out behind him, angling his foot in a most elegant manner. I heard the *clack* as he struck the ball. "Bravo, Sire!" called out a chorus of voices. I wondered if anyone ever dared beat the King. The door closed.

On the other side of the room, a game of Reversi had just finished. Large sums of gold were changing hands — fortunes were regularly won or lost in Versailles on the turn of a card. With a start, I realized that the tall gentleman who seemed intent on joining the players was none other than the Comte d'Alembert, Isabelle's father. Having never been introduced to him (I was, after all, the scoundrel responsible for the Colonnades incident), I hoped that he would not recognize me. I retreated farther into my corner. But then I witnessed something that shocked me. As he approached the card table, the three players remained seated as if he were not there, and refused to acknowledge his presence. Worse, another fellow all but pushed him to one side and proceeded to sit down in the chair d'Alembert clearly intended to occupy himself. I watched d'Alembert's back tense and his hands clench into fists, but he kept his dignity and walked calmly out of the room. I could not understand such behavior, and on Isabelle's behalf, I felt incensed at such disrespect. I was not the only one to have noticed. Half the room had seen it, and as the music played, accounts of what had happened passed from one mouth to another until the whole of the King's apartment was buzzing with descriptions of the humiliating snubbing of the Comte d'Alembert.

When Liselotte finally reappeared, I hastened to join her. She was engaged in conversation with an ancient duchess—the same whose nose the daughters of the King's surgeon had once dared me to tickle with an ostrich feather. Her dress propped up her crumbling body in such a way that her head and neck rose out of the bodice like a tortoise from its shell. When I greeted her she paused long enough to scrutinize me with her pink-rimmed eyes and yawn extravagantly. I don't believe she knew, or cared, who I was. I gathered that the two women were discussing Isabelle's father. The old duchess evidently did not hold a high opinion of him.

"I knew his wife while she was still a child, and I told her mother that he had a cruel heart. I assure you this news doesn't surprise me one jot—"

"Madame, it is not *news*," said Liselotte. "It is merely a *rumor*. How is the man to defend himself against such tittle-tattle? Gossip spreads so quickly at court—it's like smoke blowing off a bonfire."

"And there's no smoke without fire—"

"With you as judge, Madame," said Liselotte, "what need has one of a jury?"

The duchess shrugged her bony shoulders. "The proof is the guilt you can see in his eyes."

"I cannot believe there was anything suspicious in the manner of Madame d'Alembert's death. . . . I had hoped that we had put the Affair of the Poisons behind us a long time ago."

Liselotte excused herself, dragging me with her by the elbow so that we could talk in private. It was the first time I heard the calamitous rumor that threatened the d'Alembert family, although I was to hear it from different sources and in several different versions over the coming days. It was said that the Comte d'Alembert had poisoned Isabelle's mother and had bribed officials to conceal his crime. It was true that her death had coincided with the so-called Affair of the Poisons, which had erupted at court some years before, and which had scandalized the whole nation.

It started when a priest divulged some of the confessions he had recently heard to the chief of police in Paris. The ease with which one could procure poisons, the sheer scale of the murders, and the involvement of powerful and titled individuals at court was alarming. Hundreds of suspects were arrested, and by the end of the affair, dozens had been executed, burned, exiled, or imprisoned. However, when the King's mistress was also implicated, public trials ceased and the affair came to a rapid close. Many *lettres de cachet* were issued, so that many suspects still languished in prisons without hope of a trial or of release.

"It was a terrible time," Liselotte said as we made our way back to Monsieur's apartment. "Everyone suspected everyone else. A husband could die peacefully in his sleep and a fog of suspicion would hang over the grieving relatives for months."

"But, Madame, why are people accusing the Comte of this crime? And why *now*? Isabelle herself told me that her mother died of a fever when she was a little girl—"

"I dare say she did, but after all this time how can one prove it? Being innocent is not enough: You need to be able to *convince* people of your innocence. As for who started the rumor . . ."

"Could it have been Montclair?"

Unwilling to commit herself, Liselotte shrugged. "Whoever it is, if their motive is to destroy d'Alembert's reputation, they're succeeding."

"Do you think it could be true?"

"Personally, I believe d'Alembert to be innocent—though he could just as easily be guilty. After living through the Affair of the Poisons I assure you I could believe anything of anyone."

"Poor Isabelle! Even to hear such a rumor about your father—"

"If he's innocent, pity the father rather than the daughter, even though Isabelle's chances of making a glittering match are considerably lessened." A smile formed on Liselotte's face. "Although every cloud has a silver lining. . . ."

I felt ashamed, for the same idea had come, unbidden, into my own head. "I must go to her!" I cried.

Liselotte told me such behavior was inappropriate and insisted that I wait until the following morning's dancing lesson, when I could speak to Isabelle in person.

"Incidentally," Liselotte added, "I have not seen your Spaniard of late. Do you suppose he is unwell?"

I told her that I did not know.

XXII

Early the next morning Liselotte summoned me to her rooms. She announced that until the rumors concerning the Comte d'Alembert were disproved, Monsieur judged it unseemly that any member of his household should be on intimate terms with the Comte's daughter. Liselotte passed on Monsieur's remarks to me without comment, stroking the silky folds of her wide skirts as she spoke. Given that I was Monsieur's secretary, I was requested not to contact Isabelle. It was unfortunate, Liselotte said, for she knew how very fond I was of Mademoiselle d'Alembert, but in the circumstances, I had to put my own reputation first. After all, to continue a friendship with the daughter of someone rumored to be a murderer might have consequences for *my own family*. The expression on Liselotte's rosy face as she fixed me with a meaningful stare was hard to stomach. I was sorely tempted to tell her that I was not related in any way to the King. Instead, I bowed and left the room. I did not, however, attend Elisabeth-Charlotte's dancing lesson that morning and was not to do so again.

Ignoring Liselotte's advice, I started to write Isabelle a note. The words refused to flow, for how could I tell her that, thanks to the scandalous reports that put her father in such an evil light, her presence was now considered an embarrassment? I paced up and down beneath the cherubs and their garlanded goddess. I even began to wonder if the Comte d'Alembert *had* murdered his wife before scolding myself for being as weak-minded as the rest of the court.

A footman scratched at my door, as was the custom, and my irritation at being interrupted vanished when I was handed a letter from Isabelle herself. It seemed to me that someone had tampered with her seal. I opened it in a state of tender agitation. The sight of her handwriting provoked an emotion somewhere between happiness and dread. I traced the sweep of her signature, *Isabelle d'A*, and brought the paper to my face. But again there was a scratching on the door, and the footman entered a second time.

"Yes?" I demanded, slapping the letter down on my lap.

The sallow-faced footman, who never looked well, conveyed to me the surprising news that the King's *premier valet de chambre* was waiting for me in the royal stables.

"Monsieur Bontemps is waiting for me?"

"Yes, Sir."

"I am to go now?"

"At once, Sir."

I pushed the letter into the top drawer of my desk and set off in haste. Halfway down the corridor I stopped, turned around, and obeyed an almost physical impulse to go back to my desk: I could not bear to be parted from Isabelle's letter. Thrusting it into my pocket, I ran through the corridors of the palace and out into the sunshine of the courtyard.

The King kept a vast number of horses, and the royal stables were as spacious and elegant as any château. Inside, the warm air was thick with the sounds of whinnying and snorting and champing, and the stink of manure was ripe enough to make even a country boy gag. I hurried under lofty arches, and past lines of stalls, from which the arched necks of many noble horses emerged. Their melancholy gazes followed me, revealing the whites of their eyes as I passed them by. A stable boy directed me to the courtyard where I might find Monsieur Bontemps.

Here, in this semicircular space, horses, men, and carriages wheeled around in an intricate dance. I stood with my back flattened against a wall for fear of being trampled. It had been dark the last time I saw Alexandre Bontemps's coach and four, but I recognized it all the same. It was black and bore no royal insignia. I found the great man inside, his calm face wearing the resigned expression of one used to waiting. He was humming a tune and resting his legs on the opposite seat. His white-stockinged ankles, in their buckled shoes, were neatly crossed.

"Ah, Jean-Pierre," he said, sliding his feet to the floor and telling me to climb in. "I should be glad if you would join me for a short ride."

There was something in his demeanor on this occasion that failed to put me at my ease. He closed the blinds and rapped on the roof of the carriage so that I had no idea where he was taking me. Against the sounds of creaking axles and hooves striking cobblestones, we had a curious, one-sided conversation during which he seemed to be encouraging me and warning me about something at the same time. Matters had moved on apace, he said, while not specifying to which matters he referred. He informed me that the King desired to see me at Marly the following evening, at dusk. He would arrange for a carriage to take me there.

Light crept in around the edges of the blinds, though I could see nothing, and presently the horses slowed down and came to a halt. We must have been in the town for I could hear the cries of street hawkers in the distance and the rumble of wagons close by.

Monsieur Bontemps looked at me squarely in the face and announced: "I have brought you here today to see a friend."

The carriage door opened and the Spaniard was pushed into the carriage by unseen hands.

"Signor!" I gasped. "Where have you been?"

The Spaniard greeted Monsieur Bontemps (without, I thought, any warmth) and sat down opposite me. He took both my hands and pressed them between his own. Although he smiled, it was clear to me that all was not well. His eyes were glassy, and his hands, normally warm, were cold and clammy.

Monsieur Bontemps asked him if he had finished preparing for his departure.

"Departure?"

"I leave Versailles for the port of Calais at dawn tomorrow," said the Spaniard. "I am due to set sail in two days' time."

"The King himself," added Monsieur Bontemps, "has asked Signor de Lastimosa to journey to the Swedish court and report back to his Majesty on affairs that might be of interest to France. It is a great honor."

"Yes, Monsieur Bontemps," said the Spaniard. "I would go so far as to say it is an honor I feel I do *not* deserve—"

"The King is careful to reward his courtiers as he sees fit, Signor," replied Monsieur Bontemps. He adjusted the tresses of his long, dark wig and turned to me. "Time is short, Jean-Pierre, and your farewells must necessarily be brief."

With the King's *valet de chambre* at my side, I could not express the confusion and distress that I felt. Nor could I put to the Spaniard the questions I wanted to ask. Something was wrong. But whatever we had to say had to be said now, before it was too late and the moment had passed. And so, instead of demanding where he had been hiding himself, or if he thought the rumor about Isabelle's father had any truth to it, I spoke the words I felt I was expected to say. I thanked the Spaniard for everything he had done for me, congratulated him on his royal mission to Sweden, and wished him a safe journey. But all the while I had a picture in my head of the moment in the orangery when he had spoken of his desire to return to the citrus groves of Spain. He hated to be cold. I thought of all that awaited him, of continual night and of black, oily seas, of snow and pickled herrings, and a desperate sadness washed over me. Would I ever see him again? The Spaniard, in his turn, wished me well and bade me remember the teachings of Baltasar Gracián. Then, words failing us, the Spaniard and I merely looked at each other.

Monsieur Bontemps, unnerved by the awkwardness of the moment, put an abrupt end to the proceedings and opened the carriage door. Outside, a Swiss Guard stood to attention.

"It is good of you to come, Signor, when you are so occupied with preparations. I am certain you will have much of interest to recount to Jean-Pierre in your letters."

"Indeed I will, Monsieur," the Spaniard replied and, bidding me farewell, leaned forward to embrace me. I clung to him. A strange odor hung about his clothes. It was musty and damp, the smell of a cellar. And though I could not be sure of it, I thought I detected the iron tang of blood. The Spaniard climbed out of the carriage and looked up at me. I stared into his eyes, uselessly trying to impart everything I felt. He looked pale in the light of day, and his body sagged as if he had aged twenty years. He thanked Monsieur Bontemps, saying: "You are a man of your word." To me he said: "God keep you, Jean-Pierre. Make your father proud."

The door closed behind him, and when I tried to lift the blind to watch him depart, Monsieur Bontemps held it gently, but firmly, down.

On our way back to the palace I did not speak: partly because I was trying to take in this disheartening news, and partly because I guessed that what I wanted to know, I would not be permitted to ask. Monsieur Bontemps, however, had something to ask of me. Signor de Lastimosa, he said, had begged to be allowed to say farewell to me.

"I did not have the heart to refuse, but I arranged this meeting without consulting the King. When you meet with His Majesty tomorrow, I would ask you to make no mention of it. He means to tell you himself of the honor that he has accorded your teacher."

"Shall I see Signor de Lastimosa again, Monsieur? Will he return to France?"

"It is not for me to say."

To my shame, my eyes filled with tears. I felt I had been orphaned all over again. At least the King's *valet de chambre* had the tact to look away. Soon the ringing echoes of the horses' hooves on cobblestones told me that we reached the great courtyards of the palace. Monsieur Bontemps leaned in toward me, his face earnest.

"The King desires to establish you at court. Our fate, yours and mine, is to *serve*. We therefore need to be robust; we need to learn to *endure*. The alternative is far worse. To be cast out into the wilderness, away from the protection of the King, is not something I would wish for you."

He advised me to show Louis gratitude for what I had and would receive, and to hide from him any anger I might feel for what had been taken away from me.

"Remember, Jean-Pierre, that *to win* is more often than not *to lose*, for you can only fall from the highest positions. It is safer, in the end, to be satisfied with less."

To win is to lose. Words can exert a powerful hold on the immature mind. Monsieur Bontemps's words struck their mark that day. He meant well, I have no doubt of that, but in hindsight, I wonder what I might have done with my life had I never heard them.

XXIII

It was at the Apollo Fountain in the late afternoon that I finally read Isabelle's letter. Shaken by the Spaniard's demeanor and his exile to a cold, foreign land, I could not rid myself of a sense of dread. I felt that nothing was what it had at first seemed, and, that being the case, I could not rely on my own judgement. My life was sliding out of my control and in directions I would prefer it not to go. My feet had led me to the Apollo Fountain because it was here that I had felt joy, the morning after the incident at the Colonnades. Now, alone by the fountain, I braced myself for the news that Isabelle's letter contained.

My dear friend,

A great misfortune has befallen our family and I can see no end to it. I am certain that, by now, you will know of what I speak. My father has enemies at court. What they say about him is not true. My mother died when I was very young, and my memories of her are few and indistinct, but I can assure you that she died of a fever, away from the court, in the house where she grew up in Normandy.

Some weeks ago I accompanied my father to mass in the royal chapel. As we were leaving, a woman ran forward and spat in my father's face. I recognized her: She

used to be our servant when I was a child.
"Murderer!" she hissed. "May you burn in
hell for what you did to your wife!" My
father was taken aback and made no answer
other than telling her to get out of his
way. But the woman appeared again last
week, accusing him of poisoning my mother.
This time my father caught hold of her
sleeve and asked who was paying her to tell
such monstrous lies. We were in a large
crowd of people, yet no one spoke up against
her. I was sent to stay with my aunt in
Rambouillet that very afternoon.

My aunt urges my father to argue his
innocence before the situation gets out of
hand. Once, in Paris, she saw a mob tear
apart a cornered criminal and she fears that
if my father does nothing, the best he can
hope for is that scandalmongers do the same
with his reputation.

My father disagrees, and refuses to defend
himself publicly. He is of the opinion that
to do so is to acknowledge a crime that did
not take place. It is unfortunate that the
only man who could have testified on my
father's behalf—the physician who tended
my mother on her deathbed—died two years
ago. And so it seems that our family's honor
depends on whether the court of Versailles

chooses to believe my father's word or a
malicious rumor.

I wish, with all my heart, that I were
not here in Rambouillet, and that I could
talk with you, for your presence would be
a comfort to me. Alas, I fear that my stay
here will be lengthy. Is it not curious,
Jean-Pierre, how our positions at court have
been reversed? You are raised up while my
family is brought low. I only pray that you
do not think the worse of me on account of
the evil that has befallen the d'Alembert
family. I hope that your health is good and
that all is well with you and Signor de
Lastimosa.

Please believe me when I say that I am
affectionately yours,

Isabelle d'Alembert.

I folded the letter and placed it carefully in my pocket,
my mind too agitated for coherent thought. "Oh, Isabelle,"
I said aloud, addressing the air and the trees. "What can I
do?" I looked at the still fountain, at the horses that surged
silently out of green water ready to pull Apollo's chariot
across the sky; I looked up at the palace of the Sun King
in the distance, but no answer came. Isabelle asked me in
her letter not to think the worse of her. What she should

have written was: *If you* had not been so rash and stupid, *if you* had not knocked down the Prince de Montclair in the Colonnades, *his family would have had no reason to hate mine and my father would not now be wrongly accused of this terrible crime.* She was right to say that our positions at court had been reversed. I *had* been raised up, while the d'Alemberts had been brought low. And it was *my* fault.

I ran along the banks of the Grand Canal as if trying to outrun the bad fortune that had beset all those connected to me. I, who *loved* Isabelle, had brought this misfortune on her. On my account the King had forbidden my father to attend court and the Spaniard had been ordered to Sweden. My mother died bringing me into the world. Juan Pedro was killed within days of my birth. My brothers' lives were soured enough by my arrival in their family to turn them into brutes. How could I atone for the trouble I had caused? What could I possibly achieve in my life that would justify the suffering of those around me?

Only when my lungs were burning and my whole body trembled did I stop running. I bent over, retching, at the water's edge, and the notion came to me that the world might be a better place if I were to just slip beneath the sparkling surface, lie quietly on the muddy bed, and choose never to breathe air again. But if I were to do this, how would that help Isabelle?

Ludo's Theory

When Spark grates the old station wagon's gears and the engine stalls, Ludo does not even react. He has let his head fall back against the headrest and his eyes are closed. As she starts up again and jams her foot on the accelerator, the wheels spin in the deep gravel and a fine white dust rises up around them. Spark has not yet passed her driving test, but what choice does she have? The car lurches forward and she checks in the rearview mirror, half expecting to see Jacob brandishing his axe. Though it is the actions of John Stone that have truly shaken her. She'd *trusted* him. Spark steers Andy's car jerkily up the drive, every muscle tensed, gripping the wheel as tightly as if someone were trying to prise it from her grasp. What else were these people capable of doing? And she'd slept in their house! The bridge is narrow but Spark maneuvers the station wagon across it, grimacing with concentration, barely avoiding the deep ditch as she turns into the lane.

Changing up a gear, the car stalls again. Spark glances over at her passenger. Ludo is pale and still; water drips from the ends of his hair onto his soaked T-shirt, which clings to the muscles of his chest. He holds his hands clamped to his throat, crossing them at the wrist, as if simulating Jacob's brutal grip.

"Ludo? How are you doing?"

He doesn't respond. Spark turns the ignition key but this

time to no avail. The coiled spring of her panic explodes. *"Start!"* She bangs the flats of her hands on the steering wheel. As she checks the rearview mirror for any sign of Jacob, Spark feels her heart hammering wildly against her rib cage. She tries again, this time turning the key more slowly. The starter motor makes a noise like a decrepit machine gun.

"Try more choke," croaks Ludo, the irony of the phrase registering with her, though not enough to raise a smile.

Spark eases out the choke as she is told, and this time the engine roars to life. She jams her foot down on the accelerator and they speed away from a place to which, she thinks, no one could ever persuade her to return. The image of Jacob and Ludo thrashing through the water flickers in her mind's eye, overlaying her view of desolate marshland. If she follows this single-track road, it leads, via a circuitous route, to a main A-road some four or five miles away. In the rearview mirror a dying sun peeps over the mound of trees that conceals Stowney House from the eyes of the world. She drives on, and with each mile Spark breathes easier.

When they reach the nearest village, Spark pulls up outside a squat, redbrick police station.

"I'll be your witness," she says.

Ludo looks a better color, at least. "No way!"

"We should report it."

"We should get out of here before you get arrested for driving a vehicle without a license!"

"It was an emergency—"

"Tell that to the judge."

"But Jacob tried to drown you! And John Stone chucked your cell into the marshes!"

"I don't want to report it."

"But why?"

"Can we get out of here—*please*—and then I'll talk about it? Okay?"

Ludo gestures impatiently for her to get going. Spark shrugs her shoulders and moves off. Soon they reach a rest stop where there is a clapped-out caravan selling burgers and hot dogs. It must be a favorite with the long-haul drivers for there is a long line of trucks parked nose to tail. They drive through trails of blue smoke and the smell of frying onions enters the car. Spark draws up behind a mud-splattered truck with a Polish license plate.

"Man, I'm hungry," says Ludo.

"Me too," says Spark. "I'll get you something."

Spark opens the car door. Unseen, on the other side of a hawthorn hedge, lambs bleat plaintively for their mothers. She hesitates for a moment before getting out, then takes hold of Ludo's hand.

"You were only trying to help me out—me and Dan. I am *so* sorry about all of this."

Ludo smiles back at her—it is a rueful smile—and he squeezes her hand. Spark can't read what's going on behind those flecked amber eyes and before she loses courage, she leans across and kisses his cold cheek. Now she slides out of the car without looking back and lines up with the hefty truck drivers at the window of the caravan. The legs of her jeans are sodden and stick to her skin. Even in this warm breeze she shivers a little.

"There," she says, pushing greasy paper bags and Styrofoam cups onto the dashboard. "Burgers and hot, sweet tea—for the shock."

"That is *good*," says Ludo, biting into soft white bread and steaming beef.

They wolf down the burgers, giving each other sidelong looks, wiping the grease from their mouths with the backs of their hands. Spark feels strangely euphoric. She doesn't want to go home. She wants to sit in Andy's old station wagon with this American boy forever.

"What is it with you English and tea?" Ludo asks. "It doesn't *do* anything—it's *tea*." He pulls a face. "How many sugars did you put in?"

"Six. Get it down you. So are you going to tell me what happened—with you and Jacob, I mean?"

Spark waits expectantly.

Finally Ludo says: "I guess there's something I should admit to you." Spark shifts around in her seat to face him.

"I wanted to see John Stone's gallery. . . . The key was in the lock. I only had to turn it. It was too easy. I went in and closed the door behind me—"

"You did *what*?"

"Only the guy walked in on me. I'd gotten back into the house through the French windows in your room. He must have been watching me—"

Spark covers her face with her hands. "The gallery is John Stone's private place—*no one* goes in there, not even Martha. Jacob must have thought you were a thief! You weren't . . . I mean, you weren't trying to—"

"*Steal* something? No! *No!* I wanted to check out his paintings, so I just snuck in—"

"*Snuck in!* Why the heck were you *checking out* his paintings?"

"I know this must look bad." Ludo makes calming gestures with his hands. "Can I borrow your phone to show you something?"

Spark lifts up her hips and slides her phone from the back pocket of her jeans. Ludo huddles over it, sighing in frustration at the slow connection speed. The daylight is beginning to fade and a silvery glow is mirrored in his glasses. "Finally," he says, handing back the phone. "It's an app I've been developing at college. I'm going to market it on genealogy sites."

"Genealogy?"

"Family trees."

Spark scrutinizes the small screen. It's a web page. *LOOKING FOR THE NEEDLE*, she reads. *Perform visual searches on multiple images using facial recognition software.* There are two photographs: one, in color, is of a middle-aged man; the other, in black-and-white, is a high school photograph, class of '78. A circle has been drawn around one of the teenage boys. At the bottom of the page is a figure: 99 percent.

Spark looks in confusion at Ludo. "Why are you showing me this?"

"Just stay with me. When you're researching family trees, it can be hard to identify people at different stages in their lives. No one looks the same at eighty as they did at eighteen—but underneath the wrinkles they mostly *do*. What my app does is analyze a whole set of measurements—distance between the eyes, length of nose, skull size, stuff like that—and compares them to a second set of measurements."

"So the ninety-nine percent refers to . . . . ?"

"The probability that it's the same person in both images."

"Is it? They don't look alike—"

"Actually they're both pictures of my dad. It's not foolproof, but it's a useful tool. It indicates probability. I'm also working on an algorithm—with my professor, who knows a whole lot more about it than I do—that will calculate the probability that two people are *related*. Though I'm a long way from that—"

"Is that what this is about? Do you think you're related to John Stone?"

"*No!*"

Spark is becoming exasperated. "Can't you just tell me why you went into his gallery?"

"Remember the picture you left me of John Stone in New York—with the street woman?"

Spark nods.

"Great picture, by the way—"

"Thanks."

"So, I was testing my app—trying to break it, do all the dumb things you know users are going to do—and I got it to sift through every image on my hard drive looking for matches. And I've got *a lot*. What was awesome was that it matched up your photograph of John Stone with a *painting*. I can't even remember how that painting got into my image library. But it's British. It dates from the 1840s. And it's hanging on a wall in the National Portrait Gallery in London. It's *huge*. It shows a crowd of people debating the abolition of slavery. And four rows from the front is a guy who, I'm telling you, could be John Stone's *twin*. If you could see it, you'd think there's no way that the two of them *can't* be related."

Spark has turned away and is looking through the open window at the hedgerow, at the potato chip bags caught up in the thorny branches, at the cigarette butts ground into the earth. "I see," she says. "That must have been interesting for you." Her tone is flat. Ludo continues talking at her.

"If I could just prove that the guy in the painting was one of John Stone's ancestors, it would be a real breakthrough—"

"So when I told you John Stone had a gallery—"

"I couldn't resist. When we were in the kitchen, if he hadn't told me to step outside so he could talk to you, I was going to ask him if . . ." Ludo stops speaking and stares at her. "What's wrong?"

They sit in silence for a long moment. The car moves very slightly every time a truck whooshes by on the road.

"You meant to come to Stowney House all along, didn't you?" says Spark quietly.

"I would have told you earlier, but it didn't seem appropriate—you were too upset—"

"I don't think you came to England to be a friend to Dan. You came because of John Stone, didn't you?"

"One doesn't exclude the other—I *am* Dan's friend."

"You didn't come today to support me because I was upset. Did you? *Did* you?"

"Spark—it's not like that—"

"No, it was a case of killing two birds with one stone...."

Spark gets out of the car and slams the door behind her. She no longer trusts herself to speak. She doesn't even know if she's being unfair. Hugging herself, ignoring the curious glances of truck drivers, Spark strides up and down the rest stop. She is tempted to stop at the burger line and ask if anyone could give her a lift to Mansfield. Finally she walks back to the car. What else can she do?

Ludo has swapped seats. "I'm driving," he says.

A Difficult Meeting

John Stone hands over the eight green notebooks to Edward de Souza, who places them in a box file and carries them to an adjoining office. There is the sound of filing cabinet drawers opening and closing. John Stone yawns and stretches. The dawn chorus had begun in Hyde Park before the ink had dried on the final page. He regrets his choice of stationery: It was all he had on hand when he decided, all those weeks ago, to set down an account of his early years at Versailles for Spark. Strange to think that when he started to write them, they were intended for someone he thought of as no more than a potential Friend. He had planned to put the notebooks into her hands in the archive room at Stowney House. How sad that he is about to deliver a formal invitation for her to read these documents at the London offices of his lawyer. He can only hope that she will accept.

John Stone pulls up the sash window and leans out. An enormous flock of starlings is descending, cloud-like, onto a nearby plane tree, the birds dissolving instantly into the dense foliage. Lincoln's Inn Fields suddenly sounds like an aviary. Should he reveal to Edward that Spark is his daughter? No, he decides, not quite yet. His emotions are still too raw. After speaking with Mrs. Park, things will be clearer. It is enough, for now, that Edward knows that Spark's mother is Thérèse.

Presently Edward returns to his desk with the

confidentiality agreement that he has drawn up for Stella Park to sign prior to reading the notebooks. John Stone does not believe such a document is worth the paper it is written on, but does not share this opinion with his faithful lawyer.

"Would you like me to write to Miss Park inviting her to view the notebooks?"

"Thank you, no. That is in hand. But if, as I hope she will, Spark responds to my invitation, bear in mind that she has no idea that she is adopted. I would hate for her to discover the truth by accident."

"You know that I'd also be very happy to draft a confidentiality agreement to be signed by any doctor you might choose to consult." John Stone rearranges his features into an expression of mild irritation, which Edward ignores. "Forgive me, John, but how can you be happy for Stella Park to know your history while you won't even consider speaking to a neurologist?"

"Because I trust *her*! Because at some point she deserves to know that her mother was a sempervivens. As for the medical profession, doctors, more than anyone, have the most to gain from my secret. Longevity has, and always will be, a holy grail."

John Stone is not being entirely open with Edward. He's never had any faith in doctors, but he has another—more personal and more compelling—reason. In Thérèse's letter, which was so freighted with revelations, there is one passage, in particular, that preys constantly on his mind. She wrote: *And in your final judgement of me, grant me this, at least, that despite my opposing views, I never did anything to endanger the anonymity of our race—even in these final stages of my illness, when I have been sorely tempted to submit myself to a surgeon's care.* Thérèse died protecting their daughter, even while believing there were advantages to be had by revealing their existence to the world. For John Stone to weaken and consult a doctor now is unthinkable. It would be a *betrayal.*

Unusually for Edward, he continues to argue with him. "Doctors, like lawyers, know how to keep secrets. I respect your wishes, John, but I can't agree with your reasoning."

"Edward," says John Stone softly, putting his hand on his shoulder. "The subject is closed."

John Stone promises to meet with Edward again before the end of August in order to discuss amending his will in Spark's favor. Now, walking away from Lincoln's Inn Fields, he feels drained. It is as much due to a melancholy brought on by recent events as to physical fatigue. In recent days he has set himself two tasks to complete. The first—to finish writing the notebooks and deposit them with his lawyer—he has achieved. The second task, to go to Mansfield and introduce himself to Mrs. Park, fills him with dread. However, it is necessary to find out how the land lies. He also prefers to deliver Spark's invitation in person rather than send a messenger. John Stone is not looking forward to making the acquaintance of the stranger who has brought up his newly discovered daughter. It will be a difficult meeting.

He revives himself with a double espresso in a coffeehouse opposite Holborn station. As he stares out of the window, he witnesses a lovers' argument on the pavement outside. He can't avoid hearing every word. It ends with the young woman slapping the young man's face. There's something about the proud way the girl holds herself—her *spirit*—that puts him in mind of Thérèse. Of late she has often been in his thoughts: She did not fear confrontation, and could dazzle or scorch when so inclined. He had often heard her say that if she had been born a man, what could she not have done? But that was Thérèse's tragedy: She was born in the wrong age, and, in her words, suffered a lifetime of fools. He had always supposed that she thought him to be one of them, yet her last letter to him implied otherwise. It turns out that John Stone—who has always prided himself on his clear-sighted observation of his fellow man—was blind when it came to his own wife. He is still shaken by this discovery—and full of remorse. He finds that he can even forgive Thérèse for her failed attempt to set fire to Stowney House, although he likes to think that had Jacob's keen sense of smell not thwarted her, she would not, in any case, have gone through with it. Thérèse hated to feel trapped, without options. It was often enough for her to think that she *could* do a thing if she *wanted* to.

At midday John Stone calls for his driver to pick him up. He does not listen to the voice that tells him he is too weary, but heads out of London, to the north, to a mining town in Nottinghamshire that his daughter—*their* daughter—regards as home.

He phones from the car. "As it happens, it was actually you I wanted to speak with, Mrs. Park. Would it be possible for me to introduce myself? I'm parked at the bottom of your street."

After a long pause John Stone hears what he presumes to be the rattle of an ashtray as Mrs. Park stubs out a cigarette. She exhales audibly. "Well, you'd better come in. Can you give me a minute to sort myself out?"

"By all means! Shall we say a quarter past the hour?"

He should have announced his intention of visiting her days ago, but he feared she might put him off. While he is waiting, John Stone climbs out of the car and surveys the street where Spark has grown up. A light rain is falling on Mansfield, although the sun is struggling to break through the clouds. He observes the line of redbrick terraces that stretches to the brow of the hill and beyond. The front doors open directly onto the street; most of them have white PVC windows that jar with the age of the properties. A car hurtles past, bouncing over speed bumps that are supposed to calm the traffic. In its wake, an unsettling silence resumes. His heart struggles with his head: This is not a land of plenty. John Stone might have wished for an easier start for his daughter. A widowed adoptive mother with two young children, moving to a coal mining town after most of the mines have closed. He gave the son an education, but if he'd have known earlier what treasure lay in this house, what wouldn't he have done for the family? Instead, Thérèse made a cuckoo of their child—just as the Spaniard had made of him. And yet, look how Spark has flourished in this soil: She is affectionate and capable; she is unselfish and brave. A child has been playing hopscotch on the pavement in front of the house. As John Stone looks at the traces of chalk, he grieves for a childhood of which he had no knowledge. What wisdom might he have been able to pass on to his daughter? If his disease does not progress too quickly . . . If Spark will permit him to try . . . perhaps, even now, it might not be too late?

The longer he paces up and down the street, the more uncomfortable John Stone becomes. In truth, he'd sooner face muggers in an alley than confront the adoptive mother of his own child. He takes in a deep breath of air and smells the rain.

When Mrs. Park's head finally appears on the doorstep, which is painted red to match the bricks, he is surprised to find that he recognizes the way that the woman smiles. She is slim, with fair, cropped hair and wears a coral-colored top and blue jeans. Before John Stone can offer her his hand, she leads him into her neat front room. It is small, low-ceilinged, and smells of cigarette smoke and air freshener. Pine, he thinks. Mrs. Park motions for him to sit down on the squashy leather sofa; she draws up an armchair opposite him. Between them a low coffee table is laid for tea; a ring of chocolate digestive biscuits has been arranged on a green pottery plate. John Stone had anticipated a woman embittered by the premature death of her husband and the struggle to bring up a family alone, but if there are traces of pain and resentment in the set of her face, he reads warmth there too. The love of her children must have been a great consolation.

"Will you have a cup of tea?" asks Mrs. Park.

"Thank you, yes," says John Stone, who is not fond of tea. He watches her pour the dark, stewed liquid into a small cup.

"We drink it strong at our house. Help yourself to milk."

His hands feel cold. He interlaces his fingers on his lap and puts a bright smile on his face. "It's good to meet you in person, Mrs. Park. Your children are a credit to you." She nods suspiciously; accepting compliments gracefully is not, he notes, a skill she has acquired. He continues: "I was sorry to learn about Dan's health problems—"

"We don't know if there is a problem yet. Daniel's still having tests," she replies.

"Let's hope there's not. But if it comes to it, and you need any help with his medical care, I hope you will contact me—"

"*No!* Thank you. It's very kind of you, Mr. Stone, but the NHS are doing us proud."

The shrillness of her response startles John Stone. "I'm glad to hear it."

"Which is not to say that we aren't grateful for everything your charity has done for Daniel."

"He's taken advantage of the opportunities he's been given. You must be proud of him."

"He was always a bright lad. Though it's a shame his work has taken him so far away from us."

Through the lace curtains, John Stone sees someone walk past barely an arm's length from the window. It makes him start; Mrs. Park notices. "You get used to it. I can see the world going by. I dare say it's a bit different to Stowney House."

"Stowney House *is* quiet. Too quiet for many, I'm sure."

"I didn't like it in Suffolk. It might be pretty but I was

relieved to get back to Mansfield." Mrs. Park sits on the edge of her chair, gripping the arms. "What brought you here today, Mr. Stone? Is it about Stella?"

"Yes," he says. "It is about Stella—and her reasons for leaving Stowney House."

Stella. Not Spark. Daniel. Not Dan. Mrs. Park clearly does not feel John Stone has earned the right to be on informal terms with her children.

"You do know that she's not going back? She didn't hit it off with your other staff. That, and there was no one else her own age to talk to."

"Is that what she said?"

"Look, Mr. Stone, if Stella doesn't want to go back, that's an end to it—I'm not going to make her."

"I wouldn't expect you to," he says quickly. "Whether or not she chooses to stay on at Stowney House is for her to decide. Might I ask you, though, if you would be so good as to give Stella a letter on my behalf?"

"A letter?"

John Stone unbuttons his jacket and takes an envelope from the inside pocket. He pushes it across the low table toward Mrs. Park. "Stella did a wonderful job organizing my archives, but I never had the chance to explain to her what she was working on. I feel I owe her an explanation. It's an invitation to read what you might call a historical document. I believe she would find it of great interest."

Mrs. Park takes the envelope, gets up from her chair, and balances it on top of the mantelpiece above a gas fire. It sits between a postcard of the Statue of Liberty and a framed photograph of a man holding up a champagne glass to the camera. He's smiling; he looks like an older version of Dan.

"I'll give it to her when she gets in."

Mrs. Park does not sit down again; her body language indicates that the meeting is over. John Stone searches desperately for a way to broach a difficult subject. If he says nothing, the moment will have passed and it will be awkward to arrange a second meeting.

"I should like to admit something to you, Mrs. Park. Now that I'm here. I'm keenly aware of the delicacy of this matter, but, you see, I was close to Stella's birth mother—"

John Stone instantly realizes he has said too much too soon. He may as well have lobbed a grenade into the sitting room as reveal he knows the secret Mrs. Park has guarded for seventeen years. She flinches perceptibly.

"*You* knew *her*?"

For a moment he fears that she is either about to faint or attack him. She becomes defensive and her voice wavers. "Are you family? Was it on Spark's account you helped Dan?"

John Stone has no wish to lie but nor does he wish to answer. His hesitation speaks for him and she shakes her head bitterly. "I should've known! I should've known not to believe her. She said she'd tell no one." Mrs. Park makes a strange clicking noise with her tongue. "That cottage. So close to Stowney House. A charity that *happens* to select my Dan for an educational bursary . . ."

John Stone leans forward and holds up his hands in an effort to stem the flow of her words, but Mrs. Park will not stop now.

"If it weren't for Dan, I'd have put my foot down when Spark told me who she was working for. I had a bad feeling about it from the start—"

"Please, Mrs. Park. If you could listen to what I have to say—"

"No, *you* listen to me! Stella doesn't know she's adopted. *I'm* her mother—in every way that matters. It was *me* that brought her up. You don't come between a mother and her daughter!"

John Stone feels sweat pricking at him. *Is* that what he is doing? "No. Of course not!"

"Then why have you come here? Out of the blue? Interfering with something that's nothing to do with you? Say one word to our Stella about this—one word—and I'll get on to Social Services."

John Stone stares at her, appalled. "Who do you take me for? I've come to offer you—"

"*What?*" The wretched woman's cheeks have lost all their color and she grips the back of the armchair. He notices that she still wears her wedding ring. "You've come to offer me *what*? Who do you take *me* for? I've got rights. I don't want your charity!"

"Mrs. Park, I did not mean to offend—"

"I want you to leave."

John Stone stands up but his feet won't move. How can he put this right? How can he make amends? What can he say? He opens his mouth in the hope that the right words will come out.

"*Get out!*" Her voice is so shrill, it's practically a scream.

There's a banging from the neighbor's wall and a muffled shout: "You all right, love?"

John Stone retreats from Mrs. Park's burning gaze to the front door: "You have nothing to fear from me," he says. "Quite the contrary. I am sorry to have caused you distress." He lets himself out and walks unsteadily to the car. He glances back through the tinted window. Mrs. Park is on her doorstep, an expression of pure anguish on her face. Her elderly neighbor, too, carrying a plate and a tea towel, stands in solidarity at her own front door.

John Stone sees himself through Mrs. Park's eyes: a posh man in a suit who wants something from her, who's not being straight with her. A man with money to burn, getting into his rich man's car, threatening to break up her family. And what else does she have? Her precious son. Her loving daughter. And John Stone feels suddenly ashamed that he comes from a race of cuckoos.

The Anti-Slavery Society Convention

Mum has been impossible to deal with these last few days—either flying off the handle over nothing, or staring vacantly into space. And this despite the good news that the results of all Dan's tests to date have been reassuring. He's even been seeing a new—and apparently top—consultant who has volunteered to look at his case. Though all Mum could think of saying was: "Why the sudden interest in Dan?"

In need of a break, Spark has treated herself to a day return ticket to London and has caught a ride to the station. Andy was driving Dan to Nottingham Hospital this morning, in any case, so he didn't mind. It's while Andy is filling up the car with gas that a text comes through on Dan's phone.

"About time," he says.

"What is?"

Dan is in the front passenger seat. He twists around to look at her. "Ludo's sorted himself out another smartphone. He's left Paris and now he's in Florence."

"Lucky Ludo."

"He says hi. Shall I forward his number to you?"

When Spark doesn't immediately reply, Dan asks if she is still mad at him.

"A bit. He should have told me about his app *before* we went to Stowney House."

She and Ludo had both agreed to play down what happened that afternoon. As far as Dan was concerned, Ludo had got himself into a bit of a scrape. He laughed at the thought of his cool American friend being chased into the marshes by the gardener for taking pictures without permission. Not to mention dropping his precious phone in the marsh.

Spark asks Dan if he's seen the painting that, according to Ludo, depicts one of John Stone's ancestors.

"No. But he's shown me his app. It's a bit on the crude side, if you ask me. But what do I know?"

On the South Bank, with the Thames before her and the National Theatre at her back, Spark finishes the last mouthful of her egg roll. It's a relief to get away from Mum for a while. Last night, while she was drying the dishes, Mum asked her if she was positive she wanted to take out a student loan. University fees, she said, were criminal. Yes, Spark had replied, a thousand percent sure. "Well, it's your choice," said Mum, pursing her lips. "Your life." There are times when Spark wants to shake her. Why can't Mum see that if you risk nothing you get nothing? If you're too frightened to leave your burrow, all you'll ever know is darkness and dirt.

She's picked a good spot: This panorama is spectacular. The Millennium Wheel, Cleopatra's Needle, and the Hungerford Bridge all crowd into her vision, while to her right, red double-decker buses snail over Waterloo Bridge and, beyond that, the pale dome of Saint Paul's rises up, which is, she thinks, a thing of great beauty. It's breezy here in the bright sunshine, almost like the seaside. She pulls out the pocket map she picked up when she arrived at King's Cross and squints at it. From here to Tate Modern it shouldn't take her longer than ten or fifteen minutes. She slips her backpack over her shoulders and adjusts the padded straps. An edgy-looking couple stroll by, the man speaking in a New York accent that makes her heart skip a beat. Can't she go anywhere without noticing black jeans, or floppy hair, or a runner's gait? When Ludo gets back from Italy, or whichever country he's "doing," she won't make a fool of herself a second time. Earlier, she caught sight of her reflection in a shop window, only instead of seeing her own features, somehow, it was Ludo's face that she saw. This vague ache won't leave her. It hurts, though she's not sure she wants it to stop.

The smell of the river reaches her as she leans against the railings and watches sunlight dancing on the murky water. A tourist boats chugs by and floating seagulls bob up and down in its wake. Below her, a small beach has been exposed by the low tide. Pigeons peck at the water's edge and, bizarrely, four boys stand on the sand juggling oranges. She's alone, but not lonely; she observes everything through her camera lens, makes it hers. Suddenly Spark has a change of heart about Tate Modern. Instead, she'll head back across the river to the National Portrait Gallery. She decides to judge for herself if Ludo has found one of John Stone's ancestors.

Trafalgar Square is heaving with crowds that strike Spark as astonishingly diverse. How she would love to be a part of this city, to beat with its pulse, scratch her name on its rich patina. How can she stay at home forever, even for Mum? Not when there's all of this waiting for her. Past Nelson's Column she walks, past the great lions and the National Gallery and up into Saint Martin's Place. In the entrance hall of the National Portrait Gallery she plucks up the courage to ask two women in uniform if they know where she might find a large canvas whose title is something to do with the abolition of slavery. She's sorry to be so vague. It was painted in the 1840s, she thinks. The women confer. "Room twenty. But do come back if it's not what you're looking for."

Spark does not need to go back. This has to be the one. Light spills down onto room twenty from glass panels in the roof. Set against a peppermint-green wall, a huge, golden-framed canvas dominates the right side of the gallery. Spark stands to one side of it, surrounded by whispered conversations and the squeaking of shoes against polished wooden floorboards. *The Anti-Slavery Society Convention*, she reads, painted in 1840 by Benjamin Robert Haydon. There are many hundreds of faces in the great gathering that the painting portrays and she has not yet come across a single one of them that resembles John Stone in any way. Spark concludes that either it is the wrong picture (which she doubts), or that Ludo's app isn't up to much. She sits back down on the padded black bench and contemplates Henry Beckford, an emancipated slave and delegate of the Anti-Slavery Society, watching an impassioned gray-haired man make a speech in the grand conference hall. The latter raises his hand in the air to emphasize his point. Unlike most of the audience, Henry Beckford has his back to the viewer, though Spark can see his profile and the handsome luster of his skin. The faces of the delegates in the first few rows are painted in some detail, but as the rows recede into the hazy distance, the faces lose their definition. There is a scattering of women but, for the most part, the hall is swimming with Victorian gentlemen with florid faces, stiff black jackets, and white neckties. The painting must be easily four meters wide, and high enough for Mr. Haydon to have needed to perch on a ladder in order to paint the top half of the canvas. It is indeed, as the gallery notes comment, a *monumental* work of art.

Spark scans the rows of earnest gentlemen, keeping track with difficulty of where she has already looked. The name of Ludo's app, which she has been trying to remember, suddenly pops into her head. A couple of searches on her phone throw up the desired result: *LOOKING FOR THE NEEDLE: Perform visual searches on multiple images using facial recognition software.* When Spark clicks on the link, hoping to find a clue, an error message appears. It seems that Ludo's website is no longer accessible.

Frustrated, she looks back up at the painting, and it is at that instant that John Stone's kind, dark eyes meet hers from behind the shoulder of a plump, elderly man. Spark shoots up and approaches the varnished canvas, leaning forward over the low wire barrier, close enough to see every brushstroke. There is the broad forehead, the square, prominent cheekbones, the set of his jaw. The resemblance is so remarkable, she cannot believe, just as Ludo had insisted, that her employer and this Victorian gentleman are not related. Unsure if it is permitted to take photographs, she waits until room twenty's guard is preoccupied talking to someone in the corridor, focuses her lens on the canvas, and zooms in on the face in a two-dimensional crowd. Spark wonders how many generations separate this supporter of the abolition of slavery and his descendant. Could he be John Stone's great-great-grandfather? Or great-great-great-grandfather? The shape of his face, the eyes, the nose seem not just similar, but *identical*. Spark's train of thought is abruptly halted by a single idea and although her stomach muscles ache from leaning forward, she freezes. High cheekbones, hair color, skull shape—all of these are inheritable traits.

But no one inherits a broken nose.

Like John Stone, this Victorian gentleman has the look of a rugby player about him: His long nose is crooked, and twists to the right. Spark stares into the tiny face so long that the colored shapes start to lose their meaning. And then she notices the tiny flick of white paint, at the front of the dark head of hair. She sits awhile, deep in thought, before slowly gathering up her possessions and retracing her steps out of the gallery and into the street.

Spark leaves Trafalgar Square preoccupied and unsettled, no longer in the mood for sightseeing and at a loss to explain what she has just seen. Later, on the train back to Nottingham, Spark stakes her claim to one corner of the half-empty compartment, and places her backpack on the spare seat next to her. She balances her camera on her lap, flicking endlessly between the video she secretly took of John Stone at Stowney House and her photograph of the painting. Her head starts to throb and she closes her eyes. Maybe his nose wasn't broken: Maybe it was just naturally crooked. And as for the flick of white—it was so tiny, she could have imagined it. The air-conditioning is making her chilly, and Spark covers herself with her sweater. Soon, warm and comfortable, she drifts between sleep and waking, sifting through evidence that swirls about her mind. If nothing else, she can understand why Ludo's curiosity was aroused. But since it's doubtful she'll ever see John Stone or Ludo again, what does it matter?

A squeal of brakes causes her to awake. The train has pulled into Nottingham station. She has to leap up and grab her belongings, and dives through the closing doors onto the platform. It is a rude awakening, and all thoughts of John Stone vanish as she makes her way across town to the Victoria bus station. There she catches the number sixty-three to Mansfield and sits in her favorite seat on the top deck, looking out at the world and taking everything in.

John Stone's Decision

The day following his encounter with Mrs. Park, John Stone experiences three severe and prolonged attacks—a taste, no doubt, of what awaits him as this illness takes its course. He does not dare leave his hotel room but lies on top of the bed, listening to the hiss of the air-conditioning, frightened, exhausted, while he relives, over and over again, the agony of that meeting. He pictures his letter to Spark nestling among the postcards above the gas fire. She must have read it by now. What will Mrs. Park have said to her about him? Edward would have called if she had contacted him. Nevertheless, John Stone is half expecting to learn that Spark, like her adoptive mother—though for very different reasons—will prefer to have nothing further to do with him. He fails to see how to move forward in this heartbreaking game. The bond between daughter and adoptive mother is strong. How can he proceed without causing further damage? And to what end? So that the girl can watch her newly discovered father lose all dignity and die before her eyes? So that she, a sane, affectionate, capable girl who has her whole life ahead of her, can move into Stowney House with two damaged sempervivens who prefer to spurn the world? At one point John Stone vents his frustration by banging his head on a partition wall. Unlike Mrs. Park, however, he cannot count on a friendly soul to shout through the bricks and plaster to ask if he is all right.

By morning, John Stone senses that something has shifted in him. The warring impulses in his heart and head have reached some kind of resolution. The relief that sweeps over him takes him by surprise. And he remembers how, newly arrived in England, he stood on the shingle of Dover Beach, holding Isabelle d'Alembert's pearl necklace in his clenched fist. He had treasured it since her death. But now he took it and hurled it, with a great groan of a release, as far as he could into the pounding surf. It was an act neither of anger nor of despair; it was simply that he had reached that moment, like a crossroads in time, when it was right to do so. Only a life lived can teach the sense of an ending. John Stone has reached a crossroads: He does not have to go on; he has witnessed enough. It is permitted to lay down his burden. If Spark does not respond to his invitation to read the notebooks, he will act on his decision and begin preparing for his departure.

Over the following days he busies himself calling on those few people, other than Edward de Souza, in whose company he still finds pleasure. These last twenty years the number of close acquaintances he has cultivated has dwindled, for John Stone has had his fill of funerals. One afternoon he suffers a particularly serious attack as he walks past a public library. He manages to get inside, and finds a chair in the reference section between two book stacks. Although a librarian and several readers glance at his juddering limbs, they all walk on and leave him to tremble in peace. After a quarter of an hour he is recovered enough to go on his way. He decides that the time has come to confide his problem to his driver, and John Stone instructs him to cover him with a blanket on the backseat of the car if he happens to be taken ill on their travels. Henceforth he will learn to cope with the indignities that this affliction imposes on him.

The following morning John Stone breaks a rule and permits himself to be nostalgic. He stands in a street near Saint Paul's, where he perfected his English in a coffee-house demolished nearly two centuries ago. It was here that he met a man of the cloth who inspired him with his views on slavery and on the rights and freedoms of men. Later, he took him to meetings and conventions, and taught him to argue. Afterward John Stone asks to be driven to the Thames, to Petersham Meadows, close to Ham House, where Thérèse once pushed him into the water for being insufficiently attentive. As they return to the city through Richmond Park, he asks his driver to pull over at a particular spot from which he observed German planes bombard London one December night during the Blitz. John Stone strides through the bracken looking out at the far-reaching views and startles a herd of fallow deer. Today a warm wind ruffles his hair, but on a crisp, cold night over seventy years ago, there was a bomber's moon, and the blackout meant that every star hung brightly in the sky. There was the dull beat of exploding bombs traveling across inky distances, and a sickening ribbon of red that crept across the horizon as London burned.

John Stone's last port of call is Rotten Row in Hyde Park:

He wishes to be reminded of a very recent event, and one that ranks with the most precious moments of his life. He wants to celebrate the day he learned he had a daughter. His line may not end with him. There still being no word from Spark, John Stone takes out his phone and calls Edward de Souza. The time has come for him to be open with his dear friend—and to enlist his help for a final time.

Dan's Inheritance

The afternoon sun streams through the vertical blinds, highlighting silver strands in the consultant's dark, bobbed hair. Dan has heard all this already. This is a repeat performance for the family. Spark holds Mum's hand. The consultant's tone is upbeat and sympathetic, her words curiously like she's reading from a script. Arrhythmia: a disorder of the heart's electrical system. It can cause the heart to beat too fast, too slow, or—as in Dan's case—with an irregular rhythm. Mum fixes the consultant with an unblinking, laser-like stare; Spark prefers to look at her shoes, which are beautiful: navy suede with surprisingly high heels and patent-leather trimming. There's something surreal about the situation that is preventing her from taking this as seriously as she knows she should. How can it be *Dan* the doctor is talking about? The consultant confirms what Dan's doctor in New York suggested might be the case, that in all probability he inherited the condition from Dad. There's a new treatment she is going to recommend he undergoes. With luck, it might entirely cure the problem. There is a waiting list, but she will see what she can do.

Spark glances over at her big brother, who seems fine, but you can't always tell with Dan. They've been here for *hours*. Spark longs to get out of this bare consulting room with its shiny orange floor and its stupid potted plant that should be put out of its misery. Suddenly, having zoned out of what the consultant was saying, she hears the doctor asking if it is okay to call her Stella. Spark sits up straight as if she's been caught daydreaming in class. "Oh, yes—"

The consultant smiles. "Well, Stella, I think it would be prudent for you to come in for some routine tests yourself." Spark feels Mum's hand tighten around hers. "We need to find out if your father passed on this particular gene to you, too. I could arrange for you to come in next week, if you like. Get it over and done with, so you know where you stand. What do you think?"

The consultant's tone is pleasant, as if she's inviting her to come for afternoon tea. Mum disengages her hand and shifts in her seat. "Yes, that will be fine," she hears herself saying. "I'm on holiday at the moment."

Mum does a strange thing as the three of them wait by the lift on their way home. Without warning, she shoves her bag at Spark and tells them to wait for her downstairs. They watch her sprint up the long corridor and call out the consultant's name, who spins around and walks back to have a word. Mum speaks for only a couple of minutes and the consultant nods and listens, then throws a look back in their direction.

"What's going on?" says Dan.

"I have no idea," says Spark.

Mum is not forthcoming on the bus going home. Spark volunteers to do the shopping and gets off a couple of stops early to go to the supermarket. When she arrives home and heaves her carrier bags onto the kitchen table, she is surprised to find Andy there.

"Your Mum practically ordered me to take Dan to the pub," he says.

"What!" says Spark, laughing. "Are you sure you heard right?"

There's a clatter of feet on the stairs and Dan appears, followed by Mum, who is nagging him about keeping Andy waiting. Dan asks Spark if she is going with them.

Mum answers for her. "No," she says. "She's only just got in."

Spark catches Mum giving Dan a meaningful look as she slips a fiver into his hand. Dan looks quizzically from Mum to Spark and back again while Andy drags him out of the back door.

"What's going on, Mum?" says Spark as brightly as she can manage.

"I'll be back in a minute. I've got to fetch something from upstairs."

"Fetch what?"

Spark wants Dan. Has someone died? Her hand comes to her mouth. Mum couldn't be sick, could she? Spark sits listening to the kitchen tap drip. When Mum reappears at the kitchen door, a large brown envelope in her hand, it is as if she does not want to come in. She stands at the threshold, silhouetted by the hall light. Spark stares at the envelope with fear in her heart, understanding without being told that once its contents are divulged her life will be bisected into the time before she knew and the time afterward. Mum places the envelope on one side of the table then sits down opposite her. She leans over and takes Spark's two hands in hers. There is pain in her eyes. "There's no easy way of saying this." Mum pushes the envelope toward her. Her voice cracks. "If your Dad were here he'd have the right words—"

"What is it, Mum?" Spark's heart thumps wildly in her chest and it occurs to her that she really could have arrhythmia too.

"I think it's best if you read it by yourself. It's a legal document, but you're a clever girl—you'll understand. It explains everything. I'll be in the sitting room. Just know that I love you. Always have and always will. And the same went for your dad."

Mum leaves the room and closes the door behind her. Spark eyes the envelope as if it were alive. Finally she reaches for it and pulls out the document it contains. It's printed on thick parchment and there are three signatures on the last page; she recognizes two of them: They are Mum's and Dad's. She stares at letters formed by Dad's hand.

Spark reads the words several times to be certain that she understands what the document is saying. Her hands begin to tremble uncontrollably as she reads. This must be a mistake. It *can't* be true! She scrapes back her chair and walks across the chasm of the hall. Her thoughts are slow and halting as if she's taken a punch. Now Spark stands silhouetted at the sitting room door, holding the document in front of her. Now it is Spark who doesn't want to cross a threshold.

"This can't be right! I am yours, aren't I? Mum, tell me! It's not true, is it?"

Mum, who is sitting on the edge of the armchair, knees

and ankles squeezed together, stares at her lap. Spark shakes the document at her to get a reaction. "Is it?"

Mum nods. "Yes."

Spark drops the pages. They lie on the worn beige carpet between them, fluttering a little in the draft. Spark wants to be comforted, but not by Mum. And so she runs upstairs to her bedroom and hides under the duvet. She can't even cry.

Notebook 7

XXIV

Louis was nothing if not prompt. As the sun dipped below the horizon the following evening, he appeared in the gardens with his dogs. It was still light enough to see, although the torches that lined the paths at Marly had already been lit. The King came straight to the point, informing me of the "honor" he had bestowed on the Spaniard. I feigned surprise, just as Monsieur Bontemps had told me to do, and remarked that, although I should miss him greatly, I could see that it was a privilege for a Spanish-born subject to represent France in this way.

My reply impressed the King. In fact, he nodded several times. And it was only right that he approved. Under his tutelage, this innocent was learning the art of diplomacy — which is a kinder term than the art of lying, if less accurate, and, believe me, I know whereof I speak. Only the very young and the foolish say exactly what they think in all circumstances. The trick is never to lie to oneself.

When Louis informed me that I was to attend a dinner at Versailles at which members of the Royal Council for Finances would be present, and that I was to report back to him what was said, I did not need to feign surprise. Could I have refused? Although the question troubles me, I doubt that I could have, or not for long. In any case, my response was: "If you wish it, Sire."

"You will remember who said what and to whom. And you will report *only* to me. Not to Bontemps, not to Liselotte, not to Monsieur. Only *ever* to me. Be concise. A few lines will suffice. Use your ring to seal it."

For a sempervivens to chronicle the reign of the Sun King was one thing—this was quite another. Louis would have me eavesdrop on conversations, betray confidences, tell tales. Was this what Monsieur Bontemps had meant by learning to be robust, and to *endure*? I looked up at the King's shrewd, dark features, and when I saw how coolly he observed me struggling to contain my distaste, I felt diminished.

"Do you understand what I am asking of you, Jean-Pierre?"

"Yes, Sire."

I had glimpsed the future. What horse—or unicorn—does not object to that first taste of the cold, metallic bit between its teeth? But I reined in my emotions and the encroaching darkness helped conceal my dismay. Monsieur Bontemps, no doubt, would have applauded me. The Spaniard would not.

We continued to walk around the ornamental lake. When we reached the far side we stopped and sat on a stone bench. It was the King's habit to let his dogs leap into the water at this spot, and he tossed in a stick for them to fetch. A cacophony of barking and splashing echoed over the lake, although the dogs immediately lost sight of the stick. The guest pavilions that edged the water on either side were in darkness. Opposite, at the head of the lake, stood the Château of Marly. From this distance it looked like a plaything, a doll's house, its rows of windows twinkling with golden light.

The King was laughing at his dogs. "Pomme! Bonne! Nonne! You foolish beasts! Over there!"

The King threw another stick and there was more thrashing about. It occurred to me that if I were to become one of the King's creatures, I could at least try to turn the situation to my advantage.

"Sire, may I speak of a personal matter?"

The King turned to look at me, arching his eyebrows in surprise. "You are unusually *bold* this evening, Jean-Pierre." He smiled benignly. "Could it be Mademoiselle d'Alembert's current predicament that is troubling you?"

"Why, yes, Sire!" I said, recalling the cracked seal on her letter to me. "There are rumors at court, Sire—concerning Isabelle's father."

"I am aware of them."

"Isabelle's mother was not poisoned. She died of a fever."

"Is this fact or speculation?"

"I am assured it is true, Sire."

"And you have fallen for the charms of Mademoiselle d'Alembert?"

It was pointless to deny what he already knew. "Yes, Sire."

"Then you have as much reason for disbelieving the rumors as those who put them about have for insisting they have a basis in truth. Is that not so?"

The King told me that he would make his own enquiries.

In the event that the rumors proved justified, he could hardly be expected to protect a murderer. Did I have any idea who might have started the rumors? The Montclair family, for instance, he suggested. And, if so, did I have any idea what might have provoked the rift between the Montclairs and the d'Alemberts? Ah, he said, it was all *very* unfortunate. Louis was disingenuous—he knew perfectly well my role in the affair.

Presently the King stood up and called his dogs, who shook the water off their coats, splattering my stockings. Their master placed his hand on my shoulder and gripped it as we walked back to the château.

"Ridicule is a blunt instrument—and best avoided at court unless you have more experience of the world than you do. It was badly done, Jean-Pierre. And there were excellent reasons for desiring a union between those two families—"

"Sire," I said, deciding to risk the King's anger, "the Prince de Montclair does not love Mademoiselle d'Alembert, not as *I* love her!"

"Love! If love had had its way, half the crowns of Europe would have toppled by now. Wealth, power, the stability that comes from the alliance of great families: Are these to be thrown aside for an emotion that will wither like a decaying fruit? You are young and ruled by your passions—it will not always be thus, I assure you. You have inherited a unique legacy, Jean-Pierre! I advise you to fix your energies on something greater than a childish infatuation!"

His tone was severe. It was the King and not the man who stood before me now. I nodded weakly. "Yes, Sire."

We walked in silence, listening to the sound of our footsteps and the panting of dogs. Presently the King said: "I had the strangest dream last night. Versailles was made of glass and I, a giant, was eating it piece by piece, and as I ground the shards between my teeth, I bled, but still I ate. The realm of dreams is a fearful one, is it not? And not one that can be governed."

Louis asked me if I dreamed. I said that if I did I rarely remembered them. He replied that I was fortunate. When we reached the next torch, he came to a halt and leaned in toward me. Golden flames danced in his black eyes.

"I have, of late, been giving some thought to your future. With regard to your marital prospects I am *undecided*. As the son of a baron, you could expect to marry well. But it is not that that concerns me. No, what troubles me is the thought of a man who does not age marrying a woman who does." The King pulled a face as if he smelled sour milk. "It is not an agreeable thought."

I returned his gaze as evenly as I could manage, for I found his remark distasteful and disrespectful to the person I loved the most in all the world. And so I declared roundly: "I believe that I shall *always* love Isabelle d'Alembert, Sire."

"Then I must not contradict you," replied the Sun King. "Though you will allow me to remain unconvinced. You are too young to understand how time dims the brightest of passions." I did not believe him for an instant. Louis then undertook to look into the d'Alembert scandal while making no promise to intervene. In the meantime, he said, he would await my report *with interest*.

* * *

The King's veiled bargain was not lost on me: It was up to me to prove myself a reliable servant. I did what was asked of me. I did not, however, perform my task very well. To be the King's informant, to play false among respected men, filled me with shame. Yet if I did not do what was asked of me, the King might allow Isabelle and her father to sink in a tide of rumor.

As I knew little, then, of politics, and nothing of the Council for Finances, my attention was at first drawn to things of no interest whatsoever to the King. I noticed, for example, who plucked off his wig after a glass or two of wine; who grew tufts of hair in his ears; who allowed gravy to dribble down his chin. I sat between two garrulous men, one plump, one withered, who talked constantly over me, obliging me to sit back in my chair. They discussed the lamentable state of the French coffers after the War of the Reunion; they reflected on the question of the Palatine succession, and questioned if the King's deployment of the *dragonnades* against the Protestants was viewed unfavorably abroad. I nodded sagely, not knowing what else to do, which prompted my plump neighbor to ask—strictly, of course, between ourselves—if I had an opinion on the matter. He soon lost patience waiting for me to form a faltering reply, and went back to conversing with his stringy companion. Thereafter they ignored me. My one comforting thought was that no one would suspect such an embarrassingly inept and poorly informed fellow of being a spy.

The strain of remembering what had already been said,

while keeping track of the current topic of conversation, gave me a sick headache. I excused myself halfway through the evening, vomited in the corridor, and came back, green and trembling. My appearance gave rise to much merriment all around the table and there were suggestions of me being unable to take my drink. I did not contradict them.

When, finally, I returned to my room at one o'clock in the morning, I collapsed facedown and fully clothed on my bed and fell into a profound sleep. When I awoke, at dawn, I was dreaming that my two neighbors at the dinner were trying to awaken me. They were tapping their glasses with their knives, waiting impatiently for me to share my thoughts on the revocation of the Edict of Nantes.

I flung myself violently out of bed and stood, dazed and nauseous, in the middle of the room. But I could still hear the sound of knives tapping against glass. This puzzled me, and I stood very still, head to one side, listening. There it was again. I threw open the wooden shutters and, as I did so, a shower of gravel hit the window. A gardener stood down below in a large-brimmed hat. The bulky figure looked around to see if he were alone and craned up at me, removing his hat. I took a step backward in surprise. Then I came back to the window for a second look. It was the Spaniard, and he was gesturing for me to descend.

XXV

The Spaniard turned on his heels and walked toward the gardens as soon as he saw me appear. I understood that I was to follow him. He strode away at a brisk pace while I allowed a long gap to form between us. It had rained heavily overnight and my shoes and stockings became quickly sodden. With every step, as I crossed the wide parterres overlooked by the palace, I sensed rows of blank windows staring accusingly at my back. I sauntered along, yawning and stretching, trying to seem as if I were going for a stroll to clear my head. It was with relief that I reached the shelter of the groves. I guessed where the Spaniard was headed long before we got there, and soon we faced each other from opposite sides of the deserted Colonnades.

It was the first time I had returned to this *bosquet* since the night I had insulted the Prince de Montclair. The Colonnades seemed very different in that sunless dawn. Though the fountains were silent, the birds were in full voice. The Spaniard stood dwarfed by the towering marble columns that encircled us like a temple. When he opened his arms in greeting, I ran to him as if reenacting some great drama, my footsteps echoing across the stagelike space.

"Signor!" I cried. "I thought I might never see you again!"

"Ha! You thought I was no match for Monsieur Bontemps! As you can see, I am a man of parts." He seemed pleased with himself, full of life and energy. It made my heart glad. "Do you like my disguise?"

"I do! You make a convincing gardener! Does the King know you are in Versailles?"

"You think I would be skulking in the groves, dressed for digging cabbages if the King knew? No, and he would not be pleased if he knew my purpose!"

He drew me to him and thumped me on the back in the way he used to when—as I thought—we were pupil and teacher. Before releasing me, he planted a kiss on the top of my head where the rock had cracked my skull. We stood grinning at each other. The Spaniard looked thinner, and tired. Suddenly he pulled out a long blade from his belt. I wheeled around, searching for signs of an attacker, which made him laugh.

"The knife is for cutting bread! I'm as hungry as a horse!"

He offered me bread and cheese, which he pulled out of his pockets. I shook my head. He busied himself cutting off hunks and stuffing them into his mouth. "Forgive me," he said, between mouthfuls. "I have to eat. My last meal was in Boulogne—"

I watched as he chewed and gathered his thoughts. Finally he spoke, laying out his words carefully between us like a gift.

"Jean-Pierre, I propose that you leave the court of the Sun King and accompany me to England."

"*England!*"

"Yes. I have procured a house, set in marshland, far from prying eyes. The King will not wish you to leave, but his spies will not find us there. It can be our sanctuary."

"But why do we—why do *I*—need a sanctuary?"

"On the day your father died I swore to watch over you until you could take care of yourself. I begin to doubt that I have served you well."

"But you *have*, Signor! What more could my father have asked of you? I am safe and want for nothing—"

"Juan Pedro wandered the world and accrued much wisdom before he settled at the Spanish court. His character had *formed*. Juan Pedro was his own man. He could not be tamed and shaped—"

"Are you saying that I can?"

"You are young, Jean-Pierre, and Versailles is unlike the rest of the world—"

"I am not as foolish as you think, Signor!"

"Of course you are not foolish! Nevertheless, I question my own judgement in bringing you here. I fear you will be viewed as an asset, a possession—not, perhaps, as valuable as a prince of the blood who could be married off to foreign royalty, but more prized than a stud horse, or a portrait painter. The Sun King will doubtless find a use for a sempervivens, though, like wine, you will need to mature to be of value."

I considered telling the Spaniard what I had been obliged to do only the previous evening, but my pride would not permit it. He asked how I thought the King would react if I announced that it was my intention to leave Versailles for England.

"I am sure that the King would permit me to leave if I wished to do so."

"Would he?"

Misty rain fell silently onto the grove. A few feet away, a

bright-eyed crow waited patiently, head cocked to one side, eyeing the crumbs of bread at our feet. I picked up a stone and aimed at its head. It took flight, cawing, and flapped its black wings, leaving the Colonnades more silent than before. A year ago, in the cave, the Spaniard had told me that I was the master of my own destiny. And in truth, there, in the cave, I *had* been free. Was that still the case? I might not admit as much to the Spaniard, but the position of King's unicorn was unique, and the difference between protector and jailer was hard to gauge. I changed the subject.

"The day Monsieur Bontemps permitted us to say good-bye, you did not seem yourself—"

"No, as you say, I was not myself. I had been obliged to convince certain *officials* that I was not in Versailles as a tool of the Spanish court. I was released, but it is clear that the King is suspicious of my motives and of my influence on you. It therefore suits him to remove me from court. It is, I suppose, possible that there is a position for me at the Swedish court, but somehow I doubt it."

"Did they hurt you, Signor?"

"Very little. I got away lightly."

I remembered how the Spaniard's clothes had smelled that day. So I had not imagined it. I asked him how he had returned here.

"That was *not* difficult. I was given a military escort to Boulogne, where I was put on board a frigate. Once we had set sail, I simply bribed the captain to return to port."

"And you came back for me," I said.

"I did. I came back because here at court I fear you will be pruned into shape like every other plant in the Sun King's garden. Juan Pedro would not have wished this for his son, and I should have foreseen it at the start. I have returned to make amends while I can and to take you with me to England."

Despite my teacher's generous motives, and our mutual regard, I felt a swell of anger. Juan Pedro. My father. The Spaniard. The King. Did *I* not have a say in my own destiny? So now I should abandon Isabelle and leave for *England*! And for what reason? Versailles was at the center of all things— why would I prefer to spend my days in a freezing marsh in a foreign country? I recalled what Monsieur Bontemps had said to me: *To be cast out into the wilderness, away from the protection of the King, is not something I would wish for you.*

"So you advise me to live in exile away from everything and everyone I have ever known?"

"Yes. In order to become your own man."

"I *am* my own man!"

"Is that true? Do you not live your life in the Sun King's shadow?"

"No more than anyone else at court!"

"Then perhaps Versailles is not a generous soil in which to grow—"

"I am not a plant, Signor! And how could you think that I would desert Isabelle?"

"Surely you have the wit to see that there is so much more at stake than some *youthful infatuation*—"

The Spaniard and the King, it seemed, were in accord on one thing at least. I said coolly: "I will not go to England with you."

I started to walk away, and when the Spaniard begged me to stop and listen to what he had to say, I ignored his pleas, obliging him to hurry behind me.

"You are a sempervivens! Juan Pedro wrote of the heartbreak of watching wives and children die. It is not to be underestimated. Forget Isabelle—there will be *others*!"

I swung around in fury. "There will not be others! I am not too young to understand what love is. You do not *choose* whom you love!"

"Jean-Pierre, I did not mean to belittle what you feel—"

"You cannot even tell me with certainty that I *am* a sempervivens! I am grateful for everything you have done for me, Signor, but I assure you that I shall *not* be accompanying you to England. You say you fear that the King desires to bend me to his will, but do not *you* do precisely the same?"

We were close to the entrance. When I walked on the Spaniard did not follow. On leaving the Colonnades I saw a Swiss Guard headed toward me. I immediately stepped back inside the grove to warn the Spaniard, pressing my finger to my lips.

"I sail for England from Calais on the nineteenth," he hissed. "I shall wait for you there, should you change your mind."

I shook my head. "Safe journey, Signor."

His stricken expression was hard to witness. When the Swiss Guard entered the grove a moment later I engaged him in conversation, allowing the Spaniard to flee the palace like a common thief.

XXVI

In the following days I could settle to nothing, and prowled around the palace like a dog whose master has died. I missed Isabelle. I missed my father. I missed the Spaniard and felt remorse over how I had behaved. Even Liselotte, who had shown me so much kindness, kept her distance on account of my involvement with the d'Alembert family. I also dreaded my next audience with the King.

Doubt gnawed at me and I found myself constantly justifying my actions. I was *not* weak-minded. If I had agreed to act as the King's informer, it was purely for Isabelle's sake. On another occasion I might well refuse. Besides, how would living in an English marsh be of benefit to me? What could I learn there? How to harvest reeds? Make baskets? Nevertheless, the date of the Spaniard's departure from Calais, which was two days' ride from Versailles, was firmly fixed in my memory. If I were to change my mind about going with him, the evening of the sixteenth would be my last chance to depart.

On the fifteenth, Liselotte's valet woke me shortly after daybreak. He was on friendly terms with the Comte d'Alembert's valet, who had told him, not ten minutes previously, some news he thought I ought to hear. My heart leapt, and I asked if Isabelle had returned to Versailles with her aunt. She had not. However, de La Reynie himself, head of the Paris Police (it was he who had led the investigation into the Affair of the Poisons), had visited the d'Alembert residence during the night. He had come to question the Comte d'Alembert in connection with the death of his late wife and the sworn testimony of a former maid. The imminent arrest of Isabelle's father seemed likely. I immediately rose and dressed. Rather than sit patiently and wait for events to unfold, I would warn Isabelle and offer her what support I could.

Rambouillet was a morning's hard ride from Versailles. I invented an urgent errand that Monsieur required me to perform, and left the royal stables astride a sturdy white stallion with soulful eyes and a calm temperament. Save for allowing the steaming horse to rest awhile at Le Mesnil-Saint-Denis, I rode without pause, skirting around the forest of Rambouillet, which blazed with autumn tints. While the sun was still high in the sky, I caught sight of the neat, symmetrical house that sat in dignified solitude surrounded by baaing sheep. I galloped directly to the front door and dismounted. There, where I had suffered such humiliation at the hands of Isabelle's aunt, I struck the heavy door with both fists. On the other side, someone rattled open a series of bolts. The face of a weasel-like boy peered out at me.

"I must see Mademoiselle d'Alembert," I declared.

"She is not home, Monsieur."

"Then her aunt—"

"Madame is not at home, Monsieur."

I did not believe him for an instant. I gave the door a push, causing the lad to take a large step backward.

"It is *vital* that I see her. Be so good as to fetch her at once!"

"I am sorry, Monsieur, I cannot—"

I grabbed the wretched footman by the collar and shook him: "Tell me where I can find Mademoiselle d'Alembert!"

A valet, an older man whom I recognized from my previous visit, appeared. He informed me, courteously, that he was under strict orders to refuse me admittance. The valet and the footman then each took an arm and forced me back down the front steps.

"The Comte d'Alembert is about to be arrested for murder," I cried. This shocking news had a dramatic effect on the valet, who immediately let go of me. The agitated footman, however, continued to pull me toward my horse until the older man barked at him to stop.

"I apologize, Monsieur, the boy has let his nerves get the better of him. Is the Comte d'Alembert truly to be arrested?"

"Alas, I believe he will be," I replied.

"That is ill news, Monsieur, although I still cannot allow you to enter. Madame has forbidden it. However, I will say this: Had you entered, you would not, in any case, have found what you seek."

"Don't speak in riddles!" I said. "What do you mean?"

"My mistress and Mademoiselle d'Alembert left for Versailles early this morning in the carriage of the King's *valet de chambre*—"

"Monsieur Bontemps!"

"Yes, Monsieur. The King has summoned them to court."

I stared at the valet, whose confusion reflected my own.

Each time I intended to take hold of the reins of my life, it seemed that they were torn from my grasp, leaving me struggling to retain my balance and bewildered by the turn of events. The valet asked me what all this might mean for the d'Alembert family. I did not know how to answer him.

An Interesting Footnote

Once, in playful mood at a dull party, John Stone happened to find himself sitting next to an eminent historian who was more interested in writing in his small notebook than talking to him.

"If I were to tell you," he said to the generously bearded American, "that I am three hundred and fifty years old and was intimately acquainted with some of the people you've spent your life studying, would you be keener to strike up a conversation with me?"

The professor pushed his glasses back onto the bridge of his nose and smiled a lopsided smile, eyeing John Stone in that dry way perfected by certain academics. Nevertheless, a glint of interest registered behind his thick lenses.

"So," he replied in a measured tone, "you present me with an interesting proposition. How might you, a freak of nature, so to speak, be of use to me, a scholar of history?"

A *freak of nature!* The term amused John Stone very much: It wasn't so very far from the truth.

"Let us assume that you have proved to me that you are the genuine article—which would be difficult to do— what could *you* tell me that I could not discover in other ways? And, more importantly, how *reliable* would your testimony be?"

The historian went on to say that firsthand accounts of history—memoirs, letters, and the like—were interesting but unreliable. An individual, he explained, would rarely be in the right place at the right time, or, if he were, he would be unlikely to be skilled in reading situations or reporting them accurately. Most importantly, his memories would be selective, incomplete, and certainly not to be trusted.

"So," said John Stone in reply, "I wouldn't be much use to you at all?"

"In truth, no. You would make an interesting footnote."

John Stone commented that there are probably worse epitaphs.

The historian was beginning to enjoy the game. "But if it were me, I shouldn't go around talking about myself to untrustworthy fellows at parties," he said. "Longevity is a holy grail. If the truth got out, you'd be dissected metaphorically by the press, and, likely as not, literally by medical researchers and every last billionaire who wanted to prolong his miserable existence."

"But the historians would leave me alone."

"Oh, yes. You wouldn't have to worry about us."

John Stone is determined to give Edward de Souza an agreeable evening before he tells him what he plans to do. Accordingly, they have seen a revival of a Noël Coward play (not to John Stone's taste, but this is for Edward), and they have feasted on oysters, a gigot of lamb, and champagne sorbet in his favorite French restaurant in Monmouth Street. John Stone has even agreed—just for once—to reminisce about Louis XIV over a shot of *eau de vie de mirabelle*.

"How I envy you, John: to have witnessed the Sun King

progressing down the Hall of Mirrors at Versailles," says Edward. "What a spectacle it must have been—"

"Pure theatre," agrees John Stone. "Actually, it's the sounds that I remember best of all. That slow beat of his cane, then the hushed whispers and the rustle of silk as everyone bowed and curtseyed. It was like the tide coming in."

"Extraordinary—"

"I know that I am a fortunate fellow. My life has been extraordinary, even though I am not an extraordinary man."

Edward is indignant. "You *are* extraordinary, John. Your Spaniard was right: Versailles trained you too well to be reserved and modest."

"Why, thank you, Edward."

"So. Are you going to tell me what's going on? Thank you for the play, and for this delicious dinner, but if it's all the same to you, I'd prefer not to be kept in suspense any longer. You never told me the outcome of Thérèse's last communication."

"You lawyers are too clever for your own good."

John Stone would have liked to walk and talk while strolling through the city streets but, anxious in case he suffers another attack, he instructs his driver to take them to Edward's offices. Bright moonlight streams through the open window. He asks Edward not to switch on the lights. They breathe in the night air. John Stone sits on the big office desk, legs slowly swinging, while Edward perches on the windowsill. A smell of lemons rises up from the recently washed floor. How he wishes this evening were over. Below, in Lincoln's Inn Fields, a couple of drunks sing in unison, their slurred words echoing across the square. Long ago, when this was still his London house, he would look out at Saint Paul's from here; he recalls seeing forks of summer lightning strike the great dome. Everything passes. John Stone sighs deeply, reaches into his jacket pocket, and places two envelopes in Edward's hands.

"What are these? Should I switch on the light?"

"No. One is a sealed letter that should be delivered to Stella Park on her twenty-first birthday. You will understand why momentarily. The other is for you: It contains the ciphers for my journals and those written by my father. As you seem so taken by the Sun King, they'll allow you to become intimately acquainted with him. I suggest that you move them out of Stowney House before the damp from the marshes slowly destroys them."

"Why are you giving them to me now?"

Recent events, John Stone explains, have driven him to make a difficult decision. He tells Edward that it transpires, after all this time, that he is, in fact, Spark's father. He explains how, as the child of two sempervivens parents, Spark will almost certainly be sempervivens herself.

"That is *astonishing* news! Wonderful news! Another sempervivens! But why did you not tell me straightaway?"

"Because I wanted Spark to be the first to hear. Alas, this cannot now be. Henceforth, I want you to look after Spark's interests as well as my own. Will you do that for me?"

John Stone has to wait for a response. Edward has few character faults and being impulsive isn't one of them.

"Given the potential for conflict of interests, I would normally advise against such a thing—but these are unique circumstances. Yes, you can count on me: I am happy to act for both father and daughter—"

"Thank you, Edward. There are complications, however."

"There are always complications, John."

John Stone tells him about the fight in the marshes and his disastrous visit to Mrs. Park. "I doubt that either Spark or her adoptive mother will be willing to see me again. The adoptive mother is a difficult woman, but she holds my respect. Her love for Spark and her son is fierce, and I do not know when—or if—she intends to tell Spark the truth about her parentage. I will not force the issue. As for Spark, I dread to think what her opinion now is of the inhabitants of Stowney House. She left with the attitude of one determined never to return."

When he describes his conversation with Mrs. Park, Edward puts his head in his heads. "John, you should have asked for my help sooner."

"I'm sure you're right. . . . Spark can read the notebooks I've written for her when she is twenty-one. I've described that period of my life that I believe will be most useful to her, although I have avoided acknowledging our relationship. If my daughter is still ignorant of her adoption at that stage, I would ask you to break the truth to her as gently as you can. In the fullness of time you can also give her the ciphers for the journals—both mine and Juan Pedro's."

"Surely it should be you who tells Spark that she is your daughter, face-to-face? You can afford to wait a little. Can't you?"

John Stone does not answer, but looks up at the familiar figure of his lawyer, silhouetted against the sky, head bent attentively toward him. John Stone wishes he could be spared this task, wishes that someone could intercede on his behalf, but there is no one, and this is no time for procrastination. "There is another matter, Edward. This nervous disease—the same, apparently, that afflicted Thérèse and my own father—has tightened its grip on me. I no longer feel in control of myself: It seems that I have a new master. The attacks are no longer infrequent but happen several times a day, and fatigue and distress aggravate them."

Edward nods his head sadly. "I thought that was why you left your seat in the middle of the play. . . . Might you not now reconsider—"

"No, Edward. I will *not* see a doctor."

"But, John, now more than ever! You have a child!"

"Precisely! How could I take that risk?" There is anger in John Stone's voice. "Besides, I am past repair. Doctors could do nothing for me now."

"I apologize. It is only that—"

John Stone raises his hand. "I understand."

It is important to be concise for both their sakes. As every field nurse knows, better to rip off a wound dressing in one go than peel it off in agonizing stages. John Stone explains that, as the time has now come when he can no longer conceal his illness, he has made the decision to retreat from Stowney House. He is too fond of Martha and Jacob to allow them to witness a slow and distressing death. Nor does he wish Spark to get to know this diminished version of the man he was, for very soon he will be of no use to her. His journals will paint the best portrait of her father. Tomorrow he will return to Stowney House in order to make his final preparations to leave. It is best if Martha and Jacob believe that he is departing on a long trip—to America, perhaps. That way, by the time they learn the truth, they will at least have started to learn to do without him.

"You underestimate them."

"I did not come here to ask for advice, Edward."

"No."

When he gives him the word, Edward will need to put into place the contingency plans they discussed when drawing up his will. Martha and Jacob must be able to continue their lives at Stowney House in full security and for as long as they wish it. He hears Edward's deep-drawn breath and watches the line of his shoulders rise toward his neck.

"Where will you go, John?"

"I will stay in a safe house. My client has arranged it. The location will remain a secret. I can assure you that I will be well cared for until the end. I shall not be returning to London."

Edward turns his head away and looks out toward the rooftops of Lincoln's Inn Fields. "Are you saying that *this* is the last time I shall see you?"

"I'd prefer your last memory of me to be of a man who had mastery of himself. Until I leave, you can still reach me by phone."

How calm he is as he says these words; John Stone knows that his emotions will catch up with him later, in the long wakefulness of the night. As his lawyer does not reply, John Stone bows his head and sits patiently, listening to the ancient building creak and, presently, the hall clock strike the hour. There is a pale flutter, like ghostly wings, as Edward brings a white handkerchief to his face.

"The one thing I always thought I could be certain of was that you would outlive me—"

"I know."

"Will you tell me before you go? It would be very hard to be kept in the dark."

"Given the nature of the arrangements, I cannot promise. But I will try."

They walk to John Stone's car. Edward, finding no words, stands, forlorn, on the curb. John Stone embraces him and finds that his cheek is wet with Edward's tears. "You have been the best of Friends," John Stone tells him. "Prepare the way for Spark. I have told my client about her but I need you to help keep her safe. She has the perspective of youth. She will make mistakes. Can I rely on you?"

"Always."

As the car moves off, John Stone opens his window and sees that Edward has started to run. The soles of his polished brogues clatter over the paving stones, as the lawyer runs fast enough to keep pace with the car. "Wherever you are going,

John Stone," he shouts, "your friends will remember—"
Alas, John Stone does not catch the rest of his words for
the car accelerates, leaving Edward still powering along the
pavement. They turn a corner and his Friend vanishes from
sight. It is done. "Adieu," says John Stone into the night.

Such Round, Blue Eyes

Spark cranes her head and shoulders away from Mum and fixes her gaze on the stain on the wall left by a piece of Blu-Tack. It's a hard thing to find out you're not who you thought you were. Mum sits jammed up against her on the narrow bed, the wind whistling through the open window and the curtains swaying. She refuses to let go of Spark's hand. Outside tires hiss over wet tarmac and sparrows chirp in next door's hedge, familiar sounds in a world that is no longer the same.

Mum has kept repeating the same phrase: "Nothing's changed. You were my daughter before you were even born and you still are."

Spark doesn't trust herself to respond when what Mum says is plainly untrue. Something *has* changed. From this day forward, Mum is not her mum, Dad was not her dad. Only now, when she's almost eighteen, is she told she's the daughter of a dead mother and a mystery father. How dare they keep such a thing from her? Doesn't a child have a right to know the truth? Spark feels empty, disconnected.

Mum breaks a long silence. "This mattress is on its last legs. We should get you a new one—"

"Why didn't you tell me from the start?"

"I wasn't going to tell you at all—"

"So you were happy about me living a lie!"

"It wasn't like that! We were your parents—*that* wasn't a

lie. If you didn't need to know, what was the point of upsetting you? That's how I looked at it. And it's what your dad thought too. . . . We always said that if we were going to tell you we'd wait until you could understand."

"Dad didn't want to tell me either?"

"He didn't see the sense in it. He said you were his and that was enough." Spark closes her eyes tight shut. She refuses to cry. "But what with the hospital wanting to do DNA tests on you, and one thing and another . . . I couldn't risk someone telling you before I did."

"Who was she—my *real* mother?" Spark sees the hurt in Mum's eyes and at that instant she's glad.

"Your *birth* mother was your dad's landlady: He rented his restaurant from her in Suffolk. She wasn't young, but she turned heads. We never knew the details, but she'd got herself into trouble: She wasn't the first and she won't be the last to have picked the wrong man. Her name was Thérèse—"

"*Thérèse* . . . like my middle name?"

"Yes. We thought Stella Theresa Park had a good ring to it."

"What was she like?"

"I didn't know her to talk to—your dad knew her better than I did."

"And did she say who my father was?"

"No. Perhaps she never told him, or perhaps he didn't stand by her when it came to it. It's not easy being a woman."

Mum announces she is going to mash a pot of tea, and soon Spark can smell cigarette smoke drifting up from the back doorstep. Spark joins her, and they both sit on the hard concrete, nursing mugs of tea. In dribs and drabs, Mum answers Spark's questions until she can piece together how she came to be Stella Theresa Park: Mum's inability to have any more children after Dan's difficult birth; Dad arriving back from the restaurant one night with a strange proposal from the woman who owned the property; Mum's initial reluctance; Dad persuading her it would do everyone a good turn; the offer of a rent-free cottage in the marshes; the private legal arrangement. Mum tentatively puts her arm around Spark's shoulders and Spark doesn't push her away.

"You weren't born in a hospital—she didn't trust doctors. I remember that—she had a real mania about not letting a doctor touch her. She gave birth in the flat that she owned above the restaurant. No pain relief—imagine that! Well, I can. . . . Thankfully there weren't any complications. She kept you for five days, then you were swaddled in blankets and your dad brought you downstairs. The restaurant was full of holidaymakers downing roast dinners, and there I was, sitting at a corner table, our Dan wailing for ice cream, my nerves in shreds in case she changed her mind at the last minute. And then your dad appeared through the swing doors, a little bundle in his arms, a tiny face peeping out of the shawl. Such round, blue eyes you had! I would have gone upstairs to say something to her, to thank her, to say I'd take care of you like you was my own, but your dad said it was best not to. I don't know where she got the strength to give you up. I couldn't have done it. You were a beautiful baby. Anyway, the next day she was gone. She died a couple of years later. Your dad reckoned she knew she was on the way out even while she was expecting you. He said that her hands used to shake."

"Oh." Spark doesn't know how to react. She can hardly grieve for someone whose existence she has only just found out about.

"I'm sorry," says Mum. "That was a bit abrupt. I didn't mean to sound heartless. I only met her a couple of times."

"Do I look like her?"

"Very like. At least now you don't have to worry about taking after me, eh?"

"Don't be daft, Mum—"

"Sometimes I think about Thérèse and everything I took away from her. All the happiness you've given me—"

"It was her choice to give me away—"

"And her loss was my gain."

An Unexpected Visit

Life goes on. Dan is told. He tries to hide his shock and tells Spark it makes no difference to him. There are conversations behind closed doors. One surprising thing in all of this is that there is a small part of Spark that isn't actually surprised. It is as if, over the years, certain attitudes, certain carelessly phrased remarks or the exchange of meaningful looks, particular differences in physique and temperament, have all accumulated, and paved the way, inescapably, to this moment. In a sense, this disclosure has been seeded with a lifetime of clues.

Each morning Spark wakes up, vaguely aware that something is wrong, and then she remembers. She does her best to keep herself occupied: reads, goes with Dan to the hospital, does her chores, fails to find a holiday job so late in the season. Mum has been patient, supportive, and understanding; the irony of this role reversal hasn't been lost on either of them. There has been cheering news at the hospital: Somehow Dan has already found his way to the top of a waiting list. He's been fitted out with a vest studded with electrodes, which will allow the consultant to pinpoint the precise area in the heart muscle that has been causing the problem. The consultant is now confident of being able to perform a surgical procedure that could permanently correct Dan's arrhythmia.

One morning a letter arrives with an Italian stamp on

it. Mum scrutinizes it and hands it to Spark. "For you. It'll be from Ludo," she says. "Feels like a postcard." Seeing his handwriting makes Spark's heart thump, which irritates her. "He seems a nice enough lad," comments Mum, "though it's a shame he couldn't have stayed around a bit longer to keep our Dan company."

"Yes," replies Spark, noncommittally, and disappears up to her room to open it. Her letter does, indeed, contain a postcard. It is a sweeping view of Florence from the Piazzale Michelangelo, and portrays a green river and a mosaic of terra-cotta roofs. Dominating the cityscape is a great dome. *This whole town is incredible*, Ludo writes. *It's like a museum. You should see it. Dan called to tell me what's been happening. I hope you're okay—it can't have been easy. When I get back it would be great to talk.*

Spark texts to ask how long he's planning to stay in Italy. It will be a while, she says, before she gets used to the idea that she's adopted. That word: "adopted"—it's the first time Spark has used it about herself. *I'm adopted.* It feels like trying on a style of shoes she'd never think of wearing and having to buy them whether she likes them or not. Ludo texts back immediately: I get back to the UK next week. I'll be staying in London for a few days. Want to meet up? Maybe Wednesday? Hope you've forgiven me for Stowney House.

Has she? Spark resists texting back *yes*. Their trip to Suffolk—the fight, Ludo's confession in the rest stop, the awkward drive home—seems such a long time ago. As for his invitation, she's not going to read more into it than there actually is. Not this time. Ludo probably feels sorry for her.

Maybe a little guilty. *If* she decides to meet him, she could tell him that she's been to see the painting he told her about in the National Portrait Gallery—although perhaps she ought not to encourage him. Any similarity between those strokes of oil paint and the real John Stone is a fluke, just one of those things, a case of the mind struggling to make sense of random patterns. All the same, she recalls the shock of noticing that familiar face looking out at her from a crowd of Victorian social reformers.

Ludo acted like an idiot that day, but Spark supposes that she has—sort of—forgiven him. Which is more than she can say for the inhabitants of Stowney House. When she thinks about how they behaved that day—John Stone, above all—it makes her angry. And it makes her sad.

One evening, after taking a long shower, Spark lies on her stomach in her pajamas, idly flicking through the help wanted section of the free newspaper. Mum is downstairs watching a film, but right now Spark prefers the privacy of her own room. She is still consumed by a revelation that is too big to comprehend. Who is Stella Theresa Park? For now, all Spark knows for sure is that her identity is less a fact than a process.

As she circles an advert for hourly paid staff at a local hotel, a sound makes her start. There is a loud, metallic *chink* followed by a high-pitched vibrating sound. A small pebble has hit a lamp and is now spinning on top of the chest of drawers. Ludo has fixed her window so that it actually opens, and now, as she maneuvers herself off her bed and stands with her cheek against the patterned curtains, a second pebble whizzes through it and lands on her bed.

"Hey!" she calls, sticking her head through the gap.

The kitchen light is not on, so that the backyard is dark except for the small amount of light spilling out from her own window. It takes a moment for her eyes to adjust.

"*Oh!*" she gasps. "It's you!"

The pale, coarse hair that grows vertically from a weather-beaten scalp belongs to Jacob. Spark becomes aware that she has brought her hands to her face and lowers them. They regard each other.

"What are you doing here?" she whispers. Like Jacob, Spark instinctively feels that this is a private matter.

He points first at her and afterward at the back door.

"You want me to come down?"

Jacob nods.

"Are you okay, love?" Mum calls from the sitting room as Spark bounds down the stairs two steps at a time, pulling her dressing gown on as she does so.

Spark puts her head round the door. "Just putting the kettle on! Do you want anything?"

"No," comes the reply. "You're all right."

Closing the kitchen door behind her with a quiet *click*, Spark pulls the light switch and opens the back door. The fluorescent light flickers on, blue and cold, illuminating the mean concrete patio, with its hanging baskets and half-empty bag of potting compost shoved into a corner. The drain smells like it needs unblocking. In the shadows, Jacob is standing to a sort of attention. She hopes he doesn't have an axe hidden beneath his jacket. He is clean-shaven and, bizarrely, wears an old-fashioned dark suit and thin tie. She can't make out the color. From the sitting room come waves of canned laughter.

"Hello, Jacob. This is . . . unexpected."

"I have come a long way to talk with you —"

"It *is* a long way. How did you know where to find me?"

Jacob pulls out a carefully folded piece of paper from his top pocket. "I have your letter, and a tongue in my head."

Disconcerted, she realizes it is her letter to John Stone. If a panther had strolled into their backyard it would feel no odder than to see Jacob here. Spark never imagined him having an existence outside the grounds of Stowney House.

"I'm not a madman —"

"I didn't say you were —"

"You didn't need to."

"Why have you come, Jacob? What do you want?"

"To give you something. And to ask you something."

All at once Jacob leans in toward her. There's the smell of pipe tobacco on him. He reaches out and grabs her left hand, holding it in his own dry, calloused palms. The same hands that tried to throttle Ludo. Spark instinctively pulls back, but Jacob presses something into the flesh of her palm, folding her fingers over something small and solid that has been wrapped in cloth. He holds her fist tightly between his two hands so that the object digs into her bones. It is as if he is transferring ownership. He lets go.

"It is a gift."

"A gift?"

Jacob nods. "I made it for you."

"Did Mr. Stone send you?"

"You think I have no will of my own?"

"I didn't mean that—"

"John doesn't know I am here."

"Well. Thank you for my gift. I'm sure I've done nothing to deserve it."

"I do not blame you for what happened—"

Spark is at a loss to know where to begin replying to this. "*You* don't blame *me*?"

"Your arrival at Stowney House. It put things out of kilter. It changed things that can't be put right without you. Will you come back?"

"*Me?* Why would I go back? Mr. Stone will have to find someone else to help him. It shouldn't be difficult."

Jacob, who seems to have anticipated this, pauses to consider his response. He reaches deep into his pocket and takes out his pipe, then, thinking the better of it, puts it back again. "There's things you should know—"

"Like what?"

"It's not my place to say."

"So I should come back to Stowney House to find out? After what happened, do you think that's likely? *You* never wanted me there in the first place—"

"Since you left John has not been himself."

"Is that what you came here to tell me? That Mr. Stone isn't feeling himself?"

"Yes."

"Well, I'm sorry you've had to come all this way, but my answer's no. I'm not going back."

"You say that because you do not know. If you knew, you would give a different answer."

"Except you're not going to tell me what I don't know—"

"I *can* ask you to reply to the letter that John left for you here."

"What letter? Mr. Stone was never here—"

"He was. We know that the lady of the house grew angry with him and drove him away."

"The *lady of the house? Mum?* Mum drove Mr. Stone away?"

Jacob nods emphatically and his eyes shine. Spark finds his physical presence unnerving: There's something feral about him. Jacob doesn't belong in a suit and he doesn't belong in their backyard. Strangely, though, Spark believes what he says.

"If Mr. Stone *were* here, Mum would have told me."

Jacob's pale eyes, which have been fixing her intently, dart away from Spark and toward the kitchen. In one fluid movement he turns and levers himself up and over the wall with his wiry arms. As his shoes scrape over the top edge, he glances back at her and nods. Then he jumps down and lands quietly in the back alley. A moment later Mum enters the kitchen. If it weren't for Jacob's "gift" in her dressing gown pocket, Spark might wonder if she'd imagined his visit. Jacob must have acute hearing: She didn't hear anything.

Mum stands on the back step and yawns. "You didn't miss much. I don't why I carried on watching it." She rests her pointy chin on Spark's shoulder. "What a beautiful night."

There's a small patch of sky visible from their yard. Spark looks up: It is thick with stars. Even that fleeting glimpse of the infinite vastness of things is enough to take the edge off her anger. Out in the street there's the *put-put-put* of an old motorbike receding into the distance, and she wonders if that was how Jacob got here. "You should have told me that John Stone came to see you," she says.

Mum removes her chin from Spark's shoulder. "Who told you?"

"I just had a visitor from Stowney House. He wanted to know why I hadn't replied to John Stone's letter."

Mum is unrepentant, still furious that John Stone felt he had the right to invade her family home. She describes their encounter.

"*John Stone* knew that I was adopted!" Spark is outraged. "*He* knew I was adopted when *I* didn't!" Mum agrees to give Spark his letter but warns her that she's having nothing to do with him. The last thing she wants is his charity. His *charity* has cost her enough already. Spark makes no comment. "Give me the letter, Mum."

"All right," she replies, going back into the house to fetch it, "though I wish I'd burned it. Our family's business has got nothing to do with him."

Back in her room, Spark holds John Stone's letter in one hand and Jacob's gift in the other. She unwraps Jacob's gift first. There are two flat wooden ovals in hardwood, one pale as straw, the other the color of dark ale. She turns the object round and round between her thumbs and gazes at it in wonder. The ovals can slide apart or lock seamlessly into each other like a puzzle that has been solved. Jacob has carved a face, in relief, on each wooden disc. The first face belongs to John Stone; the second belongs to her. Never would she have supposed Jacob to be capable of such artistry. They are like the carvings you see in churches and cathedrals. How can he have recalled every nuance of her face? Where did he learn how to do this? It is beautiful work, yet uncanny at the same time. What is the significance of this double portrait? Is it meant to be a souvenir of her stay at Stowney House, or to lure her back? Some hope of that.

Spark folds it back inside the felt square and sits listening to the hot water pipes gurgling. Dan has come home. She can hear him brushing his teeth in the bathroom. Downstairs Mum is locking up before going up to bed. But Spark is wide-awake.

Now she tears open the envelope. John Stone's letter is short—less a letter than a note—and all it says is that he has left some notebooks in safekeeping at his lawyer's offices in London. He believes that the notebooks would be of *great interest* to her. If she wishes to read them, his lawyer can arrange for her to do so. It strikes her that if John Stone knew Thérèse, it might have been his intention, all along, to talk to Spark about her birth mother. Could that be what this is all about? Is that why Jacob was encouraging her to return to Stowney House? But if it was, why would *he* care?

Dan rattles her door handle and shouts good night through her bedroom door. "Night, Dan!" she calls back.

How can she *not* read his notebooks? She berated Ludo, that day, for killing two birds with one stone, but perhaps she could do the same: accept his invitation to meet up in London and arrange to read John Stone's notebooks on the same day.

Notebook 8
XXVII

I came early to the Hall of Mirrors and positioned myself next to the Salon de la Paix in order to see everyone who entered. I paced up and down impatiently, waiting for the d'Alemberts to appear, my task being made more difficult by the unusually large crowd that had gathered that morning. I became agitated and started to doubt the information that their valet had passed on to me in Rambouillet. When, promptly at ten, the crowd grew silent and I heard the beat of the King's cane, I pushed forward in an attempt to gain a good position, but found myself enclosed in a dense mass of wigs and fans. I stood on tiptoe and gathered from the whispers around me that the agreeable-looking man at the King's side, who had such an assured air about him, was none other than Nicolas-Gabriel de La Reynie, chief of the Paris Police. I think the King's physician stood behind them, although he was of small stature and I could see only the top of his curly wig. I saw that the King was speaking, and that he held a letter in his hand, which he tapped repeatedly for emphasis. Intrigued, I strained to distinguish his words, but to no avail. Before moving on, the King seemed to make a show of presenting the letter to La Reynie.

As the King walked briskly in the direction of the royal chapel, those who had stood within earshot of him eagerly described what had taken place to their neighbors, so that the news of it spread like a wave across the Hall of Mirrors. I spotted the twin daughters of the King's physician, whom I knew well, and ran over to them. "What did the King say?" I demanded. "What was in the letter?" They reprimanded me for my abruptness but told me all the same. The letter was written by the late Madame d'Alembert's physician shortly after her death. In it he described the symptoms of her final illness, symptoms that, according to the twins' father, were not consistent with poisoning. Thus the letter proved (here they spoke in unison, as was their way) that the rumors about the Comte d'Alembert were entirely *false*.

Instantly, the burden of guilt, which had pressed down on me for days, lifted, and a smile broke out on my face. So the Sun King *had* kept his side of the bargain.

"Look," said one of the twins, "isn't that d'Alembert?"

I swung around, and there, in the center of the room, reflected in one of the giant mirrors, I saw her. *"Isabelle!"* I cried out. What joy that familiar profile provoked in me! She walked behind the royal party and between her father and aunt, both of whom were acknowledging the greetings of those who had, until now, been perfectly happy to believe the scandalous rumors about the Comte. Bringing up the rear of the procession were the Montclair family. After spreading such a damaging rumor, I supposed that they desired to put themselves in a good light. I noted that Monsieur Bontemps (he acknowledged me from afar with a slight nod of his head) was also in attendance.

Resolving to wait for Isabelle to reappear after attending mass with the King (I wanted her, at the very least, to see my face), I installed myself in a quiet corner. There I listened to the soothing sound of heels and conversations echoing down the corridors of the palace. My daydreams were interrupted by a footman. Monsieur Bontemps had sent him to remind me of my ten-o'clock appointment. To check for messages from the King had, indeed, been the last thing on my mind. Now I hurried back to Monsieur's apartment in order to be outside the royal chapel when mass finished.

On reaching the King's study, I found three royal dogs sprawled on the floor. They knew my scent by now, and barely bothered to lift their heads. Pomme was in her usual place under the tortoiseshell desk and I shifted her out of the way with my foot. It was not a wasted journey, for inside the secret drawer was a note bearing the King's seal. I wondered if Monsieur Bontemps had known one would be there. I stared at the fleurs-de-lys and, in truth, I did not want to pick it up, for all I wanted was to be reunited with Isabelle. What might the King require of me now? Or did he merely wish to talk with his unicorn? I tore it open and found that there were only four words on the page:

Wait for me here.

But I had to go back so that Isabelle could see my face! I crumpled up the note and sank to the floor. The King never spoke to me inside the palace! The dogs dreamed on, their bellies rising and falling, their muscles twitching. *Wait for me here.* What could it mean? Covering my face with my hands, I stared into the dark hollow of my palms.

I am prone to an inconvenient reaction to acute anxiety: I fall into a sudden and deep sleep from which it is impossible to wake me. Now that I have learned to recognize the symptoms, I can sometimes prevent this from happening. But this was my first—and very untimely—experience of it.

I awoke to the sound of the Sun King clearing his throat. My eyelids slid open and I saw him standing, hands behind his back, looking down through the window at the marble courtyard. Still befuddled, I tried to stand up, and failed in my attempt. The King turned around and calmly gestured for me to stay where I was. The dogs had gone and someone had covered me with a blanket and put a cushion beneath my head.

"I believe you fainted, my unicorn. Rest awhile. You will feel better presently."

He handed me a glass of red wine and ordered me to drink, which I did, feeling very strange and not yet a part of the world. I pushed myself up so that at least I was sitting, rather than lying in the presence of the King.

Louis resumed looking through the window. "There are times when an encounter with beauty is so vivid and powerful that one feels consumed by it. And it is natural to wish to preserve that feeling—even to *possess* that object of beauty. Would you agree?"

He turned to look at me. I nodded uncertainly. Louis continued: "My life, my gardens, my palaces—all are overflowing with people and things whose charms I have been unable to resist. And yet, I have a suspicion that it is only when we ask nothing of beauty, when we let it be and accept it for what it is, that we begin to truly appreciate it. Do you understand what I am saying, Jean-Pierre?"

"Yes, Sire." I lied. I had slept in an awkward position and was trying to ignore the pins and needles in my feet and calves.

"You see, familiarity and ownership can degrade that which we love. It is the rose we do not pluck, it is the song-bird we do not cage that continues in beauty. If restraint is important for all men, it is doubly important for one with the promise of a long life."

Now that the feeling had come back into my legs I made another attempt to stand. Louis offered me his cool, smooth hand, which I took, and he pulled me up. I was still in great awe of the Sun King, and I remember that this ordinary gesture moved me profoundly. Had I guessed what the King was on the point of announcing? I wonder if, in that hidden part of the mind that is wiser than we know, I had. In any case I found myself changing the subject, as if by diverting his words I could divert his purpose.

"Sire, thank you for demonstrating to the court that the Comte d'Alembert did not poison his wife. Now no one can doubt his innocence."

"It was a *convincing* letter, was it not?" He gave me a sidelong look. "My scribe is skilled—"

"The letter was *forged*!"

The King smiled pleasantly. "Have I shocked you, Jean-Pierre? I am satisfied that the Comte is perfectly innocent. And did you not ask me to do what I could to help him? Besides, I had another motive to defend d'Alembert, which I shall explain presently."

There was an expression on the King's face that I could not read. "Tell me, my unicorn, do you long to tell someone your secret? Is it hard to be different and alone in that difference?"

"I used to speak of it to Signor de Lastimosa," I replied.

"Yes, I know it. But he is departed for Sweden and you must learn to do without him — which has led me to come to a decision that, I hope, will make the burden of your secret easier to bear. I shall permit you to have a single person to be your confidant. That person has sworn on oath, in my presence, never to divulge your true identity. She will be a Friend to you, someone with whom you can share your hopes and fears. Is this something that would please you?"

She! My heart leapt. "Who is it, Sire?"

"Your first Friend, for as long as she may live, is Mademoiselle Isabelle d'Alembert."

I gasped with the joy of it. "Sire!" I said. "Thank you!"

But suddenly I recognized the expression that played on his face, and my stomach lurched. It was *pity*.

"I chose her because she will perform the role of Friend not out of duty, nor from the hope of reward, but from *love*. As I have already told you, I am of the opinion that a marital alliance would be ill-advised: She will age and you will not. Ultimately it would be the cause of much unhappiness — for you both. You are not an ordinary man, and, like a priest, your energies must be dedicated to your calling."

The King paused to observe me; I remained mute. *My calling?*

"Jean-Pierre, I know what it is to be young. You would not have had the strength to push aside your feelings. The difference that sets you apart makes you unfit to be a husband and father. You are destined for greater things than marriage. Today, in front of witnesses, the Prince de Montclair and Mademoiselle d'Alembert were betrothed. Their union will join two great families and will heal a rift."

My mind struggled to register his words. He reassured me that my destiny would compensate for the "small sacrifice" I must now make. It was as if I stood on some precipice, and when he placed a treacherous hand on my shoulder I felt that he had nudged me over the edge, sending me spinning down, powerless to react or to stop my fall.

"Monsieur Bontemps will take appropriate steps in order to ensure that your meetings with Mademoiselle d'Alembert can take place far from prying eyes. However, I believe it is right that a period of time elapse before this new association commences in order for you both to come to terms with the change in your circumstances. I think it best if the Prince de Montclair remains ignorant of the arrangement."

The King walked away from me then; I caught a fleeting glimpse of his silhouette as he paused in the doorway, a cloud of irritation scudding over his dark features. One of the dogs scampered in, licked the tips of my fingers, and scampered out again, claws skidding on the wooden floor.

"Mademoiselle d'Alembert and her aunt are presently in my gardens by the Fountain of Apollo," said the Sun King. "If you are sufficiently recovered, you may join them and greet your Friend."

XXVIII

The fountains were, by order of the King, in full flow—a suitable backdrop for a tragic scene. He had two Swiss Guards escort me. We made our way from the King's apartment to the Latona Fountain, then walked soundlessly down the *tapis vert*, the great slope of lawn that swept down toward the Fountain of Apollo and, beyond it, the Grand Canal. The guards stopped at a respectful distance, leaving me to go on alone. My heart thumped wildly in my chest as I spotted two small figures. They stood next to the great disc of sparkling water from whose center Apollo's chariot emerged. Isabelle wore silk the color of moonlight and a formal headdress, like her aunt. She was staring into the distance but as I grew closer, something made her turn. Before she had time to adjust her expression, I saw my own pain and shock mirrored in her face. She looked as if she had not slept. Her aunt nodded coolly in my direction and retreated toward the shade cast by a long avenue of trees. I wished we could have been alone. Isabelle walked toward me and I bowed and kissed her hand. She pressed my fingers hard between her own. I looked up at her. Behind her the fountain thundered. Jets of foaming water made rainbows above her headdress.

"Are you well?" she asked.

"Is it true? Are you betrothed? Tell me!"

Isabelle nodded. "The King has told me who you are and why he protects you. . . . Why could you not have told me yourself, Jean-Pierre? Did you not trust me?"

"Yes, I trusted you—I would trust you with my life!"

"I would have told no one. I *will* tell no one—"

"I do not know for certain that I am a sempervivens. . . . Is that why you agreed to marry Montclair—because the King said that you will age faster than me?"

"No! It is because the King has commanded me—"

"But do you *want* to marry Montclair?"

"You know I do not! It suits the King to join our two families. I could see by his face that Montclair was as reluctant as I—"

"Yet you both agreed—"

"We were given no choice. Did you expect me to defy the King and my family?"

"No . . . I am sorry."

All at once the notion came to me that if we departed that afternoon we could reach Calais in time to join the Spaniard.

"What is it?" demanded Isabelle. I realized I was beaming.

"Then come away with me! Now! This very afternoon! The Spaniard has procured a passage to England. He has a house in the marshes where we would never be found. If we left for Calais tonight there would still be time."

Isabelle's face lit up and in an instant, the promise of a whole new life opened like a flower in my mind. Then I saw her lower her eyes.

"I cannot."

"But why? Montclair will not make you happy! He will not love you as I do!"

She started to speak but stopped herself.

"Come with me, Isabelle! Why can you not choose happiness?"

She held out the flat of her hand as if to push me away.

"I don't understand!" I cried.

"I *will* tell you," she exclaimed. "Even though I should not. You have heard about the letter, supposedly from my mother's doctor—"

"Yes—the King told me it was a forgery."

"You know! Yes, the letter has saved our family's reputation. But when my father said that he would prefer me to marry someone I did not actually hate, Monsieur Bontemps implied, without saying so directly, that the King desired the marriage, and that it would be unfortunate if someone were to reveal that the physician's letter had been forged—"

Suddenly all became clear to me. "It would make everyone suspect that your father had been concealing a murder all along—"

"It would become my father's death warrant. The scribe, it seems, believes his payment came from someone in our household."

I did not know how to respond. It was the first time I had seen Isabelle cry. All the sorrow and helplessness rose up inside her so that her chest started to heave.

"My father has asked me to do my duty and obey the King."

Tears ran silently down her cheeks. It was unbearable. Ignoring the presence of her aunt, I drew Isabelle to me and held her. I, who would have done anything for her, was powerless to act. We were both caught in a vise, unable to move.

Her head rested on my shoulder and when I looked up I saw her aunt staring back at me, appalled. Already she was starting to walk toward us. I thought my heart would break.

"The King told me you would need someone to confide in whom you could trust absolutely. He said that it would be selfish of me to want to keep you for myself, for you will not be like other men. He said it is for the best."

"It is *not* for the best!" I cried. "The King would make us all his creatures—"

Isabelle was calmer now. "We *are* all his creatures. But at least we have *something*. I feared that the King might separate us forever. I shall be your first and the best of your Friends."

There was something about her words that made me think she had rehearsed them. I felt a light tap on my back.

"Release my niece immediately, Monsieur!" said Isabelle's aunt quietly. "This is *unseemly*."

Isabelle lifted her head and drew away a little. "Aunt, I beg you to give us one moment more."

But her aunt shook her head and beckoned to the Swiss Guards. Then Isabelle put her mouth to my ear and whispered: "They can make me marry Montclair, but they can't make me love him."

A moment later I felt my arms wrenched behind my back at the same time as Isabelle's aunt pulled her away from me. Once we were parted, the guards stepped away and stood awkwardly to attention. I watched as Isabelle was marched back to the palace by her aunt. She craned around to look at me for as long as she could, trying to smile, keeping her dignity, doing her duty. When she had vanished from sight I stood motionless and stared absently at the fountain. I did not know what to do or where to go. Presently the guards left and a gardener came to turn the water off. My collar was still damp with Isabelle's tears. Apollo, god of the sun, still drove his chariot across the skies, giving light and warmth to the world. If I could have stopped him that day I would have, for all I sensed, and all I wanted, was darkness and cold, a sky without light.

XXIX

As I look back it seems to me that I have led not one but many lives. The first ended that day by the Fountain of Apollo. It marked the end of my youth and the beginning of a slow acceptance of what I had been put on this earth to become.

I grew up believing that I was a child like any other. These notebooks record how I learned the truth, and also contain within them the seeds of my later life. One day, it might be appropriate for you to learn more—I cannot yet say. Though only, of course, if you wish it. If the sharing of these words is to be the final transaction between us, you deserve to know, even if only in the very briefest of terms, the broad direction my life took thereafter, what became of the Spaniard, and how I came to live here, at Stowney House, with Martha and Jacob.

That I am a *homo sapiens* sempervivens, like my father and his father before him, will now be clear to you. It was a hard truth for me to grasp, and it was many years before I was wholly convinced. I had been given a stupendous, extraordinary gift. Yet what had I done to deserve it? Nothing! And did I know what to do with the life I had been given? No, I did not. But in this I was no different to any other human soul. After I left Versailles—a century and more after I arrived— there was a period when I was utterly lost. Only when I had found my way again was I able to put to good use the talents I had been born with, and the skills I had learned.

* * *

I ended my account with a description of the day that Isabelle was betrothed to the Prince de Montclair. That same day, embittered, full of hate, and convinced that I could never again speak with the King, I left for Calais, determined to take up the Spaniard on his offer. On my tail were the King's spies, though I never once noticed them. Afterward, I learned that they would have followed me to England, if necessary, their instructions being only to observe and protect me. But three-quarters of the way to the English Channel, I stopped and turned back. Isabelle exerted a pull on me like gravity: I could not abandon her. I was not alone in needing a friend: She would have to survive a marriage to a man she loathed. So I swallowed my pride and continued to perform the role the King had assigned to me, just as he knew I would.

What an ingenious stratagem the Sun King had conceived! He played us, one against the other, while tightening his grip on us all. Two great families had been brought to heel. Isabelle would marry Montclair because her father would be exposed as a murderer if she did not. The Montclair family (its empty coffers newly filled with Isabelle's dowry) also lived under the threat of disclosure, for the King had proof that it was Montclair's father who had bribed d'Alembert's maid to bear false witness against him. As for me, with the Spaniard gone and my father unwelcome at court, I could devote myself to recording the golden reign of the Sun King for posterity. If I were to tire of my task, my affection for Isabelle would tie me to Versailles. Even there, because Monsieur Bontemps was in charge of arranging our clandestine meetings, the King had some measure of control over our relationship.

Louis's energy, focus, and sheer *will*—to create over so many decades a court, a kingdom, and a country in his own image—still astonish me. I have met many leaders of men in my life, but none has surpassed Louis in his drive to leave his stamp on the world.

Monsieur Bontemps's favorite piece of advice to me was that *to win is to lose*, by which he meant that those who reach the highest positions rarely remain there for long. The trick is to *endure*. The short-lived careers of many ambitious courtiers were testament to Bontemps's good sense. As a consequence I made a point of refusing so many titles and honors over the years that the King would make extravagant offers purely for the pleasure of hearing my excuses as I refused them. If I aspired to anything, it was simply this: to learn what I could at the court of the Sun King until something better suggested itself. When nothing did, I latched on to Versailles a little more tightly with every year that passed, like a barnacle to a rock. Besides, how could I have left Isabelle? Louis always had my measure.

My days were spent in the service of the King—or, as I would tell myself, in the service of my country. I learned to observe and interpret; I understood (as the Spaniard had taught me) how to listen *beneath* what was said in order to make connections that others had not; I became an accomplished reader of character, a diplomat, a commentator. I was careful to furnish information, but *never* to give the King advice. Louis's mistakes, as I was wise enough to understand, must always be his own. My opinions I kept to myself. In short, I made myself indispensable—always ready and waiting in the wings, away from public view—sound, discreet, dependable.

The King permitted me to stay with my father every year, which was a source of much happiness. While I was at court, increasingly buried in the affairs of state, my father took to sending me a weekly letter. He painted a picture of daily life in his own small kingdom: of cabbage fields decimated by pigeons, of pregnant milkmaids and a terrier that caught more than fifty rats in one night. Those letters were an antidote to the rarefied life of Versailles, and I continued to read them regularly, for comfort, even after his death.

As for the Spaniard, the Swedish court informed the King that he had been lost at sea. His supposed drowning did not stop me from subsequently meeting with him, on several occasions, at my father's house and also in his house in the Cévennes. Unlike the King, the Spaniard accepted that, in the end, no one can dictate the course of another man's life.

I possess portraits of all my Friends. They are infinitely precious to me. When the Spaniard was an old man I commissioned a painting of him sitting in his gardens overlooking the River Tarn. The artist captured something of his spirit. When I look at that broad, lined forehead with its thick black brows, I picture him dancing a volta, or popping strawberries into his mouth one after another, far too quickly, or I see him coming after me, threatening me with his copy of Gracián when I refused to listen.

The Spaniard lived for many years in Suffolk, where he rebuilt his home in the marshes, on land that was almost an island. Always the scholar, when naming his sanctuary he put together the Saxon words for "holy place" and "island," "*stowe*" and "*ney*." Stowney House passed to me after his death, along with his house in the Cévennes and a considerable amount of gold.

Of Isabelle, what can I say when there is too much to tell? She was my life's anchor: She tied me to the world, even after she had gone. When I doubted myself, Isabelle gave my life worth. With few interruptions, Bontemps, and later his son who succeeded him, ensured that she and I were able to meet, though never as often as I would have liked. Isabelle made it a rule never to talk of her life with Montclair, and I refused to torture myself by dwelling on her arranged marriage.

My suspiciously youthful looks obliged me to change my identity during Isabelle's lifetime. I left the court and reappeared after a suitable period of time in a different wig and attire, presenting myself as a close relative of the version of myself I had left behind. Isabelle understood how much I hated living a lie. With her alone I could be myself: She knew my faults and my secrets. In spirit, she remained youthful, even though, by the end, to see us together you would have supposed us mother and son. Isabelle was, as she had promised to be, my first and my best Friend. She was tender, wise, cheerful, and true. When I took myself too seriously, she would tease me, and when the wheels of Versailles threatened to crush us, we would laugh rather than cry. Because of my Friend, I did not always feel alone.

Isabelle died at the age of forty-six, at the end of August, within a year of the Sun King, leaving behind a grieving family I saw only from afar. When Isabelle became convinced that she was going to die, she asked to meet with me, partly because she wanted to prepare me, and also because there was something she had long wanted to say.

"Jean-Pierre, I have watched you turn yourself into one of the cleverest men at court, but you are a servant, and you are not happy. Now is the time to dare leave Versailles and all its absurdities. You have given more than enough of yourself to the King. Leave. Discover what only *you* can be. Seek out other sempervivens for I cannot believe that there are not others like you in the world."

Isabelle's words troubled and convinced me in equal measure, although I recall that this was as nothing compared to the shock of hearing that she was dying. It did not seem possible that she could leave me: I needed her too much. Her illness was a long one. While she lived I would not consider leaving Versailles, and I never gave up hope that she would recover. But she did not. After her death, try as I might, I could not find the strength, alone, to do as she suggested and leave behind everything and everyone I knew. I had needed the strength of her friendship to do it, but she was no longer there to give it. Ultimately it took a revolution to convince me to leave.

I recall that it was Monsieur Bontemps's son who broke

the news to me that Isabelle had died. Unable to stay away, I rode through summer rain to the château where she had lived, and whose interior I had never seen. And so I entered her home, undisguised, for the first and last time. In the hall I met Montclair, who was, by then, heavy and purple-cheeked. If he recognized me he did not show it. I was shown to her bedchamber, where she still lay.

On entering, I saw an old woman dressed in black watching over her at the end of the bed; it was Isabelle's aunt. Her grief was raw; her eyes were sunken and red. A look of bewilderment passed over her face when she saw me, but then faded. I must have looked like someone she used to know.

My eyes refused to rest on the form that lay beneath the sheets. Perhaps I did not want to make a memory of something that would henceforth haunt me: the last sight of my Friend. When I forced myself to look on that waxen face, I found that my Isabelle was no longer there. Her body was a carapace that I did not want to touch. As soon as I was able, I hurried from the room and ran out of the château—where I felt I had no right to be—and I rode away as fast as I could. The rain still fell, and thunder growled in the distance. I galloped through fields without once turning back until I reached a stream. There I dismounted, and waded into the water and howled. All around me swifts dived and swooped, filling the air with their sibilant calls. All I knew was that I did not want to go on without her, and I questioned the purpose of life if it only ends in death.

* * *

When the Sun King died, he was succeeded by his great-grandson, Louis XV, who was only five years old. A regent was appointed: Philippe II of Orléans—the son of Monsieur and Liselotte. The Sun King had entrusted the knowledge of my existence to the regent, who swore to tell it to the new monarch, and him alone, when he came of age. In the fullness of time, the regent passed on my secret to Louis XV, who passed it on to his grandson, Louis XVI. When the Revolution came, and the guillotine put an end to the monarchy, Louis XVI took it with him to the grave.

And so I passed from one master to another, a valued and increasingly trusted servant, until the Revolution finally shook me out of my dependency like a mother bird pushing a fledgling from its nest. When the blade struck Louis XVI's head from his body, I effectively became a free man. What I would do with that freedom was another matter. I floundered then, dazed and confused, for it seemed to me that there was nothing to which I felt connected, as if I had been divorced from the human race and anything that I could call my own. For the first time, I properly considered Isabelle's advice to me, and I determined to find more of my own kind.

During my wilderness years, I traveled the length and breadth of Europe, mostly as a mercenary, always drawn to stories of those who had lived long lives. I would fight for anyone who would pay me, and found that I enjoyed danger, telling myself that I did not care if I lived or I died. With the luck of the reckless, I had a knack for narrow escapes and grew popular among the ranks.

A few years after the battle of Waterloo, an English officer befriended me and persuaded me to follow him to Dover. I determined to visit the house in Suffolk that I had inherited from the Spaniard. The captain of the frigate that took me across the Channel asked for my name. He was not fond of the French, and decided to anglicize my name for the ship's log. "I shall call you John," he said. "But you need an English surname, too." I told him that "*pierre*" meant "stone." "That will do," the captain said. "You shall be John Stone." And so I have been, ever since.

Later, fate led me to a couple, a man of the cloth and his wife who devoted themselves to campaigning for social change: for the abolition of the slave trade and for the rights and freedoms of every man, woman, and child. After Versailles, their selfless, modest lives were an inspiration. They founded a charity that aimed to educate those deprived of schooling. It was through inviting me to help in a workhouse with which they had connections that they inadvertently changed my life. I discovered a woman who, as I came to realize over the course of many months, must also be a sempervivens. It is a compelling story though one I shall not tell here. That woman was Martha. I took her to Stowney House and nursed her back to health—at least as far as I was able—for life had dealt her so many cruel blows, I doubt she could have withstood another. In turn, Martha led me to Jacob. He was being pursued by the authorities, which had become a pattern in his life, and had been on the run for some time. Martha had been feeding him what scraps she could until she was taken to the workhouse against her will. Her road back to health and well-being was uneven and very long. When I was able to reunite her with her last child, a girl of fifteen years of age, she was transformed. Martha's daughter lived nearby for almost seventy years; she never married, and lived and died in a cottage close to Stowney House where you also once resided. And so we have been a family in all but name: a curious one, but a family nonetheless. Stowney House continues to be our sanctuary, although for how much longer remains to be seen.

From time to time there was a fourth inhabitant who lived with us, a woman named Thérèse: She died some little while ago. If our paths cross again, perhaps we could talk further, face-to-face. Spark, please know that you are always welcome at Stowney House. However, after recent events, I shall understand if you prefer to stay away. If that is the case, let me take this opportunity of wishing you a long, happy, and useful life. I would also ask that, as someone who could have been a Friend to us, you respect our privacy and the sanctity of our home.

The Eternal Legacy

The idea of speaking to a lawyer worries her. Spark rehearses what she is going to say before keying in the number. Curiously, when the secretary puts her call through to Mr. de Souza—which she does immediately on hearing John Stone's name—it is the lawyer, rather than Spark, who seems briefly tongue-tied. Of course, it's easy to misinterpret people's reactions over the phone. The lawyer sounds posh: His voice is deep and mellow, and he has what Mum would call a fruity laugh. In her mind's eye Spark sees cuff links and shiny black shoes. The lawyer explains that as Mr. Stone's letter remained unacknowledged for so long, his client had concluded that Miss Park did not wish to view the documents. In the circumstances, he says, he would prefer to contact Mr. Stone directly before arranging an appointment.

"He generally checks for my texts every day, though reception at Stowney House is appalling."

"I know," says Spark. "You have to walk right up the lane to get any kind of a signal—"

"Yes, of course—you'd know. What did Mr. Stone get you to do at Stowney House while you were there?"

"I worked in the archive room. I wasn't there long in the end—"

"No, indeed. Why don't I telephone you tomorrow morning? Hopefully I shall have been able to get in touch with Mr. Stone by then."

"Thanks, but the thing is I've already reserved a seat on a train tomorrow morning. I'm meeting up with a friend in the National Gallery in the afternoon. If it's not convenient—"

"No, no," says Mr. de Souza. "You mustn't change your plans."

"How long do you think it would take me to read the notebooks?" she asks. "Presuming it's still okay with Mr. Stone."

"Oh, two or three hours, I should think. Depending on how fast a reader you are."

Spark's excitement builds as the early commuter train speeds south. She twists in her seat and presses her forehead against the glass, trying to blot out the meetings and constant phone calls, and other people's lives going on all around her. After today—with any luck—she might have a few more hooks to hang her identity on. Unwanted love child of her dad's landlady isn't a lot to go on. If John Stone knew she was adopted all along, there must be a chance, at least, that the notebooks are connected in some way to her birth mother. All the same, she is preparing herself for disappointment. Just in case. Spark screws up her eyes against the sun's glare. She's probably done the right thing not telling Mum anything about it until she's found out more.

Lincoln's Inn Fields. The name sounds a little unlikely given its location. As instructed, she gets the tube to

Holborn. She's caught up in a flood tide of people and the enforced intimacy of the London rush hour. Swaying in the crush next to the carriage doors, her nose jammed into one guy's T-shirt, treading on someone else's toes when the driver applies the brakes, Spark soon learns the rules of the game in the London underground. Like everyone else around her, she behaves as if she's inside her own invisible force field. It is a relief when she steps off the long escalator. She heads down Kingsway, her neck cricked, taking in every detail. At the corner of Africa House she spots the entrance to an alleyway that Mr. de Souza said she should look out for. A fruit seller has set out his colorful stall there. Over the rumble of the traffic he shouts out the price of strawberries. The alley leads Spark past an ancient tavern that puts her in mind of highwaymen, a café, and a gift shop; soon it opens up and she steps out of shade and into sunshine. In front of her is a great expanse of green, full of giant trees and surrounded by tall brick houses: Lincoln's Inn Fields. It is tranquil and rather grand.

The fluttering sensation in her stomach reminds her of why she is here and what she might learn. The moment comes back to her when Mum pushed the envelope toward her across the blue kitchen table. The moment when it felt like the floor had turned into quicksand and Mum had stood by while the earth sucked her down. Whatever happens today, whatever she learns about herself, it's not going to be that momentous — or that difficult. Spark takes a deep breath, glances down at John Stone's note to remind herself of the address, and sets off to find his lawyer's offices.

"Is this really necessary?" Spark asks Mr. de Souza as she studies the wording of the confidentiality agreement. Her shoulders start to tense. She must declare that she will not divulge the content of the text she is about to read to *anyone*. It's having the same effect on her as seeing a policeman—she feels guilty without having done anything. Spark can keep a secret but this is serious stuff.

"As Mr. Stone's lawyer, I have advised him that it is. It is my function to be cautious where my client is not." Mr. de Souza looks clean, pink, and wholesome. He has beautiful hands. Although he has been unable to contact Mr. Stone, he says he has taken it upon himself to allow Spark to view the notebooks. It is what he believes his client would wish.

"Have *you* read them?" Spark asks.

"Let us say that I have an idea of their subject matter."

The lawyer unscrews the top of his own black-and-gold fountain pen and passes it to her. Spark signs, wishing her signature was not so neat and childish. She slides the signed document back across the desk. Its edges flutter in a current of air and he places a paperweight onto it. Spark reaches out to touch it: It is made of heavy crystal and trapped within it is the seed head of a dandelion. She looks up to see Edward de Souza smiling at her.

"How fast a reader are you, Miss Park?"

"I'm fast."

"Good. There are eight notebooks in all. As I have explained, they may not be removed from these offices. I have made a room available for you, and my secretary will provide refreshments as required."

Mr. de Souza leads Spark down a corridor and introduces her to his secretary, a neat woman around Mum's age, who greets her politely and returns to her work. He unlocks the door of a tiny storage room, lined with shelves. It smells of dust and has the vaguely caramel odor of old cardboard; it is only just big enough for a table and chair. There is a high window glazed with frosted glass that lets in a little air and the muffled sounds from the street. There is a carafe of water and a glass and, in the middle of the small table, a neat pile of green, soft-backed exercise books.

"I'll leave you to it, then," says Mr. de Souza. "Good luck."

"Thank you," says Spark, feeling as though she is about to start an exam.

"It's a great pleasure to meet you, Miss Park," he adds, closing the door behind him and pocketing the key. "Oh, and I'd be grateful if you would return them to me in person."

Convinced that he has locked her in, Spark dives back to the door. To her relief, when she turns the tarnished brass knob, it opens. Spark returns to the table and sits, chin in her hands, staring at the ink-splattered green cover of Notebook 1. It's too quiet. Anxiety washes over her in waves. If these books are a journey, she's not sure she wants to set off right now. If she has to sign a document not to talk about them, does she want to risk going where these notebooks will take her? There's a knock on the door, making Spark jump. The secretary asks her if she'd like a cup of coffee. "No, thank you," Spark says automatically. Spark watches the secretary's eyes slide over to the pile of unopened exercise books and, guiltily, she flips open the first cover.

"I won't disturb you," says the secretary. "You know where I am if you need anything."

"Thanks very much," says Spark.

The lines of sloping letters in blue-black ink draw her in. She reads the first line: *1685, Versailles, France.* Then: *They say that the grandeur of Versailles in the age of the Sun King has never been surpassed, although, human nature being what it is, one soon gets used to anything.*

It's a story, thinks Spark, and reads on. She turns the page, and then another.

Mr. de Souza himself comes in at one o'clock, carrying a small, circular tray. He makes Spark jump. She sits up, finding it strange to emerge from her waking dream to see John Stone's lawyer and her immediate surroundings.

"How are you doing? My secretary tells me you've not surfaced since this morning."

He pushes the tray onto the table. Small triangular sandwiches—prawn, cheese, egg—are arranged on a white pottery plate. The bread smells good. There is a mug of strong, steaming tea.

"You know, don't you?" Spark says.

Mr. de Souza leans his back against the door so that it clicks shut. "I am proud to be John Stone's Friend. I am the most recent in a very long line of Friends."

"Why does he want *me* to know?"

"I really mustn't interrupt you, Miss Park. Find me when you've finished."

At a quarter past three Spark slips out of the room and finds a bathroom where she washes her face and finger-combs her hair. Sempervivens. A word that is now permanently etched in her brain. That face in the crowd in the painting in the National Portrait Gallery: It wasn't one of John Stone's ancestors, it was the man himself. Martha and Jacob are also sempervivens. Stowney House. Not a home, but a *sanctuary*, which the Spaniard built all those centuries ago. Spark looks at herself in the mirror and the tears come again: for Jean-Pierre, for Isabelle, for herself. Now she understands the cause of Martha's distress: The ancient woman in the photograph must have been her daughter. Martha has survived all of them, but her daughter, the last of her children, clung on to life as long as she could to stay with her mother. No wonder Jacob was anxious about her own arrival at Stowney House. No wonder John Stone threw Ludo's phone into the marsh. Spark weeps because by sending Ludo the photograph of the street woman and John Stone in New York, she understands how she has put them all in danger. If their secret gets out, it will be her fault. And she weeps because of John Stone's request at the end of the final notebook: Respect the privacy and the sanctity of their home, as someone who *could* have been a Friend to them. What a *mess* she has made of all of this.

Spark gathers together the exercise books and goes in to thank the secretary and say good-bye.

"Shall I take those for you?" asks the secretary.

"Oh, no," says Spark, hugging them to her. "I'll return them to Mr. de Souza myself."

He has heard her voice and comes down the corridor to greet her, his manner bright and pleasant.

"Shall I relieve you of those?" he says. "Come on through."

He closes the door behind him and locks the exercise books in his desk drawer. Spark hopes the cold water has calmed the redness around her eyes and nose. She tries not to sniff. The lawyer sits back behind his desk and gestures for her to sit down too.

"So now I know everything," she says. "Except *why* Mr. Stone wanted me to know."

"It would be more accurate to say that you know *a little*. A very small tip of a very large iceberg. I understand that it is that early period of his life that Mr. Stone most particularly wanted to share with you—"

"Mr. de Souza, there's something I've got to tell you. I gave a picture of Mr. Stone to an American friend—Ludo—when I was in New York in February. I didn't know who Mr. Stone was at the time. He was just a stranger in the street. But Ludo has taken my picture and matched it with a painting in the National Portrait Gallery. He's written this app, you see, and—"

"I know the painting you're referring to: Haydon's *The Anti-Slavery Society Convention*. We're aware of Ludo and his app. The matter is in hand."

"It is?"

"I doubt anything will come of it but, if it does, Mr. Stone has connections with people who know how to tidy up a messy situation."

"I don't understand—"

"Please don't concern yourself."

"It's Ludo that I'm meeting later—"

"In which case it would be convenient if you could convince him to forget that he ever heard of Mr. Stone."

"I'll try—though I doubt he'll listen to me. He's very excited about his discovery."

"I assure you that it's not the first and it won't be the last time someone has voiced suspicions, which are difficult to prove—"

"Can I ask you a question, Mr. de Souza?"

"Please do."

Spark pauses to take a deep breath. The lawyer gives her an encouraging smile.

"I've recently been told that I'm adopted." It hurts to say it. As if it's an admission that she's been abandoned, that she was an unwanted child. She watches Mr. de Souza's eyes widen; he picks up a paperweight and puts it down again. "I see. And how can I help you?"

"My middle name is Theresa—I was named after my birth mother. Could the Thérèse mentioned at the end of the notebooks be my mother?"

The lawyer's lips part and close again. He looks through the window and then back at Spark. "*That* is a question you must put to Mr. Stone."

So she is. The evidence wouldn't stand up in a court of law but they both know he's just admitted it. Thérèse is her mother. Spark becomes aware that she is trembling.

"Was Thérèse a sempervivens?"

"Miss Park, I have been instructed to let you read the notebooks. I am not at liberty to enter into a conversation with you about them."

"*Please!* I've got to know! You can't let me read those notebooks and then not tell me! Was Thérèse my mother? Was she a . . . sempervivens?"

Spark's eyes grow anguished. Mr. de Souza looks at the ceiling as if he wishes she were not there; a deep crease has formed between his eyebrows.

"I'm sorry," she says.

"Miss Park, I've already sent Mr. Stone a text saying that you have read his notebooks. He'll be in touch as soon as he receives it." He smiles at her. "You can *count* on that."

Spark's mind races. She struggles to recall what the Spaniard told Jean-Pierre in the cave: that only a union between two sempervivens parents ever produced a sempervivens child. She repeats this to Mr. de Souza and asks if that is correct—and if he can't answer, could she please have another look at the notebooks?

"Yes, for what it's worth, that is what Juan Pedro told the Spaniard. *Both* parents would have to be sempervivens in order for a child to inherit their longevity."

"So that explains why Martha lost all her children—she outlived them all. That's right, isn't it?"

Mr. de Souza nods briskly. "Mr. Stone will be able to answer the many questions you have."

He turns away from her to look out at Lincoln's Inn Fields. The two of them sit in silence for a moment. Spark's heart is racing. *Bong!* When the ancient grandfather clock which she passed in the entrance hall sounds, Spark checks her phone and leaps to her feet when she sees the time.

"I'm sorry, I've got to go." She gathers up her bag and jacket as she talks. "I need to be at the National Gallery café by four."

The lawyer rises from his desk. "I'll walk down with you and hail a cab. There's usually one to be found in Kingsway."

"Oh, I'm fine catching the tube."

"It'll be quicker by cab. You'll allow me to take care of the fare, of course." He walks to the door and holds it open for her. "I promise to be in touch as soon as I hear anything."

"Thank you. And thanks for . . . everything."

The lawyer takes a business card out of his wallet and hands it to Spark. "I want you to feel that you can call me at any time. After all, we have something in common now. We are links in a very long chain. The sempervivens—understandably—have told very few people the truth about themselves. The Spaniard used to call it the eternal legacy—"

"*Eternal* legacy?"

"A rather dramatic description, I agree, although I can

understand why he coined the term. You know, John tends to forget what a truly extraordinary life he has led—and how unique he is as a consequence. But I never forget."

"You really like Mr. Stone, don't you?" says Spark.

"I've devoted my life to him. How could I not?"

The National Gallery Café

The streets of London blur by, unnoticed, until the black cab deposits Spark, ten minutes early, in Trafalgar Square. It is as if the ground has shifted beneath her feet and her sense of balance has gone. How can she carry on as normal, knowing that someone who was on intimate terms with the Sun King also watched the first moon landing and now communicates by text message? Not only that, but there are—and have been—others like him. Including a woman Spark must now assume gave birth to her. And she can't say *anything* to *anyone*.

Spark sits at a small table at one end of a long marble-topped bar in the National Gallery café. Above her head is a giant floral display, all whites and red, so that the aroma of ground coffee mingles with the perfume of lilies. The high-ceilinged room is vast, and the tinkling of cutlery and murmur of conversations swirl upward into the airy space. Through the tall windows, Nelson's Column rises up into a clear sky. On any other day Spark's camera lens would have been hovering over the scene like a bee over flowers, but today her head is filled with images of another grand room, one with many golden mirrors, and windows that look out over gardens where fountains are dedicated to Apollo and to Neptune, and where lovers are told they can never marry, because the boy is likely to outlive the girl by centuries.

How can she meet with Ludo now? What is she supposed to say to him? Talk about the weather? Her actions—sending Ludo the photograph and bringing him to Stowney House—have not only put Martha, Jacob, and John Stone at risk, they have also made Ludo the *enemy*. Which means that whatever her feelings are about him (not that she's clear what they are), and even if those feelings are reciprocated (which somehow she doubts), she must ignore them. It is her *duty* to walk away. She has already betrayed the sempervivens once and *cannot* risk doing so again. She should not have come. No, she should not have come. She should go *now*, before Ludo arrives. Someone is clearing their throat next to her. Spark looks up, out of sync with the world. A waitress in a white shirt and long black apron is speaking: Her lips are painted scarlet and the words coming out of her mouth are just noise.

"I'm sorry," Spark says, "I haven't looked at the menu yet."

"I think your friend has already ordered for you," says the waitress, indicating a round table in the corner. Spark turns her head to see a slim, black-T-shirted figure in spectacles looking in her direction. When her gaze meets Ludo's, he smiles his easy smile, he greets her with that two-fingered salute of his, and he makes it impossible for her to do anything but to get up and walk toward him.

"I was wondering how long it would take for you to notice me," says Ludo, as Spark slides in next to him on the curved, red leather seat.

"Real life is elsewhere," she says. "Were you here before me? I didn't see you."

"I waved at you a couple of times but you didn't react. Not a flicker—"

"Were you watching me?"

His hair has grown. It's sun-bleached, too, after Italy. And he's tanned, a lovely golden tone. "I guess. You were so far away I didn't want to break the spell." Although he is smiling, Ludo strikes Spark as being a tad on edge. But then, she's not helping, and before he left for Florence they did not part on exactly good terms. "Are you okay?"

"Yes, I'm fine," she says.

"You don't sound it—"

"Oh?"

A silence falls between them.

"I like your choice of café," Spark offers.

"Glad you approve. So, where's the shopping?" Ludo makes a show of looking under the table. "I was expecting bags. A heap of bags. Couldn't you find anything to buy in the whole of London?"

Spark shakes her head. Ludo has already ordered a proper afternoon tea. "Is this okay for you? Can I serve you a scone? I know what to do with them now—"

Ludo splits the scones and spreads on dollops of Jersey cream, then lets teaspoons of runny strawberry jam drip onto them, like blood on snow. Spark, however, is barely paying attention. It is as if the weight and mass of this newly acquired knowledge is pressing the breath out of her. What would be the consequences if she weakened, and revealed that the painting Ludo told her about doesn't depict John Stone's ancestor, but is, in fact, a portrait of the man himself?

"Here," Ludo says, offering her a plate. "Tuck in."

"*Tuck in?*"

"Andy gave me some English lessons."

Spark looks down at her scone. Does she have the strength to bear the burden of this astonishing secret? Already, nightmarish sequences are beginning to play in her head: a press scrum outside Stowney House, the lane jammed with cars; Martha, hysterical, hiding in the kitchen; John Stone failing to restrain Jacob; journalists desperate to snatch a look at these near-immortals, wanting to tease out their secrets and their strange ways, demanding to know if they've been contacted by the big players in medical research. What price for a sample of sempervivens blood, or bone marrow, or stem cells? One slip of the tongue and all of that could become a reality. If she told Ludo, he probably wouldn't understand why he *shouldn't* announce it to the world. For the greater good. Or whatever. And it would all be *her* fault.

Abruptly she slides out from the table and stands up. "I'm sorry," she says, "I can't do this. Please don't ask me to explain. I've got to go." She pulls a fiver from her jeans pocket and places it under her saucer. "I hope that covers it."

Ludo attempts to hand back the fiver to her, but Spark refuses to take it. "What's wrong?" he asks. "What have I done?"

"It's not you. It's me. I'm sorry." Spark spins around

and walks briskly toward the drafty double glass doors that open out onto the street. Litter skitters across the pavement. Overhead a helicopter engine thrums. The crowds part for her as she strides purposefully across Trafalgar Square toward the underground. When she reaches the giant lions, Spark stops to look behind her. She is as relieved as she is disappointed that Ludo has not followed her. Around her life goes on: Red double-decker buses and black cabs wait at traffic lights, filling the air with fumes; in Trafalgar Square every other person poses, smiling their best smiles, in front of a loved one's camera; a child runs at a cluster of pigeons, scaring them so that they take off and fly over the fountains and circle back around Nelson's Column. Spark blinks back the tears: This *information* is overwhelming; she feels so alone with it locked up inside her head. How she would have liked to spread out this knowledge like a feast and share it with Ludo. Instead, her last memory of him will probably be seeing her own reflection in his glinting, rectangular spectacles. And behind the glass, in his tortoiseshell eyes, an expression of bewildered hurt.

And there is still something she doesn't know. *Why* has John Stone allowed her to glimpse these wonders? Why *her*? Is it something to do with her birth mother? As Spark descends the steep stairwell leading to Charing Cross tube, she feels a hand on the small of her back. Her heart leaps. *It's him!* But it's not Ludo. It's John Stone's lawyer.

"Miss Park," he pants. "Thank goodness."

"Mr. de Souza! Is something wrong?"

"I've been calling you for the last twenty minutes."

Spark glances at her phone: There are six missed calls. "I'm sorry, I had it on mute when I was reading the notebooks."

Mr. de Souza is out of breath and leans forward slightly while he recovers himself. He leads her by the elbow back up into Trafalgar Square.

"Do you want to sit down?"

He shakes his head. "I have reason to believe that Mr. Stone is about to go into hiding: He has been planning a journey from which he will not return—"

Spark stares at him. "What are you talking about?"

"I'm sorry, I don't mean to sound melodramatic. . . ." The lawyer has to pause to get his breath back. "Mr. Stone is not a well man. He's been suffering from a serious disorder of the nervous system for some time. These last weeks have taken their toll, and his health has deteriorated sharply. He refuses to see a doctor in case his 'difference' is detected."

Spark feels a stab of guilt. *These last weeks*—does he mean since her arrival at Stowney House?

"How ill is he? Do you mean he's going to die?"

"It is what he believes—"

"But he hasn't seen a doctor?"

"No. John is a proud and dignified man, and does not wish to be a burden to his friends. He feels that it will cause the least distress for everyone if he slips away unannounced. He has arranged to end his days in a safe house, a place where those who love him cannot find him."

"Slip away unannounced—you mean without telling Martha and Jacob?"

"He believes it's the kindest thing to do—"

"But it's not! Keeping the truth from people is cruel—everyone deserves to be told the truth!"

"I happen to agree with you, although I can also understand that to cause Martha distress, in particular, is something John would wish to avoid at all costs. Dealing with past losses has all but broken her. The point is, Miss Park, if you wish to find out more about your parentage, you need to go to Stowney House without delay."

"Why couldn't you have told me this before?"

"Half an hour ago, I didn't know. The truth is I was counting on him to change his mind as the time drew near. This afternoon my secretary took a call from the car hire firm we always use for John. They were ringing to confirm our reservation. A reservation that *we* did not make. My secretary queried it and had me return their call. It transpired that it was John himself who had made the booking—and he specified the time but *not* the destination. John has never, and would never, involve himself in travel arrangements. I did not expect John to put his plan into action so soon. Perhaps his symptoms have worsened. I'm convinced that he intends to disappear—"

"Are you saying that this could be my last chance to find out about my mother?"

"That's exactly what I'm saying. I've taken the liberty of hiring a car for you to travel up to Stowney House. It is waiting for you in Saint Martin's Place. I urge you to go."

"Why are you doing all this for me, Mr. de Souza? What aren't you telling me?"

"Time is short, Miss Park. All that I can usefully say to you is that I am acting in your best interests. And that is precisely what my client has instructed me to do."

Spark looks at the clouds scudding over Trafalgar Square, at the temple-like façade of the National Gallery and the turquoise water rippling in the fountain basin. She looks back at Mr. de Souza's expectant face. "I'll go."

As they walk up toward Saint Martin's Place, Spark's phone rings. She checks to see who it is. "It's not Mr. Stone," she says quickly. "It's Ludo. And I'm not answering."

"Probably a good idea."

Half a minute later Ludo calls again. Before he calls for the third time they've reached a large black car illegally parked opposite the Salisbury pub. Mr. de Souza signals to the driver who hurriedly gets out and opens the rear door for Spark. He asks Mr. de Souza to confirm that it's just the one passenger and that the journey is open-ended.

"Yes. Take Miss Park to Stowney House and afterward drive her wherever she needs to go."

Everything is happening so quickly: Spark has the feeling she's been strapped into a roller coaster and now that the ride's started she can't get out.

"Good luck," says the lawyer.

"I'll call you," promises Spark.

"Miss Park?"

"Yes?"

"The life John has led makes him unique and precious. He won't thank me for telling you, but if you find him, try to persuade him to see a doctor."

"Why would he listen to me?"

Mr. de Souza smiles at her: It is a heartfelt smile. "Please try." The lawyer raps on the roof of the car; Spark senses she has an ally in him. The car cruises past crowds of tourists, and it occurs to Spark that not a single one of them will have ever heard of the term "sempervivens." How bizarre. She seems to have known it forever.

The traffic is at a standstill—a giant construction truck carrying metal girders is delivering its payload in a series of delicate maneuvers—so that when Ludo calls again the car has moved less than a hundred meters. He has also sent her a text. Call me. There's something you REALLY need to know.

Spark hesitates, then answers. "Hello—"

"Where are you?"

"Saint Martin's Place."

"Where's that?"

"Just up the road from the National Gallery."

"Then don't move—I'm coming to find you."

"I'm not on foot. I'm in a car."

"Whose car? Are you with someone?"

"No, I'm on my own—in a hired car. What did you want to tell me, Ludo?"

"Can't I talk to you in person?"

"I'm in a hurry to get somewhere—"

"Trust me, you *need* to hear what I've got to say."

Spark knocks on the glass partition and has a word with the driver.

"Okay," Spark says. "The driver is going to pull over for a moment. But he's really not supposed to stop here. Can you hurry? I'm a minute away. Turn left out of the café exit."

"I'm on my way."

The car's hazard lights click on and off. In the distance a siren sounds. Spark twists around in her seat, scanning the road for any sign of Ludo or the blue flash of a police car. She spots him in the side-view mirror running toward her and opens the car door. He jogs effortlessly, dodging pedestrians, hair flying out behind him. As soon as he's inside the driver pulls away in a burst of speed, bumping down onto the carriageway from the pavement. Spark and Ludo sit either side of the generous backseat. He wipes his forehead with the back of both hands. She watches his chest heave and listens to the sound of his breathing. His eyes roam over the car's luxurious interior, but if he's puzzled, he says nothing.

"Is the gentleman traveling with you?" asks the driver.

"No," says Spark. "We just need to have a word."

"Would you like me to park?"

"No," says Ludo. "I'll find my own way back. Keep going."

The driver enquires if the air-conditioning is set at a comfortable temperature and, reassured that it is, he slides the partition shut. The car glides past Chinatown and the Dominion Theatre on Tottenham Court Road. For a while Spark and Ludo look through their respective windows, each giving the other the chance to be the first to speak.

"Well, isn't this splendid?" says Ludo in a falsetto voice, failing to sound like the Queen, and waving graciously at passersby. A young guy in a porkpie hat waves back.

Spark laughs. "I'm sorry I left like I did."

"I ate your scone."

"Don't ask me to explain."

"Okay. I won't. Are you going back to Mansfield?"

"Eventually."

They pass Goodge Street station. A new window display involving purple sofas and steel lamp shades is being constructed at Heal's.

"I can't presume to know what's going on in your head," says Ludo, "but I don't think I'm the person you think I am."

Spark looks at her hands. "I'm not still mad at you for the Stowney House thing, if that's what you mean. Now I understand. If I'd have written your app, I'd have wanted to see inside John Stone's gallery."

"I was a jerk. It was finding myself inside John Stone's house with all those paintings—I'd gotten overexcited."

"Is that what you wanted to tell me?"

"Actually, no."

"Then you'd better tell me soon, or you'll have a long trek back into London."

"It's about John Stone—"

Spark's heart sinks. "I wish I'd never sent you that picture. Can't you just forget you ever came across him?"

"No, I can't. And if you listen, I think you'll be interested too."

"I really, really don't want to talk about John Stone right now."

"Please hear me out."

Hear him out. Spark is not sure she can cope with any more hearing people out. Though after what she has just learned, anything that Ludo could tell her is going to pale in comparison. Spark sighs. "Go on, then. *Amaze* me."

Ludo frowns at her. "Do you know you can be pretty scary when you feel like it? I'm telling you this because I think you need to know, not because I'm getting some kick out of bugging you—"

"I'm sorry," says Spark. "It's been a weird day. I'm listening."

"So. One of the portraits in John Stone's gallery caught my eye. It took me a moment to realize why. Afterward, there was so much going on it slipped my mind. It was a painting of a woman in a red dress. She had eyes the exact color of yours and a cloud of blond hair like yours— the same texture, the same corkscrew thing going on. I'm not saying she was your doppelgänger, but she sure as hell looked like you."

Spark tries hard not to react. Could it be Thérèse? Could it be her *mother*? "How old was the painting? Present-day or old?"

"Old. I'm guessing nineteenth century, maybe

eighteenth. I wish I could show it to you, but I got interrupted by the swamp monster before I could take a picture—"

"Who was she?"

"There weren't any labels," says Ludo. "If that's what you mean."

Spark grips her hands so tightly in her lap her knuckles grow white. She affects interest in something in the street. To Ludo she says: "So are you saying that John Stone owns a painting of a woman who looks a bit like me? Is that the information I *really* need to know?" To herself she says: *If that was Thérèse, my mother was a sempervivens.*

"That, and something else—"

Spark brings her hand to her forehead and inhales deeply.

"You okay?" asks Ludo.

She tells him he'd better finish now he's started.

"Do you remember when we were both in the kitchen with John Stone, and he asked me not to take a picture?"

"But you took one, didn't you?" she asks.

"I did."

"I thought so."

"When John Stone made such a big deal about his privacy, I e-mailed it to myself as soon as I left the room." Ludo brings out his phone. "There."

Unposed pictures are always stronger. John Stone is walking toward the camera the flat of his palm outstretched, a stern expression on his face; Spark is looking at him, mouth half-open, a cup of tea in her hand, her brow registering concern.

"I won't be asking you for a copy!"

"It's the only photograph I have of you. You see, Dan called me in Italy to say that he'd found out that you were adopted, and that he was still trying to get his head around it. He said he'd always assumed you'd taken after your mum. So I asked him if you two were related at all. He said that my guess was as good as his, and that maybe I should run my app on you. He was joking—but I did. I used *this* picture of you and a couple I had of Dan and compared them."

Spark doesn't care for the solemn expression on Ludo's face. Her heart is beginning to thump. "So, Dan and me— *are* we related? What do our nose-to-chin ratios, or skull shapes, or whatever, imply?"

"For what it's worth—and I'm not claiming that my app is superaccurate; I've still got a lot of work to do—"

"Don't keep me in suspense, Ludo!"

"It gave a three-percent probability that you're related to Dan—"

"Oh—"

"*But* it gave a ninety-percent probability that you and John Stone are related."

Spark looks wildly at Ludo. "*What?*" she says.

"I ran it five times. I used the street woman picture too. I even adjusted the algorithm. But it kept coming back the same, give or take."

"I don't understand." This is untrue, because at some level she does. Spark feels nauseous with the shock of it. She presses her lips together to stop herself shouting the reason out loud. That must be why John Stone has told her his secret. That must be why the notebooks, which she'd hoped would be filled with recollections of her mother, were, in fact, about *him*. It was *his* story he wanted to share. *John Stone is my father!*

The safety belt locks as she tries to bend forward and Spark unbuckles it impatiently. She puts her elbows on her knees and cradles her head, covering her ears with her hands. Ludo puts his hand on her shoulder but she shoves it off. After a while she sits up and stares blankly out of the window, then refastens her safety belt. They are no longer in central London. She is vaguely aware of Ludo sitting motionless next to her and of the driver's curious glances in the mirror. Now her mind is racing, piecing together clues to a puzzle she never realized until now that she was supposed to solve. The connection she sensed with John Stone in New York, when he first held her hand and wouldn't let it go. The coincidence of Thérèse buying a property adjacent to Stowney House. Jacob's gift—a twin portrait, hers and John Stone's, as well as his parting comment: *There's things you don't know.* And today's seismic revelations. Mr. de Souza said that the exercise books covered only the tip of the iceberg of John Stone's long life, but that it was this period *he particularly wanted her to know about.*

Spark's brain tugs at her like a fretful toddler. *There's something else. Something else.* And then it comes to her. *If* Thérèse is her mother and *if* John Stone is her father—

"Stop the car!" shouts Spark, banging hard on the glass partition with the flats of both hands.

The driver slams on the brake and mounts the pavement on a busy stretch of the North Circular. Spark throws herself out of the car and vomits into the gutter. *I could be a sempervivens!*

The driver passes tissues and a bottle of water to Ludo, who hands them to Spark. They look at her, unsure what to do, and hang back while she wipes her face, rinses out her mouth, and spits into the road. That's why John Stone wrote only about his early life in Versailles: John Stone intended to *prepare* her for the discovery that she is likely to be sempervivens like her parents.

Spark asks if they can give her a moment. The driver says that this a red route—he can't stop here. But Spark is already walking away. She pulls out Mr. de Souza's business card from her pocket and keys in the number. Trucks rumble by; she struggles to hear him. They have to speak very loudly at each other.

"Mr. de Souza?"

"Miss Park?"

"Is John Stone my father?" Her voice cracks with pent-up emotion. "He is, isn't he? *That's* why he wanted me to read his notebooks. *That's* why you hired a car for me and practically bundled me into it. Isn't it?"

The lawyer seems to be considering his reply. Spark watches the driver open the car bonnet as a warning. She presses her phone hard against her ear. Then the answer comes: "That is a question you must put to Mr. Stone himself."

"Then I am!"

"I didn't say that."

"*How* can you refuse to answer me?"

"I'm sorry."

The car's hazard lights flick on and off. A truck thunders by and recedes into the distance.

"Miss Park, are you still there?"

"Yes," she manages. "What if Mr. Stone's not at Stowney House when I get there?"

"Let's cross that bridge *if* we come to it. When you arrive, could you call me to let me know whether or not you've found him?"

"Yes," says Spark. "I will do that." She hangs up.

Standing on the narrow pavement, Spark covers her mouth with her hand. She sways a little, caught in the fume-filled wake of another giant truck. The roar of the traffic compounds the roar in her head. He might not be in a position to admit it, but she sensed that he wanted to. The New York photograph—that started all this off—comes into her head. She pictures John Stone's shining eyes—so brimming with *life*—as he confronts the street woman. Everything those eyes have seen. Everything he could have taught her. By inviting her to Stowney House, he'd been trying to pave the way between them. And look how she responded. . . . The phone dangles loosely from her fingertips; her head droops forward like a doll's. Presently Ludo approaches her; he takes her arm and walks her back to the car. When the driver moves off again, a speeding van comes close to ramming into their rear. Its horn sounds again and again until the blaring, strident noise fades into a grimy cityscape.

"Are you feeling any better?" Ludo asks. "The driver wants to know what you'd like to do. Do you want to carry on as planned?"

Spark nods.

"Then I'm going to travel with you. I don't think you should be alone."

Ludo undoes his safety belt and slides into the middle seat. She leans into him and lets him put his arms around her shoulders. She is so very tired.

Spark lifts her head to look at him. "I can't talk about it."

"I get that."

Spark lets her head sink down again. "I'm going to have to trust you."

"And I'm going to have to prove to you that you can."

Beneath the hum of the engine, and the staccato bumping of tires over an uneven carriageway, Spark listens to the beat of Ludo's heart. Her eyes start to close.

"But can I just ask one thing?" he says.

Spark's eyelids snap open. Gently, he strokes her hair.

"Was it the idea of being related to John Stone that got you so upset back there?"

Every muscle tenses. Suddenly Spark is wide-awake. She looks up at him. If Ludo is curious, after all the detective work he has done, she really can't blame him. On the other hand, what does *she* think she's doing, bringing Ludo, of all people, to Stowney House? Is she on the cusp of a very bad decision? She recalls the heartbreaking downward curve of Martha's face after she mistook her daughter for her grandmother. She thinks about the beauty of the gift Jacob sculpted for her, of his guard-dog ferocity in the marshes, and of the courage it must have taken for him to come to see her in Mansfield. She is suddenly struck by the fragility of these people's secret existence, and by the humbling *trust* that has been placed in her.

Spark extricates herself from Ludo's arm, sits up straight, and shifts away from him, sliding across the black leather seat.

"You've been so kind to me today, but, you know, it's probably not a great idea for you to come along—"

Ludo stares at her. "I seem to be making a habit of upsetting you—"

She forces herself to hold his gaze. "No. You haven't upset me. It's just that things are complicated right now."

She leans forward and asks the driver to pull over when it's convenient. When she sits back, Ludo is looking incredulously at her.

"Did my question make you change your mind? You *can* trust me. I won't ask anything else if that's how you want it—"

"I think that would be asking too much."

"What? I don't understand you."

"I can't help that."

The driver turns into a suburban road and comes to a halt. Spark turns away from the hurt look on Ludo's face. She wants to grab hold of his hand and tell him to stay.

"When things have settled down for me, can I call you?" she says.

"Do you *want* to?" Ludo gets out of the car, leaning in before slamming the door shut. "Sure. Call me if you want to."

The driver opens his window to call out directions to the nearest station, but Ludo strides away without looking back. Spark curls up in the corner of the backseat as the driver does a three-point turn and rejoins the North Circular. She lowers her window and breathes in hot, polluted air. Wind ruffles her hair as she stares blankly at the rows of houses blurring by. She is emotionally spent, and desperate for reassurance that she just did the right thing, which no one could give her.

Slowly, as London is left behind and they join the traffic heading east on the M11, Spark's emotional fog lifts sufficiently for her to realize that only one thing matters now. She has to find John Stone before it's too late, and she has to ask him if he's her father. The rest can wait.

Spark sits up, dries her eyes, and catches the driver's eye in the rearview mirror. He slides open the partition and enquires if she's feeling any better. She is, she says, though she's getting a bit thirsty. Not that that's important. What *is* important (she says this as matter-of-factly as she can manage) is that if they don't reach Stowney House before John Stone's driver does, she will regret it, every single day, for the rest of her life. She's not asking him to break the law—though she doesn't mind if he does—but could he *please* drive as fast as he possibly can?

The driver roots around in the glove compartment and passes back a bottle of mineral water over his shoulder, still chilled. Spark takes it with thanks and presses it to her cheek.

"Always happy to put my foot down," the driver says. "Though, if you like, I can make a call. Mr. Stone usually asks for me but, as it happens, it's my mate who's picking him up today. He won't mind taking his time, so we can get there ahead of him. Not if I ask nicely."

A Sky Without Light

John Stone has planned a guillotine departure: If he is to sever himself from this sanctuary, he wants a clean cut. Presently a car will collect him and remove him forever from Stowney House. He thought he had prepared himself well for his final exile. But now that it comes to it, he recognizes that it was always an impossible ambition. He does not feel old, although he knows he is; he does not feel wise, although he knows, by rights, he should be. All he is sure of is that the throb and mystery of life lure him on—even now, in this pitiful condition. A heron wades toward him through the shallows of the muddy bank, and regards him down the length of his long beak, as if astonished to find him here.

John Stone has fled his house: The sight of his luggage, neatly stacked in the hall, was proving too painful. Unexpectedly, it has been Thérèse's example that has given him most courage these last days. He accepts that a part of him has doubts, and that another part of him threatens to kick and scream, and cling on with bloodied fingernails. But he will release his grip all the same. The best he can hope for is that he finds the strength to deliver his farewell with love and dignity.

The preparations for his imminent "long trip" have unsettled Martha and Jacob. There have been tender words and angry words, and today, as the time of his departure is almost upon them, there has been a kind of withdrawal. The last time he saw them, they were both tree walking. Later, he hopes, they will come to understand how these past days have been one long good-bye.

He came to the boathouse an hour ago. Here, on the veranda, he sways in his hammock. The water laps beneath the rotting wood. John Stone hooks his fingers over the edge of the canvas and pulls it down so that he can see his beloved marshes. The river beckons to him; the clouds and the wind soothe him. A tune comes into his head. He recognizes it. It is the song of the Swiss Guards. He starts to sing quietly to himself, for comfort, under the shivering leaves. The song describes a journey through winter and night. It speaks of finding your way under a sky without light. There is something in the words that makes him want to weep, and he tells himself that the recent discovery of a daughter has made him sentimental.

Soon the car will be here. It is time for the endgame to start. John Stone removes his gaze from the luminous landscape and swings his legs over the hammock. He sets off for the house without looking back.

Sensitive to the tiniest jangle of his nerves, John Stone registers a twitch in his little finger and an accompanying pang of fear in his chest. *Not now!* By the time John Stone reaches the formal gardens, he is certain that an attack is building. He hears a vehicle coming to a halt in the lane. A car door closes with a dull *thud*. Why hasn't the driver parked in the yard? There are far too many suitcases to lug them up into the lane. He would have asked for his usual driver, but it seemed more fitting that a stranger collect him.

Pausing under the yew arch, he hears the crunch of footsteps on gravel and, in the greenish shade at the end of the drive, he spots a slender figure in jeans heading toward the house. A slanting golden ray of sunshine pours onto the yard. One more step and the light catches in her hair like a flaming beacon. It is Spark! It is his *daughter*! A cry rings out from the house, and Martha's voice echoes over the lawns: "Jacob! She's come!"

John Stone retreats through the arch and cries out in desperation, for his arm is already jerking violently. He cowers against the hedge until Spark disappears toward the house. At the first opportunity, John Stone lollops across the lawn, skirting the fountain and pinning his bad arm to his side. He enters the house through the breakfast room and slips into the long gallery.

The attack is a bad one—they are always bad nowadays. To distract himself, he drags himself along the full length of the gallery, past all the portraits of his Friends, until he reaches his first. It is as Jean-Pierre that he looks into Isabelle's storm cloud eyes and, with his good hand, blows her a kiss, as he always does. As he retraces his steps, each face becomes a kind of bridge to a previous life. When John Stone arrives in front of his sometime wife's portrait, it occurs to him that Spark is now a bridge that leads him back to her mother. Thérèse wears red; her hair is loose. For a moment he lets his forehead rest on hers.

* * *

There is a window at one end of the long gallery, which has a view of the intersection between lawn and yard. John Stone positions himself here while he waits for the attack to pass and tries to decide what to do. Using the curtain to shield him, he peeps out, hoping to catch a glimpse of Spark—the heel of a shoe, a wisp of golden hair, her moving shadow. No doubt she's gone to the boathouse with Martha.

These attacks weaken him and he sinks to the floor, pulling on the curtains. He takes in frequent, shallow breaths. As much as he is able, he thinks of nothing and attempts to be indifferent to his situation.

The Long Gallery

A quiet knock on the door wakes him. It is still light: He can't have been asleep long. No one ever disturbs him in the gallery. The hinges creak open and it is his daughter's voice he hears from behind the door.

"Mr. Stone?"

"Spark?"

He raises his head a fraction from the cold limestone floor where he is still slumped. His lower back aches; his good hand is numb; his bad arm lies limply at his side. The attack is almost, but not quite, over.

"I couldn't leave without speaking to you. Jacob saw you come into the gallery. The car you ordered has arrived. . . . Can I come in?"

He cannot permit her to see him like this. Even if she does not know it yet, her last memory of her father must not be this one.

"I'm sorry—I'm not myself at the moment—"

"You want me to go away?" Spark's tone reveals an intense disappointment. Anger even. Why *has* she come here today? After the fight in the marshes, surely she cannot wish to resume her holiday job! Has Mrs. Park complained to her about his unwanted visit? John Stone stares at the gap in the door. Somehow it reminds him of the confessional.

"I honestly think it would be best, Spark—"

"I've been to see your lawyer," she says. "I've read your notebooks."

John Stone's gaze burns into the back of the door; he lets out a groan as he tries to heave himself up with his good arm. "You've read them!"

"Please don't send me away. You owe me that much—"

The tips of Spark's fingers are curled around the door as she holds it ajar. Where will he get the strength to leave if he see his daughter's face?

"Tell me, does your mother know that you're here?"

"My mother's dead. And I'm told my father's dying."

"What did you say?"

"Mum told me I was adopted after you paid her a visit. The rest I've worked out."

Spark enters the gallery. John Stone tries to get up but is as helpless as a beetle on its back. Spark's eyes betray her distress as she sees him laid out by the window.

"Should I fetch Martha? Can I help you up?"

"*No!* No. Thank you. Could you just give me a moment?"

Averting her gaze from his sprawled figure, Spark walks to the opposite end of the gallery. John Stone observes the back of her golden head as she examines the paintings. She stops in front of his portrait of Thérèse. "My mother?"

"Yes."

"And *are* you my father?"

He draws a breath. And another. "Yes . . . *Yes!*"

"And am I a sempervivens, like you?"

"I think you must be. Though I cannot say for certain."

Spark utters a small, strangulated cry. John Stone

supposes he should comfort her, but cannot move.

"How did you find out?" he asks.

Spark clutches the hem of her T-shirt as she speaks. "With a little help from Ludo. And Jacob."

"*Ludo? Jacob?*"

"Ludo took a photograph of us that day. His app picked up the connection."

John Stone shakes his head in disbelief. "I see. . . . But Jacob—he doesn't know."

"He made this for me." Spark unzips her bag and hands over the double portrait.

Did *Jacob know*, John Stone wonders, *or was he guessing?* He turns the object over and flips it back again. It is very fine. How easy it is to underestimate Jacob.

"When did he give you this?"

"Last week. He came to Mansfield—"

"He went to *Mansfield*!" John Stone thinks back. It must have been while he was still in London. The cunning fox!

"Mr. de Souza has told me you're going away. For good. And he says you won't see a doctor. . . ." Spark struggles to rein in her emotions. John Stone hears her voice crack. "I love Mum very much, and life's been hard on her. But she's sometimes made some poor decisions, and it's been me that's had to pick up the pieces—"

"You've been a good daughter to her. I know that."

John Stone finally succeeds in levering himself upright. He grabs hold of a chair back for support.

"And now that I discover I've got a father who's at least

three hundred and fifty years old, it turns out that nothing's changed!" She's beginning to sob.

"*Spark—*"

"How *could* you let me read your notebooks and then plan to disappear? How *could* you walk away without telling me to my face that you're my father?"

John Stone walks unsteadily toward Spark and offers her both hands, even the trembling one. Spark takes a step backward.

"I don't understand why *everyone* had to lie to me. Didn't I have a right to know?

"It was for your adoptive mother to tell you—I did what I thought was best for your family."

"But you knew I was probably a sempervivens! Didn't it occur to you that I might deserve a bit of *help*? Didn't you think it might be tough to lose a mother and *two* fathers?"

John Stone stands next to Spark and tries to offer her his handkerchief while she perseveres with a rolled-up ball of tissue.

"Spark, I wish with all my heart that I'd known sooner—"

Spark bursts into tears. He guides her to an armchair.

"And *why* won't you see a doctor?"

"I'm trying to protect you—"

"Do you think I care if you shake?"

"This is a cruel disease. I wanted to spare you—"

"And do you think going off to die alone is *sparing* me?

"I don't believe there's a doctor alive whom I could trust with my—with *our*—secret."

Spark listens calmly, dabbing her nose.

"Your mother died from the same affliction. She wouldn't take the risk of seeing a doctor. I won't allow her to have made that sacrifice in vain."

Gripping the damp tissue, Spark bangs down her fist onto the table. "You're going to orphan me so that my mother didn't die in vain! You think keeping all of this a secret matters more to me than spending time with my father! Who else can advise me? Who else can tell me who I am?"

Tears prick at John Stone's eyes. "And twenty years from now, when your life is an unending circus, you will curse the day you let the world know you were sempervivens—"

"At least I'd have known my father—even if only for a short while. You didn't."

No, he thinks. *I didn't.* "My dear Spark, they'd show you no mercy. They would tear into you like hyenas. It would be a *vile* existence. How can I let that happen to my own daughter? Besides, you have more faith in the medical profession than I do. I don't believe there's anything they could do for me. No. The risk is unacceptable—"

"But it's acceptable for you to disappear because you can't bear for anyone to see you ill!"

Spark realizes she's gone too far, and hangs her head. But she's not ready to apologize. The line of golden frames gleams in the soft evening light. Outside, Martha and Jacob are walking across the lawn toward the fountain.

"You are your mother's daughter. You have a passionate nature. I can see how frustrated you are with me."

Spark walks to the window and leans her shoulder against the pane. He observes her while endeavoring to regain his own composure. That profile, that hair, that strength of purpose. What turmoil she must be in. With her last gift, Thérèse surpassed herself. There's a change in her demeanor. Spark turns to look at him.

"As you intend to go away today, from now on, it will be up to me to make my own decisions. Perhaps I shan't want to live a lie. Perhaps telling the truth would be the right thing to do. After all, just think of the good my DNA could do. Maybe my privacy is something mankind can't afford. I could go into the lane and announce my secret right now! And it's not like Versailles; the whole world could know by tomorrow morning. What's to stop me?"

Spark makes as if to get up and leave.

"You're not serious!"

"I am. If the world already knows about us, I shan't need your protection. You'll have nothing to lose by going to see a doctor."

"Is that a *threat*?"

"I want to keep my father alive!"

John Stone stares at his defiant daughter's face and it is Thérèse that he sees. And a pulse of hope and pride, like a comet shooting across the blackness, stirs him into action. Spark, sensing a shift in him, takes a step backward. *My daughter*, he thinks, *is a risk-taker.*

"Come with me," he says and, taking Spark firmly by the arm, leads her out of his gallery of dead Friends.

Send or Delete

John Stone pulls his daughter through the house to the front door. Spark does not resist. The speed of his recovery astonishes her. As does his strength: He grips her arm tightly as if frightened to let her go. This grip, and the determined set to his jaw, provokes in her a vague dread. She wants to ask her father what he intends to do but does not dare. When they reach the threshold he stops abruptly and it occurs to Spark that he could be saying a last good-bye to Stowney House. It's dusk. From the orchard comes the sound of songbirds marking the close of day. Swifts swoop low over the lawn, harvesting insects in the fading light. There is a smell of earth and newly mown grass. At first, the two figures in the garden do not notice them. Martha sits primly on the rim of the fountain basin. In her black dress (for once, she has taken off her apron), she holds herself rigid, steeling herself for what is to come. Spark looks from John Stone to the still figure patiently awaiting her fate. She cannot begin to imagine what Martha has endured in her life. John Stone still hesitates on the threshold as if once he crosses it there will be no going back. She tries to extricate her arm from her father's grasp but he won't let her go. This is unbearable. How can Martha and Jacob survive without John Stone? Jacob flanks Martha; he stands puffing on his pipe, resting his weight on the handle of a long broom. All at once John Stone steps over the threshold onto the gravel path. The sound alerts Martha to their presence and she immediately gets up. Jacob, too, stands to attention, scrutinizing his friend's face, while barely acknowledging Spark's presence. John Stone asks her for Jacob's medallion. Then, without releasing her arm, he walks them up to Jacob and dangles the double portrait from its cord in front of his nose. Tobacco smoke laces the cooling air.

"John," says Jacob. His tone is cool, his back straight as a soldier's. Maybe he used to be a soldier. Jacob's life appears to Spark as a deep, dark mystery. Those pale blue eyes of his are not old, they are *ancient*.

"How long have you known that Spark is my daughter?" In this company Spark feels absurdly young.

"The day we caught her biting the dog's nose I reckoned the pair of you smelled the same."

Spark does not know if she should be offended.

"And you didn't care to mention it?"

"I was biding my time."

"And you shared your thoughts with Martha?"

"No, John. He did not," says Martha. "Not then."

"If the girl was who I thought she was," says Jacob, "there'd be plenty of time. If she wasn't, I had to protect Martha from herself."

The girl, thinks Spark. *I have a name!* She's not the only one to be offended: Martha, too, glares at Jacob before turning back to John Stone.

"Jacob told me what he suspected after all the shenanigans with the boy." Now Martha turns to Spark, her face softening. "I always thought there was something special about you."

Spark reaches out her hand to Martha, who holds it briefly in her own cold fingers.

John Stone continues to address Jacob: "So, while I tried to protect the ties that bind Spark to her family—because I judged the time was not right to do otherwise, and because these matters are *delicate* and *precious*—you took it upon yourself to go to Mansfield and shatter the illusion?"

Spark opens her mouth to speak but changes her mind. She wants to say that it wasn't like that, that Mum had already told her she was adopted when Jacob turned up out of the blue. But how can she interrupt? Nevertheless, it strikes her that if it weren't for Jacob, she would not have seen her father again—not even for this short time.

"You forced the issue," continues John Stone, "without telling me what you knew. Without thinking to ask my permission."

"What'd have been the sense in that, John, since you would've said no?" Spark feels her father's grip tighten. "Who was it that went to Mansfield in the first place? All I did was relight a fuse you'd let go out."

Jacob aims a gob of spittle at the flower bed and Martha puts a restraining hand on his arm. "We were anxious about your health—and this *long trip* you've been talking about—"

"Do I truly deserve to have decisions I've agonized over disregarded? As if I possessed neither judgement nor foresight?" Spark senses the deep well of his distress and is glad she remained silent. "Do you truly not see what you have done here?"

"You'll be glad I did it before your end comes," says Jacob.

Spark feels a tremor in her father's fingers. Martha falls silent and glances at Jacob, who is still looking at the spot where his spittle fell. She lifts her head toward John Stone: "It's because we love you that we acted how we did—"

"*Love* does not impose its will on its object—"

"*L'amour!*" cries Martha. "*Je sais très bien ce que c'est l'amour!*"

Spark gives her father a sharp look.

"Martha is rebuking me. She says that she doesn't need me to tell her what love is."

Spark's arm is returned to her as John Stone breaks away to walk over the lawn. A breeze enters the circle of tall trees that watch over Stowney House. The agitated leaves release a long sigh. No one speaks. Her father's white shirt glows in the twilight. Presently John Stone turns and asks Martha if his bags have already been loaded into the car.

"Yes, John," Martha replies in a defeated voice. It seems to Spark that she has shrunk into herself. "The driver is ready and waiting in the lane."

"Come," says John Stone, holding out his hand to Spark. She walks toward him and takes his arm. They walk away from the fountain and Spark cranes her head to look back at Martha and Jacob, who are staring after them. She looks up at her father but he presses determinedly on.

Her father walks quickly, taking long strides so that Spark is obliged to hurry to keep up with him. They pass through the deep shade of the drive, cross the little bridge with its sound of burbling water, and turn into the lane, where a stiff breeze ruffles her hair and makes her T-shirt flap against her midriff. Past the two parked cars they go, both empty, and, presently, come across the drivers, who stand smoking and talking at the edge of a reed bed. Behind them, a band of scarlet marks the horizon. John Stone acknowledges them with a nod but keeps on walking. Spark does not even try to respond to her own driver's puzzled stare.

"There, I have a signal," says John Stone.

Spark watches him touch the screen and wait. Finally he passes the phone to her.

"I don't trust my fingers today. Will you help me?"

A cursor blinks on a blank screen. "Of course."

Spark awaits instructions, but she sees that he is staring at the glistening marshes, as if grappling with some inner argument. A gust of wind blows the hair from his forehead, revealing the thin stripe of white.

"I've witnessed countless deaths in my time—of the young and old. And one thing I've noticed is how easily the very young leave this earth. Often, it is as if death merely blows out their life like a flickering flame. But when the old die, even those tormented by pain, they will mostly struggle to hold on to every last second that remains to them. And why? Because a lifetime has taught them how precious life is—"

"Oh, please don't! I can't bear it!"

John Stone's eyes soften but he won't stop. "Which is why I had decided to spare my friends the sight of it. I've loved the world and I *don't* want to leave it . . . especially now." He takes Spark's hand and squeezes it. "No matter that I've had more than my fair share: It's only made me love

515

life more. I foresee a difficult end with precious little dignity. It is not something I would wish you to witness. The best of me you will find in my journals."

Her father's gaze is so intense, Spark dare not take her eyes away. She tries to be brave, but her throat continues to constrict and, despite her efforts, a tear rolls down her cheek. John Stone wipes it away with his thumb.

"I'm so sorry," he says. "Will you type my words now?"

Spark nods. Her fingers tap as John Stone dictates. Letters appear on the tiny screen. As the words accumulate, Spark's heart begins to lighten. Her father seems to be withdrawing his request for a safe house. At the same time, he appears to be accepting a previous offer of help with regard to access to a surgeon.

Spark looks up at him round-eyed. John Stone takes back the phone and indicates the two options at the bottom of the screen: send or delete.

"This is my gift to Thérèse, your mother, who thought of me as a considered and cautious man. I am giving *you* the decision. I will take that risk. Because I can see it's what you would *want* me to do. I undertake to abide by your decision. You, of all people, must learn to trust your own judgement. Yours will almost certainly be a very long life."

John Stone holds out the phone for Spark. Her finger hovers over the send button and her eyes slide back up to her father's. "Can I?"

"If that's what you judge to be the *right* thing to do."

Spark hesitates. "Is the surgeon trustworthy?"

"You mean, if he found out that a patient under his care

had lived hundreds of years, would he take that piece of information to the grave with him? What do you think, Spark?"

"He might not find out."

"True. I've never permitted myself to be examined, so I
could not say."

"Why would you leave that decision up to me? How am
I supposed to know?"

"I was about to disappear and abdicate all decisions.
Where's the difference? At least I am able to stand at your
side while you make this one."

Spark turns away from him and stares at the marshes. If
she were a doctor she knows what she'd do.

"And just suppose the doctor did find out you were different, would it *really* be so bad?"

John Stone looks at her. "I don't know what would happen. I can only imagine. Just like you."

She closes her eyes, and imagines. She thinks of the
Spaniard, and Martha, and Jacob, and everything her father,
and all his Friends, must have done over the course of the
centuries to keep his secret safe. Then she imagines her
father dying alone in a strange place. She wonders if *anything* could be done to help him.

"I *can* see why you haven't ever taken the risk."

"It's your decision, Spark."

She turns and bends over the phone, then, glancing at
her father for a moment, brings down her finger firmly onto
the screen. "Send," she says and continues to look at the
screen as if following its path into the ether.

John Stone's face falls; he brings his hand to his heart.

"I deleted the sentence about the surgeon." She looks up at him. "But I've said you won't be needing the safe house."

Spark hands him back his phone and watches him sway slightly. She links her arm through his, sensing the rawness of the many emotions that scud, one after another, across his face. How can she presume to understand what he must be feeling, but she thinks—she hopes—she can discern a trace, at least, of relief.

"I don't want to lose you. Whatever that might mean."

In the wood, an owl hoots. Men's voices are carried to them by the marsh wind. Presently Spark's father says: "I'd better tell my driver he can head back to London."

The Silence of Fountains

Only a few minutes of light still remain. On the lawn next to the fountain, four sempervivens stand in a circle, heads bowed, silent and attentive. Spark feels her father's and Martha's arms draped around her shoulders. She feels their warmth. How many thousands of times must this simple ritual have taken place? It is a shared moment of intimacy, a statement of kinship and intent. "Nothing," says John Stone, "is as important as this day."

Once they break apart, Jacob announces he has something to show them. He disappears behind the yew hedge and presently runs back cupping his hands to his ears.

"Listen," he says.

Water glugs along pipes buried beneath the lawn. Closer it comes, the pressure building, the gurgling increasing. Martha, Spark, and her father exchange glances and look expectantly at the fountainhead. All at once foaming jets of water shoot upward and gush over the garlanded river god until the garden, almost dark now, is filled with the sound of splashing water. Spark laughs out loud at the sight of it. John Stone claps his hands for, as he has told Jacob enough, he could never abide the silence of fountains.

"Well, it's taken you long enough, Jacob," says Martha. "But I think it was worth it."

There is a movement among the weeds. It is the ghostly white koi carp, whose name no one can any longer remember. It surfaces for a moment and flicks its strong tail.

"Bravo, my friend," says John Stone. "Thank you." And he plucks an imaginary hat from his head, steps forward, and bows low, as gracefully as only those who have bowed before the Sun King can bow. And Spark can almost see his stockings and his red-heeled shoes, can almost see the boy who was father of the man, who is, in turn, father to her, and she can almost hear the words that Louis himself gave to him: *In me the past lives.*

Abundant Harvest

Late September, Stowney House.

"A penny for your thoughts—"

"Martha! I didn't hear you."

Martha places an enamel bucket on the grass and sits down with Spark next to the fountain. They have to raise their voices above the splashing water.

"Is everything ready? Can I do anything to help?"

"No, everything's done, thank you. I'm just waiting for Edward to arrive. He won't be long. He's a punctual man. But I came to ask you if you could tell your father that I'll be serving at one o'clock. Be sure to tell him there's no hurry, mind. We'll wait on him. We're having cold cuts and I've made a pork pie. . . . There's nothing wrong, is there?"

"Dan's invited me to visit him when he starts his new job. I can't decide what's best to do."

"You like New York, don't you?"

"I love it."

"So?"

"Ludo will be there."

"Ah."

"He's not as bad as you think."

"I can't advise you on that. Why don't you sleep on it? You're a clever girl. You'll know what to do for the best."

"The thing is . . . I can't stop thinking. . . . Because of who I am, it can't go anywhere—"

"Bless you, you can't work out life before it's happened! The only sure way to protect yourself from hurt is to protect yourself from living. There never have been and there never will be any easy answers."

"Are you saying I should go?"

"No. I'm saying only you can tell if he's worth it."

"Do you think there are any other sempervivens, Martha?"

"Your father thinks there must be. He's always searched among the vagrants and the beggars, people who've lost their place in society. It's where he found me and Jacob, after all. But I've always tried not to think about it—you could send yourself mad."

Martha gets to her feet and picks up her bucket. She lifts off the lid, revealing scraps of vegetables, and shows it to Spark.

"So your brother can feed Bontemps. I think he's smitten with that tortoise."

Spark watches Martha set off for the orchard.

"Martha!"

"Yes?"

"I do understand that I've got to be careful now. You don't have to worry about me."

"I'm not worried."

As Spark sets off for the boathouse, a car pulls up in the yard. It is Edward de Souza. He waves to her and Spark jogs back to the house to greet him. She notes that he's wearing jeans— neatly ironed, naturally. He extends his hand formally, but at least he has started calling her by her first name.

"I hear you've turned down your university place."

"I wanted to be with my father."

"I think you're very wise. John tells me that you won't let him forget that he educated your brother and not you!"

Spark laughs. "He deserves it. I'm trying to drag him into the twenty-first century!"

"I'm glad I've caught you on your own. I wanted to congratulate you on getting a prescription for your father—I gather the drugs are having some effect. You're a miracle worker! He's never listened to me."

"They're not a cure, but it's something. The neurologist we contacted said that if he refused to undergo any tests these might be worth a try."

"Well, if he's more comfortable, that's wonderful news." Edward de Souza smiles. "I also wanted to take the opportunity to invite you to come to see me in my offices when you can. I'm accumulating quite a pile of papers for you to sign."

It's so weird, she thinks, that along with everything else, she seems to have acquired the services of Mr. Edward de Souza.

"So, are you my lawyer?"

"The short answer—and there is a much longer one—is: I am."

"Can I afford you?"

"Oh, yes."

"Do I *need* a lawyer?"

"You certainly do."

Spark looks at him and thinks that he is a nice man, and that she can trust him.

"Listen, Spark, I know this is a day of celebration, but I wanted to say to you that, sooner or later, you're going to have to make certain decisions regarding your future. And I believe that the kind of things you will face, won't have been faced by your father."

"You mean because it will be so much more difficult to conceal things?"

"I mean precisely that."

"And I can't live in Stowney House forever—"

"You *could*, but I can see that you might not want to—"

"But we've got to keep it going for Martha and Jacob."

"Absolutely. It goes without saying—it's their home."

Spark finds half-articulated thoughts rushing to the surface; she hesitates, then decides she may as well say what she thinks. "If it's at all possible that there are other people like me, I want to do everything I can to find them."

"If I were in your position, I'm sure I'd be thinking along the same lines."

Spark looks at him, surprised. "Oh?"

"Naturally your priorities aren't going to be the same as your father's. The only thing I would say is that perhaps *now* is not the time."

"No, of course not. It's just that I don't want to be trapped inside this secret. I want who I am to open things up—not close me in. Do you understand what I mean?"

"Yes, I do."

A floating seed, a tiny gossamer parachute, drifts in a current of air between them. The lawyer tries to catch it but misses. Spark brings the palms of her hands together and captures it before opening up her hand again and blowing the seed away.

"You've got a lot to consider. But you're not alone, Spark, and you can always count on me. Use me as a sounding board. I promise you that I will do everything in my power to protect your interests and help you adapt to change on *your* terms. Remember that as well as being your lawyer, I am your Friend."

Spark steps forward and kisses him on the cheek. "Thank you, Edward."

"Dad. *Dad.* . . ." John Stone wakes to the kiss his daughter plants on his stripe of white hair. He blinks, dazzled by the light on this warm September day. He shades his face with his hands.

"I didn't mean to fall asleep again." The hammock rocks from side to side as John Stone stretches out.

"How are you feeling now?"

"Better, I think. Rested." He regards Spark with one eye and gives her a wry smile. She is backlit by the noon sun so that her hair, stirring in the breeze, has become a halo around her head.

"Martha says lunch is ready when you are. She's made the table look so pretty. And she's let Bontemps out of his cage to roam free."

"Jacob will be pleased!"

"I think she's teaching him a lesson for disappearing when Mum asked him to show her the kitchen garden."

"Jacob hasn't offended her?—"

"No, no—she knows what he's like. *Cantankerous*, she calls him. I think she's got a soft spot for him."

John Stone laughs.

"Will you tell her?"

"One day I'll tell Mum—and Dan. But not yet. . . ."

"Do you mind if I lie here a moment longer? I'm still a little groggy."

"Take as long as you like," says Spark. "Martha says there's no rush. Can I wait with you?"

She lowers herself onto the edge of the veranda, dangling her legs above the water. The rippling river slides by; along its margins, tall reeds swish and sway.

"I can see why you come here," she says. "I love it too. You must never let this old boathouse fall down."

"I could build you a new one—"

"No! I love the peeling paint and the rickety decking."

"It'll collapse eventually."

"I don't care."

They sit peaceably. Spark tells her father that she's decided to go to New York, after all, when Dan starts his new job. Just for a few days—if he doesn't mind.

"Of course," says John Stone. "I'm not going anywhere." He pulls down the canvas with one finger to look at her. Silhouetted, against the marsh, all blues and greens, she's shading her eyes, and looks upward.

"How do geese learn how to fly in a V formation like that?" she asks. John Stone looks up at the flock of dark-bellied geese propelling themselves across the shimmering sky. There is a whistling sound as they beat their wings in unison. They have come to spend winter here. It has been several years since they last sought sanctuary. He is happy to see them back. He is happy to be here to see them back.

"Geese are born with the knowledge of what it is to be a goose," he says.

"Are we?"

"I believe we know more than we think we do. It takes time to trust oneself."

"Dad?"

"Yes."

"Do you see my mother in me?"

"Yes, I do. Every day."

John Stone raises his left hand to the sky and stretches out his fingers, opening and closing them like a fan, squinting at their outline, black against the sky. There is currently no tremor.

"It's helping, isn't it?" Spark is looking over her shoulder at him. "Even if it's making you tired."

John Stone nods. "The symptoms are less severe. . . . We'll see. Would you run ahead before Martha gets impatient? Tell her I'm on my way."

Spark jumps up, making the decking creak, and John Stone raises his neck, straining to watch her golden head disappear out of sight.

Presently John Stone rolls out of his hammock. He walks slowly back toward the orchard, not because he feels weak, but rather because the world is beautiful. He is fiercely grateful for each new day that dawns. Reengaging with his past these last few months has stirred up the sediment of his life. Clarity has been replaced by richness. Each place connects with another, each feeling with another, each thought with another, so that, finally, everything resonates and chimes with meaning.

Yellowing, heart-shaped leaves fall around him. He seems to catch the smell of rosewater, and sees shadows tracing patterns on a slim back; he stares down at the ground from the height of his father's horse; he hears the thunder of hooves and a voice calling for his unicorn; he feels the cool spray of fountains on his cheek. There is no end to scratching away the layers of memory.

John Stone no longer has any doubt that his daughter is sempervivens. Like Martha and Jacob, he does not need to be told. Spark believes that nowadays secrets are impossible to keep and he is beginning to agree with her. She says that if her father came of age in a hall of mirrors, she must live in a house of glass. What will she want, this astounding daughter of his, he wonders, and what she will do? They will disagree, but while he can, he will protect her. And he will tell her all he can about her mother's life, and help her to find out more.

When he reaches the orchard he stops for a moment under a spreading damson tree, draped with clusters of deep purple fruit. Wasps drone drunkenly around the wrinkled windfalls. He remembers some of the desolate moments of the past year and it is with joy that he now observes a long table beneath the trees, garlanded with flowers and fruit, and peopled with friends and family. After so long, the boundaries of Stowney House have miraculously opened up. Edward stands at the head of the table, opening wine; Mrs. Park helps Martha arrange plates; Dan leans backward in his chair, feeding red apples to Bontemps. Jacob is nowhere to be seen though he can smell pipe tobacco. He scans the taller trees for telltale signs. Everywhere, apples, plums, pears hang from branches weighed down with fruit. Spark looks up at him and waves, giving him the loveliest smile. She pats the empty seat next to her. His long life, he knows, is now tilting toward darkness, but for now John Stone emerges into the golden sunshine and walks toward his daughter, marveling at this abundant harvest.

Acknowledgments

My sincere thanks to David Gale and Liz Kossnar at Simon & Schuster for their inspiring professionalism and editorial expertise; to the Royal Literary Fund for generously awarding me a fellowship 2013–2015; to Professor Anthony Grafton of Princeton University for an illuminating conversation on seventeenth-century Versailles and for his views on the predicament of John Stone; to Dr. Mark Bryant of the University of Chichester for casting an expert eye on my historical detail; to my sister novelists—Emma Darwin, Essie Fox, and Caroline Green—for their invaluable support and advice; and a special thank-you both to Susannah Cherry for her notes on a final draft, and to Margot for her advice on my protagonist's legal affairs, for suggesting the giant tortoise, and, most importantly, for her insights into the moral world of John Stone; to all (both currently and formerly) at the wonderful A. P. Watt Ltd. at United Agents, but in particular to: Caradoc King, Mildred Yuan, Amy Elliott, Louise Lamont, Elinor Cooper, and Christine Glover; to the dramatist John Retallack for helping me put flesh on Jacob's bones; and to Rachel Robinson for a psychologist's take on a three-hundred-and-fifty-year-old man. Finally, and above all, my thanks to R., L., and I. Archer, without whom this book could not have been written.